CAN BLESSED
Aisling Elizabeth

To Sarah

Aisling Elizabeth

Copyright © 2024 by Aisling Elizabeth

All rights reserved.

No part of this publication may be reproduced, distributed, or transmitted in any form or by any means, including photocopying, recording, or other electronic or mechanical methods, without the prior written permission of the publisher, except as permitted by U.S. copyright law. For permission requests, contact [include publisher/author contact info].

The story, all names, characters, and incidents portrayed in this production are fictitious. No identification with actual persons (living or deceased), places, buildings, and products is intended or should be inferred.

Book Cover by Mythical Worlds Publications

Acknowledgments

I have enjoyed working with the other amazing authors in this epic shared world. You should check out their stories as well.
My lovely PA Nicole has been a rock in the last few months, and I couldn't imagine getting by without her.
My friends, Jen for being there when I needed, and Kayla and Charlotte for letting me talk your ears off on our walks.

Contents

Dedication	VII
Content Warning	VIII
Prologue	1
Chapter 1	3
Chapter 2	15
Chapter 3	23
Chapter 4	33
Chapter 5	42
Chapter 6	51
Chapter 7	57
Chapter 8	64
Chapter 9	74
Chapter 10	82
Chapter 11	91
Chapter 12	97
Chapter 13	107
Chapter 14	117
Chapter 15	124

Chapter 16	136
Chapter 17	145
Chapter 18	154
Chapter 19	165
Chapter 20	174
Chapter 21	183
Chapter 22	191
Chapter 23	200
Chapter 24	208
Chapter 25	220
Chapter 26	232
Chapter 27	244
Chapter 28	253
Chapter 29	261
Chapter 30	272
Chapter 31	282
Chapter 32	290
Chapter 33	300
Chapter 34	311
Chapter 35	320
Epilogue	332
Dawn of the Zodiac	339
About Aisling Elizabeth	341
Also By Aisling Elizabeth	343

To my children, who are my own destiny.

Content Warning

This book contains the potentially triggering elements listed below. If any of these elements are triggers for you please be cautious when reading. I try to be sensitive with the content and nothing is included for gratuitous reasons.

- Sexual, physical and emotional violence, including elements of dub con.

- Death of character.

- Manipulation.

The book is set in the UK and is written and edited in UK English.

Prologue

A long time ago, when the universe was first born, so were the Constellations, beings of great power who watched over the universe. The Dark Ages brought around the time of the supernaturals and unleashed magic across the universe.

The Constellations watched as Earth's inhabitants abused their newfound power, causing a rift to open many light years away–a speck at first that grew larger until it consumed the very stars around it. The Constellations knew if Earth's inhabitants didn't stop their misuse, the rift would consume everything.

A prophecy was released telling those on Earth that if they did not change, then twelve Zodiacs would be born to make the change for them. But those with power were greedy. They refused the prophecy and instead twisted it for their own nefarious purpose, pushing it on the masses in its' bastardised form to suit their version of the future and secure their power.

No one, not even the Constellations would take what was theirs, and thus the true prophecy was lost to all but a few, leaving only the twisted version in its place:

At the dawn of an era
Twelve Zodiacs will rise
Swiftly and fiercely
They will change the tides

The divines have bestowed
The daughters with power
They come for your children
To destroy and devour

Hear the call of their magic
Hear them cry and decree
The dawn of the Zodiacs is here
No one is safe, no one is free

Chapter 1

Serena

The bitter scent of chamomile filled the air as I lifted the mug of tea to my lips. On the small television mounted in the corner, a balding scientist droned on about the effects of the black hole swallowing up Mars. His monotone voice and excess of technical jargon made it hard to pay attention, so I found my gaze drifting around the cramped storeroom I now called an office.

The shelves were cluttered with books, candles, incense, and various occult trinkets. My inheritance from Gran, along with this little new age shop tucked away in the twisting alleys of Whitby. Gran used to tell me that this place held a power all its own, that the veil between worlds was thinner here. I guess that's why she chose to settle down in this seaside town after a youth spent travelling the globe, seeking magical hotspots.

A child of the 60's, they called her. A truth seeker. The type attracted to eastern religions and psychedelics. Not that I could imagine Gran doing drugs, she was far too practical for that. But she did have her crystal pendulums, tarot cards, and books on every spiritual tradition under the sun, and of course she was well known as a powerful psychic, not just to our little town, but also beyond. I remember being a little girl and watching with awe as people from various parts of the world came to visit Gran to take counsel of her amazing powers.

I smiled sadly, glancing at the photos of Gran on the shelf. We may not have been related by blood, but she was the only real family I'd ever known. The woman who took me in when my mother abandoned me, leaving a weeping, frightened seven-year-old orphan on her doorstep. I didn't know much about my parents, but Gran said my mother had been a misguided youth. Apparently being a mum was too much hassle for her and she passed that duty onto my poor Gran. And Gran took that duty seriously. She taught me everything she knew about the hidden world of magic and spirits. How to open my mind and my heart. I didn't always understand her esoteric wisdom, but I soaked up every word. Gran awakened things inside me I'd never known were there. A sixth sense. An awareness of forces beyond the physical realm.

When I was nineteen, Gran passed away peacefully in her sleep, just two weeks shy of her seventy-fifth birthday. Her shop and all its treasures became mine. For the past eight years, I've done my best to continue her legacy...with mixed results.

I glanced down at my worn Megadeth t-shirt and ripped jeans. Hardly the image of a mystical shopkeeper. My tattoos and piercings tended to scare off the older, New Agey crowd. But the emo and goth teens seem to dig my vibe, so that's something. Gran would probably get a laugh out of the fact that I'm now serving as an "occult expert" in her stead.

On TV, the segment had switched to an interview with Donovan Wilder, distinguished leader of the Supernatural Council. The volume was muted, but I could easily imagine his pretentious tone and the rubbish spewing from his lips. More propaganda about the Zodiacs, no doubt.

Supposedly they were evil beings who wanted to destroy the world and steal all the magic for themselves. Utter hogwash. I may not know much firsthand about the Zodiacs or the prophecy surrounding them, but I trusted Gran's conviction that they were good souls, meant to heal the tear caused by the greed of magic practitioners. She had nothing but contempt for the Council and their smear campaign. In her eyes, they were blinded by their addiction to power.

My powers of perception may not live up to Gran's, but I knew she was right about this. The Council had created a scapegoat, inciting fear and hatred to maintain their control. Now independent groups were taking it upon themselves to hunt down and kill any suspected Zodiacs. Senseless violence endorsed by Wilder's dogma.

I grimaced as Wilder pontificated on-screen, the camera zoomed in tight on his stern face. Gran would've thrown a shoe at the telly if she were here now. As for me, I settled for a derisive snort. Arsehole.

I leaned back in my chair with a sigh. As much as I tried to ignore it, Wilder's fear-mongering was getting to me today. I'd been feeling strangely unsettled for weeks now, like a nervous energy was building inside of me. It reminded me of how antsy I'd feel whenever Gran was expecting an important visitor to the shop. I could sense a shift coming, a charge in the air heralding change. I felt that same way in the months before Gran passed too. A disquieting intuition that her time was coming to an end.

Perhaps this unease was just my body reacting to the longer nights and colder weather. I always got a bit melancholy when the darkness crept in earlier and the tourists deserted our coastal town. The vitality seeped from Whitby as autumn edged toward winter. Or maybe I was picking up on the tense, frenetic energy infecting the entire world as the black hole expanded. They said it had swallowed Mars whole on the TV. How much longer until Earth met the same fate?

People tried to hide their fear behind anger and hatred. Like those who bought into the Council's CLAIM that the Zodiacs were responsible for the black hole. Cast enough blame, and you can avoid facing your own helplessness in the situation. I worried humanity wouldn't realise the truth in time to make a difference. The Council had them all brainwashed, conditioned to see the Zodiacs as evil harbingers of the apocalypse. What if we passed the point of no return before enough to wake up to reality? With a frustrated huff, I rose from my desk and headed back into the main shop, hoping to distract myself with menial tasks. As I tidied a display of healing crystals, my eyes kept straying to the muted television screen through the door into the office. The Council really knew how to put on a good propaganda reel. Wilder stood at a podium, his image projected on massive screens behind him as he addressed an enormous crowd. The camera panned over hundreds of angry, fearful faces yelling and waving signs decrying the Zodiacs. Like torches and pitchforks 2.0. My stomach turned watching the frenzied mob calling for the extermination of innocent people. I wished I could show them who the real monsters were, the council standing by as hatred and violence festered. But how could I open their eyes when they refused to see? With a scowl, I smacked the power button on the remote, plunging the screen into darkness. The silent shop seemed to breathe a sigh of relief at being freed from the Council's toxic rhetoric. Even Carnelian, who'd been watching intently from his perch on the counter, relaxed once the TV went quiet.

"We don't need their fear-mongering here, eh?" I murmured, scratching the cat behind his ears. He leaned into my hand, a deep, satisfied rumble emanating from his chest. The big ginger cat had been a present from my Gran, along with his brother Obsidian, who was around here somewhere. I knew they were a way of appeasing the lost little child that my Gran suddenly claimed as her own, but he always knew how to provide comfort when I was feeling low.

I moved on to straightening up the section of new tarot decks,though my thoughts kept returning to the worrying state of the world. Gran had tried to teach me to clear my mind through meditation and breathing exercises, but serenity eluded me tonight. Sighing, I paused to rub my temples. A headache was starting to build behind my eyes. Perhaps I'd been staring at screens too long today. I could use some fresh air to clear the stagnant energy from my system. I grabbed my jacket and flipped the sign on the door to "Closed" before stepping out into the night. Two blurs shot past me as both of the cats followed me out into the night. It wasn't unusual for them both to follow me on my walks. The air bit at my cheeks, carrying a hint of smoke and sea salt. I shrugged deeper into my coat, hands shoved in pockets as I wandered the twisting cobblestone streets.

Whitby looked like a town straight from the pages of Dracula at this time of year. Shadows gathered thick in alleys and archways, the darkness broken only by the occasional pool of yellow light spilling from a pub or inn window. Winding steps and narrow passages tunnelled through the little town and only added to the charm that this place held. Gran said Whitby existed between worlds, a threshold between land and sea, past and present. In the gathering gloom, it felt timeless...and yet impermanent. Would it still stand a year from now? Or would we all be consumed by the hungry void devouring our universe? I shook my head sharply, as if I could physically dislodge the grim thought. I refused to accept that fate. There had to be hope. If only I could find some way to reignite it within people's hearts. Gran told me once that the darkest nights produce the brightest stars. As I wandered the shadowed streets, I prayed for even a lone star to pierce this darkness. A sign that all was not yet lost. We needed a miracle...now more than ever.

After about an hour of walking my mood was no brighter and the cold was beginning to seep into my skin. I had walked in a big circle and landed back at the shop before really knowing that was my intended direction. Obsidian greeted me by winding his way around my legs, his deep black fur giving him the perfect camouflage in the night, while Carnelian sat on the doorstep watching me with a look so disdained that it could only come from a cat. I unlocked the door and chuckled as both cats shot into the darkness of the shop.

I unlocked the door and chuckled as both cats shot into the darkness of the shop. After securing the lock, I flipped on the lights and turned to survey the space. Obsidian was already curled up on the vintage armchair in the reading nook, ready to resume his nap. Carnelian sat near the display of healing crystals, gazing at me expectantly.

"Don't give me that look," I told him wryly. "It's dinner time soon." The cat slowly blinked his green eyes in response. I shook my head and moved further into the shop, ready to close up for the night.

A thunderous crash made me scream, heart lurching. Whirling around, I saw Carnelian standing over a pile of shattered quartz crystals, shards glinting under the lights. He knocked an entire display onto the floor.

"Carnelian!" I yelled, hand pressed to my still racing heart. "What did I tell you about jumping on the shelves?" The cat flicked his tail, clearly unrepentant. He gave me an offended look, as if I was scolding him for no reason at all. I blew out an exasperated breath and carefully stepped around the mess to switch off the main lights. The soft glow of the fairy lights along the ceiling and walls provided just enough illumination to see by without murdering my electric bill overnight.

Approaching the destroyed display, I slowly crouched down, wary of more toppling crystals. I gathered up the large chunks, dumping them in an empty box to deal with tomorrow. As I scooped up the final shards, the overhead lights glinted off something among the debris.

Frowning, I picked up the small object and wiped residual dust from its surface. It was a delicate silver necklace with an oval pendant. Encased within the oval was a carved white flower. I held it closer, examining the realistic details. It was as if a real flower had been frozen in time, perfectly preserved in some kind of glass or resin. Intricate

Celtic knotwork marked the edges of the oval setting. The entire pendant seemed to glow with an ethereal luminescence.

"Where did you come from?" I muttered, glancing around the shop for clues. This was no cheap trinket; I would have remembered putting out something so unique. Carnelian watched me investigate, diligently cleaning his paw as if the broken crystals were already forgotten.

"Did you knock this off a shelf too?" I asked wryly. His steady green gaze told me I wouldn't get an answer. With a resigned huff, I returned my focus to the mystifying necklace.

The more I looked at it, the more captivating it became. The silver gleamed brightly, seeming to pulse softly in my hand. I brushed a fingertip over the carved flower. A thrill of energy swept through me at the contact. Without consciously deciding to, I found myself clasping the delicate chain around my neck. The pendant came to rest perfectly in the hollow of my collarbone. For a moment, nothing happened. Then blistering heat exploded against my chest, making me gasp. My senses were flooded by vivid images bombarding my mind... Twelve shadowy figures standing hand in hand beneath a sky ablaze... An ominous tear ripping through the darkness of space... Millions of stars swirling into a gaping black abyss... A majestic feathered serpent coiled around a glowing orb, eyes blazing...

The onslaught ceased abruptly, leaving me breathless and dizzy. Gripping the edge of the counter for balance, I fought to regain my bearings as the shop swam back into focus.

What the hell was that? Some kind of waking vision? I hadn't experienced anything so intense since I was a child, before Gran helped me erect mental barriers to tune out spiritual phenomena. For years, my extra senses had been muted to a mere whisper. Now this pendant had blown open the floodgates without warning. I shuddered, nerves still tingling with remnants of power. Carnelian leaned comfortingly against my leg, grounding me. After a few deep breaths, I found the strength to stand upright again. I reached tentative fingers to the pendant resting innocuously above my pounding heart. The engraved silver was smooth and cool to the touch. No more scorching heat or disturbing visions.

Yet I knew there was more to this necklace than met the eye. Something about it had called out on a soul-deep level, piercing through my protections as if they were gossamer. I still didn't understand the meaning behind those fleeting images...but I felt certain this was a catalyst for change I could not ignore. I tucked the pendant out of sight beneath my shirt. Until I figured this out, I would keep it close and keep it secret. I had enough to handle with the Council's vitriol; no need to add fuel to that fire.

With a shaky exhalation, I began rebuilding my mental walls. The spirit realm would still be there when I was ready to let it back in. For now, I had a shop to run and bills to pay. The mundane world required my full attention. But the pendant's presence persisted, a whisper in my mind, both foreign and familiar. I had a lot of research and meditation ahead to make sense of it all. This was far bigger than me; I could feel that intrinsically. But Gran taught me to walk my own path in my own time. So one step at a time it would be.

After sweeping up the remaining debris, I grabbed the empty cat food bowls. "Dinner time, boys!" Carnelian trotted after me eagerly while Obsidian blinked awake from his catnap. In the small upstairs apartment Gran left me, I filled their bowls and changed their water.

The comforting sounds of contented munching followed me as I fixed a quick microwave meal for myself. Too wired for bed, I settled onto the secondhand sofa with my laptop, determined to dig into the mystery of the feather pendant. Maybe I could find some info on the symbols engraved around the edges. They seemed Celtic, but my knowledge of that mysticism was minimal. An hour of fruitless searches later, my eyes were strained and I was no closer to answers. The symbols remained inscrutable, and nothing I found online resembled the pendant. With a huff, I shoved the laptop aside and slouched back against the cushions. Obsidian jumped up to join me, curling into a black furry ball on my lap. I scratched under his chin absently as I wracked my brain. There had to be some clue to unlocking this puzzle.

My gaze fell on the bookshelf crammed with Gran's extensive occult library that I'd inherited. Maybe the answer was right in front of me in her writings.

Invigorated by the new direction, I grabbed a hefty stack of her journals and notebooks. Obsidian grumbled in protest when I dislodged him to spread the materials across the coffee table.

"Sorry buddy, I'm onto something here," I told him as I eagerly flipped through page after page of Gran's cramped scrawl. Detailed accounts of her global travels, spiritual musings, paranormal encounters - my gran had documented it all faithfully in these journals spanning decades. Some passages were in English, while others shifted to French, Latin, or Greek when she wanted to ensure privacy. I skipped past those, focusing only on entries in English. An hour later, my neck was cramping, I was no closer to answers, and discouragement was setting in. Until a symbol inked in the margin caught my eye. There it was, one of the identical symbols engraved on the pendant! Heart leaping,

I traced it with a fingertip. The rest of the page was in Greek, but the paragraph above the symbol mentioned the Moon and the High Priestess tarot card.

I grabbed my phone to pull up the Moon card image. And there circled around the large crescent moon were the same symbols etched into the pendant.

"No way," I whispered, sitting back with wide eyes. This couldn't be a coincidence. The Moon card represented illusion versus reality, inner consciousness and wisdom. Feminine energy and the subconscious realm. Gran used these same symbols as markers in her journals related to the Moon, intuition, and divination. She must have known their origin and meaning.

What did it all have to do with my pendant? I touched the spot over my shirt where it rested, and almost felt the silver warming beneath my fingertips. There was some connection between Gran and this necklace; I could sense it. And her journals might hold the key to decoding the mystery.

With renewed fervour, I kept reading through the night, searching for more clues. The cats eventually grew bored of my obsession and wandered off to nap, but I was too wired to sleep. The first glow of dawn was peeking through the curtains when I finally sat back, bleary-eyed yet thrumming with excitement.

I now knew the symbols were some derivative of Celtic astrological glyphs representing the twelve zodiac signs. The flower pendant was connected to one such sign along with three other strange symbols, though I still didn't know which. And it seemed to hint at some kind of ancient prophecy involving twelve young women. The Daughters of the Zodiac.

Gran never came right out and explained it all, but reading between the lines of her cryptic journal entries gave me enough pieces to get the basic gist. We could be facing some serious supernatural shit soon if the whispers and dreams Gran documented were true. And my sudden psychic vision and mysterious moon pendant sensationally pointed to me being one of these foretold Daughters connected to the moon itself. Assuming I wasn't just grasping at straws in a sleep deprived haze. I rubbed gritty eyes with a groan. This was some next level insanity I'd landed myself in. How could I possibly be part of some arcane destiny prophecy thing? I was just a small town eccentric shop owner who was always told that I wore too much eyeliner, not a destined saviour of the world!

The sun was properly up now, golden rays streaming through my curtains to shine onto the couch where I sat dumbfounded by my apparent cosmic fate. I carefully gathered up Gran's journals, returning them to their proper places with reverence. Their secrets would keep for now. Exhaustion finally catching up, I shuffled to my bedroom and face-planted onto the quilt. Maybe things would make more sense after some sleep. As I drifted off, fingers curled around the pendant at my neck, I sent up a prayer to Gran and the universe: please let me find the guidance and strength to walk the path ahead, wherever it may lead me.

Chapter 2

Serena

I jolted awake, feeling disoriented as my bleary eyes took in the darkness of my bedroom. For a moment I wasn't sure what roused me from sleep. Then intuition prickled along my skin. This was no ordinary awakening. The quality of the shadows felt different...denser somehow. And an expectant hush filled the air, like the world was holding its breath, waiting for something to begin. I sat up slowly, blinking away the last cobwebs of exhaustion from my mind. Sunlight had been streaming through my curtains when I finally collapsed into bed, utterly drained from a night spent piecing together occult research. Now, an impenetrable night pressed against the window.

Comprehension dawned as I absorbed these unnatural details. This was a dream. But no ordinary dream. As a psychic medium, my encounters with the spirit realm often manifested through visions as I slept. The pendant's awakening of my psychic senses yesterday must have opened the way for communication while my conscious defences were down. Anticipation thrummed through me. What message was I meant to receive? The spirits didn't send dreams without reason. Slipping from bed, I moved silently to the bedroom door. The hallway beyond was swallowed in shadows. Yet somehow I knew that stepping through would take me where I needed to go. I turned the knob and passed through, leaving the simulated reality of my apartment behind.

Cool night air kissed my face as I emerged onto the dark streets of Whitby. My breath caught at the sight of the town rendered in moonlight and shadows. The winding alleys and arched stone buildings looked hauntingly beautiful, monochrome under the star-flecked indigo sky. Whitby often had a timeless, haunted air about it, but never more so than now in this dreamscape. I spotted two shadows slinking ahead and felt a rush of affection. "Carnelian, Obsidian!" I called softly. My spirit cats turned, eyes luminous, and padded back to entwine happily around my ankles. Their presence grounded me, easing away the last of my disorientation. Together, we began descending the quiet streets. I didn't know where we were headed, but my feet seemed to. I let them guide me along the path laid out by my dreaming mind.

We walked unhurriedly through the labyrinthine alleys and archways of Whitby, our matched sets of footsteps echoing faintly off the stones. The further we went, the thicker the mist grew, erasing the world around us until we seemed to walk among the clouds. Still we descended, the air growing heavier and colder. I drew my cardigan more tightly around myself against the chill.

The never-ending steep hill downward should have tired me, and it certainly seemed longer than what it was in reality, but in the dream I felt no fatigue. At last, we reached the bottom of the hill and emerged onto Church Street. My breath caught as I spotted the imposing spire of Whitby Abbey towering atop the cliffs on the other side of the River Esk. During waking hours, the ancient Gothic abbey was a popular tourist destination that I often visited myself. But now it loomed like the decaying manor of a ghostly lord, stones weathered and darkened by centuries. I craned my neck to take in its impressive height, then hurried my steps toward the old stone bridge leading across the river. The insistent tug in my spirit told me the abbey was my destination tonight.

The river was shrouded in mist that swirled over its inky surface. Passing a hand through it, I shuddered at the bone-deep chill. The silence pressing around me was profound, broken only by my soft footfalls crossing the bridge.I continued through the small winding streets, a sense of anticipation drawing me ever closer to my destination. No human souls stirred in this dream version of Whitby. The abbey stood utterly isolated atop the cliffs. My cats paced by my side as we climbed the legendary 199 Steps to the abbey ruins. Each steep staircase was carved from weathered stone worn smooth by thousands of feet over centuries of pilgrimage. I tried counting them as I always did when I walked this route, but lost track in the moonlit fog. At last we reached the clifftop, my breath coming faster from the long ascent. I paused a moment to take in the striking view of Whitby Harbor and the North Sea sprawling below us to the horizon. Up here on the cliffs, the salty wind blew brisk and strong, tugging at my hair and clothing. Turning my back to the hypnotic expanse, I faced the abbey's entrance.

During waking hours, the public could only access the interior on paid tours via a strict path. But in the world of dreams, no gates or ropes barred my way. Passing beneath a crumbling archway, we entered the roofless nave open to the elements. Moonlight poured down to wash the interior in silvery blue. Slivers of mist drifted through the abbey's skeleton, adding an ephemeral quality to the hallowed space. The pounding of the nearby surf echoed distantly off stone walls with an eternal rhythm. Obsidian and Carnelian kept close as I slowly walked the length of the nave. Our matched sets of footsteps were the only sounds breaking the profound stillness. Reaching the end, I turned and gazed back the way I'd come. The cats sat side by side, focused on me with knowing looks. My dream was leading me onward. I faced forward once more and continued into the shadowy chambers beyond the main chapel. The cats' presence at my heels reassured me as we navigated lightless corridors by some unseen guidance. Gran used to tell me Whitby Abbey was a thin place, a site where the veil between worlds faded to near transparency. The cleansed energy from centuries of devotion allowed elevated communication to flow freely. Now in this dreamscape, that metaphysical membrane felt diaphanous. A breath was all that separated me from piercing through.

I slowed to a halt in what originally must have been a small circular chamber, but now was only a ring of stones in the middle of these beautiful and ethereal ruins. This felt like my destination, though I didn't know why. Moonlight streaming through an arched glassless window provided the only illumination. I turned in a slow circle, waiting for a sign. As I faced the window again, the quality of light began to change. The white glow intensified, then started cycling through the colours of the rainbow. The mechanical brightness felt sentient somehow. The chamber filled with the rainbow light, and all other details faded into the background. I had the sensation of standing outside my body, viewing a play. Awe blossomed within me. I was in the presence of an ancient spirit. Ageless, cosmic, and infinitely wise. Though it had no tangible form, its essence pressed tangibly against my psychic senses.

A rich, melodic feminine voice echoed through my mind.

"Daughter blessed by the Moon. I am the one who set your sign to shine eternal in the heavens. The era foretold is dawning, and you play a vital role." My breath caught at the confirmation. Gran was right about everything. "Long have I observed your maturing, preparing for this moment when your destiny blooms." I shivered, nerves thrumming with exhilaration and trepidation. Was I really this Zodiac, one of twelve in a world of over eight billion people? Licking dry lips, I whispered,

"What must I do?"

"Serve as my earthly hands, acting to heal the wounds inflicted on our worlds. Join your spiritual sisters and help to reweave the torn tapestry of fate. You hold a fragmented piece of my celestial magic within the pendant. When combined with the other Zodiac relics, it will grant the power to seal the devouring abyss."

My head spun as I tried to grasp the meaning behind her words. Gran believed the Council had it all wrong about the Zodiacs, that we were meant to save the world somehow, not destroy it. This dream confirmed we were on the brink of a cosmic drama foretold ages ago. And I was fated to be one of its protagonists.

"How will I know what to do?" I asked the swirling rainbow spirit. "I'm just a shopkeeper and part time psychic." The ageless voice took on a maternal note.

"Destiny's call comes to all in due time. Trust your heart's wisdom, and you will walk the right path." I chewed my lip, uncertainty rushing through me, even as those simple words resonated through me. My entire life had prepared me for embracing my intuitive gifts, if only I could believe in them fully.

The spirit's glowing aura began to dim, signalling the dream was ending.

"The hour is late, but the dawn of your destiny is almost here. We will speak again, Daughter. Be strong and be vigilant."

"Wait!" I cried out as the light continued fading. "Tell me more!" But my plea went unanswered. Instead a voice that felt like a thousand breathes circled me and echoed through the the chamber.

> "At the dawn of an era
> Twelve Zodiacs will rise
> Swiftly and fiercely
> They must change the tides
> The divines have bestowed
> The daughters with power
> To right that which is wrong
> To destroy all who devour
> Hear the call of our magic
> Awaken in our time of need
> The dawn of the Zodiacs is here
> To undo the faults of your greed."

I had heard the prophecy of the Zodiacs many times over the years, but these weren't the words that I had heard, this was another version, a more pure version. I could tell by the warmth of the words against my skin. Like the gentle caress of something much bigger than me, something much bigger than any of us.

The chamber returned to mundane moonlight once more. Blinking against the abrupt darkness, I took a steadying breath. The cats twined comfortingly around my ankles, grounding me. I gave each a grateful caress between the ears. Their vibrant gazes reflected the wonder and trepidation swirling within me.

"Well, that was…cosmic," I finally murmured with a nervous chuckle. I hoped my humour would calm the fear inside me, but it did nothing other than ring out into the night. My cats responded with slow blinks, exuding calm assurance. With their steadying presence, I was able to gather my reeling thoughts and emotions. This was a lot to process, but the core truth rang clear as a bell: my destiny was unfolding, and I could not hide from it any longer. Dark times lay ahead, but I would face them with all the courage and wisdom I possessed.

Gran taught me not to fear the unknown, but to open myself to learn and grow. Now was my opportunity to truly embody those lessons. To stand strong with faith in my inner light against gathering darkness. If only she was here to help me in this cosmic battle. I shook my head and caressed the pendant resting over my heart. Its once-dormant power now thrummed through me, an embodiment of my link to the celestial realm. Strange as my path appeared, I knew with bone-deep certainty that I was exactly where I needed to be.

With that sense of resolution warming me, the last misty threads of the dream began to unravel. But the renewed sense of purpose and direction they provided would remain when I awoke. The first step of my journey was taken. I was ready for whatever lay ahead.

As the abbey faded around me, I kept my eyes fixed on my spirit cats, letting their presence guide me back through the dissolving dreamscape to the familiar environs of my little flat above the magic shop.

Back to my ordinary life, so soon to be transformed in extraordinary ways.

Chapter 3

Serena

I jolted awake to the sound of loud banging. Disoriented, I blinked against the sunlight streaming through my curtains as the previous night's dream came flooding back. The mystical encounter at Whitby Abbey still felt vividly real, sending a renewed thrill of exhilaration and trepidation through me. Destiny was calling, but was I truly ready to answer?

More impatient banging from downstairs made me abandon that unsettling line of thought for now. Tossing back the covers, I stumbled out of bed and hurried to pull on rumpled clothing from my floor. The noise was definitely coming from the shop's front entrance. Who could be knocking with such urgency at this hour? My eyes widened in alarm as I noted the time, nearly noon. I never slept this late! The dream must have plunged me into a deeper slumber than I realised. Hopefully no customers had been waiting too long on the doorstep. Further thunderous knocking propelled me out of my flat and clattering down the stairs to the shop's ground floor, still trying to smooth my bedhead into some semblance of order.

Flinging open the front door revealed Alec looming on the threshold, hand raised to deliver another barrage. I recoiled at the sight of his grim expression, fearing bad news. But then he broke into a relieved grin.

"There you are! I was getting worried when you hadn't opened the shop yet," he declared, enveloping me in a brisk hug before I could respond. His bulk lifted me right off my feet for a moment.

"Oof! Okay, you can put me down now," I wheezed, swatting the broad shoulder currently squeezing the air from my lungs. Chuckling, the bear of a man set me gently back on my feet. Alec was a long-time family friend Gran had known since her travels in Greece decades ago. They had bonded over their shared knowledge of the arcane and mystical. He now ran an occult bookshop on the other side of Whitby, and we stayed in close contact. His familiar face was comforting to see after the intensity of last night's dream encounter.

"Sorry if I scared you pounding on the door like that," he said sheepishly, hoisting up a grocery bag. "I thought I'd bring some breakfast, make sure you're eating properly." I shook my head, torn between exasperation and affection. Alec had apparently appointed himself my caretaker since Gran passed. I opened my mouth to tease him for acting like my dad, then paused as his words fully registered, of course it was late.

"I had no idea I slept so late. Let me throw on the kettle and I'll explain," I said as I headed towards the back of the room. Alec followed me through the beaded curtain into the back room I used for storage, bookkeeping, and tea breaks. While I filled the kettle from the mini fridge sink, he began unpacking the groceries. Scones, cream, jam, sausages, eggs, mushrooms, bread, bacon - enough for a feast. Soon delicious scents filled the cramped space. My stomach gurgled eagerly despite the unsettled emotions still swirling inside me. Alec stole a scone, slathering it with cream and jam before passing it to me with a knowing look.

"Here. Food first, then talk." I accepted the scone with wry gratitude. He knew me too well. The first bite of fluffy sweetness cleared away the last cobwebs of exhaustion. Alec busied himself frying up eggs and meat, keeping watch until I'd finished every crumb. When I sat back contentedly, he prompted.

"So what happened last night?" I took a bracing sip of black tea.

"You might want to make your own cup for this." Once he'd prepared a second steaming mug, I launched into the full story of last night's vision quest. The mystical voice and prophecy at Whitby Abbey. My apparent cosmic destiny as one of the prophesied Zodiac daughters. Alec listened intently, grey eyes bright with interest.

By the time I finished, the food was ready, so he transferred the feast to the small bistro table in the corner. Over hearty bites of sausage and eggs, I asked,

"Have you ever heard anything about those exact words of prophecy I recalled? The part about healing wounds and reweaving the torn tapestry of fate?" Alec frowned thoughtfully as he chewed a bite of toast. After washing it down with tea, he mused,

"It's been ages since I read Gran's journals mentioning the Zodiac mythos. But that section sounds familiar. I believe she theorised that the commonly known prophecy. the one about darkness and destruction, had been altered over time. That the original was more benevolent." I snapped my fingers.

"Exactly! The voice said that dawn was almost here. Like the true prophecy was meant for this current era all along. To heal the tears caused by magic overuse." Alec nodded slowly.

"And your ancestor pendant holds a piece of this power. Fascinating." He leaned back to study me across the table. "You've been given quite the cosmic responsibility, Serena. How do you feel about that?" I grimaced, dropping my gaze to shreds of egg yolk soaking into my toast.

"Mostly terrified," I admitted around the lump in my throat. "This is all so huge and mystical. How can plain old me possibly play a part in arcane prophecies and saving reality?"

"Look at me." Alec gently tilted my chin up until I met his kind grey eyes. "You are anything but plain. You just haven't embraced the full extent of your gifts yet. But you've been preparing for this all your life under Gran's tutelage. She chose you as her successor for good reason." He gave my shoulder a reassuring squeeze. "When the time comes, you'll be ready." I offered a small but grateful smile. Alec's steadfast faith soothed my rattled nerves and insecurities, reminding me I wouldn't walk this daunting path alone. Gran made sure I had allies like him before she passed.

"We'll figure this out together," he promised. "I'll hit the books, reach out to my contacts abroad. You see what more you can learn from Gran's journals about the true prophecy."

"Good idea." I rose to give him a fierce hug. "Thank you for being here. Gran would be glad you're looking out for me." He patted my back gently.

"She was the closest thing I had to a mother too. It's only right that we take care of each other now." Releasing me, he gestured at our cleaned plates. "And that starts with a solid breakfast! Here, help me with these dishes." We quickly washed up, settling into easy chatter about his occult bookshop and other mundane topics. The warm normalcy of it helped calm my remaining anxiety over destiny's call. By the time Alec left with a promise to be in touch soon, I felt ready to begin my ordained purpose, whatever that entailed. Watching his bulky figure stroll down the street with a final wave, I whispered a heartfelt thanks to Gran and the universe for bringing him into my life when I needed him most.

After securing the front door, I headed upstairs to shower and change into proper clothing. The refreshing hot water finished sweeping away the last vestiges of disturbed sleep. As I combed out my wet hair, the events of yesterday and last night replayed in my mind, underscoring how profoundly life had shifted overnight. Less than twenty-four hours ago, my priority had been keeping this little shop afloat and trying to ignore the Council's poisonous vitriol. Now, if Gran and the celestial voice were to be believed, I bore a direct tie to a cosmic destiny meant to somehow heal the damaged fabric of reality itself. No pressure, right? I shook my head wryly. Whatever the scope of the unknown road ahead, I must walk it one step at a time. My first step was learning all I could about the true Zodiac prophecy. I dressed quickly in ripped jeans, a heather grey sweater and my go-to leather jacket. After a swipe of mascara to combat the pallor of stress and lost sleep, I declared myself ready to face the day. My pendant rested cool and smooth against my sternum, its mystical presence a tacit reminder of last night's revelation. Together we descended the stairs back down to the shop.

The space felt clearer now, as if it too had shed the last lingering remnants of restless night energy. Golden late afternoon light poured through the front windows, catching dancing dust motes. The crystals and trinkets glinted cheerfully on shelves and displays. At the crooked bistro table tucked by the beaded curtain, my notebooks and laptop awaited, along with the comforting scents of chamomile and sage from the diffuser. I breathed deeply, letting the tranquillity of my quaint shop fill me with serenity. This space had always felt like home, but now took on new significance as a haven where I gathered my strength before venturing forth into the wider unknown. Obsidian dozed curled in a sunbeam by the altar space, but Carnelian trotted over to greet me with a bump against my ankle. I smiled and obligingly scratched under his chin until he purred.

"Ready for another day of mystical adventures, boys?" I asked wryly. Two slow blinks answered me. With my feline companions overseeing, I settled in at my workspace with a fresh cup of tea. The scattered pages of Gran's handwritten notes and journals surrounded my laptop. I cracked my knuckles, inhaled deeply, and began to read.

Several hours later, my eyes were strained and gritty, my neck and shoulders knotted painfully from hunching over the tiny table. But I finally felt like I was making progress decoding Gran's encrypted research into the Zodiac prophecy. Her writings obliquely referenced "the true account seldom spoken aloud due to lost pages and elder tongues." She cited fragmentary evidence of alternate origin accounts passed down through oral tradition and hidden records, stories that contradicted the commonly known narrative portraying the Zodiacs as harbingers of doom. Gran hypothesised that vital portions of the prophecy had been deliberately altered or destroyed centuries ago. Perhaps by those like today's Council who sought to taint the Zodiacs' image to retain power. Her efforts to learn more through global contacts were stymied by fear and mistrust. But she remained convinced the Daughters had a sacred destiny "to heal wounds between worlds." I now knew her instincts were correct.

Too restless to sit any longer, I decided to walk and process this new information. After locking up the shop, I found myself following the same route my dream-feet trod the previous night through Whitby's cobbled streets. But under the setting winter sun, no haunting magic lingered. Just the cries of gulls wheeling over the harbour and the tang of salt on the breeze. Tourists milled along the sidewalks, bustling in and out of shops and restaurants. Familiar faces called cheery greetings to me as I passed by. My hometown looked utterly ordinary, giving no indication of the extraordinary cosmic events about to unfold here.

I paused on the bridge crossing the River Esk, gazing downstream toward the harbour mouth opening onto the steel-grey North Sea. The cries of gulls and the chug of boat engines carried faintly on the brisk breeze. In the daylight, the 199 Steps climbing the cliff to Whitby Abbey looked far less ominous than in the dreamscape. Still I hesitated, drumming my fingers on the worn stone railing. I wasn't sure I was ready yet to revisit the site of last night's vision. The faded daylight magic might pale in comparison to the luminous encounter with my destined birthright. Turning my back on the iconic ruins, I instead followed the river path to Pannett Park. Sunlight filtering through bare branches dappled the trail. The cold winter air gradually cleared the heaviness from my mind. By the time I looped back around to the magic shop, I felt centred mentally and emotionally. Ready to continue pursuing my strange destiny, one day at a time.

The lights were on inside the shop when I returned, flickering faintly through the windows. Frowning, I cautiously tried the front door and found it still locked. Had I forgotten to flip off a lamp before leaving? I took care unlocking the door in case someone had broken in. But the space inside looked undisturbed. Obsidian sniffed my hand in lazy greeting from his spot by the altar while Carnelian wound between my ankles. If there had been an intruder, the cats clearly no longer sensed a threat. My eyes scanned the room, seeking the light source. There. The antique stained glass lamp on the counter softly glowed, though I distinctly remembered switching it off earlier. I crossed behind the counter to examine it. The crystal pendulum suspended from a nearby stand began oscillating as I approached. My own psychic senses subtlety prickled too, though nothing malicious lingered in the atmosphere.

"Alright, I know you're trying to get my attention," I murmured aloud. "What is it?" The pendulum stilled, then slowly began swinging along a deliberate path, tapping certain stones lining the countertop. Jade...moonstone...obsidian... Finally it came to rest, indicating the rose quartz near the lamp. I adjusted the rocks until they were aligned with the lamp in the centre. The pendulum swung faster in approval. I chewed my lip thoughtfully, pondering the meaning.

Rose quartz signified unconditional love and healing. With the jade for wisdom and moonstone for intuition, they formed a triangle around the lamp, symbolising...illumination. My eyes widened. "Light to guide me forward in darkness," I realised aloud. The lamp glowed brighter, as if in confirmation. I huffed a soft laugh, shaking my head. Even in death, Gran found ways to send me subtle messages of encouragement from the spirit realm. This was her way of affirming I was on the right path. I stepped back from the impromptu spirit altar with a lump in my throat.

"Thank you, Gran," I whispered. "I miss you, but I'll make you proud. Wherever destiny takes me, your light will shine the way." A warmth filled my chest, like phantom arms embracing me. Then the lamp slowly dimmed back to darkness as the unseen presence faded. But Gran's love remained woven through the shop's foundations, through all the gifts and wisdom she had imparted to me. A bittersweet comfort as I continued reading the signs and portents guiding me toward my fated purpose. There was much still to learn about the obscured truths of the Zodiac prophecy. But thanks to Alec's staunch support and Gran's enduring guidance, I knew I would unravel the mystery one step at a time.

I was gathering my notes, prepared to dive back into research, when a knock at the shop door made me look up. Through the glass I saw Violet, my bubbly friend who ran the floral shop down the lane. Her vivid blue ponytail bounced as she waved enthusiastically. I waved her inside, wondering what brought her by.

"Hey you, what's up?"

"I just closed up the flower shop for the day and realised I'm craving fish and chips something fierce," she said, absently playing with the crystal windchimes. "Want to pop over to the pub for some dinner? My treat!" I hesitated, gaze drawn back to the messy stack of journals. But further reading would have to wait; food and friendship took priority now. I smiled warmly at Violet.

"That sounds brilliant. Let me grab my purse." Violet cheered, looping her arm through mine to escort me out the door. As we walked to the pub, her colourful energy washed away the last grim remnants of prophecy research. She chattered about her latest floral creations while I made the occasional comment, content to simply listen. The fresh sea air and Violet's sunny presence were just what I needed to lift my spirits after the heavy revelations of the past twenty-four hours.

Over piping hot plates of fish and chips at our favourite outdoor table overlooking the harbour, we laughed and talked about nothing consequential. For now, destiny could wait. This bright moment with my dear friend was a gift to be savoured before tomorrow plunged me back into the cosmic unknown. But I knew that as long as we had each other's light to brighten the gathering shadows, we would find our way through whatever lay ahead.

Chapter 4

Jake

The worn wooden sign above the door creaked as it swayed back and forth in the sea breeze. A faded painting depicted a mermaid sitting upon a rock, though the edges had long since curled and the colours muted. I eyed it distrustfully as I approached, the mermaid's demure smile at odds with the roaring laughter and music pouring from the open windows. A pub. Of course it had to be a pub. I suppressed a scowl, bracing myself before pushing open the carved oak door. Everything I disliked about small towns was encapsulated in these quaint, claustrophobic drinking holes. But the intel my uncle provided indicated this was the best place to begin gathering information on the local supernatural community.

I paused just over the threshold, allowing my senses to adjust to the assault. The mingled odours of old beer, sweat, and fried food turned my stomach. Raucous conversations battled with the jukebox's twangy country music for auditory dominance. My eyes scanned through the dimly lit space, cataloguing exits and any potential threats.. Fighting the urge to turn and leave, I waded into the fray. Locals turned to inspect the newcomer with blatant curiosity. I kept my head high, refusing to show weakness. Their attention would pass once they categorised me into one of their simplistic boxes: outsider, threat, prey. None realised I was the wolf that came to hunt among their flock.

My uncle advised me to pose as a tourist, allowing their guards to lower. But I couldn't stomach the inane questions and contrived wonder required for that role. Better to play the strong, silent outsider just passing through. I claimed a stool at the far end of the bar, back to the wall so I could monitor all approaches. The overweight bartender waddled over, tattoos and piercings fighting for space on her exposed skin.

"What'll it be, stranger?" Her broad Yorkshire accent betrayed her at once as a local. Hopefully her loose tongue would prove equally beneficial. I ordered a whiskey, neat. She delivered it wordlessly, likely picking up on my lack of desire for small talk. I nodded my thanks and sipped the smoky liquid, steeling myself for the night ahead. My handler would expect a progress report soon. Hopefully I could provide the name of one of these backwater dwellers whose trust I could exploit for information. But so far, the inhabitants defied any such categorisation. My nose wrinkled at the sticky residue on the bar top as I set down my glass. The establishment's façade promised quaint local charm, but it seethed with the same shallow appetites and petty disputes I witnessed in too many dives before it. A brawl was likely to break out soon, judging by the belligerent shouts from the pool table area. No one here would welcome an outsider into their circle.

As the bartender passed by again, I decided to nudge fate along.

"Quiet night?" I asked casually, hoping to bait her into conversation. She snorted, wiping the bar with practised swipes. "Aye, 'til the weekenders roll in. Reckon you're a bit early for all the fun." I shrugged.

"The off-season has its perks. More likely to have a quiet drink without the crowds."

"Can't argue with that." She nodded approvingly. "Whatcha bring you to Whitby anyhow?" There it was, the fishing hook cast out. I carefully considered my response for maximum gain.

"A friend recommended the seaside views and historical sites. After too long in the city, the fresh air is welcome." I lifted my glass in a mock toast. "Even on quiet nights like this. Though it seems I'm more likely to get a view of the tavern floor if I stay too long," I replied wryly. Her laughter was startlingly loud in the crowded room. "Too right! We may be small, but we know how to have a good time 'round here." I forced an answering smile, hoping it reached my eyes. She seemed inclined to linger, hungry for gossip, so I reeled her in further.

"Anywhere in particular you'd recommend checking out?" As she enthusiastically listed off sights, I nodded along, feigning interest while focusing my attention on the room reflected in the mirror behind the bar. Locals drank and chattered in small groups. My eyes were continually drawn to one table near the back where two young women sat chatting animatedly. Even in the dingy reflection, the vibrant hair colours of one's blue locks and the other's golden waves stood out. Their laughter carried clearly, even above the rest of the noise. Something about the blonde woman stirred an odd instinct in me, though I couldn't pinpoint why. An inexplicable gravity seemed to surround her, subtly bending the energy of the room. It put me on edge. As the bartender finished her recommendations, an idea took root.

"Are there any shops in town that cater to more spiritual interests?" I kept my tone light and curious. "Crystals, herbs, that sort of thing." Her eyes turned wary, smile dimming.

"Not sure I can rightly recommend any such places. Most around here keep to the old religions, nothing dark or dangerous." I lifted my hands in a placating gesture.

"No offence meant. Just curious what services are offered for spiritual folks. I'm simply interested in expanding my knowledge of holistic practices." I offered a self-deprecating smile. "City living makes me appreciate the simpler joys." My reassurance only deepened her frown. She crossed her arms, posture radiating protectiveness. Realisation struck that this woman likely knew or even was one of the witches my uncle mentioned. Interesting. Perhaps we could make a mutually beneficial deal.

"Apologies for prying," I said earnestly, holding her gaze. "It's clear you have reasons to be cautious around a stranger asking too many questions." I lowered my voice just enough to avoid being overheard. "And I understand, being...gifted...myself. It's why I hoped to connect with fellow open-minded types during my stay. No harm intended."

Her shoulders relaxed fractionally, though suspicion still lurked in her expression.

"Aye, well...I may know of a few places for those seeking spiritual guidance." She eyed me a moment longer before leaning in closer.

"Serena's place just down the way has what you're looking for. Inherited it from her gran." She nodded toward the blond woman. "She does card readings and the like. Harmless, but folks say she's got real talent." I tracked her gaze to the blonde, thoughts turning rapidly. A psychic witch was exactly the sort I should investigate further. She could have valuable insights. I needed to learn more about this Serena without rousing suspicion.

"She seems lovely," I remarked casually. "How long has she lived in Whitby?" The bartender shrugged.

"Most her life, as far as I know. Took over her gran's shop maybe...oh, seven or eight years back? Keeps to herself mostly, after..." She faltered, glancing away. I leaned in curiously.

"After what?" But she shook her head firmly.

"Never you mind that. Talk of strangers isn't my place." She busied herself wiping the bar, refusing to meet my eyes. I suppressed a scowl at the abrupt end to our conversation. The woman clearly knew something significant about the girl's past but refused to gossip further. Pressing the issue would only make her withdraw more. I had learned enough for one night. Instead I offered a placating smile.

"I understand completely. Thank you, truly." I extended a hand. "I'm Jake, by the way."

"Millie." Her handshake was brief but firm. She looked me over with consideration. "You seem a decent lad. But steer clear of trouble, you hear? Whitby takes care of her own." The implied warning was clear. Causing any harm would not be tolerated. I lifted my glass in a mock toast.

"I only aim to broaden my horizons, nothing more." I filed away that curious information for later investigation. If this Serena had secrets, they may prove useful leverage. Finishing my drink, I laid some bills on the bar and rose to leave.

"Appreciate the guidance, ma'am. I'll be sure to check out the shop you mentioned." I made sure to thank Millie again for the guidance, playing the part of the deferential newcomer seeking her wisdom. She preened under the attention, entirely unaware she had already betrayed one of her own kind and set me on the scent of my prey.

My mood lifted exponentially as I left the cloying tavern air behind and set off into the night. While the evening had not gone precisely to plan, I now had a solid lead in this Serena. And Millie's protective reaction suggested Serena likely had abilities beyond the ordinary. Plus, operating a magic shop provided the perfect front and access to arcane materials and lore. Yes, this young shopkeeper showed real promise as a source of information. I inhaled deeply of the briny air, cleansing the tavern's stale odours from my lungs. The breeze off the sea soothed my agitated nerves in a way the alcohol had failed to accomplish. Out on the darkened streets, my confident stride and neutral expression fit far better than amidst the rabble I'd just left behind. The night felt full of possibility now that I had a direction for investigation. One of many long nights ahead, to be certain. But I would be patient. Slow and steady won the hunt. And when I finally cornered my quarry, the kill would be all the sweeter.

The winding streets running downhill toward the harbour made navigation difficult, but I welcomed the challenge. It focused my thoughts, bringing clarity of purpose. I belonged out here stalking evil, not stuck blending in with oblivious civilians back home. The Zodiacs' corrupted powers endangered all humans and supernaturals alike. Someone had to take a stand against them. Too many stood idly by, even defended the Zodiacs and their false prophecy. My uncle said complacency and confusion ran rampant, which allowed these witches to move freely. But we in the Council knew the truth. Saw the danger they posed. And so the task fell to us to remove the threat before more innocent lives were lost. My hands flexed unconsciously, craving the comforting weight of my blades. Being forced to rely only on words and charm tonight left me feeling exposed. But I would do whatever it took to complete this assignment. No matter how distasteful pretending benign interest in these small-minded provincials became, I could not fail again. The Council's patience was not infinite.

As the proud arches of the nearby abbey came into view, I redirected my steps uphill. While the ghostly ruins held little appeal personally, their height would provide an optimal vantage point to survey the surrounding area. I could see now how generations of rulers and conquerors chose this clifftop to oversee the harbour and town. The view granted a kingly perspective. From up here, the streets below appeared like veins mapping the living organism that was Whitby. And like a skilled surgeon, I need only identify the right vessels to sever in order to drain the life from the infested body. Serena and her little shop seemed a promising artery to target first. Cut there, and vital resources feeding the Zodiac would be compromised. Without access to protective charms, obscuring potions, and whatever dark magic empowered their inhuman abilities, the Zodiac would be left exposed. Easy prey for my blades. A chilling gust whipped my coat around me as I ascended the long staircase to the abbey entrance. I barely noticed the cold. A growing sense of fierce purpose ignited my blood better than any hearth fire or stiff drink could manage. I did not fool myself into thinking this hunt would prove simple. Powerful forces moved against me in the shadows. This Zodiac likely had allies among the witches and other foul beings infesting the area. To defeat them, I could not rely on strength alone. No, I would need cunning to match...and a ruthlessness they could not begin to fathom. I was merely the outward face of a vast, ancient order. Its true depth and influence extended further than these provincial dwellers could comprehend. They only saw a lone man. Not the uncompromising might standing immovably behind him.

My shoes scraped over stone worn by thousands of feet over hundreds of years as I reached the abbey entrance. Twining my hands behind my back beneath my coat, I began a slow circuit along the perimeter walkway. Far below, the town lights glittered, deceptively quaint and inviting. But I knew the truth. Hidden among the innocuous streets and friendly faces lurked a monster. A demon in the fold. This Zodiac and their kind threatened everything we as a Council stood for, everything generations before us had fought and died to build in order to keep humanity safe and ignorant of the supernatural forces poised to prey on them if left unchecked. I could not, would not, allow more innocent blood to stain my hands due to failure or inaction. Not as my uncle had with my parents, even if his role went unacknowledged, unpunished. The guilt and shame of that loss still haunted me, a yawning abyss threatening to swallow me whole if I let memory take hold. The only absolution lay in spilling Zodiac blood. Cleansing the earth of their unique poison, as I had been trained since youth to accomplish with detached precision. So why then did my usually steady hands tremble now with more than just the cold?

Furious with myself, I clenched them tighter behind my back, nails biting into calloused palms. Now was not the time for doubt or distraction. Lives depended on my success here. I could not find redemption until my mission was complete. And once this Zodiac was confirmed and eliminated, I would be one step closer to the absolution I craved. Chin lifted, I stared north toward the black sea, imagining it spreading to swallow all light and life should I fail.

Turning abruptly on my heel, I descended the steps rapidly with renewed conviction. The time for observation and patience had passed. Action and answers were needed now. And I knew just where to start hunting for them come sunrise. I had a promising new angle of investigation in this Serena. One that required closer scrutiny. Come morning, I would pay her shop a cordial visit to take her full measure in person. Her reactions could prove most illuminating. For now, I forced myself to be patient. I was playing a subtle game here, not rushing in with blades drawn. Not yet, anyway. But if this witch proved to be concealing the cancerous Zodiac I sought? Her fate would be sealed. With care and cunning, I could transform that silken thread into the noose with which to hang the Zodiac. The Council demands results, and I aimed to deliver.

Chapter 5

Serena

I awoke with a groan, the midday sun piercing through my eyelids like daggers. My head pounded furiously, protesting the one too many ciders I'd indulged in with Violet last night. Apparently my tolerance wasn't what it used to be. Rolling over with a muffled whimper, I noted the time on my bedside clock: nearly noon. I never slept this late! Or not until recently it seemed. The shop should have opened hours ago. Thankfully it was winter season, and a weekday so hopefully I wouldn't have lost too many potential customers.

Cursing under my breath, I sat up slowly, willing the room to stop spinning. How on earth was I going to make it downstairs and function today? The very thought of customers and noise made my stomach lurch warningly. I cradled my aching head in my hands, trying to recall the blurred events leading to my current state. Ah yes, staying out far too late at the pub with Violet, laughing and drinking without a care, simply living in the moment. No cosmic destinies or mystical prophecies to weigh me down. Just the joy of dear friendship. Well, until Millie had dropped the bombshell about some newcomer in town asking questions about me and my shop. I groaned again recalling her words. Apparently the man had seemed very interested when she mentioned my psychic talents. He even asked for recommendations on spiritual shops to visit during his stay in Whitby, which in itself wasn't unusual. And helpful Millie went and gave him my name and location, thinking she was sending business my way. I understood her intent was good, but the whole thing put me on edge. Whitby was well known for the spiritual community but I wasn't a fan of being singled out, even if I did need the business. In my experience, mysterious strangers poking around in mystic matters rarely meant anything positive. My only clear memory of the man was the sight of his broad shoulders and dark blond hair reflected in the tavern's dingy mirror. I hadn't gotten a good look at his face. Something about him bothered me, though. An instinctual wariness I couldn't quite pinpoint. Gran had taught me to always trust those subtle intuitions even if the conscious mind didn't grasp the reason yet. They hinted at deeper knowings recognising danger on an energetic level. But in my cider-soaked state last night, I'd pushed the concern aside, not wanting to ruin the lighthearted mood.

Now in the harsh clarity of a vicious hangover, unease twisted my gut again. This man's sudden interest seemed too convenient on the heels of my Zodiac awakening. I doubted it was mere coincidence. But was he an ally, like Alec, come to help guide me, or something more sinister? Until I had answers, I would be wise to proceed with caution. Starting with a very strong cup of coffee before attempting to open the shop.

With another groan, I slowly levered myself upright, bracing against the nightstand as the room swayed dizzily. Coffee, shower, fresh clothes. Priorities first. Answers about the mysterious newcomer would have to wait until I could stand upright without wanting to vomit. I shuffled slowly toward the kitchen, each footfall jarring my aching skull. Today was going to be a long, painful road indeed. But I had survived hangovers before, and lived to tell the tales. Plus, I now had an air of destiny about me. Surely I could face this ordinary challenge with at least a scrap of cosmic grace, right? The amused voice in my mind sounded suspiciously like Gran's as it teased me for overdramatizing. Smiling ruefully, I conceded her point. Once the coffee kicked in, I'd be fine. After all, a little hangover was nothing compared to the mystical trials ahead. I just needed to take things one mundane step at a time today. Starting with liberating the caffeine to revive my poor crushed mortal form into facing the day and all its mysteries. Prophetic destiny could wait until after my shower.

After the restorative powers of coffee worked their magic, I managed to shower and get dressed in preparation to face the day. My head still throbbed dully, but at least the room no longer tilted dangerously when I moved. Progress. I slowly descended the stairs, one hand braced against the wall just in case. Obsidian and Carnelian twined around my ankles in greeting as I reached the shop floor.

"Morning boys," I murmured, leaning down to scratch their ears. Their affectionate presence steadied me. I flipped the sign on the door to 'Open' and unlocked it, hoping I wouldn't have to disappoint too many customers who arrived earlier expecting prompt store hours. Gran would likely admonish me from the spirit realm for the lapse. The thought made me wince as I turned to survey the shop. To my immense surprise, I found Ophelia already inside, smiling brightly. In her hands she held a large steaming paper cup and a small white bakery bag.

"Good morning, Serena! I had a feeling you could use a pick-me-up today, so I brought reinforcements." She held out the offerings. The rich aroma of fresh coffee enveloped me as I accepted the cup, sighing blissfully at the first sip. Still hot and perfectly creamy. Ophelia knew my tastes well. Despite her claiming to not be gifted, she always seemed to know what I needed to get me through the day.

"You're an angel for bringing this, truly. I slept right through my alarms." Ophelia waved off my gratitude.

"What are friends for? Besides, I sensed you could use some extra support today." Her tone grew more sombre. I tensed.

"Regarding anything in particular?" She tilted her head thoughtfully.

"A shift is coming. But take comfort that you aren't walking alone." Before I could ask for clarification, the cats began meowing loudly, pacing around her feet. Ophelia laughed.

"Don't worry, I didn't forget you two!" She disappeared into the back room, returning moments later with two plates of fresh fish from the morning market. The aromatic smell made my queasy stomach rumble unexpectedly. Ophelia handed me the bakery bag with a knowing look.

"Eat. It will help settle you." I peered inside and my mouth watered at the sight of a perfect apple cinnamon pastry. The first bite of warm, sugary apple and flaky crust almost made me moan. Ophelia chuckled, sipping her own tea while the cats gobbled their treat. The familiar comforts of food and friendship in my cosy shop already lifted my spirits and strengthened my resolve. I had a feeling Ophelia's arrival this morning was no coincidence either. Whatever awaited me today, I could handle it with help from loved ones. For now, I savoured this quiet moment of calm before the storm. Ophelia and I drank our beverages in serene silence, with the occasional chat, gathering our strength and courage for the unknown road ahead.

A few hours into the day I was feeling better. Ophelia had decided to start cleaning around the shop while I worked on some paperwork at the counter. Our casual conversation about town gossip and happenings was interrupted by the bell above the shop door, announcing a customer's arrival. I looked up from my herbal tea, words dying on my tongue as I took in the tall stranger now stepping inside.

It was him, the newcomer that Millie and others had spoken of. Though we had never met, his rugged features stirred a peculiar sense of familiarity in me, like a half-remembered dream. He moved with understated grace, exuding subtle power and intensity. Dark wash jeans encased muscular legs while a black leather jacket stretched across broad shoulders. His black t-shirt clung appealingly to a toned chest. No wonder he was stirring interest among the locals. I could appreciate firsthand how his commanding presence would draw eyes and set tongues wagging in our small town. When his gaze met mine, an inexplicable jolt passed between us. His eyes were a striking silvery grey, forceful and astute. They seemed to look directly through me in an unsettling yet intriguing way. I had to repress a shiver at the potent awareness sparked by our unexpected connection. Ophelia made a small sound, recapturing my attention. I realised I had been staring rudely. Heat flooded my cheeks. Clearing my throat, I adopted a polite smile.

"Good morning, welcome in. Let me know if I can help you find anything." The man approached the counter with graceful strides, assessing me with interest.

"I believe you can. Are you the owner, Serena?" I tensed slightly at hearing my name on this stranger's lips. Up close, the thrum of power and purpose surrounding him was unmistakable. He did not simply stumble upon my shop by chance, I felt certain.

"Yes, I'm Serena," I replied cautiously. "Have we met?" One corner of his mouth lifted in a hint of a smile that did not reach his cool eyes.

"Not yet. But I've heard many promising things about your shop and skills." He extended his hand across the counter. "I'm Jake. A pleasure to make your acquaintance." His firm grip seemed to sear my skin as we shook. Everything about this intense newcomer intrigued yet discomfited me. I glanced over at Ophelia who was watching Jake with a suspicious look. I could tell she wasn't as impressed with this guy as everyone else was. The man, Jake, coughed bringing my attention back to him and I realised that I was still holding his hand. He had a smirk on his face and amusement shone in his eyes. I released his hand in horror and blushed at my sudden complete social malfunction. Jake's smirk grew, obviously aware of my embarrassment.

Kill me now, was it too late to climb into some deep hole and hide? I didn't know what had come over me, it wasn't like I was someone who was swayed by a pretty face. We had plenty of attractive guys come through town in the summer months, and I handled all sorts of attempts of charm from some of them who thought a single girl with a little extra weight would be putty in their hands. Some I indulged but on my own terms, and knowing that it was only temporary. But for some reason this man was different and made me feel all flustered. And that just in the first two minutes of meeting him.

I struggled to regain my composure after that awkward first interaction with the handsome newcomer, Jake. His bold scrutiny and strong handshake had flustered me in a way I wasn't accustomed to. I wasn't some blushing small-town girl to be so easily ruffled. Clearing my throat, I smoothed my features into a politely detached mask.

"So how can I help you today?" I asked in my best customer service voice. Jake's eyes gleamed with subtle amusement, likely at my transparent effort to act unfazed.

"I was hoping you could assist me in finding someone," he replied. "A woman who I believe resides in Whitby, though I don't have her name or description." I blinked in surprise. That was certainly an unusual request.

"I'm afraid it will be difficult to locate someone with so little information," I said carefully. "Whitby has many residents and visitors. Do you know anything else about this woman that could narrow it down?" Jake shifted, suddenly looking uncomfortable. He cleared his throat before answering.

"She's connected to my late mother in some way. I'm afraid I don't have much else to go on." He gave a self-deprecating shrug, not quite meeting my gaze. "When my mother passed, she mentioned a friend living here in Whitby that I should seek out. But she didn't provide any names or specifics. I realise it's not much to work with, but finding this person was important to my mother. I had to try and fulfil her wish."

His voice carried a note of genuine regret and sadness that gave me pause. My earlier wariness faded as empathy rose within me. I knew too well the pain of losing a beloved parental figure and trying to honour their memory.

"I understand," I said gently. "I lost my own grandmother several years ago. She was like a mother to me. I still miss her every day." Jake's expression turned solemn, his keen eyes softening faintly.

"My condolences. It's a difficult loss to endure." I nodded, a bittersweet pang in my heart despite the years that had passed. We shared a moment of poignant silence for those no longer with us except in spirit. Strange that I should feel such an instant sense of kinship with this intriguing newcomer. But grief was a powerful bridge. It whispered that perhaps not everything was as it seemed with Jake. There were hidden depths beneath that cool exterior.

Clearing my throat again, I straightened and met his gaze directly.

"I'll certainly do what I can to help you find this woman, even with minimal information. May I ask what brought you here to Whitby now to search for her? It seems like a long time to wait after your mother's passing." Jake shifted again, buying time by brushing some imaginary dust from his leather sleeve. I noted the avoidance but didn't press. Everyone had parts of their past they preferred not to revisit.

"It's complicated," he finally replied. "But with the world's current instability, the timing felt right to finally honour this request." He shrugged, regaining his nonchalant air. "I happened to be travelling through the area on business, and Whitby came highly recommended as a place to visit. Two birds, one stone." I nodded thoughtfully, sensing there was much he wasn't saying but not wanting to pry deeper.

"Well, lucky for you, mysticism and the paranormal are our specialties here in Whitby. I'm sure between myself and others in town, we can uncover something to point you in the right direction." Jake's expression warmed a fraction.

"That would be greatly appreciated..." He trailed off as Obsidian suddenly leapt up onto the counter, wings of black fur spread dramatically. Before I could react, his inquisitive sniffing sent my steaming tea mug toppling over the edge. I gasped in horror as fragrant liquid spilled across the worn wood surface and directly onto Jake's expensive looking shoes.

Chapter 6

Jake

The hot tea splashing on my boots made me freeze in shock. I stared down at the growing brown stain in disbelief before my eyes snapped up to glare at the culprit - a smug looking black cat now preening itself on the counter. The damn thing seemed proud of its antics. My hands fisted at my sides, fury rising. This was my favourite pair of boots, made of expensive imported Italian leather. Ruined by some foolish animal!

Before I could react, Serena rushed into the back room with a cloth. "Oh no, I'm so sorry! Here, let me help-"

I checked my temper before she could glimpse it. "No bother," I said through gritted teeth. Keeping up polite appearances was crucial, no matter how much I currently loathed her trice damned pet. The other woman in the shop made a quiet sound of amusement. I felt my jaw clench. She'd been watching me like a hawk since I walked in, suspicion evident in her shrewd gaze. Now the blasted cat had seemingly confirmed something for her, if that knowing glint in her eye was any indication. Wonderful. Just what I needed, more obstacles interfering with my mission.

I stretched my lips into what I hoped resembled a smile and turned toward her. "Clumsy things, aren't they? No harm done." The lie tasted bitter. These had been my favourite boots. But losing my temper would not win me any trust here. The woman's eyes narrowed fractionally.

"Yes, animals are excellent judges of true character." I barely repressed a scowl at the insinuation. To prove her wrong, I reached out a cautious hand to pet the preening beast. Quick as a viper it hissed and swiped at me, claws outstretched. I jerked back my throbbing hand just in time.

"Blasted creature," I growled. The woman failed to muffle another laugh. My forced smile became more of a baring of teeth. Everything in this shop grated on my nerves, the cloying incense smell, the absurd crystals and charms lining the shelves, and most of all these two confounding females seeing far too much. I needed to regain control of this situation, and quickly.

Serena returned from the office with a towel in hand and frowned at the cat.

"Obsidian! Mind your manners." She cast an apologetic look my way. "I'm so sorry. He's normally quite friendly."

"I'm sure he didn't mean any harm," I said evenly, flexing my hand to ease the stinging scratches. I stroked a finger over my talisman, seeking any advantage to sway things in my favour again. The moonstone felt cool and calming against my skin. My mam said it had protective powers against magical forces. Though apparently not enough to guard against fate and fickle felines. I took a slow breath, calling on years of training to exude harmless charm once more.

"Please, think nothing of it," I told Serena with a rueful smile. "I've dealt with far worse than some spilled tea." Like the blood of the supernaturals that dared to defy the council and side with the evil Zodiacs, I thought to myself. "Only sad to ruin such fine boots." I kept my tone light, hoping she would soften towards me again. Her lovely eyes filled with sympathy, some of that wariness fading. Good. She was my best avenue to glean anything useful in this confounded town. I just needed to isolate her from the other woman's meddling influence. And the damn fleabag who chose that moment to hiss at me again.

"Obsidian! We do not hiss at customers, that is very rude," Serena scolded in a cringeworthy high pitch voice. The cat remained unmoved by her admonishment, continuing to groom itself. Serena shook her head and came around the counter.

To my shock, she dropped to her knees in front of me and began wiping at my boots and the spilled tea on the floor.

"I'm so very sorry about this," she said again, scrubbing furiously. Having her on her knees before me sent an unexpected spike of heat through my veins. I could see straight down her top and the way her breasts bounced as she scrubbed. In my mind's eye, I saw her glancing coyly up at me from that position... but with less clothing and as her stroking was more gentle and around my hard cock. What the fuck, where the hell did that image come from. I shifted uncomfortably as my body reacted, desire stirring despite my attempts to suppress it. What the fuck was wrong with me? I normally preferred leggy, athletic blondes for the occasional fuck and run, not this softly curvaceous woman exuding gentle spirituality. And yet, the sight of her on her knees stirred me in a way I didn't anticipate. Before I could stop myself, I reached out to touch her golden hair where it fell across her flushed cheek. The silky strands glided beneath my fingertips. More vivid images assaulted me, of tangling my hands in the golden silk as I rammed my... I dropped my hand quickly, shocked by my own actions and the direction of my thoughts. Get control of yourself, man!

I forced a smile to my face, hoping the panic, or the lust wasn't showing. I needed her to get off the floor and away from that alluring position, before I felt the need to take advantage of it

"Please, don't trouble yourself. It was just an accident, no real harm done." Serena looked up with a relieved smile. It was exactly what I didn't need. Our gazes locked and the breath left my lungs. Even on her knees, her eyes were so vibrantly alive and expressive. Beautiful. Stirring a primal hunger I did not understand. I had to grip the counter tightly against the urge to touch her again, or worse. Then her smile faltered, eyes dropping. I knew my cock was straining hard at the material of my jeans, begging to be released so I could ruin the woman's makeup. Fuck! The urge was so strong. I never reacted like this for a woman. But I suddenly wanted to dominate this woman and carve my name into her soul, making her mine and ruining any experience she would ever think of having with any other man. My thoughts really must have been all over my face because When she looked back up at me crimson flooded her cheeks. She quickly looked back down but I noticed when she peeked again helplessly at my crotch before wrenching her gaze away. Mortification surged through me. What was happening to my legendary control?

Serena mumbled something that I couldn't understand and scrambled hurriedly to her feet, fleeing into the office without meeting my eyes again. I stared after her, stunned and disturbed by my lack of composure. I was normally adept at keeping my baser urges suppressed during missions. But something about this woman obliterated my restraint, and I did not like it one bit. Taking a slow breath, I struggled to regain my customary poise. I could not allow carnal desire to distract me from my duty. Finding and eliminating the prophesied Zodiac was all that mattered. I refused to fail out of lust for some artlessly appealing girl.

Clenching my jaw, I smoothed my features as the other woman approached, her gaze far too assessing. I could tell she was going to be trouble. But I would complete my mission here in Whitby, no matter the obstacles. And I would not let a piece of ass sway me from my purpose again. I just needed to tell my raging boner that. With an inward scoff, I straightened my shoulders. I was in control. Always. I repeated it to myself, hoping my body would get the message as well. These confounding witches were no match for my resolve.

Serena emerged from the office a few moments later, cheeks still endearingly pink.

"I'm so very sorry again about the mess," she said, not quite meeting my gaze. I waved off her apology with a friendly but strained smile.

"Not at all, it was just an accident. No harm done." We stood there awkwardly for a moment, the peculiar energy still crackling between us. When Serena finally lifted her eyes to mine again, the world seemed to stop. We stared at each other, frozen in the moment. Something deep and inexplicable passed between us, setting my pulse racing. What was it about this woman that caught me so easily off guard? I cleared my throat gruffly, breaking the spell. Get it together! I reminded myself harshly.

"So, do you think you could still help me with that reading?" I asked, rubbing the back of my neck. "To find the mystery woman my mother mentioned?"

"Oh, well I..." Serena trailed off, blushing. The other woman interjected smoothly.

"Actually Serena and I have plans this evening that simply cannot be changed." I bit back a surge of irritation. Of course this meddlesome woman would thwart me. Serena gave her friend an exasperated look before turning back to me with an apologetic smile.

"I'm afraid Ophelia is right, we do have an engagement tonight." Dammit! I tried not to scowl. "But I am sure I will have availability tomorrow if you wanted to come back for a reading then?" Serena said quickly. Ophelia made a quiet huff of disapproval. I ignored her, focusing on Serena's lovely, earnest face. Tomorrow was not ideal, but better than nothing. I would make it work. Plucking a pen from the counter, I quickly jotted down my number on a scrap of paper.

"Here, take my mobile number," I said, flashing her my most charming smile. "Give me a ring whenever you have an opening." Serena took the paper, blushing prettily again. "Of course, I'll call you tomorrow then." She smiled, shy but intrigued. Perfect. I had planted the hook well. Satisfied I had made progress despite the obstacles, I bid Serena a warm goodbye and left the incense-choked shop, the meddlesome Ophelia glowering at my back. I was determined that Serena would aid my mission one way or another. The Zodiac could not evade me forever. And neither could the hold this girl seemed to have on me, maybe I could schedule in some fun activities, it would surely make her open up in more ways than one. The rush of lust coursed through me again, reminding me that I needed to get it under control, and maybe figure out why this woman caused such an effect. Though I dared not examine it too closely. Not yet.

Chapter 7

Serena

The scent of melted cheese and tomatoes filled the air as I pulled the glass baking dish from the oven. My stomach rumbled eagerly, even though I'd already sampled the spinach and mushroom lasagna earlier. It was one of my favourite comfort foods, and the perfect meal to share with Alec and Ophelia tonight. Speaking of, the sound of heavy footsteps coming up the stairs signalled Alec's arrival. Right on time, as always.

"That smells heavenly!" he exclaimed as he shoved the door wider with his foot. His arms were laden with the baguettes I'd asked him to pick up from the bakery on his way over.

"Lasagna just out of the oven," I told him with a smile. "Here, you grab that, and I'll take the salad downstairs to start setting up." Alec deposited the warm, crusty bread on the counter while I pulled the big bowl of mixed greens from the fridge. Balancing it carefully in my hands, I headed down the narrow stairs into the shop, Alec followed close behind with the lasagne.

The cosy back room was already set up for our dinner, with its round bistro table and mismatched chairs in the centre. Ophelia stood nearby, studiously examining the array of vintage plates and cutlery she'd pulled from the shelves. She looked up with a smile as we entered.

"Ah good, I was just about to come up and hurry you slowpokes along," she teased.

I stuck my tongue out at her in response as I set the salad bowl down. "If you're so impatient, you can cook next week."

Ophelia waved a hand airily. "And subject you to my burnt offerings? I think not."

Chuckling, I helped Alec get the lasagne situated while Ophelia poured us each a generous glass of the merlot she'd brought. I quickly ran back up the stairs and cut the bread into pieces and smeared them with lashings of garlic butter. I was carrying it back down when I heard Ophelia and Alec talking.

"I dunno," Alec's gruff tone sounded, "I am sure she can handle herself."

"But you didn't see it," Ophelia said, "The guy was oozing manipulative charm all over the place. He even tried to charm me but I can spot his kind a mile away. You know we have to look out for the girl, especially with-"

"I know," Alec interrupted Ophelia, sounding irritated. "I'll talk to her later, okay?" I sighed to myself. It was bad enough that Ophelia had made herself perfectly clear on her thoughts of Jake to me, but now to bring it up to Alec, and treat me like some fragile piece of glass, I mean I was almost thirty years old, not five. I grimaced and forced a smile on my face and called loudly as I came down the stairs. I noticed the awkward look on both their faces, but acted like all was normal. I just wanted to enjoy dinner and not have to worry about epic world destiny or anything else.

Soon we were all seated comfortably and filling our plates. Alec immediately scooped out a big square of the cheesy pasta.

"This looks incredible as always, Serena," he said before taking an appreciative bite.

I smiled, warmed by the praise. Cooking had never been a great skill of mine, but this recipe was a personal favourite I'd perfected over the years.

We ate in contented silence for several minutes, simply enjoying the food and wine. I loved our cosy family dinners, just the three of us gathered here after hours in the shop. Gran used to host friends for weekly meals as well, keeping her myriad of eclectic acquaintances close knit. In my grief after she passed, it had been Alec and Ophelia who stepped in to fill that void, basically adopting me into their little circle despite our age difference. Their unwavering support these past years meant everything.

Glancing around the shop, lit softly by strings of fairy lights, I could almost imagine Gran sitting right there at the table with us, shrewd eyes twinkling as she listened to the latest gossip and dispensed advice. Everything from the crystals reflecting rainbows on the shelves to her collection of vintage tarot decks felt infused with her steadying presence. This space had been Gran's true home for decades before becoming mine. Holding our weekly gatherings here kept her spirit close even now.

I must have drifted into melancholy silence thinking of Gran, because Ophelia gently touched my hand.

"Everything alright, dear?" I offered her a small smile.

"Yes, just missing Gran a bit extra tonight for some reason."

Ophelia's expression softened with understanding. She gave my hand an affectionate pat. "I'm sure Iris is still keeping an eye on you from the other side. In fact-" Her sharp gaze turned mischievous. "I'd bet good money she even checks in on our dinner conversations." Alec snorted mid-bite of lasagne.

"Knowing Iris, she's heckling every word and complaining about the lack of whiskey."

I laughed aloud at the perfect impression of Gran's acerbic wit. The sombre spell broken, warmth spread through me again. Gran would scold me for brooding when I was surrounded by loved ones and delicious food. She'd tell me to enjoy the gifts in front of me now.

"You're absolutely right," I conceded, lifting my wine in a toast. "To Gran and the good memories."

"To Iris," Ophelia and Alec echoed, clinking their glasses to mine. The merlot paired perfectly with the rich lasagne, the crisp bite of the salad, and the savoury, garlicky bread.

We were enjoying the leisurely meal, chatting casually about our days. When Ophelia finally dabbed her lips and fixed me with her piercing gaze, I suspected what topic was coming next.

"So tell me truthfully," she began, "what did you make of that odd newcomer in the shop earlier? Mr tall, dark, and up himself, stranger." I suppressed a sigh, having expected this line of questioning. Ophelia had made her opinion of Jake abundantly clear through subtle looks and noises of disapproval all afternoon after he left. And I honestly couldn't blame her guarded reaction. Everything about him set my senses on high alert even as an undeniable magnetism drew me in. But that didn't mean I could afford to turn away what might become a regular paying customer.

"Jake seems...intriguing," I hedged, chasing a bit of tomato around my plate. "And he's willing to pay for a reading, which I can't afford to pass up with winter being here and all. The cold months are always slow for business." Ophelia just tsked, clearly unconvinced by my pragmatism.

"There's something dangerous about that man, mark my words. He pretends at politeness, but it's just a mask."

"You can't know that for certain though," I countered half-heartedly. In truth, every one of my finely tuned instincts screamed similar warnings, despite my undeniable attraction to Jake's rugged good looks and hot as fuck body. But facts were facts, the rent and bills still had to be paid regardless of mysterious strangers.

"Perhaps not for certain," Ophelia conceded, though scepticism remained etched on her face. "But any woman with sense would be foolish to ignore the signs. You'd do well to be cautious, that's all I'm saying." She took another drink from her wine glass before pointing her glass at me. "Besides, even Obsidian didn't like him. That's gotta count for something." I glanced over at the black fur ball who was currently curled up in the chair in the corner. He opened his eyes and watched me before closing them again. I couldn't argue with that one. Cat's really were especially intuitive.

I turned to Alec, hoping he would provide a more balanced, moderate viewpoint. But his bushy brows were drawn together in an uncharacteristic frown.

"I have to say, from what I heard, I agree with Ophelia on this one," he rumbled at last. " I only saw him briefly in the street but there's something...cold about him. Calculating. Gave me an uneasy feeling right off." Alec had good instincts when it came to reading people, so his validation of Ophelia's concerns gave me pause. While the logical part of me still clung to justifying taking Jake's money, my gut whispered to be wary of getting further entangled with this man, no matter his allure. I chewed my lip uncertainly, feelings torn. Sensing my indecision, Ophelia reached over again and patted my hand.

"Just trust those keen instincts of yours, dear. And if anything feels off, send him packing. Your safety is what matters most." I nodded slowly, knowing she spoke wisdom.

"You're probably right that I should be careful. I'll make sure to keep the reading very professional."

Alec and Ophelia exchanged a knowing look that suggested they guessed professionalism had already lapsed earlier today when I was on my knees before Jake, transfixed by his heated gaze and evidently sizable manhood that was inches from my face. Even now, a secret thrill coursed through me remembering our charged encounter. What was it about him that drew such a powerful, almost primal reaction from me? I took a quick gulp of wine to cover my flustered expression.

"Well, professional or not, the point is be vigilant," Ophelia said briskly, topping up our glasses. "That one seems like a man accustomed to getting what he wants by any means."

"I promise to keep my guard up," I assured her, hoping to ease their concerns. I knew they just wanted to protect me, and I loved them for it. Alec cleared his throat loudly in the brief silence.

"Right, well, why don't I dish up seconds? Can't let this delicious lasagna go to waste."

He efficiently redirected the conversation to lighter topics as we finished off the decadent meal. Laughter and wine flowed freely as we lingered long after the food was gone, simply enjoying each other's company. Sitting contentedly among these dear friends in Gran's space, their worries over Jake's intentions seemed easily swept aside for now. The cosy intimacy of our family dinner nurtured me, bolstering my courage. I knew in my heart I was ready for whatever lay ahead on my fated path, no matter how dark or dangerous. Whatever this stranger Jake was truly seeking here, with my loved ones' support, I could handle it. And who knew, maybe I could even help guide him toward the light if he proved worthy. For now, I decided to trust my intuition tomorrow regarding both the professional reading and my perplexing personal reactions to him. One way or another, I sensed this newcomer would have an impact on my destiny's direction. Though whether for good or ill remained to be seen.

Chapter 8

Jake

The night air was frigid against my face, but I barely felt the sting as I peered through the large shop window. Inside, golden light spilled from strings of small bulbs, casting everything in a warm glow. My eyes were immediately drawn to Serena. She sat at a cosy bistro table set with plates of food and glasses of wine, chatting and laughing with her companions. The sight made something uncomfortably tight knot in my chest, though I refused to examine the feeling too closely. I was crouched outside this shop well past dark for one reason only: gathering necessary intel on potential Zodiac allies. The fact that seeing Serena relaxed and happy with other people sparked an unwelcome ache meant nothing. She was a means to an end, no more. At least, that's what I repeated like a mantra, determined to make it true through force of will.

Shifting to regain feeling in my numb toes, I continued surveying the scene playing out before me. Serena's laughter rang out again, clear even through the glass, and my traitorous gaze fixed on her smile. Annoyance flared that I was again distracted by this woman I barely knew. With effort, I wrenched my focus to the other people at her table. The older woman, that I now knew was called Ophelia, still watched Serena with that shrewd, maternal air, as though worried she might disappear if not monitored constantly. I fought back a scowl recalling how she had obstructed me at every turn earlier that day. A meddlesome wretch, though clearly cunning. The man was unfamiliar to me, and my eyes narrowed taking in his large stature and close, relaxed rapport with Serena. He touched her hand familiarly, like an affectionate relative. Yet a flare of some ugly, unnamed emotion rose in me at witnessing their easy intimacy.

Were they involved? Lovers? The thought stirred a vile brew of anger and... could it be jealousy? Impossible. I harbored no claim over this stranger that would give me any right to resent her affection for another. Did I? Gritting my teeth in frustration, I forced myself to catalogue the man in pragmatic terms. He seemed near the same age as the older woman, perhaps late forties or so. Strong build but carrying some extra weight, especially across the midsection. His food disappeared rapidly from his plate to confirm an appreciable appetite. Faded tattoos marked his forearms and peeking above his shirt collar - military perhaps? The bearing and watchful eye certainly fit. If he also had combat training, he could be a dangerous opponent despite age and bulk slowing him down. I would need to invest time learning all I could about him and verifying whether he posed a threat. To my mission, I mean, a threat to my mission. Not to the feelings that I shouldn't be having about the woman he was so comfortable with. I could almost hear an inner voice laughing, yeah keep telling yourself that.

For now though, they seemed merely three close companions enjoying a cosy dinner. Harmless on the surface. My brow creased as I noted again how perfectly at ease Serena appeared in their company, her expression open and unguarded. Like she had let down all masks and defences, trusting these two completely. They clearly shared an intimate bond that stirred an ache of longing I quickly smothered. I hadn't known true friendship or belonging for many years now. Not since my parents died and Uncle took me in to train with the Council. Emotional attachments were seen as liabilities in my world. Yet some small, broken part of me yearned to experience again that level of inner circle acceptance. To simply relax and laugh with others, letting the ever-present weight lift temporarily off my shoulders. Perhaps in another life.

No. I could not afford sentimentality. Not when I had a job to do. These fanciful wishes were pointless distractions that weakened my resolve. With renewed determination, I focused again on the back room tableau. The remains of their meal littered the table amidst partially emptied glasses of wine. As they chatted, smiles and gestures animated, I scrutinised their body language and interactions for anything of value. But it was only a warm familial scene, no obvious clues leaping out. Perhaps I had been too hasty pressing Serena earlier about a reading today. If I had exercised more patience, she may have invited me to this gathering, allowing me to directly observe her among allies. Though in truth, imagining myself trying to fit into this intimate circle was laughable. Their easy rapport would wither under my presence, their laughter turn to wary silence. I was a killer, not a friend. The permanent stain on my soul would corrupt their light.

No, better to remain out here objectively analysing from the shadows. Detachment was my sanctuary, obsession my downfall. Remember the mission. Yet even as I repeated the cold creed that ruled my life, my eyes strayed back to Serena again and again as if compelled by an unseen force. The way silken hair spilled over her shoulders when she threw her head back in laughter. How she nibbled her full lower lip when listening intently. The curve of her smile and sparkle of her eyes. Far too many pointless details for an impartial observer. Realising I was more fixated on watching Serena than gathering useful intelligence, I forced myself to turn away from the window's revealing insights.

Nothing more could be learned from pointless mooning. I had confirmed she was close with the other two, and that they did not fully trust me, hence blocking my reading request. I would need to tread carefully in handling them to win Serena's trust and cooperation. Rising slowly, I stamped some feeling back into my numb feet and legs. The cold from the pavement had seeped into my bones, matching the chill settling around my heart once more. Sentiment was making me weak, distracted from duty. I needed to clear my head and refocus.

Hands shoved deep in my pockets, I slowly began walking the twisting streets that ribbons through Whitby, following the downward slope toward the harbour. I kept my head down against the biting wind, the hood of my jacket drawn up for anonymity. The fresh sea air helped revive me from the cloying warmth of the shop and the distraction of dangerous yearnings best forgotten. I repeated the Mantras drilled into me by years of training, like hammer blows pounding my wavering hope and weakness back into cold, hardened determination. There is no passion, only clarity of purpose. Kill the heart, keep the mind lethal. You have no name beyond the Council's will. I was a blade honed to exterminate evil. Nothing more.

My steady pace carried me along the cliffs overlooking the harbour mouth where the River Esk met the North Sea. Despite the late hour, the sounds of drunken laughter echoing up from the pubs along the waterfront carried on the wind. I turned my back on the taint of frivolity, instead looking out at the vast expanse of the sea. Under the cavernous dome of night sky dusted with stars, the dark water stretched endlessly to the horizon. The immense power and timelessness of this view centred me, putting my troubles in perspective. What did it matter if I was distracted by a pretty face or camaraderie I could never share in? All beauty and life would be obliterated if the black hole set by the Zodiacs was allowed to consume Earth as it had Mars. I could not fail in my duty to stop the prophesied extinction. At any cost.

The wind whipped my coat violently as I stood at the precipitous cliff edge. The cold did not touch me now, filled as I was with renewed icy purpose. I had wasted enough time and mental energy on inconsequential. Starting tomorrow, I would be focused solely on my objective: verifying Serena's role in concealing the Zodiac, then eliminating them both if confirmed. My uncle taught me well that conscience must be sacrificed for the greater good. I would do what was necessary, no matter how distasteful. Failure was not an option with so many innocent lives at stake.

Satisfied I had regained proper perspective, I left the blustery clifftop vigil and headed to my rented room. I needed rest tonight so I would be ready to present harmlessly charming cover tomorrow as just a man seeking spiritual guidance, ignorant of the danger. Serena had called while I was speaking to my uncle, leaving a message about an opening tomorrow evening. I would use the reading to gauge what secrets lay protected behind that gentle smile. My mission compelled me forward, no matter the cost. Tomorrow would reveal if Serena had chosen to stand with demons and defy the Council's authority. If so, she would share their fate. No one could protect her from my blades.

Steam from the shower still clung to the small bathroom's mirrors and tiles as I secured the towel around my waist. Scrubbing a hand across the fogged glass, I leaned in to inspect my reflection. Cold eyes devoid of emotion stared back at me. Good. The mask was firmly in place again. No hints of weakness or inner conflicts to exploit. I was a weapon forged by duty and honed by death. Let Serena and her cohorts see only the indifferent killer, not the man. Satisfied, I crossed into the cramped bedroom just as my mobile started vibrating loudly on the rickety dresser. I tensed for a split second before forcing my muscles to relax. Paranoia was my constant companion after so many years living among shadows. But I was safe here. For now. Casting aside the towel, I quickly donned clean boxers and trousers before snatching up the phone mid-ring. The name on the Caller ID screen had me relaxing marginally. Not a threat, just an expected annoyance. I took a breath to brace myself before accepting the call with a brisk,

"Yes Sir?" My uncle's clipped tones filled the speaker. "Status report. What progress have you made in identifying the target?" I sat on the edge of the creaky mattress, letting the familiar mix of respect and dislike that defined our relationship settle over me.

"I'm still narrowing down options, sir," I answered evenly. "This place is overrun with witches and other supernaturals complicit with the false prophecy. It will take time to discern who is hiding the Zodiac."

"We are nearly out of time," he snapped. "The void spreads daily, consuming everything in its path. Mars is already lost." His normally cold voice held an uncharacteristic note of strain. Our window for preventing catastrophe was closing rapidly.

"I understand, sir. But we only get one chance for the kill shot," I pressed urgently. "I can't risk taking it without certainty. I just need a bit longer to gather evidence and confirm." He grunted, displeasure evident even without seeing his stern face. We both knew I was right, though. If I assassinated the wrong target, the real Zodiac would be driven further into hiding, perhaps permanently out of reach. I had to be absolutely certain before I struck. Silence extended between us before he conceded gruffly.

"Very well. But time is a luxury we do not have. Report back the moment you have confirmation on the target's identity. Do not engage until the Council sanctions the kill. Understood?"

"Understood, sir." The line went dead without further pleasantries. I set down the phone with a vexed exhale. My uncle was under tremendous pressure from above to eliminate the Zodiac threat before catastrophe struck. But he also hammered the lesson into me that no kill was better than a rushed, botched job on an unverified target. I just needed to buy a little more time and trust my instincts to identify the correct prey. Starting with Serena tonight. My gut said she was the key, if only I could get her to lower her guard and open up.

I stood and began dressing for the evening, considering how best to present myself. Benign, but with enough allure to tempt her into letting slip any useful knowledge. Despite my misgivings, Serena's evident attraction to me could prove advantageous if expertly manipulated. Though the memory of that charged moment yesterday when raw hunger nearly overwhelmed my restraint made me hesitate. Playing with fire was dangerous when one's control proved so precariously fragile around her. But the approaching apocalypse left little room for restraint or uncertainty. I would use every weapon at my disposal, no matter how unorthodox, for the sake of the mission. A sudden buzz from my phone interrupted my strategic thinking. I snatched it up, breath catching when I saw the message was from Serena. So she hadn't lost her nerve yet. I quickly scanned the words, lips curving as her meaning sank in. She had an opening tonight at 7pm for the reading and wanted confirmation that the time suited me. Perfect. I rapidly typed a response.

Serena, 7pm tonight works perfectly for me. I look forward to seeing you again and hopefully regaining some insight into this mystery woman from my past. Please let me know if I need to bring anything special to prepare for the reading. Otherwise, I will see you at your shop this evening. Regards, Jake

I hit send and set down the phone with a renewed sense of anticipation. Everything was falling into place now. Tonight I would have Serena alone and vulnerable. The time was ripe to push for answers about whether she had any knowledge of or ties to the Zodiac I hunted.

A successful interrogation could provide the confirmation I needed to take my kill shot before disaster struck. The phone buzzed loudly again just as I finished getting dressed - a response from Serena already. Eagerness spiked through me, quickly suppressed. Get it together, man. This is reconnaissance, not a social call. I kept my face impassive as I read her reply.

Jake, 7pm tonight is perfect, no need to bring anything! Just your open mind and any details you can remember about this mystery woman and your mother's connection to her. See you soon! - Serena

Despite the polite, distant tone, I could tell she was also anticipating our meeting. A promising sign that my presence disarmed her, opened her up beyond wise caution. I just needed to ensure that empathetic instinct worked in my favour tonight. With the trap set, my uncle would expect contact. I hit redial on his number, unsurprised when he answered before the first ring ended. We had trained each other well over the years to be constantly vigilant.

"Yes?" The same curt greeting, demanding swift facts. I provided them concisely.

"The shopkeeper I told you about has agreed to a private meeting tonight for the reading. If she is harbouring the target as I suspect, she may let slip something to confirm it."

"And if your suspicions prove true, you are prepared to carry out termination immediately?" His severe tone brought no softness. I did not hesitate.

"Yes sir. You may trust the threat will be eliminated by morning."

"See that it is." A pause, then uncharacteristic uncertainty entered his voice. "And Jake...take care. Do not allow emotion or temptation to sway you from duty again." I flinched at the use of my name, a low blow reminding me of past failure. Jaw clenched, I bit out, "I won't fail this time."

"I look forward to your report," he said grimly before terminating the call. I slowly lowered the phone, his underlying message clear. If I wavered from my duty again due to soft sentiment, the consequences would be severe. There could be no room for doubt or weakness tonight. One way or another, this ended with Serena's blood on my hands.

Chapter 9

Jake

I took extra care dressing for my meeting with Serena, donning one of my nicer fitted black shirts that showed off my muscular build. I hoped the casual yet sharp look would make her see me as intriguing and attractive. This "reading" was about far more than glimpsing the face of my target, it was a chance to connect with Serena, gain her trust. Our apparent chemistry could prove useful if I made her feel comfortable lowering her guard around me. I wasn't above using seduction either if fucking her brains out was going to get me closer to what I wanted. You know what they say, loose legs can lead to loose lips. The idea should have seemed distasteful, but I found myself anticipating time alone with her, even if pretence was required on my part. I was more than willing to sample what bodily delights this woman had to offer.

When I arrived at the shop, I could immediately sense Serena's nervous energy, noticing how she shuffled the papers on the counter and avoided direct eye contact. Time to turn on the charm. I gave her my most disarming smile.

"Good evening, Serena. Thank you again for taking the time to see me, especially after hours." She glanced up, looking slightly flustered as if I had caught her off guard.

"Of course, I want to help if I can. I thought closing the shop would give us more privacy and concentration for the reading."

"That was very thoughtful of you." I injected warm appreciation into my tone. I could tell that my charm was working, and watched as her eyes raked over my body as she unconsciously wet her lips. She suddenly looked up at me, a blush appearing on her cheeks. Fuck, she looked so innocent and enticing. I almost wanted to forget the reading all together and slam her body into the counter she stood behind and just try and fuck the information out of her. The thought must have shown in my eyes because her eyes widened and her cheeks reddened further. I allowed a smug smile to lift the corners of my lips, knowing that I had her right where I wanted her.

"So..." I asked, allowing a hint of amusement to show, "what do we do now?" When she still hesitated, I gestured at the rows of shelves behind her.

"Perhaps you could show me some of the wares, before we get started? I'm very interested to browse what you have available." That did the trick. Serena visibly rallied herself, falling smoothly into her role as shopkeeper.

"Of course, let me give you a quick tour." As she led me further into the modest shop, I catalogued the various occult paraphernalia lining the shelves. Crystals, candles, incense, tarot cards, all the usual accoutrements. My lips thinned in distaste, but I was careful to keep my true sentiments concealed. No need to arouse her wariness when she was finally lowering her guard around me.

Serena gestured to each section as we walked, keeping up a stream of enthusiastic commentary about the items. I made sure to nod and ask occasional questions, maintaining a guise of innocent interest. In truth, the very presence of such unholy objects set my teeth on edge. But I could not afford to reveal that yet. Not until I had confirmation this woman posed the threat I suspected or outlived her usefulness, despite her friendly manner. My duty demanded I remain open to all possibilities. We paused before a display of various dried herbs and roots. Serena picked up a bundle tied with twine, holding it up for me to examine.

"For example, this is a protection charm I make using rosemary, dittany, and black salt." She unwrapped a corner to release a pungent herbal aroma. "I harvest the herbs myself out on the moors. They're infused with the intention to defend against negative energies or magic." I made an effort to lean closer and inhale the scent, keeping my true revulsion hidden. Just the thought of unnatural magic being used nearby made my skin crawl with the urge to cleanse the taint. But I forced myself to smile benignly.

"Fascinating. It seems you have quite the extensive collection of specialised items." Serena re-wrapped the bundle, setting it back in its place, her expression thoughtful.

"My Gran was the real master when it came to crafting charms and potions. I'm still learning all she knew through trial and error." A shadow of grief passed over her face, there and gone. I filed away that reference to her deceased grandmother for later consideration. Grief could be exploited as easily as any other emotion, if necessary.

Clearing her throat, Serena gestured to the curtained-off back section of the shop.

"Beyond the reading nook is where I offer psychic services like tarot readings, seances, and such." She gave me a warm smile. "It may help in your search for more information about this mystery woman." I hesitated, weighing how to respond. Allowing her to wield her unnatural powers on me was unappealing at best, dangerous at worst. But refusing might rouse her suspicions after I had feigned such interest.

"I confess I'm sceptical about such mystic arts," I hedged. Serena's expression remained neutral and open.

"Perfectly understandable. It's wise to approach these things with care." She paused delicately before continuing. "Although in some cases, tapping into forces beyond the mundane can offer real insight, if done properly." Her wording intrigued me. She seemed to acknowledge the risk of venturing beyond mortal limits. Perhaps she was not as corrupt as others of her kind. I could potentially use that nuance to my advantage. But first I needed confirmation of her role as a believer.

"You raise a fair point," I conceded. "I pride myself on keeping an open mind despite my scepticism. If you believe your skills could aid my quest, I'm willing to try." I held up my hands disarmingly. "No obligations if it doesn't feel right." Serena's smile held approval and an enthusiasm that seemed genuine.

"Wonderful! An open mind is all that I ask. Why don't you take a seat inside and get comfortable. I'll prepare some tea to help relax your focus."

She drew back the beaded curtain screening off the reading nook. Mystical symbols adorned the walls within the snug space. Candles and crystals covered nearly every surface. Incense saturated the air with cloying sweetness that turned my stomach. But I forced myself to settle comfortably onto the plush purple armchair as Serena busied herself preparing tea. I saw a blur of something from across the room and a ginger cat had the audacity to jump into my lap, circling before deigning to curl up, rumbling like a small engine. I tensed, ready to dump the presumptuous animal to the floor. But Serena glanced over with a smile.

"Carnelian seems quite taken with you, at least. He's an excellent judge of character." Her subtle emphasis on that last word stayed my hand from ejecting the cat. I forced myself to relax and even stroke the soft fur. How many of these blasted things did she have? But anything to keep Serena's trust for now. Soon enough, the charade would no longer be necessary.

Serena finished steeping the tea and poured two mugs, adding honey to mine before handing it over. I took a cautious sip, detecting nothing amiss in the earthy flavour. She settled across from me on a cushioned bench, cradling her own mug.

"Now then. To start, I'd like you to close your eyes and focus on your breath." Her voice took on a rhythmic, lulling quality. "Allow your mind to open, releasing any tension or resistance. Let the sounds and smells soothe your spirit." I followed her guidance, modulating my breaths while expanding my senses as stealthily as possible. A psychic's mental defences were often lowered in these trance states. If I could slip past her protections, perhaps I could discern her true nature before she gained similar access to my own closely guarded thoughts.

"Picture your intention forming clearly in your mind's eye." Serena's voice floated softly across the space between us. "The face of the one you seek here in Whitby. Call her image into focus." I concentrated on summoning a vague feminine silhouette, not having much to go on as it was, I was also careful with my intentions and also wanting to expose my actual objectives and target. I couldn't imagine sweet Serena here being so willing to help if the reading she was giving me was to result in the bloody death of potentially one of her friends. I heard Serena's soothing voice continue to tempt me further.

"Think of your mother, and the connection that you wish to claim through her." Then a force beyond my control suddenly seized hold, forcibly guiding my visualisation. I could feel myself falling into the black abyss of my unconscious mind. I knew that this would lead to things that even I didn't want to see. But before I could react, a lifelike image coalesced within my mind's eye. Serena stood across from me, wreathed in a luminous aura, eyes aglow with ethereal light. No! How had she managed to infiltrate my consciousness so easily? I pushed back violently, trying to dispel the vision, but her radiant image persisted. And a scene unfolded out in front of me, starting with the lifeless eyes of my mother as she lay in the ruins of my childhood home, and shielded by the broken body of my father. I felt the pain of their loss ripping through me all over again. But then the scene blurred and shifted to another night that was seared into my memory. The night of my first kill. With my uncle by my side as barely an adult at eighteen I snuffed the light from the eyes of an elderly woman accused of conspiring with the Zodiac believers, and of Thaddeus Morgan, the leader of the resisters himself. Then the scenes kept coming, faster and more pronounced. All of them, all the lives that I had taken in the name of the council and in my mission to seek out and find as many of the bastard Zodiacs as possible, before they did to the whole world what they did to my family. And all the time Serena stood there in some ethereal glow watching the scenes unfold, her features becoming more twisted with horror. Finally Serena looked up at me, her eyes pooled with tears and only served to enhance the play of the green blue that swirled within them.

"Who are you?" she asked in a choked voice, "What are you?" She thought that she was looking at a monster, a ruthless killer. But I wasn't the monster here. I was protecting her from the monsters.

My eyes flew open with a gasp, breaking the trance. Serena blinked slowly, appearing drained and unsettled. Her tea had spilled unheeded, soaking into her skirt. Carnelian lifted his head, green eyes piercing as they shifted between us.

"What did you see?" Serena whispered. I could see the horror forming in her eyes as she spoke. I rose abruptly, dislodging the cat from my lap, causing the fleabag to dig his claws into me in some effort to hold on. I winced as I felt his claws pierce through my shirt into my chest. But it didn't matter, I had revealed too much already. I needed to get out of here and regroup.

"Forgive me, I need some air." I strode rapidly from the reading nook without meeting Serena's eyes. I could feel her troubled gaze following me as I left the shop onto the street, but I did not stop until I was several buildings away. Only then did I lean against a shadowed alley wall to catch my breath, heart pounding erratically.

So the psychic witch was more powerful than she let on. I had felt her alien power firsthand as it forced its way into my mind. And though I I wasn't sure how much she had actually seen before had halted the connection, she now knew I was not merely a tourist seeking family history. I may have ruined my best opportunity to get close and catch her unaware. Cursing under my breath, I slammed a fist against the rough bricks until pain helped clear my chaotic thoughts. I would need to proceed with far more caution around Serena now. She was clearly stronger than expected. And was going to be more suspicious of me. But I had overcome far greater foes during my decade of hunting the supernatural. I refused to fail my duty because of one witch, no matter how unusual her abilities seemed.

I just needed time to regroup and determine my next move. For some reason she was clearly the key to my target, but I couldn't risk pushing too far. Perhaps observing her from a distance for a few days while I strengthened my mental wards against psychic intrusion. There were still avenues left to explore in this hunt. I had no intention of returning to my Council contacts empty-handed. Not when so much depended on my success here. Serena could still be useful to me, and as long as I was careful she would lead me to the evil incarnation, so that I could end them for the good of all mankind. Whitby's peaceful streets would soon run red to cleanse this infestation from the earth. For now though, I would bide my time. A hunter knew when to wait in the shadows for the perfect moment to strike. Straightening from my slumped position, I shook out my tense limbs and resumed my confident stride. There were preparations to be made. Contacts to call on for information, charms and potions. When I returned to face the witch Serena again, it would be on my terms, with victory assured. This was merely a minor setback, not a defeat. The Zodiac's days were numbered now. My patience would be rewarded soon enough. Until then, I had work to do. Without a backward glance at the innocuous shop, I melted into the dark cobbled streets, just one more face in the crowd. But though they did not realise it, these people now walked alongside a hunter who had caught a scent of his elusive prey. And I would not stop until my duty was fulfilled.

Chapter 10
Serena

The silence rang in my ears after Jake's abrupt departure. I sat motionless on the cushioned bench, shaken to my core by the vision we had apparently shared. Though his hasty exit left me uncertain precisely what horrors he might have glimpsed within the psychic connection. Visions were annoying like that. They only told you what you needed to see, not what you wanted to see, and even in the same vision you would see different things. After all, even in life two people looking at the same object would see it from a different point of view given their circumstances and experience. I only knew that the battlefield strewn with bodies that culminated in Jake's own gruesome death would haunt me. The glimpse of the potential future had taken place on the iconic 199 steps ascending to Whitby Abbey. I couldn't shake the image of his broken body as it lay across some of the steps. Ominous significance, given the site's role in my previous premonition. What fatal dance were Jake and I destined to play out upon that ancient stone stage? And to what end? The fragmented vision alone offered more dread portents than answers.

My hands trembled, causing the remnants of my spilled tea to ripple across the already soaked fabric of my skirt. I scarcely noticed the scalding heat. Absently, I reached for a tea towel that say by the hot teapot and laid it on my lap. It wouldn't mop up everything but it was the best I could do while My focus remained trapped in those terrible images now seared into my mind. Jake, a man I barely knew yet felt intrinsically linked to, torn apart by an unseen enemy upon the cliffs I loved. His silver eyes devoid of life, just like all the other bodies scattered around him. I hugged my arms tightly across my churning stomach, struggling not to be sick. How could I have foreseen something so horrific? Was it the truth or merely a warning? Gran always said the future remained malleable, each choice altering its course. But the vision's visceral details haunted me. Every vivid sensation had felt cruelly real. The tang of blood and smoke in the air, the screams and clash of combat washing over me. I knew with bone-deep certainty I had witnessed a tragedy soon to unfold unless the vision spurred change. But how to prevent events already in motion? And what role did I play in this cosmic drama? The glimpses I had been granted so far seemed only to breed more fear and confusion.

I flinched as a sudden weight impacted my lap and sharp claws pricked my thighs. Blinking rapidly, I focused on the ginger cat now kneading my legs with concern in his piercing green eyes. Carnelian's unexpected pounce jolted me from the waking nightmare replaying in my mind. My hands moved automatically to stroke down his back. His rumbling purr soothed my jagged nerves as nothing else could.

Steadying as always, my spirit cat seemed to sense the disquiet left in the wake of Jake's swift departure.

"Thank you, friend," I whispered shakily. Carnelian butted his head against my hand as though in reply. I leaned into his warm, living presence, so comforting after the death I had witnessed. He bore mute witness as scattered tears escaped despite my efforts at control. I let wave after wave roll through me, releasing the heart-wrenching emotions the vision inspired. Carnelian's purrs remained a constant rumble grounding me until finally, the flood subsided. I sat quietly then, focused on the simplicity of stroking soft fur until my breaths came evenly again. The calm after the storm. When I felt reasonably composed, I gave Carnelian a final scratch under his chin.

"Right. I suppose sitting here falling to bits won't solve anything." The cat chirped approvingly as I set him aside and stood on still-unsteady legs. Lingering fear and sorrow haunted my heart, but I refused to surrender to their paralysing effects. If destiny had granted me these glimpses of possibilities, there must be purpose behind the pain. I need only have faith and courage to walk the path revealed one step at a time. Gran's teachings echoed in my mind, her belief that each person's future remained fluid, changing with every choice. My visions offered insight, not inexorable fate. It was up to me to parse their meaning and use it for good. Starting now. I inhaled deeply, gathering my scattered determination. Breaking the deadly chain of events seemed improbable, but I must try. Somehow, I knew Jake was key. Our fates had become entwined for a reason. I only prayed that by keeping him close, I could prevent the dark tragedy foreshadowed.

Filled with renewed conviction, I headed up to my flat and changed from my wet clothes. The sting from the hot tea still left red blotches on my skin. I applied some aloe to the burn and pulled on a pair of joggers and a simple top. I pulled my hair up into a bun and headed back down into the shop and the reading room beyond. I needed to clean up the mess from my tea and worked quickly and tired to think of anything but the horrific vision that played over and over in my mind. Finally, I turned toward the office at the back of the shop to start a pot of strong coffee. No rest would come easily tonight after bearing witness to such havoc. It was better to keep my nervous energy productively focused. I had research to do and preparations to make. But my steps faltered as Carnelian insistently butted his head against my ankle. I looked down to meet his expectant green gaze.

"What is it?" His eyes shifted pointedly to the corner where Jake had sat during the reading. I followed his stare to see an oval pendant laying half-hidden beneath the chair. Carnelian trotted over and batted it closer. The moonstone amulet, I realised with a start. Jake's necklace that I had noticed earlier. It must have snapped off in his haste to escape. I remembered how his sudden movement had caused Carnelian to cling to him, maybe that had caused the delicate chain to break.

I hesitated, then slowly bent to retrieve the pendant. Power thrummed against my palm the moment I touched the cool silver setting. This was no ordinary token. The energy resonating from it felt intrinsically linked to Jake himself. I lifted the amulet higher, examining the moonstone's distinctive glow. Definite magic dwelled within this piece. I found it interesting given Jake's admittance of being sceptical in the supernatural arts, but then maybe he wasn't aware of the potent magic that was contained in this trinket. As my fingers brushed over the carved sigils along its edges, the oppressive air of the reading nook seemed to lighten around me. The comforting scents of sandalwood and bergamot bloomed. my Gran's favourite perfume. A familiar presence enfolded me in phantom arms, whispering wordlessly against my hair. Gran, here with me as she had been so often when I needed guidance from beyond.

"Little moon, your destiny intertwines with this man, though his own path remains shrouded in shadow," she murmured, her smoky voice threaded with sorrow and hope. "Guardian and guide him, but tread carefully. Heed both your mind and heart, for balance is needed to weather coming trials." Gran's embrace slowly dissolved until only faint traces of bergamot lingered. I stood rooted in place, clutching Jake's talisman as understanding pierced me. For all his secrets and stoic surface, his soul called out to me. Whatever darkness drove him, I was meant to be a light guiding him back. But the journey would not be easy for either of us. Gran's words hinted at the winding course destiny had arranged. Much more than romantic attraction bound me to this enigmatic man. Our joined fates would require patience and wisdom to unfold safely. I must walk a narrow line, nurturing Jake's humanity while shielding my own. Clearly it was fate that he had been brought to my door.

Sensing the truth of it in my core, I looped the moonstone amulet's chain safely around my own neck, tucking it out of sight beneath my top. The magic thrummed warmly against my heart, bound now to me through fate and free choice rather than its creator alone. When Jake returned seeking what he had lost, this compass would lead him back to me once more. And I would be ready to stand by his side and guide us both through the gathering darkness. Steeled by new understanding, I moved at last toward the office doorway. I had research to do and mental preparations to make tonight. But through it all, an inner calm persisted. Whatever the path ahead, with Jake's talisman over my heart, I would help him find his way. Together, bonded by destiny's design, we would face the menacing future. And with luck and trust, prevent the tragedy foretold. For now, it was enough simply to wait in faith and plan in hope.

The coffee pot gurgled and steamed cheerfully in the office kitchenette, its mundane noise oddly soothing after an evening of intense mystical encounters. While I waited for the brew, I dug a worn leather notebook and my laptop from my desk. Settling onto the lumpy second hand sofa with pen in hand helped to anchor my still scattered thoughts after the reading's upheaval. Recording insights and questions always clarified my process after such intense spiritual experiences. The familiar ritual comforted me now. I wrote first of the initial vision up on the cliffs, that I had only a couple of days ago. The twelve shadowy, feminine figures joined together surrounded by celestial bodies in agony. A glimpse of the Zodiacs' intended role as healers of cosmic wounds. I added a note to research the details and timeline of the original prophecy later. For now, I focused on documenting tonight's vision involving Jake's gruesome fate at Whitby Abbey. I wanted those ominous images captured in words before time blurred the disturbing details.

The images threatened to overwhelm me again as I recounted the mayhem and violent death that could come to pass on those ancient steps. But the sheer act of witnessing them differently through the lens of written description seemed to dilute some of their visceral power. By the time I set down my pen, the tremor had left my hand. I breathed a soft prayer of thanks to Gran for teaching me this processing ritual. Seeing the vision transformed into neutral words on paper restored much-needed objectivity. I could now review what I had seen with clearer eyes, search for meaning rather than just emotion in the haunting scenes.

When the coffee finished brewing, I poured a generous mug and returned to the lumpy couch with it cradled between my palms, savouring the heat. Several long sips of the fragrant, bracing brew helped sharpen my tired mind before I opened the journal again to reread my documentation of the shared vision with Jake. Details I had scarcely absorbed in the moment stood out now with glaring significance. The obscured, faceless figures locked in combat around Jake's broken body. His eyes staring lifelessly skyward. My own perspective as a helpless witness to the death and destruction. Most ominous of all, the backdrop of Whitby Abbey and the 199 steps leading up to its ruins. That specific site recurred too often now to be chance. Whatever the original Zodiac prophecy foretold, that hallowed landmark clearly played a pivotal role. I added this observation to the pages concerning the vision. But a single troubling question circled endlessly through my thoughts. What catastrophic chain of events could possibly culminate in such gruesome violence upon Whitby's iconic steps? And how might I stop the tragedy before it began? Gran's words echoed that Jake himself was instrumental to fate's design in ways I did not yet fully grasp. I jotted down her cryptic advice to keep him close and act as guardian and guide. Though where precisely such guidance might lead us both remained nebulous.

I could only imagine Jake's turmoil after the shared vision plunged him into the heart of impending disaster. Small wonder he had fled without a word or backward glance. Being confronted with one's own potential death would unsettle even the steeliest soul. And whatever secrets Jake harboured beneath his reserved exterior, I sensed profound humanity within him, wounded perhaps, but still redeemable. His moonstone talisman over my heart seemed to resonate agreement with that intuitive impression. I added a final note in my journal to reach out first thing tomorrow and see if he had regained some equilibrium after the shock of the reading. He would need compassion, not fear or blame because of disturbing glimpses vouchsafed by powers beyond his understanding. I opened my laptop in hope to search out more information on Jake. Maybe knowing his past would help me save him from the future that I saw. But what did I know about this elusive stranger that had so evidently invaded my life? I wasn't even sure I knew his last name. Shaking my head, I closed the laptop again. I would need to ask around to see if anyone knew any more about him. I got the impression that Jake would not take too kindly to me snooping in on his personal life, so it wasn't like I could ask him directly. I leaned back into the worn cushions with a sigh. My mug sat empty on the side table, the caffeine doing its work to sharpen my mental acuity. Lingering wisps of bergamot reminded me I did not face this uncertainty alone. Gran continued guiding me from beyond the veil, never far. And though Jake had retreated into his darkness for now, our crossing paths seemed destined to continue until fate's design was made clear. I touched the hidden moonstone briefly, comforted by its subtle magic aligned now with my own. Just as its creator would be again soon, led by consecrated bonds.

Weariness dragged at my bones as the adrenaline of mystical revelation receded. But my spirit felt more centred and resolute. The future remained unwritten, always in motion. And I had been granted the gift of insight in order to shift that course toward hope rather than devastation. Blessing the visions despite their darkness, I finally rose to prepare a simple dinner and turn in for whatever rest the night might allow. Calories and sleep would fuel the body and spirit for the trials to come. And the light of dawn would bring fresh determination to rewrite fate and rekindle Jake's inner radiance. United with shared purpose, we could yet prevent the grim future glimpsed. Tonight, the first steps were taken. Tomorrow would unfurl in its own time, shaped by courage, faith, and work yet to be accomplished.

Chapter 11

Jake

After an absolutely fucking terrible night's sleep plagued by visions of my past kills, I woke up in a foul mood with my nerves still shot to hell. The bloody images raking across my mind left me wired and on edge, though I'd never admit it aloud. I hadn't experienced dreams like that for years. I had conditioned myself to shut that side of myself down and they trained me to lock down any weakness and keep a mask of cold purpose in place no matter what. Any cracks in that armour were vulnerable spots enemies could drive a blade, or a bullet, through, and I had plenty of those bastards eager to take me down. So I swallowed down the chaos ruling my thoughts and prepared to face the day ahead. I groaned at the thought of leaving the safe haven of the covers but I knew that I still had much to do before I could leave this bloody town and its temptations behind.

The image of said temptation formed in my mind and seeing the soft curves of her body and the pink of her lips stirred a more primal urge in me, and my cock along with it. Idly, I stroked my hardened length while the thoughts of the devious witch played in my mind. Images flashed through of her on her knees in front of me again, looking up at me with those wide eyes that were anything but innocent. I imagined forcing my cock between those rosy lips and pushing slowly to the back of her throat, before pulling out again. As my hand found its rhythm, stroking my aching length, the image of Serena's succulent lips and enticing body consumed my thoughts. Her sweet scent intoxicated me. I sank deeper into the fantasy, imagining her on her knees in front of me once more. Her rosy lips parted, her eager stare setting my heart racing. My cock head teasing her warm, wet mouth, begging to be taken. She would have no choice but to take me deep in her throat as I thrust myself back in causing a startled and muffled yip from her. Her tongue pushing at the underside of my cock and her warm breath brushed against my skin, sending tingles through my body. And she would love it. Her enthusiastic moans vibrating against my shaft as she took me deeper, her fingers clawing at my thighs. Her eyes now wet as I pushed myself deeper into the back of her throat. I pumped furiously at the vivid image in my mind feeling the first signs of my impending climax.

I was closing in on the edge when I was startled by the sound of my phone on the nightstand.

"Fuck!" I hissed as I was pulled from the fantasy. I grabbed the phone and looked to see who would be ringing me so early. I groaned at seeing my Uncle's name on the screen. I took a deep breath and answered the call, forcing an even tone.

"Yes, Sir?" My uncle's gravelly voice came through.

"Status report. Have you identified the target yet?" I suppressed a sigh, my unsatisfied arousal still throbbing.

"Not yet, but I'm making progress. I have a solid lead I'm pursuing."

"This witch you mentioned seems to have caught your attention," my uncle said sceptically. I hesitated, something in me bristled at the comment, like Serena being on my uncle's radar was something I wanted to avoid. Or at least my feelings for her.

"She's proven to be... an intriguing case."

"Don't let yourself get distracted, boy," he warned. "Emotions cloud judgement. Remember what happened with Clara." I flinched at the mention of her name. We all knew what happened with Clara and the remorse that she lives with every day because of it.

"That was different. I know my duty."

"See that you do it. We're nearly out of time before the bloody Zodiac ritual, whatever the hell it is. How can one witch give you so much trouble?" His condescending tone made my blood boil.

"She's elusive, but I assure you I will have results soon."

"For both our sakes, you'd better." He paused. "Don't forget who you serve, boy. The mission comes first, always. Keep your feelings in check." I dug my fingers into my thigh, biting back an angry retort.

"I know my role, Sir. My focus is clear."

"Keep me informed," he ordered curtly and hung up. I cursed and threw the phone down. The interruption had killed the mood, but I was still wound up. A cold shower would have to do for now. I couldn't let Serena distract me from my mission, alluring as she was. I would do whatever it took to complete my task and make my uncle proud, no matter how much his scorn stung. I would sort out these unwelcome desires afterwards.

I dragged myself out of bed and headed for the shower. I turned it too low temperature and stepped in. The cold water did little to quench the irritation in me as I stood in the shower. I braced myself against the cold tile wall, the chill barely registering. My mind wandered again to thoughts of Serena despite my attempts to focus it elsewhere. I imagined her lithe body pressed up against me, her soft curves moulding to the hard planes of my chest. I pictured trailing kisses down the slender column of her throat as my hands explored her supple flesh. A groan escaped my lips as my traitorous cock stirred back to life. This witch had me under some kind of spell, that was the only explanation. I had never lost control like this before. With an angry grunt, I turned the water colder, seeking to shock my system out of the haze of lust. I refused to give in and stroke myself to climax while imagining her writhing beneath me. But then another image invaded my mind. The image of Serena's horrified expression from last night, and the vision I had came roaring back like I was still stuck in the nightmare. I tried to push it away, focus on the water on my skin but the icy chill did little for my frayed nerves. Slaughtering monsters was one thing, the kills I was forced into by the Council haunted me the most. The visions from yesterday's session with Serena had cracked open that door in my mind, exposing the rot I usually kept locked away. I should have known a psychic as powerful as her could slip past my defences.

I turned off the water and climbed out of the shower and stared at myself in the mirror. But all I saw was a monster looking back at me. I knew that I was only a soldier in this war against those blasted Zodiacs. But I was starting to wonder what sort of man I was turning into. My fist slammed into the bathroom wall before I could stop it, leaving a sizable dent in the plaster. I cursed under my breath. So much for keeping a low profile at the inn. Serena was a complication, no doubt about it. I couldn't afford any entanglements with my target so close. And yet...the way she had looked at me with those sea-green eyes, so open and compassionate, made my chest ache. I didn't deserve her empathy or her beauty. But some deep, broken piece of me wanted it desperately.

I shook myself and headed into the bedroom and pulled some clothes from my bag. I started getting dressed, my thoughts still consumed by Serena despite my attempts to refocus on my mission. As I went to grab my t-shirt, my fingers brushed against my bare chest, finding nothing but skin where my pendant usually hung. I froze, panic gripping me as I realised my protective amulet was gone.

"Shit!" I cursed, immediately tearing the room apart searching for it. I looked under the bed, in the sheets, in every pocket and bag I had. But the pendant was nowhere to be found. My pulse pounded as the implications set in. That amulet was specially enchanted to shield me from magical influence and psychic manipulation. Without it, I was exposed and vulnerable. It was also the only thing that I had from my parents. My only connection to the people ripped away from me as a child. The emotional attachment meant more to me than the protection it offered.

My mind raced, retracing my steps, trying to pinpoint when I'd last seen it. The answer came in a flash, yesterday at Serena's shop. When her blasted cat had scratched me as I jumped up to escape the horror of the vision, the chain must have broken and fallen off without me noticing. I traced the scratches still on my chest from the vile creature and scrubbed a hand over my face, dread sinking into my gut.

This wasn't good. Serena was already more powerful than I had anticipated. And now, without my protective ward, I was completely susceptible to her psychic talents. She could slip into my mind, discover my mission, my past, everything. The thought of being so defenceless, so open to attack, made my skin crawl. I had to get it back, and soon. Cursing under my breath, I quickly finished getting ready and headed out.

As I made my way to Serena's shop, I tried to calm my racing mind. I would simply explain that I'd lost the pendant and politely ask for its return. Surely she would understand its importance and have no issue giving it back. At least, that's what I told myself. But my instincts said she would not part with it easily. I steeled myself for a fight as her shop came into view. This witch had gotten under my skin in more ways than one. I only hoped she hadn't yet discovered all my secrets. The amulet had to be recovered, no matter what it took. Failure was not an option.

Chapter 12

Serena

I sat with Ophelia and Alec, wrapping my hands around a mug of chamomile tea to try to calm myself after recounting everything that had happened with the vision and Jake. Going over it again made my heart race all over.

"So you both saw the same events?" Alec asked, his sharp grey eyes focused on me. Ophelia just shook her head, lips pressed tightly together.

"Not exactly," I explained. "I think some details were different. But there was definitely something that upset him." I shivered, remembering his haunted look. "He left so quickly." Ophelia made a dismissive noise at the mention of Jake's name. It was pretty obvious that she didn't like him. I shot her a warning glare. However rattled I still was from seeing Jake murdered, I knew that there was good in him, even if others didn't see it.

"Gran said it herself, Jake has a vital role to play," I insisted. "Whatever he's battling, she told me to help guide him." Ophelia clearly wasn't convinced.

"I still think you should be careful around him?" she said with a disgruntled frown. "He's hiding something and I don't like it."

"Aren't we also hiding something?" I countered, and she took a deep breath.

"Yes, but what we are hiding will stop you from getting killed," she said, "How do we not know that what he's hiding won't get you killed." My fingers tightened around the hot ceramic mug.

"I trust Gran's spirit and wisdom, it's got me this far safely. I can't dismiss her message now."

Sensing Ophelia gearing up to argue more, Alec jumped in as referee, ever the peacekeeper in our trio.

"Maybe the answers are in Iris's journals upstairs," he suggested calmly. "I can help look if you want." I smiled, grateful for his effort to get us back on track. I gulped down the last of my tea and stood abruptly.

"Searching Gran's archives is a great idea. She knew way more about this obscure Zodiac stuff than anyone." Inspiration hit me suddenly. "Oh wait! When I found the first relic, it led me to a page on some objects connected to the prophecy." Ophelia seemed to perk up at this bit of new intel.

"Well now, that could be useful! Perhaps we can figure out details on the other three you'll need to complete the ritual."

"Exactly!" My earlier fatigue vanished, replaced by adrenaline. Maybe pinning down specifics about the ceremony would make everything feel less overwhelming. I started toward my office.

"I have Gran's journals in my office, I will get them now."

I collected the journals from my desk and just as I was about to walk back into the shop I noticed the Pendant hanging on one of the hooks. The white flower seemed to shimmer as I picked it up, but that was probably more my lack of sleep than anything else. The thought of it brought my attention to the amulet around my neck. The one that Jake had left last night. I wondered if the two were connected, after all Gran said that Jake was connected to my destiny, it didn't seem too farfetched.

I headed back into the shop with the journals as Ophelia came downstairs with some cakes from my apartment, and a fresh pot of tea. Alec was already set up at the table reading something in one of the books.

"What's that?" I asked as I put the journals down. He looked up and smiled at me and lifted the book. It has a colourful cover and I could see the signs of the zodiac on the front.

"It's a book I picked up in York a while back," he said. "It's supposed to be written by one of the resistance." I looked again at the cover and saw that the author's name was just the word Zodiac.

"They would say that," Ophelia said with a laugh, "It would sell more books that way." Alec gave Ophelia a curious look before shaking his head and looking back down at the book.

"You see it says here about the four relics," he said and pointed out a passage. 2It says that the ritual is different for each of the twelve daughters but the essence is the same."

"Hmm interesting," I said as I picked up a piece of flapjack from the plate that Ophelia had set down.

"Well, maybe we can cross reference everything with the journals," Ophelia said, and I nodded in agreement. I sat down and grabbed the first journal in the pile and flipped open the page. Obsidian jumped up onto my knee and purred as her turned once and settled down to sleep. I smiled as I idly stroked his head while I began to read Gran's neat handwriting.

It was a good few hours later and my eyes were beginning to hurt from the strain. We had gone through a few of the journals and each of us had a good number of pages of notes written down. Most of the journals were Gran's travel notes as she travelled from different exotic locations to the next. On the face of it, it looked like everything was just about the travel and the interesting things she found, but there was something niggling inside me that made me think that there was more in the journals than what was written. Like something on the edge of my eye line that I couldn't quite see. It was already past lunchtime and heading into the evening and we still hadn't found anything concrete about the Zodiacs or the relics. I sighed and leaned back in my chair and rubbed my eyes.

"How many more are there?" I asked and Alec glanced over at the box with a frown.

"I don't even think we are halfway through yet," he said. I groaned and rubbed my face with my hands.

"It's very fascinating though," Ophelia said, as she scribbled something down. "This one talks of something that had happened in Paris, and she keeps mentioning warehouses."

"Yeah, I saw something similar in Egypt," Alec said.

"Well, maybe-" I began but at that moment Carnelian jumped up onto the table and knocked my tea over.

"Oh no," Ophelia jumped up as hot tea splashed her way, and over the book she had been reading.

"What the hell is it with these cats," I muttered as I rushed for a cloth. They weren't usually so clumsy. I grabbed a cloth and ran back into the other room and began to try to soak up the liquid from the book.

"Cats will be cats," Ophelia said with a smile as she stroked Carnelian's fur. He looked at me like he dared me to defy his godliness. I rolled my eyes and patted at the book again, hoping that it wasn't too damaged.

"Well, it looks like the damage is only minimal," Alec said. I nodded as I glanced down at the blurred ink.

"Yeah, just the one book," I said but then looked at the pages again. The ink had dispersed under the effects of the tea and created a mess of black ink spots, but as the pages began to dry, it looked like something was forming in the ink's separation. I looked like there was something under the words, I squinted to see what it was, wondering if it was a trick of the light when I saw one word forming. I was about to show the others when the bell above the shop door sounded and we all looked over at the entrance.

My breath caught at the sight of Jake's tall frame filling the entrance, broad shoulders backlit by a streetlight outside. Standing there in a fitted black t-shirt with a leather jacket over was Jake. His cheeks were flushed from the cold but I could see the intent in his eyes, even from across the room. He hesitated on the threshold for a tense moment before stepping inside; the door falling shut behind him. Our eyes met across the space, the air suddenly electric. He looked drawn, shadows smudged under those piercing eyes, but jaw resolutely set. Before the heavy silence could lengthen, I marshalled my most reassuring smile. I glanced back down at the pages quickly, trying not to react to the words that were now clear as day, before dropping the cloth on the book hiding it from sight. I stepped away from the table and towards the door.

"Jake, what a pleasant surprise. Please, come in." My deliberately warm welcome seemed to disarm him slightly. He moved further into the shop, as he looked around with suspicion. His gaze remained guarded.

"Can I get you anything? Tea, coffee?" He considered it for a moment, glancing at the pot on the table before shaking his head, a wry quirk to his lips.

"No, thank you. I've had my share of mystical brews lately." Ah yes. No wonder he eyed the offer askance now. I gave a small self-deprecating huff, hoping to put him further at ease.

"Too right, after that reading got so intense. Probably best to avoid any magic potions or trances today." I infused my tone with gentle humour but also sincerity, trying to demonstrate compassion for his discomfort with navigating unknown mystical forces. The subtle tension in his shoulders eased a bit more at my candour. Jake glanced at Alec and Ophelia, who were doing their best to act like they couldn't hear us. I shook my head and gestured to my office. I walked in knowing that Jake was following. I turned as I got in and almost bumped straight into him. My hands landed on his chest.

"Oh crap, sorry," I said, snapping them back. I saw Jake's lips quirk again, clearly amused at my lack of grace.

"It's alright," he said.

Then the smile faded, and I saw the same haunted look in his eyes that I had seen last night. I reached out again, in an offer of comfort, but stopped myself before I made contact.

"In all seriousness, how are you holding up after last night?" I asked gently. Jake's eyes shuttered slightly at the question, jaw tightening. But after a pause, he responded gruffly.

"Managing, thank you for asking. It was...unsettling." His stark words belied the bone-deep fear the grim scenes must have kindled. I ached to offer comfort but resisted the urge to reach out and touch his arm. Too much, too soon. Instead, I summoned an understanding smile.

"Of course. I imagine it's a lot to process." Jake grunted noncommittally, clearly not keen to linger on the topic. I redirected the conversation to safer waters.

"Well, I'm glad you stopped by regardless, even just to say hello." The subtle emphasis reminded him his presence was not merely tolerated but welcomed here. Jake's eyes warmed fractionally at the edges.

"I appreciate you saying so after I left rather abruptly last night." He cleared his throat awkwardly. "Actually, I came by hoping to recover something lost in my haste. The, ah, necklace I was wearing." Of course the missing talisman had drawn him back. I reached automatically to touch the spot beneath my blouse where it hung concealed, and it suddenly felt warm against my skin. Before I could reply, Obsidian chose that moment to saunter out from the beaded curtain and twine himself sinuously around Jake's ankles. I froze, astonished by this rare show of affection after his hostility yesterday. Jake scowled down at the cat even as he reached one hand tentatively to stroke the raised tail.

"Seems your little beast is warming up to me after all," he noted sardonically. Obsidian's approving chirp elicited the slightest uptick to Jake's lips. I hid my own smile, struck by how vulnerability softened the usual sternness of his handsome features. Allowing my perceptive familiar access past his fortified walls felt like progress, however small.

Their bonding sparked hope that Gran was right and there was good in him.

"He's normally an excellent judge of character," I remarked mildly with a smile of my own. Jake's eyes snapped to mine, traces of his subtle smile already smoothing away. His hand hovered slightly before he pulled it back, much to Obsidian's disappointment.

"So, I wondered..." he trailed off. I looked into his eyes and saw something in them. I wasn't sure what. "My necklace, did you see it?" Oh yes, the necklace. Suddenly for some reason I felt awkward about the idea that I was wearing his necklace and wasn't sure how he would take it. It seemed a tad strange in hindsight.

"Oh, erm," I hesitated before I smiled brightly. "I haven't, but I will have a look around for sure." Jake's smile looked a little disappointed. "I promise," I said, reaching out, only this time taking his hand, and instantly feeling a warmth spread through me. "If it is in this shop, I will ensure you get it back." Jake looked down at my hand holding his and I went to pull it back, but he held on.

He looked back up at me with another look in his eyes, a more carnal fire that caused my breath to stutter.

"Thank you," he said with intent, "That piece of jewellery means so much to me." I nodded with a smile, suddenly feeling so connected to the man in front of me. I tried to pull away my hand again, but Jake still held on.

"For some reason," he said, his voice lowering to a husky tone, "I feel like it isn't the only thing that could be important to me in this little shop of yours." His eyes seemed to search my face, like he was looking for the secret to the universe in it.

"I feel like I need to get to know you better, Serena." I tried to respond, but I seemed trapped in his intense gaze. What the hell was wrong with me.

"Erm, well," I stuttered and Jake smiled, causing my face to redden as the embarrassment of my lack of control of my own self.

"Would you go for dinner with me?" Jake asked. He looked away, and I finally felt like I could breathe. I saw him glance at the clock and then back at me. "It's not too late is it?" I looked up at the clock and saw it was barely 5pm, and shook my head.

"Erm, no," I said. A frown crossed his face, and he released my hand and I realised what I said. "Oh no," I said quickly, "I meant, no it isn't too late for dinner, not that I don't want to go for dinner." I realised that I was rambling and stopped quickly and shut my eyes and shook my head at myself. What the hell was wrong with me. I opened them again to see Jake watching me with an amused look. I tried to smile and not glare at him as I spoke.

"I still have a few things to deal with though, so I would need about two hours, would that be okay?" I asked and Jake smiled and nodded.

"That sounds perfect," he said, amusement still glinting in his eyes. "Until then." I nodded with a smile as he turned and headed out of the office. I followed him to the door, avoiding the eyes of both Ophelia and Alec as I went. Jake turned and smiled again as he left the shop.

I closed the door behind him and rested my head against the cold glass, as I tried to regain my composure.

"You're going on a date with him." I heard Ophelia's voice and groaned. Of course they were listening. I shook my head at the disapproving tone and turned to face them. Ophelia was frowning but Alec was grinning.

"Never mind that now," I said and hurried back to the table and lifted the cloth from the book.

"Serena," I don't think that it's a good idea that you go on a date with that man," Ophelia said. Alec scoffed at her.

"Don't be so worried," he said, "the girl needs to relax a little."

"Guys," I said, interrupting their conversation about my social life. "That's not important right now. I found something." I lifted up the book that was still damp from the tea. The ink was all smeared, but I could still see it plain as day. Under the ink looked like a second set of writing. I held the book up to show them. Alec came over and took the book from me and his eyes widened as he read the previously hidden text. He looked back up at me with a gleam in his eyes.

"Oh well done Carnelian," he said, glancing over at the cat.

"What?" Ophelia asked and Alec passed her the book. Ophelia scanned the page and read the title out loud with a smile on her face.

"The ritual of the Cancer Zodiac."

Chapter 13

Serena

The clock struck seven as I stood in front of the mirror, applying the finishing touches of mascara. My hands trembled, smudging the wand against my eyelashes. I cursed under my breath, wiping away the excess with a tissue. Why was I so nervous? It wasn't as if this was my first date with a new guy. Living in a seaside town meant a lot of holiday makers came through here, and some of those were looking for more than sea and sand. Sometimes I indulged, and sometimes I didn't. But tonight felt different. Charged. Like we were teetering on the edge of something bigger, a precipice I both longed for and feared.

I sighed, tossing the mascara aside. My aquamarine eyes stared back at me, uncertainty swirling in their depths. My heart raced, a flurry of butterflies swarming in my stomach.

It didn't help that after spending all day going through my Gran's journals I had finally discovered the ritual for the Cancer Zodiac. Alec, Ophelia and I had gone through the text at length, after Jake had left.

It was much the same that we knew. Four relics, one I already had, and was now nestled between my breasts as I got ready. But the key difference was the location. The text said the ritual site was at the top of the sacred journey, almost two hundred levels above. Ophelia got it straight away, the two hundred levels was the 199 steps that Whitby was so famous for, meaning the ritual took place at the Abbey, which made perfect sense as in my dream, that was where I first saw the Constellation. But tonight wasn't about prophecies or destiny. Tonight was about Jake.

"How about this dress?" Violet drew me from my thoughts as she held up a slinky black number, crimson lace tracing the neckline and hem. "It'll drive him wild."

"I'm not trying to drive him wild." I ran a brush through my hair, glancing at her reflection. "Just dinner."

"You've never been this nervous over a guy before." A coy smile curled her lips. "Admit it, you like him." My cheeks warmed as I thought of Jake's rugged features and stormy grey eyes. "I barely know him."

"Exactly. So go have fun and get to know him." She winked. "In every way possible."

"Violet!" I tossed the brush at her, fighting a smile of my own. She ducked, cackling. The doorbell jarred me from my laughter. Violet's laughter faded.

"This is it." She squeezed my arm. "Be yourself and enjoy it." I took a deep breath.

"Right." I inhaled deeply, steadying my nerves. You can do this, Serena. Just take it slow.

Heart pounding, I descended the stairs into the shop and opened the door. Jake stood on the porch, looking sharp in a charcoal blazer and light blue button-down that matched his eyes. His cropped brown hair shone in the fading light.

"Hey," he said, lips quirking into a crooked smile.

"Hi," I breathed, drinking in the sight of him. Strong, solid, yet somehow soft around the edges. "You look nice."

"So do you." His gaze traveled down my figure, lingering on the curve of my hips. "Stunning as always." Heat rushed to my cheeks. I couldn't remember the last time someone had looked at me with such raw desire. It terrified me and set my blood aflame.

"I'm Violet, by the way," Violet said, all chipper, with amusement ringing in her voice. I grimaced at how she was clearly having fun at my expense. Jake turned to Violet with a smile.

"It's very nice to meet you Violet," he said with such an ease of charm. Violet practically giggled, and I rolled my eyes. And she called me the flirt.

"Well, you two have a good time now," she said as she picked up her bag. "Don't do anything I wouldn't do." She winked at me and then left the shop and practically skipped down the street.

"Colourful girl," Jake mused with a smile.

"And then some," I said as I picked up my own coat and shrugged it on.

"Shall we?" He extended his elbow in an old-fashioned gesture. I looped my arm through his, my skin tingling where it met the solid muscle of his forearm.

We stepped outside into the cool evening air. My anxiety melted away with each step we took together, our easy conversation flowing as naturally as the river winding through Whitby. Jake guided me along the cobbled streets toward the Magpie Cafe, a popular seafood restaurant perched along the harbour.

"I hope you like fish and chips."

"My favourite," I said. "Nothing is more quintessential than fish and chips by the sea."

"Excellent." Jake smiled down at me, eyes glinting silver in the moonlight. "Then you're in for a treat." We arrived at the restaurant bustling with locals and tourists alike. Jake held the door open for me, his hand brushing the small of my back as I passed through. A spark ignited at his touch, warming my skin. I glanced over my shoulder to find his gaze fixed on me, a hungry look in his eyes. The dining room glowed with amber light, shadows dancing across exposed brick walls. A hostess in a black dress greeted us with a smile.

"Table for two?" Jake's hand found the small of my back again, guiding me through the intimate space. I inhaled the mingling scents of grilled fish, garlic, lemon. My stomach rumbled. We settled into a booth beside a window overlooking the harbour. Jake ordered a bottle of white wine and I sipped it slowly, savouring the crisp mineral taste.

"So," Jake said, leaning forward, "tell me about yourself, Serena." I traced my finger around the rim of my glass, considering. "Not much to tell, really. I'm just a small-town girl." He arched an eyebrow.

"Somehow I doubt that. A beautiful, mysterious woman who sees the future?" His eyes glinted. "There must be more to you." A nervous laugh escaped my lips. "I'm really not that exciting."

"I find that hard to believe." Jake's voice dropped lower. "I want to know everything about you." I folded my hands in my lap, suddenly nervous under the intensity of his gaze.

"So, for example, what else do you like to do for fun around here?" One corner of his mouth quirked up. "What would you like to do for fun?" A blush crept into my cheeks at the implication. I averted my gaze to the harbour stretching endlessly before us. Boats bobbed in the inky water, their reflections dancing across the rippling surface.

"Well," I said slowly. "I do enjoy getting lost exploring the old alleyways, shopping at the local stores, having a drink at one of the pubs..." I trailed off with a shrug.

"All perfect date activities." Jake reached across the table, fingertips brushing over my knuckles. "We have all night to explore whatever you like."

The server arrived with our appetisers, briefly interrupting the intensity of the moment. I averted my gaze to the plate of garlic bread and calamari, my heart pounding. Jake and I made light conversation as we ate, discussing our interests and hobbies. He was well read and enjoyed exploring the countryside. We talked about our favourite books and TV shows, discovering we had more in common than I expected. With each topic of conversation, my nerves eased into a warm comfort. Jake listened as much as he spoke, asking questions and following up on the details I provided. He made me laugh with witty observations and stories of his own. By the time our main courses arrived, a deep connection had formed. We talked as if we'd known each other for years instead of a few days. His foot nudged against mine under the table, sending a spark through my veins.

"You know," he said, pausing to take a bite of his steak. "I haven't been able to stop thinking about you since we met."

"Really?" I traced my fork through the remains of my pasta, heat flooding my cheeks.

"Yes, really." He reached across the table again, covering my hand with his own. "There's something about you, Serena. A light, a fire I'm drawn to. I want to get to know you better, in every way possible."

My breath caught at the intensity in his eyes, the promise of passion unspoken. "I feel the same way," I admitted softly.

Once the check was paid, we headed out into the cool night air. My earlier visions crept into the edges of my mind, a dark foreboding I pushed away. Tonight was about living in the moment, embracing a connection I never expected to find. Jake slipped his arm around my waist, pulling me close against his side.

"Where to now? We could walk along the harbour, or find a quiet spot to sit and talk. I'm not ready for this night to end just yet."

"A walk sounds perfect." I leaned into him, matching my stride to his unhurried pace. We wandered down cobbled streets illuminated by the soft glow of streetlights. After a few blocks, we approached the stone steps leading up to the churchyard and my chest tightened. The memory of Jake's lifeless body flashed behind my eyes and I faltered, panic swelling inside me. He gave me a questioning look.

"Are you alright?" I forced a smile. "Just got a bit lightheaded for a second. Maybe we could avoid the steps tonight?" Jake nodded, but his eyes were fixed on the winding stone staircase ahead. I bit my lip. Clearly my subtle suggestions were lost on him. My mind raced as we drew inevitably closer. I had to steer Jake away, but how? His superhuman strength meant I couldn't forcefully drag him elsewhere. I had no rational reason to avoid the abbey that he would accept. I was running out of time.

Acting on impulse, I grabbed Jake's arm, pulling his face towards mine. Before he could react, I pressed my lips to his. He stiffened in surprise. My bold action stunned even me, but I had to keep Jake distracted. Jake's shock quickly melted into desire as he wrapped his arms around my waist, pulling me tightly against him. His lips moved urgently against mine, warm and insistent. I sank into the kiss, the rest of the world falling away. My hands slid up his muscular chest and locked around his neck. His scent overwhelmed me, woodsy and masculine. The stubble on his jaw grazed my skin as our kisses deepened, sending shivers down my spine. His hands roamed my back, tracing my curves. I arched into him instinctively. We broke apart, breathless. Jake's grey eyes smouldered as he gazed at me.

"Serena..." he murmured, his voice rough with need. Before he could continue, I silenced him with another searing kiss. We stumbled backwards until my back hit the railing overlooking the water. Jake's body pinned me in place as his lips trailed passionate kisses down my neck. A soft moan escaped me. We shouldn't be doing this, not here, but I was powerless to stop. The desire coursing between us felt primal, inevitable. Jake's fingers tangled in my hair, tilting my head back further. His teeth grazed my fluttering pulse. My nails dug into his shoulders as liquid heat pooled in my core. Somewhere in the recesses of my mind, I knew we had to stop. Jake's stubble scraped against the sensitive skin of my neck as his lips explored lower, each kiss igniting sparks across my flesh. My breaths came in short, ragged gasps, drowned out by the crashing waves below us. Jake's hands slid down to grip my hips, pulling me tighter against him. I could feel his growing arousal and it only heightened my own feverish need.

"We shouldn't...not here..." I managed to gasp, the rational part of my mind clinging to propriety even as my body cried out for more. Jake lifted his head, his smouldering gaze holding mine.

"I know," he rasped, his voice thick with unrestrained longing. Yet neither of us made any move to step away. The energy swirling between us had taken on a life of its own, an irresistible force that overpowered reason. Jake's thumbs traced slow circles on my hipbones and I shivered, arching into him wantonly. His mouth claimed mine again in a searing kiss that stole my breath. My hands gripped his muscular shoulders, nails digging in. Jake's passion seemed barely leashed, a wildness in him awakened by desire. I revelled in it even as warning bells continued to sound in some distant corner of my mind. With reluctance, Jake broke the kiss, pulling back to meet my dazed gaze.

"Not here," he repeated hoarsely. Taking my hand, he led me quickly away from the waterfront, towards the winding streets and shadowed alleyways of Whitby. I followed in a sensual haze, my blood burning, ready to give myself over completely to this dangerous man.

Jake led me through the darkening streets, his firm grip on my hand both guiding and possessive. I stumbled along breathlessly, my thoughts lost in a fog of arousal. The rational part of my mind tried to reassert itself, questioning where exactly he was taking me and what would happen when we got there. But my body thrummed with desire, drowning out the faint warnings. We turned down an especially gloomy alley, the high brick walls blocking out the last fading rays of dusk. Jake pressed me back against the rough stone, his hard body pinning mine as his mouth found the sensitive spot on my neck. I gasped, tangling my hands in his hair to pull him closer.

"We shouldn't..." I whispered again, the words at odds with the way I arched into him wantonly. Jake made a low sound of need against my throat.

"I know somewhere... not far..." Through the haze of passion I realised just how compromising our current position was. Anyone could stumble upon us, wrapped around each other in a public alleyway. The thought made me flush even as it sent a spike of excitement through me. With a groan, Jake pulled back, his breathing ragged. Taking my hand again, he led me swiftly through the maze of narrow passages and empty streets. I followed blindly, my heart racing with mingled apprehension and anticipation.

Jake's grip on my hand was firm as he guided me through the darkened streets. I stumbled once or twice on the uneven cobblestones, my heels catching on the ancient rock. He caught me effortlessly each time, his strong arms keeping me upright. I shivered, acutely aware of his hard body pressed against mine as he steadied me. The night air was cool against my flushed cheeks. My lips still tingled from Jake's passionate kisses. I licked them nervously, tasting him there. My body ached for more of his touch, even as my rational mind screamed warnings I could not heed.

We rounded a corner into an even narrower alley, the old buildings leaning together as if sharing secrets. Jake paused, pulling me into a shadowed doorway. I briefly noted that we had stopped at a bed-and-breakfast, one I didn't know too well, I went to mention this when I looked up at Jake. His eyes gleamed in the darkness, filled with desire and something more complex I couldn't name.

"Jake..." I began, unsure what I even wanted to say. But his mouth silenced any further words, claiming mine in a searing kiss. My reservations burned away, lost in the fire of wanting him. I was dimly aware of him fumbling with a lock, and then we were through the door and stumbling up a dark flight of stairs. At the top was a small studio apartment, sparsely furnished. Moonlight spilled through a large window, illuminating a wide bed tucked against the far wall. We stood for a moment, the significance of where we were sinking in.

Jake's chest rose and fell rapidly, matching my own erratic breathing. His eyes searched my face, looking for any sign of reluctance. But I knew we'd passed the point of no return, for better or worse, I had to see where this night led.

Chapter 14

Jake

The room was dim, the only light emanating from the moon that streamed in through the window, highlighting the woman in front of me. She looked around the room with a nervous tension that I could almost taste. I had half a thought to be concerned about the mess I had left the room in, but it vanished as Serena turned and looked at me. Despite the dark she seemed to glow in her own ethereal light and I knew there and then that it didn't matter about the mission, or anything else for that matter. This woman had to be mine, body and soul. Something must have shown on my face because I saw Serena's eyes widen and her breath hitched slightly. Something akin to lust filled her eyes, and she darted forward into my arms. Serena's lips crashed into mine, hungry and demanding. I grasped her waist, pulling her flush against me. Her taste was intoxication, her scent an aphrodisiac, jasmine and sandalwood with an underlying hint of primal female musk. A groan rumbled in my chest as her hands roamed over my torso, nails scraping against my skin. The beast within strained to break free, fueled by lust and the urge to dominate.

"Jake," she whispered, her lips brushing against my ear. The sound of my name on her lips was euphoria. "I want you...now." What could I do but to comply? The assassin might resist such base needs, but the man craved her with an intensity that eclipsed duty or reason. My hands slid down to cup her ass, grinding her hips against my hardening cock. A strangled moan escaped her, echoing my own. In that moment, nothing else mattered but satiating the inferno raging between us. The assassin and the Council be damned. I would follow Serena into the depths of hell itself.

"On the bed. Now," I commanded, my voice rough with overwhelming lust. She grinned, a wicked curve of her full lips, and sauntered toward the bed, stripping out of the black dress that she wore as she went. The sway of her hips was mesmerising, an invitation I fully intended to accept. I followed in her wake, already shucking off my shirt and boots. By the time I reached the bed, I wore only my pants, and those wouldn't last long.

Serena lounged against the pillows, completely bare apart from the black lacy panties that looked like a crime against nature against the pale of her skin.. The pale moonlight filtering through the window, shadows caressing her skin illuminated her curves.

A goddess. My goddess.

Crawling onto the bed, I hovered over her, bracing my weight on my forearms. Her eyes reflected the depths of midnight, fathomless and filled with promise.

"You're overdressed," she purred, her fingers dancing along the waistband of my pants.

"Patience," I chided. If she thought to rush me, she would be sorely disappointed. I intended to savour every moment, explore and conquer at my leisure. Her eyes narrowed, a spark of challenge glinting in their depths. My lips twitched, unable to contain a smirk. If she wanted to play, I would oblige. Dipping my head, I brushed my lips over hers in a fleeting caress. A frustrated sound escaped her, fingers tightening around my waist. I deepened the kiss for a breath before pulling away once more, trailing my lips along her jaw. A sharp nip at my shoulder, and I growled.

"Behave."

"Or what?" Defiance laced her tone, though her body betrayed her need. I could feel her trembling, the pounding of her heart matching my own.

"Do you really wish to find out?" An idle threat, and we both knew it. I would never hurt her, but a bit of discipline might be required. A wicked smile and another nip, this time at my neck, and my restraint shattered. My hands slid beneath her, grasping her hips and flipping our positions in one smooth motion. She gasped, eyes widening as she found herself pinned beneath me.

"I warned you," I rasped, desire burning through my veins like molten fire. She squirmed, testing my hold, and I tightened my grip.

"Jake, please." The plea in her tone nearly undid me. Nearly. I bent to nip at her collarbone, grazing my teeth along the delicate bone.

"You'll take your punishment and learn to behave, or I'll stop." A whimper escaped her, back arching to press her body more firmly against mine.

"I'll be good, I promise."

"Too late for promises now," I tsked, shifting to cup one full breast in my hand, kneading the soft flesh. She cried out, head falling back to expose the long line of her throat. An invitation I couldn't resist.

I latched onto the curve where her shoulder met her neck, sucking hard enough to leave a mark as I rolled her nipple between thumb and forefinger. Her nails dug into the skin of my shoulders, holding me in place even as her body bucked. Releasing her breast, I slid my hand down to trace the waistband of her panties.

"These are in my way. Take them off, Serena." She scrambled to comply, pushing the scrap of lace down long, shapely legs. I sat back on my heels to admire the view, primal satisfaction flooding me before I dove back in, crashing our mouths together as I eased her onto her back. Her fingers curled around my biceps, blunt nails digging in. Our tongues duelled and twined, a dance as familiar as it was new. One that left us both panting for more. For everything. My lips trailed down her neck once more, leaving a constellation of marks on sun-kissed skin. A claim. A promise. One she arched into, soft cries urging me on. I cupped the weight of one breast again, rolling the nipple between my fingers until it pebbled. Only then did I close my mouth over it, laving and sucking until she writhed beneath me.

"Jake, please," she sobbed, hands fisting in my hair to hold me in place. "I need you." I gentled my touch, looking up at her through the veil of my lashes.

"What is it you need, sweet Serena?" A flush stained her cheeks, but she met my gaze unwaveringly.

"You. Inside me." She rocked her hips against mine, evidence of her need pressed against my abdomen. "Now, Jake." A growl rumbled in my chest at the demand.

"So impatient." I nipped at her jaw, relishing her gasp. "Not yet. I'm not done with you." She whimpered, desire and frustration at war on her face. I took pity on her, sliding a hand between our bodies to stroke over slick, swollen flesh. She cried out, back bowing.

"Jake!" I caught her mouth in another searing kiss, swallowing her pleas and protests both. We had all night, and I was going to take my time. After all, she needed to be taught a lesson in patience. And I was just the man to teach her.

My fingers dipped inside her, curling to find that spot that made her keen. Her inner walls fluttered around me, greedy for more, but I kept my strokes light and teasing. She tore her mouth from mine with a gasp.

"Please, I can't, Jake, please!" I shushed her, brushing a kiss over her forehead. "Shh, I've got you." Another finger joined the first, stretching her deliciously. "Just feel, sweetheart. Let go." A broken sob escaped her as I began to move, thrusting deep and sure. Her hands flew to my shoulders, nails biting into my skin again. I welcomed the sting, my own pleasure heightened by her need.

"Look at me," I commanded softly. Dazed eyes flickered open, pupils blown wide with desire. I held her gaze as I quickened my pace, watching greedily as her expression shifted from pleasure to ecstasy. Her mouth opened on a silent cry, back bowing off the bed as she came apart around my fingers. I gentled my touch, drawing out her release until she collapsed bonelessly against the mattress. Only then did I withdraw, ignoring her whimper of protest.

My fingers glistened, coated in her essence, and I brought them to my lips without thinking. The taste of her burst across my tongue, and I groaned.

"Jake." My name on her lips was a plea, hands reaching for me beseechingly. "Please, I need you inside me." How could I deny her? Especially when it was all I wanted to do. I settled between her thighs, positioning myself at her entrance. One sharp thrust seated me deep within her, and we both cried out at the sensation.

Perfect. Whole. Home.

Our bodies moved as one, a dance as old as time itself, and I lost myself in her warmth. Her nails scored down my back, urging me on as I pounded into her. The coil of heat in my gut tightened with each slick glide, pleasure rippling outwards until I thought I might burst from the ecstasy of it.

"Serena," I groaned, fighting for control. "Look at me." Her eyes opened, and in their depths I saw my undoing. With a shout, I came apart, spilling into her in hot, wet spurts. Her inner walls clamped down, milking my release as her own pleasure crested once more. For endless moments, we clung to one another, hearts pounding against each other's chests. I buried my face in the crook of her neck, breathing in her scent. Mine. She was mine. And I would kill any man who dared try to take her from me.

We lay entwined for a time, exchanging lazy kisses and soft caresses. Her fingertips traced idle patterns across my chest and shoulders, a feather-light touch that ignited sparks along my skin. I stroked her hip, content to simply hold her close with no thought of letting go. A bone-deep satisfaction had settled into my limbs, sated in a way I'd never known before her.

"You're thinking too loudly," she mumbled, nuzzling into my throat. A wry chuckle rumbled in my chest.

"Just committing every moment to memory." She lifted her head, aquamarine eyes peering into my own, a look of uncertainty brimming along the edge.

"Regretting it already?" I caught her chin, tilting her face up for a searing kiss. "Never," I vowed. "You're mine, Serena, in this life and the next. I won't let you go so easily." A slow, Cheshire cat smile spread across her lips.

"Possessive, aren't we?"

"With you?" I smoothed a stray lock of hair away from her face. "Always."

Chapter 15
Jake

The first thing I saw as I opened my eyes was the winter sun pouring in through the small window at the other end of the room, casting a pale glow into the room. From the way it filtered in I guessed that it was still early. The light painted Serena's body in shades of soft blue and grey; her curves like rolling hills beneath the thin sheet that had slipped down to our waists during the night. Her breath was even, calm; her chest rose and fell against my side with an entrancing rhythm. Her head rested on my chest, blonde hair splayed out like a halo, strands teasing my skin with every exhalation. In the stillness of the morning, I felt something unfamiliar, a warmth that seeped into my marrow, a sense of peace that dulled the sharp edges of my existence. This woman, this striking, curvaceous being entwined with me, she stirred an emotion I'd long thought assassinated alongside my morality.

"Beautiful," I murmured to no one but the lingering shadows. My fingers traced the outline of her tattoos, symbols and sigils that marked her as much more than what met the eye. They danced over her shoulders, down the dip of her spine, each inked image a testament to the otherworldly knowledge she bore. My hand glided over her skin, revelling in the softness of her flesh. She was plush where women in my past had been all angles and hard lines. Her body was a landscape of sensuality, each curve a promise of unspoken pleasures. My fingers lingered at her waist, drawing lazy circles before venturing lower, exploring the generous swell of her hips.

"Jake..." Her voice, groggy with sleep, broke the silence, but she didn't stir, lost in the haze between dreams and wakefulness.

"Shh, love," I whispered, not wanting to break the spell just yet. "Go back to sleep, it's still early." I marvelled at the way she filled my hands, the way her body seemed crafted for pleasure, both mine and her own. A surge of desire pulsed through me, raw and urgent. It was a primal need, a craving to worship at the temple of her form, to prove that every inch of her deserved adoration. Her lashes fluttered against the pale skin of her cheeks as she slowly awakened, and for a moment she lay perfectly still, her body a gentle rise and fall against mine. But as awareness returned, her smile faded to a tentative curve, and with a self-conscious motion, she reached for the sheets, pulling them up to cover herself.

"Hey," I murmured, my voice still rough from sleep. "Don't hide from me." She laughed, a sound tinged with embarrassment.

"It's just... you know, morning-after talk. You don't have to keep up the compliments."

"Serena," I said, serious now, catching her chin with my fingers and turning her face back toward me. My thumb traced the soft fullness of her lower lip. "I meant every word. You're beautiful."

"Jake," she protested weakly, but her eyes couldn't conceal the vulnerability she felt about her body.

"Look at me," I insisted. Her gaze met mine, and there was a raw honesty in those aquamarine depths that nearly knocked the wind out of me. "You are fucking exquisite." The words were more than mere compliments; they were an oath, a vow to make her understand how profoundly she affected me. With purpose, I let my hands roam over her curves, taking in the softness of her skin, the plushness that made her so incredibly womanly. She shivered at my touch, and I could see the doubt flicker across her face. I kissed the delicate curve of her neck, whispering my reverence into her skin.

"Every inch of you is like a work of damn fine art, sculpted to drive me mad with wanting." My hands glided down, mapping the topography of her torso, lingering on the soft swell of her hips, drawing circles over the velvet expanse of her stomach.

"Jake..." Her voice was hesitant, uncertain, but I could feel the tremor of anticipation that rippled through her body.

"Shh," I hushed her softly, my lips trailing lower, paying homage to the divine. "Let me worship at your altar." I captured a nipple between my lips, teasing it with the flick of my tongue, rough and gentle all at once. She arched beneath me, a silent plea for more, and I obliged, lavishing attention on her breasts, savouring each moan that spilled from her parted lips.

"God, love, do you have any idea what you do to me?" My voice was ragged with lust as my mouth descended, marking her with my need. "Your curves are a fucking revelation, every dip and rise a chapter in the sexiest story ever written."

"Jake," she gasped, her fingers grasping at my arms, pulling me closer.

"Tell me you can feel it," I growled against her skin, nipping and sucking a path across her chest. "Tell me you know you're perfect."

"Y-Yes," she stammered, surrendering to the raw desire that crackled between us.

"Good." I felt a surge of triumph. This was my mission, my purpose, to show her, make her believe. "Because every fucking moment, Serena, I'm going to make sure you never forget it." My hand travelled lower, skating over the softness of her belly, a terrain I could explore for hours. But there was a heat pooling between her thighs, her body's silent confession that she wanted me as fiercely as I craved her.

"Ah, love," I murmured, my lips trailing down her stomach, feeling her muscles quiver under my touch. "Can you feel how wet you are? That's all for me, isn't it?"

"Jake…" Her voice was a desperate whisper, thick with arousal.

I settled between her legs, inhaling the scent of her desire. My tongue flicked out, teasing the swollen nub of her clit, and her hips bucked in response. She tasted of salt and something intoxicatingly feminine, a flavour I was quickly becoming addicted to.

"Fuck me, you're delicious," I said against her. The coarse words were a stark contrast to the tenderness with which I worshipped her body.

"God, more, please…" Her plea was barely audible, lost in the heaving breaths that fell from her parted lips. I obliged, sliding two fingers inside her, revelling in the slick warmth that welcomed me. Slowly, I began to move them, curving to stroke the velvet walls that pulsed around me. At the same time, my mouth latched onto her, sucking and licking with an unrelenting hunger.

"Christ, you're tight… so fucking perfect." I groaned, the sound vibrating against her flesh. My thumb circled her clit in time with the languid thrusts of my fingers, orchestrating a symphony of sensation that had her writhing beneath me.

"Jake... oh god..." Serena's hands scrambled for my hair, attempting to tug me closer, urging me on. But soon she settled for gripping the sheets beside her, I reached up with my free hand and laced my fingers in hers.

"Let go, baby. I want to feel you come apart for me," I urged, my voice ragged with the effort of holding back my own need. Her body tensed and I felt her clench around my fingers, her legs trembling as wave after wave of pleasure crashed over her.

"Fuck yes," I hissed, my dick hardening as I drank in every shudder, every moan that escaped her lips.

"Jake... Jake!" Serena's cries filled the room, her orgasm a raging inferno that consumed us both.

"Look at me," I demanded, my gaze locking onto hers, wanting her to see the raw emotion etched into my face. "You're mine, baby. Every fucking inch of you." Serena trembled beneath me, her body a tempest of pleasure as the waves of her climax continued to crash over her. Her sounds filled the air, raw and unrestrained, a symphony I had composed with the flick of my tongue and the slow dance of my fingers inside her.

"Jake... please," she gasped between breaths, her voice ragged with need. "I need you inside me." Her plea was a siren's call, irresistible and urgent. I pulled my fingers out from her gripping embrace and moved back up her body and between her legs, I positioned myself at her slick entrance, the heat of her arousal scalding against my skin.

"Your thighs," I growled as I teased her entrance, revelling in the whimper of need from her, "they're the gates to heaven, and I'm the sinner who gets to pass through." I kissed her deeply, our mouths a tangle of tongues and promises. And then, in one powerful thrust, I buried myself within her welcoming depths, eliciting a cry from her lips that was both shock and ecstasy entwined.

"Fuck, baby," I growled into her ear as I held myself still for a moment, savoring the tight clasp of her around me. Her inner walls pulsed, gripping me like a vice, and I fought the urge to lose myself in the sensation. The velvet clasp of her sweet pussy was a vice of pleasure around my cock, and for a moment, I simply revelled in the feel of her, in the way she pulsed around me.

"Jesus," I groaned, the baseness of my voice reflecting the primal nature of our coupling. "You're so fucking tight, baby."

"More," she breathed out, her aquamarine eyes dark with need. "I need more, Jake. Please." Her plea was my command. Withdrawing almost to the point of escape, I thrust back into her, setting a rhythm that was both relentless and reverent. Each penetration was a prayer to the carnal gods, an ode to the curves and swells of her plus-size body that I worshipped with every fiber of my being.

"Fuck, yes!" I hissed as I drove into her faster, harder. "I can't get enough of your deliciously thick body."

"Harder, Jake! God, yes, just like that!" Serena's nails raked across my back, dragging lines of fire that only fueled the inferno burning within me. I felt her walls tighten, her body coiling once again for release. And then, with a bite to my shoulder sharp enough to draw blood, she came undone beneath me.

"Fuck!" I roared as the sting from her teeth sent me teetering over the edge. I pounded into her with a need born of both lust and something deeper, a connection that defied my own understanding. I growled, my thrusts becoming erratic as I chased my own climax. Her pussy clenched around me like a fist, wringing me out until I was nothing but a vessel for the ecstasy that shattered through me.

"Serena!" My shout was guttural, a savage sound that filled the room as my orgasm tore through me, hot spurts of cum painting her insides in a mark of possession that went beyond the physical.

For a long moment, we were locked together, panting, the air between us heavy with the scent of sex and sweat. I collapsed on top of her, my weight supported by my elbows so as not to crush her, yet unwilling to sever the connection that still hummed between us.

"Fuck me," I muttered against her lips, kissing her with an intensity that bordered on reverence. "I've never... Christ, you're incredible."

"You're not so bad yourself," she chuckled breathlessly, the sound vibrating against my chest.

I finally gathered the strength to untangle from her embrace and collapsed beside her on the bed. I pulled her back into me, unwilling to allow the connection to break just yet. We lay there, the gritty reality of our lives momentarily forgotten, lost in a haze where desire reigned supreme and duty had no dominion. But even as I held her, the spectre of my existence loomed, a shadow across the glow of our spent passion. The silence of the room was a heavy, pulsating thing, echoing with the remnants of our cries and the ragged draw of our breaths. The sweat on our skin gleamed in the pale light, serving as a sheen testament to the raw intensity we had shared. Serena's head rested on my chest, and her heart beat against my own. I found myself lost in the feel of her body against mine. The calm sereneness of it. The almost normalness of the scene that we lay in. I tried to fight it off, but I couldn't help the shadows that edged in from the side. The truth of who I was and how this could never be a part of my reality.

"Jake?" Her voice was a soft whisper, yet it cut through the haze in my mind with ease. "What are you thinking about so intently?" I smiled, a facade to mask the turmoil brewing within.

"I'm planning how to spoil you with breakfast," I confessed, or at least, I offered the part of the truth that was safe to share. She snorted, her laughter tickling my chest.

"If you think your cooking can compare to what we just did, you've got another think coming."

"Trust me," I said, my voice low and husky, "one bite of my English breakfast will have you screaming my name all over again."

"Oh, now that is a confidence that I hope you are able to back up," she said with a teasing grin.

"You better bloody believe it," I grinned. I knew my cooking skills were almost as good as my assassin ones. But a shadow lurking at the edges of my contentment. It wasn't the doubt of my abilities in bed, nor the kitchen, but rather the gnawing reality of who I was, an assassin whose hands were stained far beyond what any amount of scrubbing could clean. The dark thought slithered through my mind. This wasn't a life for someone like her, someone pure and full of light. What future could there be between a killer and a psychic medium who sought peace?

"Jake?" Serena's voice pulled me back, a gentle tether to the present. "You're doing that brooding thing again."

"Can't help it," I admitted, allowing myself a small, wry smile. "It's part of my charm."

"Charm, huh?" She raised an eyebrow. "Well, as long as you channel some of that into breakfast, I suppose I can deal with a little brooding."

"Deal," I promised. Then I smiled at her, turning the charm back on and attempting to push away the dark thoughts.

"Go ahead and take the first shower," I murmured, my voice still husky from our morning exercise. "I'll get started on breakfast."

"Are you sure?" Serena queried, her aquamarine eyes sparkling with a mixture of mirth and mischief.

"Absolutely." I pressed a soft kiss to her forehead, a silent promise of things to come. With a reluctant smile, she rose, her curves swaying hypnotically as she padded toward the bathroom, the tattoos etched over her skin like ancient arcane symbols that told of her deep, spiritual connection to the world beyond. As the sound of running water filled the cramped space of the apartment, I turned to the small kitchenette, the utilitarian surfaces cold and uninviting. My hands moved mechanically to gather the necessary tools for the meal, pots, pans, eggs, but my mind was elsewhere, caught in the sweet web of Serena's embrace. I would cook for her, play the part of the perfect lover, if only to keep the shadows at bay for a while longer. Because in these stolen moments, with her laughter ringing clear and true, I could almost believe in fate, even if it was a luxury I knew I could never afford.

A buzz from my phone disrupted the domestic tranquillity I was creating. The screen displayed several missed calls and messages, all from the same sender: my uncle. Each vibration was a call back to the reality I had momentarily escaped from—the reality where I was not Jake, Serena's lover, but an assassin on a mission that could very well be targeting one of the friends of the woman who was working her way dangerously into my heart. My thumb hovered over the device, an itch beneath my skin urging me to unlock it and delve into the words that would undoubtedly drag me away from this ephemeral peace. But I couldn't, I wouldn't, not yet. I shoved the phone aside with more force than necessary, the metallic clang a sharp note of defiance. Serena deserved my undivided attention, even if only for a stolen morning.

"Everything alright out there?" Serena's voice floated from the bathroom, slightly muffled by the cascade of water.

"Perfect," I called back, pouring myself into the act of cooking with an intent that belied my dark thoughts. A sizzle erupted as bacon hit the hot pan, the aroma enveloping me, a comforting cloak that shielded me from the creeping dread of my other life. Would she understand? Could she ever truly accept what I was? Or would the knowledge of my deeds be too much for her tender heart to bear? The warmth of her body was still a ghostly presence against mine, and I clung to it desperately as a shield against the biting chill of my own nature.

The steam from the shower seeped out like a silent spectre as Serena emerged, tendrils of my sandalwood-scented shower gel wafting around her. The aroma clung to her damp skin, marking her with my essence in an invisible, intimate way that stirred something possessive within me.

"Breakfast is almost ready," I said, watching as she moved gracefully, her curves wrapped in a towel that did little to hide the voluptuous form beneath.

"Smells good," she said.

"Wait until you taste it," I replied, my tone light, though inside, turmoil churned like a stormy sea.

"Your confidence is sexy, you know that?" Her laughter was a balm, and I allowed myself to drown in it, to forget who I was outside these four walls.

"Confidence is all I have when it comes to you," I admitted, flipping the eggs with a deftness born of years of living alone.

By the time that I had plated up the food Serena had, much to my disappointment, already dressed. We sat at the small table I'd set up in the corner of the kitchenette, knees brushing as we leaned into each other's space. The intimacy felt natural, unforced, as if our bodies were conversing in a language only they understood. Serena took a bite of the English breakfast I'd prepared, a mess of eggs, bacon, toast, and tomatoes, and let out a moan that was almost carnal in its satisfaction.

"God, Jake, this is incredible. Best English breakfast I've ever had." Her praise sent a flush of pleasure through me, warming parts of my soul that had long been shrouded in shadows. "I aim to please," I replied, watching her lips close around another forkful.

"Clearly, you're not just skilled with your... hands," she teased, a glint of mischief in her aquamarine eyes.

"Multi-talented," I affirmed with a smirk, though my chest tightened at the thought of talents best left unspoken between us. Her gaze held mine, searching for something I wasn't sure I could give.

"You're full of surprises, aren't you, Jake?"

"Only the pleasant kind, I hope." My voice was gruff, betraying the roiling emotions beneath my calm exterior.

"Very pleasant," she murmured, reaching across the table to brush her fingertips against my hand. The simple contact sparked a current that surged straight to my core. The clink of our forks against the plates and the soft murmurs of satisfaction were soon the only sounds in the small kitchenette, a symphony of domestic bliss that I never thought I'd conduct. Serena's lips parted in a contented smile as she finished another mouthful of the English breakfast laid out before us.

"Seriously, Jake, this is bloody amazing," she said, her voice lilting with genuine pleasure.

"Nothing but the best for you," I replied with a wink, watching the way the morning light played across her features.

A knock shattered the serenity like a hammer through glass. I tensed, every muscle coiled tight as instinct surged through me. Who the hell could it be at this hour?

"Expecting someone?" Serena's brow furrowed in concern, echoing my own unease.

"No, that I am aware of," I muttered, pushing back from the table. I approached the door, every step heavy with dread and reluctance that seemed to grow all of a sudden. Bracing myself, I twisted the knob and pulled open the door. His face was as grim as a headstone, the lines etched deep by years of blood and secrets. Uncle Stephen. His grey eyes, so much like my own, bore into me with an intensity that belied his calm demeanour. He was the last person that I wanted to see, especially with Serena sitting in the room.

"Jake," he greeted me, his voice a low rumble of thunder threatening to break. "We need to talk."

Chapter 16

Serena

I watched Jake's back stiffen at the sight of his visitor, whoever it was. His lean muscles, moments ago so relaxed and confident around me, now coiled tight like a spring. He stood taller, his posture rigid, as if bracing himself against an invisible force. I didn't like it, and started to get a bad feeling in the pit of my stomach.

"Jake?" I asked softly, my question hanging unanswered in the tension that suddenly filled the room.

"Give me a sec," he muttered, voice low and strained, not looking at me. The murmurs from the other side of the door were indistinct, but the edges of their voices were sharp enough to slice through the thick air between us. Even without hearing the words, I knew the conversation was laced with discord. Jake cast a hesitant glance over his shoulder, eyes clouded with trepidation. With a heavy sigh, he pulled the door open wider, surrendering to the intruder's silent demand for entry.

An older man stepped across the threshold, his gaze sweeping the room with a thinly veiled disdain. He was dressed in a crisp shirt that looked ironed to a fault, his grey hair cropped in a military fashion. His eyes, a cold steel blue, missed nothing, least of all the slight wrinkle in the throw blanket on the couch or the solitary coffee mug sitting on the countertop.

"Place could use some tidying up," he commented, each word clipped and precise. I instinctively glanced around the space that had seemed so welcoming moments before. Now, under his scrutiny, it felt suddenly inadequate. Jake's room was spotless, aside from the bed which was still a mess from our morning activities. Just thinking about the way I had woken up this morning was almost enough to chase the cold feeling that was invading my thoughts right now and I felt a small smile playing at my lips for a brief second before I was brought back to reality.

"Uncle Stephen," Jake said, his voice betraying none of the weight that seemed to press down on his shoulders. "What brings you here?"

The man, I guess the Uncle Stephen that Jake had mentioned in conversation last night, gave no immediate answer, and instead turned his imposing gaze toward me. I shrank back slightly, feeling the full force of his domineering presence. Everything inside me told me that this was not a good man, I couldn't say why, but all i wanted to do was to get away from him. I could sense the years of authority behind his stance, and suddenly a lot of the way Jake acted made sense, especially if this was the man who raised him. It was as if I could see the strings of control stretching between them, invisible yet palpable. A dance of power and obedience that Jake had long learned to perform.

The man continued to stare right through me. His eyes, sharp and assessing, found mine after a slow, deliberate survey of the room. His lips curled into what might generously be called a smile, but it held the warmth of a winter's frost.

"And who do we have here?" he asked, his voice carrying the weight of authority and expectation. Jake's response came haltingly,

"Serena, this is my Uncle Stephen, Captain Kirkland." He offered an apologetic look that didn't quite meet my eyes. I could tell from the way he glanced between me and the man that he wasn't happy, like he had broken some sort of rule.

"Charmed," Kirkland drawled, extending a hand that seemed more like a command than a gesture of greeting. I took it, his grip firm and unyielding, as though he could squeeze the truth from my bones.

"Serena runs the local antique shop that I told you about," Jake continued, his voice unsteady and rushed. "It's been... helpful."

"Ah," Kirkland nodded slowly, releasing my hand but not his scrutiny. "So, you're aiding Jake in our little search, are you? With psychic abilities, I hear." His words dripped with a contempt that tightened my chest. It was clear he viewed my gift as a parlour trick at best, and probably evil at worse.

"Every bit helps, I suppose," I replied, masking my discomfort with politeness. Jake shifted beside me, a silent current of tension running through him.

"Indeed." Kirkland's gaze flitted to the tattoos curling along my forearm, symbols of protection and insight inked into my skin, a visible declaration of my connection to the unseen. "And how long have you two been...collaborating?"

"Recently," I answered, cautious but honest. Jake's silence spoke volumes; his jaw was set, a muscle ticking as if he were grinding his teeth.

"Interesting," Kirkland mused, his eyes narrowing just so. They were the calculating eyes of a man accustomed to moving chess pieces in a game where lives were at stake. I felt suddenly transparent under his gaze, his piercing blue eyes attempting to unravel the threads of my purpose, my connection to Jake.

"Your shop," Stephen said with a quirk of his head, his eyes scanning the room before settling on me, "it isn't the Wonders and Whispers is it?" I felt my eyes widen in shock and I glanced at Jake who had seemed to tense further, if that was even possible. The cold settling in my stomach felt like it was growing with each moment. How did this man know my shop? There were any number of antique shops in Whitby, and more than one boasted an owner with different gifts.

"Yes, it is," I said with a cautious tone. I was trying to maintain my politeness, even as the intuitive alarm bells were ringing loud. "How did you know?"

"Ah yes," he said, in less of a reply and more of a dismissal of my question. I could tell that this was a man that wasn't concerned with answering questions. "That shop has always intrigued me. A quaint little place brimming with curiosities."

"Yes, well, antiques tend to have that effect on people," I said, aiming for lightness but catching the edge of sarcasm. I didn't like that he was insinuating that he had been to the shop. He certainly hadn't while it had been mine.

"More than you can imagine." There was a knowing glint in his eye. "I knew the original owner, Iris, quite well." A jolt went through me at the mention of Gran's name. I caught Jake staring at me from the corner of my eye. Evidently this little revelation was news to him as well.

"You knew my Gran?" My voice was a whisper, disbelief colouring it.

"Indeed. She was a remarkable woman, resourceful, discreet, and extremely knowledgeable about... certain matters." My heart hammered against my ribs, betrayal stinging my cheeks. She was everything he said and more. But why had Gran never mentioned this man? How did she know this man, and was Jake connected? Jake said he was looking for someone connected to his mother, could the person he was looking for be my Gran?

"Remarkable doesn't begin to cover it," I managed to say, my mind a tempest of confusion and curiosity. "How did you come to know her?"

"Let's just say, we were... associates, in a manner of speaking." His words were deliberate, each one dropping like a lead weight into the silence.

"Associates?" Jake echoed, his tone wary. I looked over at him and he turned his head and avoided my eyes.

"Indeed," Stephen affirmed, a shadow of a smile playing on his lips. I could tell that he was enjoying the discomfort that both I and Jake were feeling. The room seemed to contract around me, the air thickening as if charged with a storm's approach. My heart pounded a treacherous rhythm against my ribcage, threatening to betray the calm demeanour I struggled to maintain.

"What do you mean by associates?" I asked. I wanted answers. I assumed my Gran had always run the shop, or at least she had once he had stopped travelling so much. What sort of journey could have caused her to be associated with this man.

"Your grandmother, Iris," Stephen began, his voice carrying the weight of history, "she wasn't just known to me. We worked closely together on several Council endeavours."

"Council?" I asked the surprise clearly in my voice. "You work for the council?" Now I understood the dread that had been building. If this man worked for the Council, then I needed to be as far away from him as possible. The Council were actively seeking out the Zodiacs, they made that very clear. They were the reason for the public hatred towards us, and I could only imagine what would happen if he knew that I was one of them. I stepped back involuntarily, wanting to put distance between us. I would need to talk to Alec, the last thing I needed was for me to remain on this man's scent. I half wondered if there was something that Ophelia and I could do, like a spell to put the guy off or something.

I should have made my excuses and left there and then. But there was another question playing on my mind and I knew I had to clarify.

"Are you saying that my Gran worked for the Council?" I asked. I hoped that he would say no and that maybe it had been a passing arrangement. How could Gran, with her gentle smiles and stories that smelled of lavender and old paper, be entwined with the Council, a group whose reputation among the supernatural community was as murky as the shadows they operated in?

"Your disbelief is palpable, Serena dear." Stephen's gaze was unyielding, an ironclad bridge connecting our pasts. "But it's true. Iris was instrumental in many of our operations. She had abilities that were... invaluable."

"Abilities?" My voice cracked, the single word splintering into a thousand unspoken questions. How much did they know about my Gran? Did they already know about who I was?

"Ah, yes." He nodded, the corners of his eyes crinkling with a respect that seemed at odds with his usual stern countenance. "She hid them well from the mundane world, but to us, she was a beacon.

She used her gifts for the forces of good, helping us in our mission to protect our world. She really was quite remarkable" A hand instinctively rose to the locket that lay against my chest, the one I had found recently, its contents a mystery I'd yet to solve. Was this another piece of the puzzle? Another secret tethered to my own bloodline?

"Remarkable?" I asked, the feeling in my stomach making me feel nauseous. I knew my Gran was extremely remarkable, she was practically my idol growing up. But for the same words to be uttered in some connection to the Council was a concept that I was struggling to grasp.

"Oh yes," Stephen replied. He had a smile on his face that seemed to actually show signs of warmth. "She was quite the Commander. She trained operatives, offered guidance on matters beyond the understanding of most." The room tilted, reality skewing as I absorbed his words. Gran, my Gran, training operatives? Guiding the hidden hands of the council? It was too much, too far removed from the woman who had baked cookies and hummed lullabies, taught me everything I knew about my own gifts as a psychic.

"In fact, she trained me herself," he continued, ignoring or perhaps not noticing the tremor that took hold of my hands. "Had a mind sharp as a tack and a spirit fierce enough to tame the most unruly of energies. Didn't think anyone could fill her shoes until..." His gaze flickered to me, loaded with something that I couldn't quite grasp.

"Until what?" I asked, my voice a threadbare thing amidst the heavy air.

"Until she left," he said. His words were simple but I could tell that the meaning behind them was more. Like my Gran leaving the Council was some sort of disloyalty or unfathomable thing.

"W-why did she leave?" I asked, the tremor taking control of my voice.

"Serena," Jake interposed, his hand reaching out as if to protect me in some way. But the action wouldn't protect me from my mind, or the thoughts that were crashing through it with these revelations. "We don't have to do this now. We can-"

"No," I interrupted him as I realised that there was comprehension in his eyes. Like there was more that he knew and that he wasn't telling me. "What are you not telling me?"

"N-nothing," he replied quickly. I could see him shutting down in front of me. He was already trying to shield himself, "I just think that you have had quite the revelation right now and maybe you need some time to process it."

"Nonsense boy," Stephen snapped. "I hardly think that knowing her grandmother was one of our best people is something that needs processing. The girl should feel proud of being related to such an amazing woman." I scoffed without thought but quickly covered it with a cough when Stephen's eyes narrowed on me. I felt anything but pride at what I was hearing. I needed answers about the woman that raised me, and the one I thought I knew. I wasn't going to get those answers here.

The air in Jake's room had grown dense, heavy with secrets that clung to my skin like a shroud. A pressure built within the walls of my chest as I rose from the couch, the room tilting slightly as if reality itself was off-kilter.

"Jake, I am very sorry but I need to go," I said, my voice a mere wisp amongst the storm brewing within me. I tried to force a smile on my face and a light tone in my voice. "The shop won't open itself." My change of tone caused his grey eyes to widen before they narrowed again. They searched mine, clouded with worry.

"Serena, are you sure? You look..." He trailed off, the sentence unfinished, but the concern unmistakable.

"Like I've seen a ghost?" I quipped, attempting to inject some levity into the gravity of the moment. But it fell flat, dissolving into the tension that hung between us.

"More like you've been hit by a freight train," he corrected gently. "At least let me walk you."

"No." The word sliced through the air, sharper than I intended. My heart clenched at the sight of him, so willing to anchor me when I felt adrift in a sea of revelations. "I need to clear my head, feel the morning chill, make sense of... everything." I turned to Stephen and tried to smile.

"I apologise for my hasty departure, but it was... erm... nice to meet you." Stephen nodded slightly as he regarded me with the deep scrutiny that was anything but warm. I turned away, grabbing my bag like a lifeline, and made for the door. I stepped out of the room and into the hallway, instantly feeling a release of tension as I closed the door behind me. I leaned against the wall and let out a deep breath as I tried to centre myself and the mass amount of thoughts that were crowding through my head.

A couple with two children came out of another room, the children chattering excitedly about going to the beach. I smiled at the woman as concern flashed through her eyes as she passed me. I let them get down the first flight of stairs before following them out of the building and into the streets below. It was still early, and the cobbled narrow streets were mostly deserted as I rushed through them towards my shop. I knew I needed answers and if Gran thought being dead would stop her from answering them, then she was in for an unwelcome surprise.

Chapter 17

Serena

My boots slapped against the rain-dampened cobblestones as I bolted through the early morning alleyways, my breath coming out in sharp puffs visible in the fresh air. The dense cloud of dread that loomed over me was pierced by a spear of determination; I couldn't let Jake's Uncle's words be the end of it. Gran, my sweet, secretive Gran, entangled with the Council, I couldn't even imagine that being possible?

The dark front of my shop came into view, the familiar sight offering no comfort. I fumbled with the keys, my fingers numb and awkward, and pushed the door open with more force than necessary. The bell above gave a plaintive jangle, announcing my arrival to the empty space.

"Alright, Gran, it's time we had a little chat, because you have some explaining to do." I said to the silence, picturing her twinkling, knowing eyes. Did I expect her to answer? No, but it would have been nice. I flicked on the lights and was immediately embraced by the warm hum of electricity. Shadows sprawled across the walls like dark fingers, mimicking the tendrils of uncertainty that curled around my heart. The shop's familiar scent of old paper and incense did little to comfort me as I moved with purpose, ignoring the chirrup of my cats as I passed them. I knew they probably weren't happy that I was out all night, but right now I needed answers and the only place that I could think to get them was Gran's journals. They were records of her travels, or so I had always believed.

"Let's see what you were really up to, Gran," I murmured, reaching for the stack of books that I had always believed to be innocent chronicles of her adventures. My fingers tingled with a psychic's sensitivity as they brushed over the embossed spines, a silent prayer escaping my lips for something, anything, that would shed light on her ties to the Council. I flipped open the first journal, its pages crisp and filled with her looping script.

"Morocco, 1972," I read aloud, the words falling flat in the quiet room. "The spice markets, the call to prayer... beautiful, but not what I need." I turned page after page, each one a vivid account of cities and deserts, mountains and seas. They were the stories I had grown up with, tales that once sparked my imagination, now taunting me with their mundanity. I sighed, letting the book fall closed.

"Why is there nothing here?" My voice was laced with frustration, the sound echoing off the shelves crammed with mystical artefacts and ancient tomes. I rifled through another journal, more hastily now, the action punctuated by soft thuds as I tossed the unsatisfying volumes aside. Paris, Rome, New Delhi, each city a dead end, each entry a brick in the wall that seemed to be closing in around me.

"Come on, give me something to work with," I pleaded to no one, though somewhere deep inside me, I hoped she might hear. I leaned back in my chair, rubbing my temples where a headache threatened to bloom.

"Gran, I don't understand. If you were part of the Council, why is there no trace of it here?" My eyes scanned the room, half-expecting to find an answer hidden among the crystal balls and tarot decks that lined the shelves. The room started to feel colder than before, as if the very air had been sucked out along with the hope that I clung to. My fingers trembled slightly, betraying the steadfast front I attempted to maintain. Page after page of Gran's neat script flipped by, a testament to her worldly adventures, but not a single whisper of the Council or their clandestine affairs.

"Gran, I need you," I murmured, my voice cracking like thin ice underfoot. "Please, just... give me something, anything." The plea hung in the space, desperate and raw, my own words sounding foreign to my ears. My gaze swept over the empty shelves, the half-open drawers. Then, I looked upwards, half expecting, half hoping for a spectral sign, a shadow to shift, a wisp of ethereal energy, Iris Ashmoor's spirit reaching across the divide to offer guidance.

"Was it all just lies? The stories, the relics... your love?" The last word was a dagger, self-inflicted, plunging deep into the core of my grief. How could I not feel at a loss when the woman who had raised me with such love was a part of such a dangerous organisation? I needed to understand, or something to tell me that it wasn't true. Anything. But silence was my only answer, oppressive and mocking. The journals in my hands suddenly felt like nothing more than bundles of paper bound in leather, heavy remnants of unspoken truths. In a swift motion, frustration boiling over, I slammed the latest journal down on the floor. The sound it made, a soft thud, was a pathetic echo of the chaos whirling inside me.

"Damn it!" I shouted, the force behind my upset sending the remaining journals skittering across the surface. "You can't leave me in the dark like this. It's not fair!"

A shiver crept up my spine as Obsidian's sleek, black form emerged from the shadows. His one good eye gleamed in the dim light of my shop, reflecting back my own restlessness. With a grace that seemed almost human, he leapt onto my lap and nestled into the curve of my arm. The soft vibration of his purr was grounding, a gentle reminder of life amidst the chaos.

"Hey, big guy," I murmured, my fingers gliding through his velvety fur. "Wish you could tell me what's real." The room was heavy with silence, broken only by the rhythmic sound of Obsidian's contentment. But my mind was far from silent; it was a cacophony of doubt. Could Stephen be weaving lies, spinning tales to ensnare me? My Gran's life, her secret dealings with the Council, how much of it was a fabrication?

"I don't like that he knows too much," I whispered, half to myself, half to the cat whose cloudy eye seemed to see right through me. "But why would he lie about knowing Gran? What would he gain from it?" Obsidian shifted, his purring a gentle rebuke to my troubled thoughts. It was then that my caress faltered, my hand falling away as my mind raced. He let out a soft, protesting chirrup, the feline equivalent of a reprimand, before slipping off my lap to join Carnelian up on the shop counter.

I watched, a smile tugging at my lips despite everything, as the two of them began their dance of mock combat. Obsidian landed a gentle swipe on Carnelian's ginger flank, who responded with an acrobatic twist and a playful counterattack. Their movements were a fluid ballet of feline agility, a momentary escape from the gravity of my situation. Their antics continued, oblivious to the storm brewing within me. For a fleeting second, I envied them, free from the weight of destiny, from the burden of intuition and grief. They lived in a world of simple pleasures, untouched by the complex weave of mysticism and fate that tangled around my life.

"Maybe there's wisdom in your carelessness," I mused aloud, watching as Obsidian playfully batted Carnelian's twitching tail. They seemed to speak a language of their own, one rooted in the present, where each moment was just a moment, not a piece of some grand prophecy.

"Easy for you to say," I sighed, pulling myself out of the brief respite their play had granted me. "You don't have a legacy to unravel or a destiny to accept." The cats paused, their gaze meeting mine, and in that shared look, there was a spark of something unspoken, an understanding that transcended words. Then, as if nothing had happened, they resumed their playful scuffle, leaving me to ponder the enigma of my grandmother's life and the secrets that she could possibly be holding.

The serene quiet of the shop shattered as Carnelian's paw caught the edge of a glass, sending it hurtling towards the floor. It hit with a sharp crack, splintering into a starburst of shards and spilling its contents in a wild torrent over the aged wooden planks.

"Obsidian! Carnelian!" I cried out in exasperation as I leaped to my feet, my heart pounding not just from the shock but also the mess they'd made. The water spread quickly, seeping into the stacks of books and assorted paraphernalia that lined the shelves of my shop.

"Of all the times..." I dashed to the back room, yanking open the cupboard to retrieve an old towel, stained from countless previous mishaps, and hurried back to the scene of chaos. The spilled water glinted in the dim light like a pool of liquid mercury, mocking me with its silent, creeping advance.

"Look at this mess," I muttered under my breath, dropping to my knees and beginning to sop up the water. The fabric of the towel darkened as it drank thirstily from the puddle. Wet stock in hand, I couldn't help but scold the two feline culprits who seemed more interested in licking their paws than feeling any guilt for the havoc they caused.

"You two are driving me mad. Couldn't you have spared me this one extra headache?" I addressed the cats, knowing full well they were oblivious to the depth of my turmoil. But I needed to voice it; to release some of the pressure building within me like a storm cloud ready to burst. Obsidian simply blinked at me, his black fur a stark contrast to the white towel in my hands. Carnelian, on the other hand, cocked his head, ears twitching as if actually considering my plea.

"Fine, be that way," I sighed, tossing another soggy tome onto the growing pile. I wrung out the towel, water dripping back onto the floor with a sound that was too much like laughter. The irony wasn't lost on me: In seeking control, I was merely spreading the water further. I glanced towards Obsidian and Carnelian. The two of them were now preening, tongues licking fur with meticulous strokes, their earlier mischief forgotten. Their indifference was a stark contrast to the tumult in my heart. "Don't bother to help or anything?" I spoke to them half amused with myself, knowing full well they wouldn't answer. Carnelian paused, mid-lick, and met my gaze with those deep emerald orbs. For a moment, I fancied I saw a flicker of understanding, or was it mere cat curiosity, before he resumed his grooming, unconcerned with the human world's troubles.

I reached further back on the shelf, my fingers grazing over the old stock that seldom saw the light of day. A sigh escaped me as I pulled out dusty trinkets and faded books, setting them aside with care despite the urgency clawing at my insides. Each item held history, stories, secrets, just like the ones I was desperate to unearth from Gran's journals. Water had seeped further than I had anticipated, wicking into the cardboard boxes that housed unsold inventory. It wasn't just the shop's stock that was soaked—it was as if the spill sought to penetrate every corner of my life, leaving no stone unturned.

"Damn it, how much bloody water was in that glass?" I cursed under my breath, pulling the saturated items out. They left a trail of droplets behind, marking their reluctant journey from darkness to light. The scent of wet paper and must rose to my nostrils, both acrid and oddly comforting. It was the smell of old secrets, of things hidden away and forgotten. My gaze returned to the felines, who were now curled up together in a yin-yang of black and orange fur. Their peaceful slumber was enviable, free from the weight of prophecies and hidden truths. Yet their serene presence was a balm to my frayed nerves. I returned to the mess in front of me. The damp cloth in my hands was heavy with spilled water as I reached towards the back of the lower shelf, where the shadows clung to yet more forgotten trinkets and dusty memorabilia. The air was thick with the scent of mildew and age-old secrets, a tang of metallic fear lingering on my tongue.

"Of course," I muttered to myself, "it just keeps going." Dragging out an antique snow globe, its flakes long since settled into a stagnant blizzard, I nudged aside a stack of yellowed paperbacks with cracked spines. That's when the outline of something unexpected caught my eye. An anomaly in the architecture of my sanctuary. A small, unassuming door, perfectly flush with the wall, almost indistinguishable save for the faintest gap along its edge.

"Hello, what's this then?" I spoke softly, my curiosity piquing as I set the globe aside. Was there a door back there? My fingers traced the outline, it was a door. How the hell did I not know about this? I ran my fingers further along the seam, feeling for a catch or a hinge, and flicking it when I found it. With a gentle push, the door creaked open, revealing darkness within. I hesitated, my breath quickened, heart thudded against my ribs. Every instinct I possessed screamed at me to be wary, but the pull was undeniable.

"Secrets upon secrets, eh, Gran?" I whispered to myself, reaching into the void before me. My hand made contact with something solid, notebooks. The texture was unmistakable, the familiar feel of worn leather and frayed edges brushing against my skin. I pulled out the top one and immediately recognised the familiar handwriting as belonging to my Gran.

"Gods..." My voice was barely audible as the enormity of the revelation hit me. These weren't just any notebooks; they were Gran's, created by her hand, sheltered here for reasons unfathomable. Her elegant script danced across the covers, intimate and secretive, beckoning me deeper into a history I thought I knew. I immediately went back to the cupboard and pulled out more of the notebooks. Dozens of notebooks, their spines cracked and worn, jostled for space on the wooden shelf. The air grew thick with dust as I reached in, an electric charge of anticipation coursing through me.

"Gran, what have you been keeping from me? Why would you hide these" My voice was barely above a whisper, the thumping of my heart loud in my ears as I cradled the first journal.

"Did you two know about this all along?" I glanced back at Obsidian and Carnelian, their golden eyes fixed on me with an unnerving focus. Their tails flicked in unison, a silent communication I couldn't decipher.

"Ha! As if you'd tell me," I laughed, shaking my head at my own absurdity for expecting some sort of confession from a pair of cats. I looked back down at the notebook in my hand and took a deep breath. I opened the cover revealing the first page and with a sinking feeling deep in my stomach, the first thing I saw was the familiar insignia of the Council mark. My hand tremored slightly as I read the neat writing below the one thing that confirmed what Jake's uncle had been saying. That I didn't know everything about the woman who raised me.

"Commander Iris Ashmoor, field notes," I muttered the line with the sinking feeling only getting worse, as I traced the faded ink with my thumb.

"Alright then, Iris Ashmoor," I said with a deep breath, invoking her name like a talisman against the darkness creeping at the edges of my consciousness. "Let's see what truths you've hidden amongst these lies."

Chapter 18

Serena

I sat cross-legged on the floor for I don't know how long, surrounded by my grandmother's journals. The air was thick with the scent of old paper and dust. I couldn't believe the sheer number of them; over twenty, each filled with her neat, formal handwriting. As I flipped through the pages, I noticed a stark difference between these journals and the ones I was used to seeing. My Gran's usual scrawl was replaced with a more formal script, as if she were writing official reports rather than personal reflections.

I picked up the top journal from the pile and began to read. My heart raced as I realised that these journals contained accounts of my Gran's missions with the Council. The entries were chilling; detailed accounts of her work for the Council, including missions to capture or eliminate supernaturals who were deemed threats to society. It was clear from her words that she had been deeply involved in spreading hatred and fear towards those who possessed magical abilities, including myself. My stomach churned as I read about how she had participated in spreading the twisted version of the prophecy that was now being fed to the public as truth. The Zodiacs were portrayed as evil reincarnations of the constellations, bent on destroying humanity and stealing their magic because of that blasted prophecy.

As I continued reading, I felt a growing sense of betrayal towards my Gran. How could she have been involved in such heinous acts? How could she have used her own gifts to help those people hunt down those like her, like me? And why had she never told me about any of this before? Had she truly believed in what she was doing all those years ago? Or had she simply been following orders?

Tears welled up in my eyes as I closed the current journal with a heavy thud. The revelation that my own flesh and blood could be capable of such cruelty left me feeling utterly devastated and confused. Being told that she was a part of the Council was one thing, but seeing it in her own words… How could someone who claimed to love me be so blindly complicit in spreading hate and fear? I leaned back against the wall, feeling overwhelmed by everything I had just discovered. My mind raced with questions; what else had my Gran kept hidden from me?

As I sat there lost in thought, Obsidian jumped onto my lap and began purring contentedly against my chest. Carnelian joined him soon after, curling up beside him on the floor next to me. Their warm bodies provided some small measure of comfort amidst this sea of confusion and pain. As they snuggled close to me, their soft fur brushing against my skin, I felt a sudden surge of love for them both; they were my constant companions through thick and thin, always there for me no matter what happened in my life. I sighed and picked up the next journal and opened it to the first page. I knew I needed to know more about what was going through Gran's mind and find out why she left the Council.

My heart pounded in my chest as I began to read about a mission to hunt down a vampire. The entry was chilling; Gran described the creature in detail, its piercing red eyes and sharp fangs, and how it had to be destroyed at all costs because it was believed to have a connection to some important relic or other. The way she described the vampire was horrific, like he was some grotesques monster. I had met enough vampires to know that this account was completely wrong. They rarely resembled the stereotype that they had been given as ruthless killers, or at least no more than humans were.

Just as I was about to close the journal, the bell above the shop door jingled, signaling that someone had entered. I looked up to see Alec walking in with a smile on his face. But as soon as he saw me, the smile dropped and a look of concern crossed his face. Alec rushed over to me, kneeling beside me and gently took my hand, his touch comforting in its warmth and strength.

"Serena," he said softly, "what's wrong? You look like you've seen a ghost." I took a deep breath and tried to steady myself before answering him.

"Alec... I found something... something that changes everything. It's awful." I tried to contain the tears that were threatening to fall from my eyes as I told him what I had found. His eyes widened with concern as he picked up one of the journals.

"What is it?" he asked urgently. "Tell me." I hesitated for a moment, unsure of how much I should reveal. But then I decided Alec deserved the truth; after all, we were friends and Alec was the closest thing to family that I had right now, him and Ophelia. So I showed him the journals; all twenty of them, filled with accounts of my Gran's missions for the Council.

Alec's face paled as he read through the entries; he could see just how deeply involved my Gran had been in spreading hatred and fear towards those who possessed magical abilities. It was clear that she had been blindly following orders all those years ago, believing that she was doing what was best for humanity. But now... now she knew better. Now she understood the true nature of her actions and their consequences. And now... now she was gone, leaving behind a legacy of pain and confusion for those who loved her most.

As Alec finished reading the last entry of one of the books, he looked up at me with tears in his eyes.

"Serena," he said softly, "I'm so sorry for what your Gran did... but please know that you are not responsible for her actions." I stared at Alec, my heart pounding in my chest. He didn't seem all that surprised by what he had read. Upset, sure, but not surprised.

"Alec," I said slowly, "what are you not telling me?" His eyes flickered towards the journals, and I could see the guilt etched on his face.

"Serena," he said softly, "I knew about your Gran's involvement with the Council. That's how we met in the first place." My mind raced as I tried to piece together what he was saying. How could they have met because of Gran's work for the Council? And why hadn't he told me before?

"You worked for the council as well?" I asked, the feeling of dread growing inside me. Was everything I knew about everyone a lie? Alec shook his head quickly and the look of panic spread across his face.

"Oh god, no, Serena, no," he rushed out, and I felt the weight in my stomach lift in relief. "I mean I met your Gran, while she worked with the Council. She wanted to get out, and she wanted the help of the resistance to do it."

"The resistance?" I ask, my eyes widening. "Like the Zodiac believers?" Alec nodded his head and a small smile crossed his lips.

"Yep," he said with almost a hint of pride in his voice. "Both my parents were believers, and I was brought up with the same values. I was working with Thaddeus Morgan himself when your Gran reached out to us."

"Thaddeus?" I exclaimed. I didn't know much about the man, other than he led the resistance against the Council and was a very wanted man because of it. Alec grinned, the pride clear on his face. I sat there stunned, trying to process everything Alec was telling me. My grandmother had been working with the Resistance? The same Resistance that was dedicated to protecting magic users like myself from the Council's persecution?

"I know this must be a huge shock," Alec said gently, placing a hand on my shoulder. "Your grandmother was always very secretive about her past." I let out a shaky breath.

"I just can't believe it," I murmured. "All this time, and she never said a word. Why didn't she tell me?" Alec gave my shoulder a comforting squeeze.

"My guess is that she was trying to protect you. Iris knew how dangerous the Council could be. She didn't want you getting caught up in any of it." That made sense. No one who was even remotely supernatural wanted to be in the Council's spotlight. They either used you for your gifts, or got rid of you for them.

My head was spinning with a million questions. Too many for me to grasp onto.

"So how exactly did you two meet?"

"Well," Alec began, "it was about 30 years ago. I was still pretty new to working with the Resistance back then, only a lad myself. One night my father got an urgent message from Thaddeus saying that someone from the Council wanted to pass us some vital information. He told him to meet with the informant and find out what they knew. My father took me along to get some field experience." Alec paused, seeming to gather his thoughts.

"That informant was your grandmother. We met at an old warehouse just outside the city. She was so nervous, looking over her shoulder the whole time. But Iris was determined to share what she knew in order to save one of our own." I listened intently, hanging on Alec's every word.

"She told us the Council had discovered the identity of a Resistance member - a young psychic named Willow Barton. They planned on capturing Willow and making an example out of her to scare other magic users into submission." Alec shook his head, his expression darkening at the memory.

"Iris knew it would be a death sentence for Willow if the Council got their hands on her. So she offered to give us information to help keep Willow safe, in exchange for our help getting your grandmother away from the Council for good." My pulse was racing as the pieces started coming together. My Gran had risked so much to help Alec and the Resistance. Maybe the fact that the girl was a psychic was too close to home for herself. And from my guessing, my mum couldn't have been much different from this psychic. What if my gran thought the Council would do the same to my mum?

"Obviously, we took the deal," Alec continued, pulling me from my thoughts. "Iris gave us details about Willow's location and the Council's plans to capture her. Thanks to your grandmother's intel, we were able to get Willow to safety before the Council could find her."

Relief washed over me. My Gran had saved that girl's life by standing up to the very organization she once served.

"After that, we held up our end of the bargain," said Alec. "We helped Iris stage her disappearance and took her someplace the Council would never find her." He waved his arm around the shop with a smile. "Here, in fact. She was free to live out the rest of her days in peace, away from their influence." I felt a swell of gratitude for what Alec and the others had done for my Gran. Thanks to them, she'd been able to leave that dark chapter of her life behind for good. Alec gave me a bittersweet smile.

"She was so grateful, Serena. Iris wanted a chance to make up for the harm she'd caused with the Council. Helping Willow was her way of starting to set things right." I reached out and took Alec's hand, giving it a grateful squeeze. He squeezed back and smiled at me.

"Your grandmother was a complicated woman. But in the end, she chose to stand up for what was right. It's why I stayed in contact. I wanted to make sure that she stayed safe. Well that, and other reasons," Alec said, with a blush in his cheeks. I quirked my eyebrow, and he laughed, a small nervous laugh.

"I met your mother," he said and my eyes widened. It had never occurred to me that Alec would even know my mother. From the look on his face, he knew her more than a little.

"My mum?" I asked, unable to contain the shock in my voice. "You...you had a thing for my mum?" I finally managed to get out. Alec chuckled, though there was a tinge of sadness in it. "Ah yes, your mother was quite the beauty back then. But it was just a crush. At the time, it felt like she was the brightest light in the world." He gazed off, as if picturing her face. "We were just teenagers at the time. I remember thinking she was the most enchanting girl I'd ever seen. Those bright blue-green eyes, always so full of light and laughter. And her hair was like spun gold, the way it shone in the sun. You look a lot like her." I listened intently, hanging on his every word. It was so strange to hear him speak of my mother as a young, carefree woman. I had only known her briefly, and what I did remember was fleeting, before she dropped me on Gran's doorstep and disappeared.

"We became friends shortly after your grandmother came to us for help. Iris thought it would be good for Clara to have some mates her own age who understood what it was like to have magic." Alec smiled wistfully. "Your mum was still getting a handle on her abilities then. She would accidentally repeat what she had heard in someone's thoughts, not knowing that they hadn't said it out loud." I nodded, picturing a younger version of my mother struggling to control powers so much like my own. It made my heart ache, knowing she had dealt with the same burden.

"I tried my best to help her accept her own gifts, and see that they weren't the evil that the Council painting them as." Alec chuckled. "Of course, my crush on her made me all the more eager to spend time together. Your grandmother picked up on it right away. She told me as much one day when Clara was off practicing a new technique." I raised my eyebrows in surprise. Gran playing matchmaker was not something I ever expected. Alec shook his head, still grinning.

"Iris made sure to give me a stern talking to. She said not to go getting any foolish notions, that Clara's only focus needed to be her training. Of course, that didn't stop me from pining after her." His expression grew wistful once more. "Your mother was always kind to me, but I could tell her heart lay elsewhere. She had feelings for..." Alec trailed off, his face clouding over. I sensed there was more to the story he wasn't sharing. The way his tone shifted made it clear this tale did not have a happy ending.

"Alec?" I asked gently. "What happened between my mum and this other person? Please, I want to know." My stomach coiled at the very thought of who it could be. I had never met my father. When I was young, I asked my Gran if she knew him, but the look on her face had been one of hurt that I had complied when she had brushed off my question and told me to go play. Now Alec had the same expression, and I was sure that this other person was important to him. Alec shook his head and squeezed my hand again.

"Maybe another time," he said before standing up from the floor. He held out his hand to help me up, and I accepted it. I knew the walk down memory lane was over, at least for now.

Together we began to gather the journals from the floor in silence and stacked them neatly on the counter so that we could go through them some more. After a few moments Alec turned to face me with a curious look on his face.

"How did you find these?" he asked, and I nodded to the cats who had curled up in a patch of sun.

"Those two," I said. "They were playing and knocked water on the floor. I pulled out the stock to clean up and found the cupboard." I stopped and thought over the whole occurrence. I then narrowed my eyes on the cats.

"What is it?" Alec asked, and I shook my head with a chuckle.

"Just that I had been desperate for information about Gran being connected to the council when they knocked over the glass." I looked back at the cats and up at Alec. "And then I find the books. That can't be a coincidence, surely?" Alec shrugged and looked at the cats.

"Maybe," he said thoughtfully, "You never know with Iris. I wouldn't be surprised to hear that she found actual familiars."

"Familiars?" I asked, my eyes widening. I knew that the existed of course, but a familiar was a magical gifted animal that attached themselves to important gifted humans. But it was few and far between, given how rare they were. Carnelian looked up at me and gave a quiet meow before snuggling back down with his brother.

"Why were you looking, anyway?" Alec asked me, interrupting my wonder about the cats.

"What?" I asked, not sure what he was talking about.

"You said that you were looking for information on your Gran, that you knew she was connected to the Council. How?"

"Oh," I said as I realised that there was so much that I hadn't told him. "Jake's uncle. He works for the Council." I went into detail about how Jake's uncle had turned up at the place Jake was staying and had recognised the shop and my Gran as the original owner. Alec didn't look happy at the revelation, in fact he looked rather concerned.

"What was his name, this uncle of his?" he asked and I shrugged.

"Stephen Kirkland", I said. I was sure that there were plenty of Council Operatives, what was the chance of Alec knowing this one. But when I said his name the way Alec paled told me I was dead wrong about my assumption.

"Oh Fuck," he hissed, "Are you sure?" I nodded my head, the dread returning in my stomach,

"Why?" I asked.

"He's bad news, Serena," he said. He pulled out his phone and began typing something in quickly. "If the Council and especially him, know that you are a Zodiac then you are in a lot of danger."

"How would they know?" I was trying not to panic, but Alec's expression was serious and I didn't like the growing feeling that I had.

"I don't know," he said, putting the phone away. "But it seems too much of a coincidence that his nephew turned up just before he did."

"Jake? I'm sure he has nothing to do with all this," i said, although the little seed of doubt was beginning to grow.

"Nevertheless, it might be best to make some preparations." Alec went to look out of the window, before coming back to the counter. "You should pack a bag."

"A bag!" I exclaimed. "Alec, I'm not going anywhere." Did he think that I would up and leave so quickly?

"Serena, please," Alec pleaded. "I'm just trying to protect-"

His sentence was cut off as the bell above the shop door sounded and we both turned to look at the person that walked in. I started to smile, to plaster a sense of welcome in my stance, but instead my jaw dropped as I laid eyes on the woman standing in the doorway.

"Mum?"

Chapter 19

Serena

I stood frozen, staring at the woman who walked out of my life over twenty years ago. My mother, Clara Ashmoor, was here in my shop as if it was the most normal thing in the world. I hadn't seen or heard from her since I was seven and she dropped me off on Gran's doorstep with nothing but a small suitcase. The life of a mum was apparently too hard for her.

"Hello, Serena," she said softly. My heart pounded in my chest. I wasn't sure if I wanted to hug her or slap her. I felt so conflicted and confused.

"What are you doing here?" I asked sharply. My mother glanced around the shop, not even reacting to my tone. She took in the shelves of crystals, candles, and incense, mixed in with the strange and wonderful objects. The disdain on her face barely covered the ways her eyes gleamed as she took everything in, like there was something in particular that she was looking for.

"I heard you had taken over the shop. It looks... lovely." Lovely? That was all she had to say after over two decades of absence? I shook my head in disbelief. Alec stepped forward, putting himself partially between my mother and me.

"Serena asked you a question Clara, what are you doing here?" he asked in a low voice. She turned her gaze to him and something akin to hate flashed through her eyes.

"We have some family business to discuss. This doesn't concern you." I looked between them both and could tell that there was some serious history here. This wasn't the woman that Alec had been talking about less than an hour ago.

"I"m making it my concern." I put a hand on Alec's arm. As much as I appreciated him defending me, I knew I had to handle her myself.

"It's okay," I whispered to him. I looked at my mother, steeling myself. "Why are you here, Mum?" She winced at the word Mum, like it was something dirty. In that moment the pain of abandonment went through me again. What was so awful about me, that she hated being my mother so much.

"I'm here to pick up something important," she said, glancing around the shop with that same calculating look in her eyes. I stared at my mother in disbelief. After all these years, she had the audacity to come into my shop and demand something?

"Clearly it's not your daughter," I muttered, not even trying to hide the bitter sarcasm in my tone. "Please tell me what is so important, more important than your flesh and blood even, that it graces us with your presence." My mother glared at me the look of contempt on her face.

"It's a private thing between me and my mother," she spat. "It's nothing to do with you."

"If it's in my shop, then it has everything to do with me," I snapped back. The anger was simmering below the surface of my being and I was doing everything I could to contain it. I felt movement to my side and saw both cats had uncurled from their spot and had come to stand by my side. It could have looked like a casual coincidence but it looked like they were flanking me along with Alec, standing by my side. From the look on my mother's face as she frowned at the cats, she noticed the gesture as well.

"Well this is mine," she said as she looked around the room. Her eyes lit up as she looked behind me and she took a step in my direction. Both cats stopped what they were doing and hissed at her, stopping her in her tracks.

"Bloody pests," she muttered glaring at them. I couldn't help the bitter laugh that escaped my lips, it was like my mother was afraid of the cats.

"Nothing here is yours, Mother. Gran left everything in the shop to me in her will after she died. But I guess you wouldn't know that since you didn't even bother to come to her funeral." My mother's eyes flashed with anger for a brief moment before her expression smoothed over.

"It was for the best that I stayed away," she said tightly. "Some things are better left in the past." My hands curled into fists at my sides. How dare she act like her absence was no big deal? Like it didn't completely devastate Gran and me when she abandoned us without a word.

"If you cared so much, you would have at least visited sometime in the last twenty years," I shot back. My mother glanced over at Alec again, her lips pursing.

"I had my reasons for staying away," she said vaguely. I looked between Alec and my mother, confusion swirling through me. What did Alec have to do with any of this? I could tell that there was clearly some history between them, more than what Alec had told me. Alec's expression was stony, his jaw clenched tight.

"I think you should leave, Clara," he said in a low voice. "You're not wanted here."

My mother let out a cruel, bitter laugh in response to Alec's demand that she leave. The tension in the room was palpable and I could sense there was far more history here than I realised. Alec moved to stand partially in front of me, as if to shield me from my mother's cruelty. She scoffed derisively at his protective stance.

"Oh Alec, you're still just that pathetic little boy, with your pathetic little crush, from all those years ago. No amount of wishing will ever make you Serena's father." I gasped in shock, my eyes widening. Father? What was she talking about? I glanced over at Alec, looking for some sort of answer to why my mother would even say such a thing but his jaw was clenched, with anger flashing in his eyes, trained on my mother.

"I may not be her father, but I'm the closest thing to family she has left thanks to you," Alec spat angrily. My mother's lip curled in a sneer.

"Please, I was trying to protect my daughter from the bastard and the evil shit that he was spouting. I was just doing my duty when I made sure he was never in the picture." Alec was shaking with fury now.

"You need to leave, now, before I do something we'll both regret." I had never seen Alec this angry before, his large frame felt so much bigger now. My Mother turned and looked at the cats and then sneered at me.

"But my attempts to stop the corruption didn't work anyway, did they, my dear child?" The look on her face was pure hatred, and it took everything I had not to take a step back.

"I- I don't know what you are talking about," I whispered. I really thought that the woman abandoning me was the most hurtful thing she could have done, but right now, despite not seeing her for so long, the look she was giving me cut right through to my bones. I had to fight the tears that threatened to fall.

"You know exactly what I am talking about," my mother hissed. She nodded at the cats and then looked back up at me. "These vermin are proof of your evil." I tried to understand what she was saying, but her words were wrapped up in so much disgust.

"You're a disease, Serena," she spat. "A parasite just like all the other Zodiacs, sucking up magic that doesn't belong to you." I shook my head in disbelief. This twisted propaganda sounded just like the Council's rhetoric, not the woman who gave birth to me.

"That's not true!" I cried. "The Zodiacs are meant to bring balance, not destruction." My mother let out a cruel, mirthless laugh.

"Oh yes, that's what you'd like everyone to believe. But I know the truth - the Zodiacs will bring nothing but death and ruin." Her words felt like a physical blow. I stumbled back, grasping the counter for support as her vitriol continued pouring out. "As soon as I realised what you were, I wanted to hand you over to the Council. No child of mine could be one of those monsters." Tears blurred my vision. The woman before me was nothing but a stranger wearing my mother's face. Alec moved to block her path, shielding me from her venom.

"I think you've said quite enough," he growled. "It's time for you to go." But my mother ignored him, her gaze fixed on me with that same twisted hatred. "Oh, I can't wait to get out of this wretched place, just give me my mother's journals." Journals? Was that what she was really after?

"What do you want with her journals?" I asked, the emotion clear in my voice.

"I told you," she spat, "That is my business." My fists clenched at my sides and I glared at her and shook my head firmly.

"Well, you can't have them," I said, "They're mine. Now get the hell out of my shop before I make you."

"GIVE ME THE FUCKING JOURNALS YOU LITTLE BITCH!" The scream that came from my mother's mouth was so raw and guttural that for a moment it stunned me and I felt frozen on the spot.

Before I could react, she lunged towards me, clearly intending to get past and get the journals herself. But she didn't make it more than a step before Carnelian and Obsidian were there, hackles raised and claws out, hissing furiously. My mother stumbled back with a shriek as the two cats swiped at her ankles.

"Get away from me, you filthy beasts!" she cried. But they stood their ground, placing themselves firmly between us. I found my voice again.

"Don't you dare speak about them that way!" I said angrily. I gently picked up Obsidian while Carnelian wound himself around my ankles, as if sensing I needed their comfort. My mother's lip curled in disgust.

"Look at you, consorting with demons," she sneered. "You always were an unnatural child." Her words cut deep but I refused to let her see it.

"The only demon here is you," I said coldly. Inside I was shaking, the adrenaline coursing through me. But I stood tall. My mother started to say something else but her words were cut off as one of the large crystal pieces on the shelves seemed to fly from the shelf and straight at my mother. Alec pulled me back and my mother jumped out of the way as the crystal went crashing into the wall behind her. I looked around the room in shock but realised from the familiar scent of my Gran's perfume that she was here in spirit form.

I stared in shock as my mother shouted angrily at the air, cursing my grandmother's spirit.

"Oh here she is," my mother spat into the direction of where the crystal came from. Her words were cruel and hateful, "The old witch is meddling again. Don't think for one second that you will stop me from finishing what I started twenty-one years ago you old hag." What did she mean, finishing what she started? My mind raced, trying to make sense of it all.

"What are you talking about?" I demanded. "What did you start twenty-one years ago?" My mother whipped around, her eyes flashing with malice as she turned her venom on me. A nasty smile spread across her face and she opened her mouth, clearly about to reveal something sinister. But before she could speak, Alec cut in sharply.

"Enough!" he bellowed. "Shut your fucking mouth and get the hell out of this shop, Clara!" I jumped, startled by the force in Alec's voice. I had never seen him so furious before. He was shaking with barely contained rage as he stood protectively in front of me. My mother recoiled briefly before collecting herself. She smoothed her clothes and raised her chin haughtily.

"No Alec, I want to know," I said. "What did you do?"

"Serena, please don't," Alec said as he tried to move me away from my mother. But my mother simply laughed, the sound hollow and chilling.

"Oh come now, the girl wants to know the truth. Who am I to deny her that?" She fixed me with a mocking smile. "It's quite simple, really. When I realised what an abomination you were, I knew I had to cleanse your evil while you were still young. So I took you to a secluded grove and began the ritual to purge your wickedness."

"Purge my wickedness?" I asked, although I knew exactly what she meant, I felt sick at the thought, surely there was no way that she could mean... Alec tried to comfort me but I pulled out of his arms and stared at the woman in front of me, the one who was supposed to love and nurture me, who had tried to murder me as an innocent child. My stomach twisted in revulsion and rejection. Alec made a move as if to physically remove my mother from the shop, but I put a hand on his arm to stop him. As much as it pained me, I had to hear the whole truth.

"What ritual?" I asked through numb lips. "How could you do that to a helpless child?" her smile turned cruel.

"Oh, I had my ways, and my resources," My eyes widened as I released what she meant. The Council of Supernaturals, my mother was one of them and had used their resources to try to take my life.

"But just as I was finishing, your meddling grandmother showed up." Her face contorted with bitterness. "She claimed she wanted to help 'save' you, but I see now it was just a ploy to take you from me. Once you were in her grasp, she put a spell on me to prevent me from ever trying again." My head was spinning as I tried to process my mother's words. Gran had saved me from being murdered by my own mum. And then she'd ensured that she could never try to hurt me again. My mother hadn't left me with Gran, Gran had taken me from her.

"You're sick," I choked out. "What kind of monster tries to kill their own child?" My mother's eyes blazed with fanatical zeal.

"A monster who knows what must be done for the greater good! I see that now more clearly than ever. The Zodiacs cannot be allowed to fulfil their destiny." Her gaze bored into me. "And I, Clara Moore, will do whatever it takes to stop them." She narrowed her eyes at me, "To stop you."

Alec had heard enough. He grabbed my mother roughly by the arm.

"I think it's time you left, now" he growled. She tried to wrench herself from his grip, but Alec held firm. He steered her forcefully to the door. But just before pushing her out onto the street, she turned and fixed me with a chilling smile.

"This isn't over, Serena," she purred. "I have plans for you, my dear. This is just the beginning. Once I get my hands on those journals and break this damn spell, I will finish what I started, and the next time you see me will be when I am plunging my blade into your poisonous heart."

I watched as she walked out of the door, slamming it shut behind her. My body felt frozen to the spot and my chest felt heavy as I struggled to pull in a breath. My mother, my own mother had just threatened to kill me. How awful, how disgusting must I be for the woman who gave birth to me and was supposed to love me unconditionally had such a murderous hatred towards me. A thousand thoughts rushed through my head as I tried to comprehend what had just happened. I felt something touch my arm and looked up to see that Alec was talking to me, but I couldn't hear anything over the rushing in my ears. The simple gesture was enough to bring everything crashing on inside me, and I collapsed to the floor in floods of tears, the feeling of rejection ripping through my soul crushing any light inside me.

Chapter 20

Jake

I stormed down the cobbled streets of the small seaside town, fuming after the conversation I'd just had with my uncle Stephen. That man had no sense of boundaries or etiquette. Interrupting my morning with Serena like that, and dropping that bloody bombshell on her as well. And man was it one hell of a bombshell. Serena's Gran was a Council Operative. I was guessing by the look of horror on Serena's face that she really wasn't happy with that. Part of me felt hurt by the reaction. Would Serena react like that towards me, when she found out that I wasn't just one of their operatives, but also one of the best assassins they had. The very thought of those pretty aquamarine eyes having any sort of disgusted feelings towards me made my stomach twist in a way I didn't like.

I kicked an empty can down the street in frustration. Dammit! This assignment was proving more difficult than I'd expected. Serena wasn't just another mark I could seduce and discard. She was different.

Intriguing. I hadn't been able to get her out of my head since our first meeting in her occult shop. She seemed to stare right through me, sending a jolt through my system. The curve of her hips and swell of her chest that stirred an unfamiliar longing inside me. But it was something deeper than that. I had never felt like this before. It was like I was under some sort of spell or something. I reached up absently to grasp at where my pendant usually lay against my chest, only to find it still missing. Another wave of annoyance washed over me. That pendant was the only thing protecting me from the forces of evil that we were dealing with in this world, and it was all I had left of my mother and Serena still hadn't returned it. She hadn't even mentioned it last night. Was she hiding it from me? Did she know the power that it held? Or had she simply just not found it? I'd have to go back to the shop again to retrieve it. The thought of seeing Serena again eased my frustration slightly. Plus I wanted to make sure that my uncle hadn't made her cautious of me, and that she was still willing to help me. Yeah that was it, I thought to myself as my dick twitched at the very thought of seeing her again.

I shook my head, irritated at my own distraction. I had to stay focused on the mission. Serena was a means to an end, a source of information, nothing more. I couldn't afford attachments or distractions. Not when I was so close to finally getting vengeance for my parents' deaths and wiping the blight of the Zodiacs from this earth forever. My phone buzzed in my pocket. I pulled it out to see a text from my uncle.

"Any progress?" it read. I scoffed and switched the phone to silent, shoving it back in my pocket. I'd deal with Stephen later. Right now, I needed to ensure that he hadn't done any damage with Serena. I turned the corner onto the street where Serena's shop was and saw the lights were on inside. I felt a sense of relief that Serena was telling the truth when she said she needed to open the shop.

I pushed open the door to Wonders and Whispers, the little bell above the door announcing my presence with a cheerful tinkle. The charming smile I had plastered on my face faltered as I took in the heartbreaking scene before me. Serena was kneeling in the middle of the cosy occult shop, her beautiful face buried in her hands as she sobbed uncontrollably. Shards of broken glass and other debris littered the floor around her, evidence of some violent outburst. The tall man I recognized as Alec, one of Serena's closest friends, was crouched next to her, one arm wrapped comfortably around her shaking shoulders as he murmured gentle reassurances. Anger flared hot and unexpected in my chest at the sight of Serena's distress. What could have possibly happened to reduce this normally vibrant, strong woman to such a pitiful state? Who had hurt her so badly that she was left weeping amidst the wreckage of her cherished shop? I had to clench my fists tightly at my sides to stop myself from stalking across the room and demanding answers from Alec. As far as he could have been concerned, I was just a client, a friendly stranger really. I had no right to pry into Serena's private troubles, no matter how fiercely protective I felt. But seeing her like this made my heart ache in a way I didn't quite understand. All I knew was that I wanted to wrap my arms around her, soothe away her tears, and promise that everything would be alright.

"What the fuck happened here?" I growled out and Alec's head jerked up at the sound of my voice, his expression morphing to one of suspicion as he recognized me. He shook his head slightly, as if warning me away.

"It's fine," he said quickly, "I got it." I knew he was brushing me off, but I wasn't going to let him get rid of me that easily. I stalked across the room and dropped to my knees in front of the beautiful sobbing woman.

"Hey beautiful," I whispered and reached out my hand towards her face. Alec growled at me, but I ignored him as I cupped Serena's chin and encouraged her to look up at me.

"Serena, sweetheart, what's wrong?" Serena looked up from her hands, and despite the rim of her eyes being all red and puffy, the aquamarine colouring swirled like great stunning pools of water that I would happily drown in.

"Oh Jake," Serena sobbed and threw herself into my arms. She mumbled something else in his shoulder, but the sobs seemed to drown out her words. Alec looked shocked at her reaction, but instead of saying something, instead he sat back on his heels and watched me closely. I stared back at him, challenging him to say something, but he didn't, he just watched me with a calculating expression.

"What the hell happened here?" I demanded, and he raised an eyebrow at my tone.

"It's complicated," he finally answered before standing up and heading towards the back of the shop.

I could hear him in the back and from the brief glances as he paced by the door I could see that he was on the phone to someone. I kept a hold of Serena as she continued to cry on my shoulder. I tried to soothe her but whatever it was that had upset her had cut a wound so emotionally deep. The very thought of what it could be filled me with a quiet rage that surprised me. I wanted to find the bastard who dared to hurt her and rip them apart so they could hurt even half as much as I could feel this woman was hurting right now.

Alec eventually came out of the office at the back of the shop with a frustrated and concerned look on his face.

"I have to go and deal with something," he said, heading over to us. He knelt down beside me and lightly touched Serena's shoulder.

"Serena darling," he said in a gentle tone. "I have to go out, but I left a message on Ophelia's phone for her to come over straight away." He looked mildly concerned that Serena didn't answer him. Alec glanced at me, the concern turning to suspicion.

"Watch her," he said, "Don't leave her alone."

"I'm not going anywhere," I assured him. He nodded, obviously satisfied with my commitment to comforting the woman in my arms. I watched as he headed to the door and just as he reached for the handle he stopped and turned his head slightly in my direction.

"You hurt her and I will hunt you down and kill you." The certainty in his voice took me by surprise and he was out the door before I could form a response.

I held Serena close as her sobs quieted to soft hiccups and sniffles. My shirt was thoroughly soaked with her tears but I didn't care. All I cared about was comforting this amazing woman who had somehow conquered my heart in such a short time.

"Shh, it's okay. I've got you," I murmured, gently stroking her hair. She clung to me like I was her lifeline, her face still buried in my chest. I wanted nothing more than to protect her, to slay whatever demons were haunting her and threatening her light. But I knew the wounds that cut the deepest were often invisible.

After a few more minutes, Serena lifted her head and looked up at me with those stunning aquamarine eyes, still shimmering with tears.

"I'm sorry," she whispered hoarsely.

"You have nothing to apologise for," I assured her. Using my thumb, I tenderly wiped away the tears staining her cheeks. Her skin was so soft. She closed her eyes and leaned into my touch, a tiny sigh escaping her lips. My heart clenched. She looked so weary, so broken. I had to do something to help take her mind off whatever had caused this pain.

"Come on," I whispered. "Let's get you upstairs and settled on the couch. I'll make you some tea." Serena nodded and allowed me to help her to her feet. She swayed slightly and gripped my arm to steady herself. Without thinking, I swept her up into my arms, one arm under her knees and the other supporting her back. She let out a small gasp of surprise but didn't protest, instead wrapping her arms around my neck and nestling her head against my chest once more.

I carried her effortlessly up the stairs to the cosy apartment above the shop. Using my foot, I nudged open the already ajar door and made my way inside. The space was charmingly decorated, with shelves of books, clusters of crystals and candles, and plush rugs strewn about. It reminded me so much of Serena. I headed for the living area and gently laid her down on the plush sofa. She immediately curled into a ball, hugging one of the pillows to her chest. My heart ached at how small and vulnerable she looked.

"I'll go put the kettle on," I said softly. Serena grabbed my hand as I turned to leave.

"Don't go," she pleaded, her eyes wide. I nodded and sat down on the edge of the couch next to her. She shifted so her head was resting in my lap, those aquamarine eyes gazing up at me. I stroked her hair soothingly, and she closed her eyes again, fresh tears leaking from beneath her lashes.

"It's going to be okay," I murmured. "I'm here. You're safe." She clutched my other hand to her chest like it was her anchor. We stayed like that for some time, me gently running my fingers through her hair while she held onto me as if I could protect her from the demons in her mind.

Gradually, her breathing slowed and her grip on my hand relaxed as she drifted off to sleep. I continued stroking her hair, marvelling at how peaceful she looked. The furrow between her brows had smoothed, and the sorrow had left her face. She was so beautiful it made my heart physically ache. I had no idea how long we stayed like that; her sleeping with her head in my lap while I kept watch over her. The light faded outside the windows as afternoon turned to evening. Still, I didn't move, unwilling to disturb her. Instead, I resolved myself with planning on finding out who had destroyed my girl like this, so I could rip them a new one. The promise of violence consumed me long enough that it was a while before I realised I had referred to her as 'my girl.'

Sometime later she began to stir, nuzzling her face against my stomach before blinking her eyes open slowly. She looked confused for a moment before her gaze found mine.

"Hey," I said with a soft smile. "Feeling any better?" She gave a small nod and started to sit up. I helped ease her upright, though I immediately missed the warmth and weight of her head in my lap.

"Thank you," she said hoarsely, tucking a strand of mussed blond hair behind her ear. "For taking care of me. You didn't have to do that."

"I wanted to," I told her honestly. And I realised at that moment, I really did. Her pain had become my pain. Her tears had shattered my heart. I would move heaven and earth if it meant seeing her smile again.

"Can you tell me what happened?" I asked but the shine of tears in her eyes had me regretting that I had brought it up again. I quickly backtracked when I saw the hurt look in her eyes at my question.

"Hey, it's okay. You don't need to talk about it if you don't want to," I said gently. Serena gave me a small, grateful smile and nodded. She pulled her knees up to her chest and wrapped her arms around them, staring blankly across the room.

I studied her profile, taking in the dark circles under her eyes and the slump of her shoulders. She looked utterly defeated, a far cry from the vibrant, confident woman I had come to know. It made my blood boil to think someone had reduced her to this.

"Whoever did this to you is going to pay," I growled through clenched teeth. Serena's head snapped towards me, eyes wide with surprise.

"Jake..." she started, but I cut her off.

"No, I mean it. I'll make them suffer for what they did. I'll hunt them down myself and-"

"Jake, stop," Serena interrupted, placing a hand on my arm. Her touch was like a splash of cold water, instantly cooling my rage.

"You don't need to do that," she said firmly. "Revenge won't change anything or make me feel better." I opened my mouth to protest, but she silenced me with a pleading look.

"Please, violence will only breed more violence. That's not what I want or need right now." I let out a frustrated huff but nodded. As much as I wanted to tear apart whoever had hurt her, I respected Serena too much to go against her wishes.

"Then what do you need?" I asked softly. "Tell me how to help and I'll do it. Anything for you." Serena gave me a sad smile.

"I just need to feel loved right now. To be reminded there are still good people who care about me." Her words struck a chord deep inside me. I wanted nothing more than to show her just how much she meant to me, how deeply I cared, though we'd only known each other a short time. Before I even realised what I was doing, I reached out and cupped her face in my hands. Her lips parted in surprise but she didn't pull away.

"I care about you, Serena," I said thickly. "So fucking much." Then I kissed her. Gently at first, giving her the chance to stop me. But when she melted into me, I deepened the kiss, pouring every ounce of passion and longing I felt for her into it. She wrapped her arms around my neck, fingers tangling in my hair as she returned the kiss with equal fervour. The taste of her, the feel of her soft lips moving urgently against mine was pure ecstasy. When we finally broke apart, breathless, I rested my forehead against hers.

"I promise, I'll remind you every day how much you mean to me," I whispered. Serena's answering smile warmed me to my very core. In that moment, nothing else mattered but her. Not my mission, not the Council's orders. All I wanted was to stay by her side and keep her safe.

Chapter 21

Serena

Everything hit me all at once. My mother, the Zodiac legacy, everything. More importantly, Jake's declaration just moments ago that he cared about me ran rings around my thoughts. Hearing tell me that was something that I didn't know that I needed to hear and to hear him saying it out loud was enough to know that I felt it too. This man had walked into my life and changed everything, almost like fate.

I could feel the tears brimming again, but this time it was for a completely different reason. But I was sick of crying and ready to be happy. I pulled on Jake's shirt and met his mouth again with mine. At first he seemed surprised by the move but then Jake's lips were so soft yet demanding against mine. I sighed into his mouth, letting the kiss deepen as he wrapped his strong arms around me. All the hurt and anger I'd felt earlier melted away, replaced only by desire. When we finally broke for air again, Jake rested his forehead against mine.

"I'm sorry, I shouldn't have..." he started, but I silenced him with another brief kiss.

"Don't be sorry," I whispered. "That was..." I trailed off, unable to find the words.

Jake's grey eyes bored into mine, dark with want.

"Serena, I..." My heart pounded in my chest. I knew I should stop this, that getting involved with Jake was dangerous, but I couldn't bring myself to care. All I wanted was more of his touch, his kiss, the safety of his arms. I shifted closer, running my hands up his broad chest. Jake's breath hitched, his body taut as a bowstring. Slowly, gently, I drew his head down until our lips met again. The kiss was hungrier now, almost desperate. Jake's hands roamed my back, my hips, leaving trails of fire in their wake. I tangled my fingers in his short hair, revelling in the softness. We fell back against the sofa cushions, Jake above me. His stubble scraped my cheek as he trailed kisses along my jaw, down my neck. I gasped at the sensation, arching into him. Jake groaned, his mouth finding mine again. His weight pressed me into the sofa but I didn't care. I wanted him closer, as close as possible. My hands moved to the buttons of his shirt. I fumbled with them briefly before simply ripping the fabric apart, sending buttons bouncing across the floor.

Jake gave a throaty laugh.

"Impatient, are we?"

"You have no idea," I purred, running my hands over his now bare chest. Jake shivered at my touch, his muscles quivering. He kissed me hungrily again, one hand trailing down to grasp my thigh. I hooked my leg around his hip, enjoying the feel of his body against mine, separated only by our clothes. But even the thin veil of clothing was too much distance away from him and I reached down to pull my own top over my head. Jake's eyes blazed with lust as they travelled down my chest.

"Fuck," he muttered. "You are fucking beautiful." I tried to pull him back down to me, wanting, no, needing, to feel the connection of his skin against mine, but with a sly grin Jake pulled me up from the sofa and onto his knee where I ended up straddling his legs on the sofa. My heart pounded in my chest as Jake's lips trailed down my neck, leaving a trail of fire in their wake. I could feel the lust inside me growing with each passing second, the need to be whole with him almost too much to bear. I gripped his shoulders tightly, my nails digging into his flesh as I arched my back, pressing myself closer to him. Jake's breath was hot against my skin as he continued his worship of my body. My breath hitched as Jake unhooked my bra, letting my breasts fall free. I watched in a daze as he leaned forward, his eyes hungrily locked on my chest. The anticipation was almost too much to bear, and I could feel the heat building between my legs. Without another word, Jake took one of my breasts into his mouth, his tongue swirling around the sensitive nipple. The sensation was electric, sending shivers down my spine and making me cry out in pleasure. I arched against his mouth, my hands tangling in what part of his hair that I could grab at as he continued to lavish attention on my breast. His other hand palmed the other breast, squeezing gently and sending more waves of pleasure through me. I moaned softly, unable to resist the intense sensations coursing through my body. Jake's teeth grazed over my nipple lightly before he bit down gently, sending a jolt of electricity through me. I gasped at the sudden pain mixed with pleasure, arching even further into him. His tongue flicked over the bite mark, soothing the sting while driving me wild with desire.

"Oh god," I moaned. "Jake, please." Jake looked up at me without releasing his hold on my breast and there was a devious mischief in his eyes as he sucked more of my breast into his mouth. Finally he let go with a pop and before I could readjust my thoughts Jake was standing up, hooking his arms around my legs to my ass and looked around the room.

"What are you-" I started to ask but then his eyes fell on the only closed door in the apartment and with a resolved grunt he headed towards my bedroom. Jake kicked the door open and dropped my on the end of my bed with a bounce. He was on his knees in front of me and kissing me again before his lips began to trail down my neck and back to my chest. His lips moved lower, trailing kisses down my stomach until they reached the waistband of my skirt. With a swift motion, he hooked his fingers into the elastic and pulled it down over my hips, leaving me naked beneath him except for a pair of lacy panties that matched my bra that was left in the living room.

"So fucking beautiful," he repeated again, more to himself than to me. Jake's eyes roamed over me hungrily as he pushed the panties aside and ran his fingers along the sensitive skin of my inner thighs. My heart pounded in my chest as Jake's lips trailed up my thighs, leaving a trail of fire in their wake. I could feel the frustration building between us, the need for release almost too much to bear. With each kiss he placed on my thighs, I moaned softly, and I arched my back, pressing myself closer to him.

"Jake," I begged, not knowing how much longer I could take the teasing. Jake's eyes locked onto mine, his grey irises dark with desire.

"Don't worry baby, I got you," he whispered hoarsely. His words sent shivers down my spine and I knew that I wanted him more than anything in this world. With a devious smile, Jake pushed a finger into my pussy without warning, it sliding in to my wet embrace with ease. The sudden intrusion sent waves of pleasure through me and I cried out in surprise and delight. Jake's finger slid in and out of me slowly at first, each thrust sending another jolt of pleasure through me. He added another finger as his other hand found its way to my clit, rubbing it gently and he continued to finger fuck me. I gasped at the sensation, my hips bucking against his hand as the pleasure built inside me. Jake's eyes never left mine as he continued to work his magic on my body. His fingers moved faster now, each thrust deeper and more intense than the last. My breath came in ragged gasps as the pleasure built higher and higher within me.

Jake's mouth found its way to my clit once more, his tongue flicking over it hungrily as he continued to finger fuck me. The sensation was overwhelming, and I knew that I was close to climax. My hips bucked wildly against his hand as the pleasure reached its peak and then... I exploded, crying out loudly as wave after wave of pleasure washed over me. He didn't stop even as I came apart at the seams; instead, he continued to work his magic on my body until every last drop of pleasure had been wrung from me. When it was finally over, I collapsed back onto the bed, panting heavily and utterly spent. Jake crawled up beside me, pulling me into his arms where we lay together quietly for several long moments before he finally spoke up again.

"Oh my god, that was incredible," I muttered, slightly incoherent. "You certainly know how to take my mind off thing."

"Oh, I haven't finished yet darling," he growled in my ear and the words sent a shiver of excitement down my spine.

My heart pounded in my chest as I watched Jake stand up from the bed and undo his trousers, stepping out of them. His hard cock sprang free, standing proud and erect against his body. I couldn't help but feel a thrill of excitement at the sight of him, my pussy clenching in anticipation. Without breaking eye contact, Jake crawled up the bed and positioned himself between my legs. He rested on top of me, his cock pressing against my pussy entrance. I stared up at him, my heart pounding in my chest. I could see the emotions swirling in his eyes - hurt, love, lust. It was clear that this wasn't just about physical desire for him; there was something deeper going on.

"I don't know how," he whispered, his voice barely above a whisper. "Or even how it is event possible so quickly. But there is one thing that I know for sure right now and that is I am completely in love with you." The words hit me like a ton of bricks. I had been so focused on the danger and the mystery surrounding us that I had forgotten about the simple fact that there was a man lying on top of me who cared for me deeply.

"Jake..." I breathed his name, my voice barely above a whisper as well. "I... I don't know what to say." He smiled softly, his grey eyes filled with warmth and affection.

"You don't have to say anything," he murmured, leaning down to kiss me gently. "Just feel." And he kissed me again, a slow, lingering kiss that left me breathless and wanting more. His lips were soft yet demanding against mine, and I could feel the passion simmering beneath the surface. As our tongues danced together, I felt a warmth spreading through my body - a warmth that had nothing to do with his cock pressed against my entrance, and everything to do with the connection between us. I was just as certain as he sounded when I knew I was in love with him too. I broke the kiss as I felt tears prickling at the corners of mine. Ready to tell him, it was a sudden and overwhelming realisation that took me by surprise, but it was the truth. But before I could say anything, Jake pushed his cock into me with a low groan of pleasure. The words of love ready to come from my escaped in the cry of please that smashed through my body. The sensation was intense, every inch of him filled me up as he slid deeper inside me. It was more than just physical pleasure; it was an emotional connection that went beyond anything I had ever experienced before.

I wrapped my legs around Jake's waist, pulling him closer to me as he began to thrust into me with a rhythm that matched the pounding of my heart. Our bodies moved together in perfect harmony, each movement bringing us closer to each other both physically and emotionally. The pain from earlier had faded away completely; all that remained was the intense pleasure that radiated through every inch of my body with each thrust from Jake's cock. As we moved together, our breaths came in ragged gasps and our eyes never left each other's gaze. It was as if we were sharing something sacred, a moment that would be etched into our memories forever. And then... it happened, a wave of pleasure washed over me like a tidal wave crashing onto the shore, leaving me breathless and utterly spent as I cried out in ecstasy around Jake's cock buried deep inside me. Jake soon followed me over the edge and joined me in the waves of pleasure, in a sound so guttural and so primal that a fresh climax hit me and I screamed out his name to the gods listening above.

Jake finally collapsed partly on top of me, his body a mass of deep breathing and sweat. Once again he fell to my side and pulled me into his arms. I was vaguely aware of something covering my body and looked down to see he had pulled my blanket over us. I tried to move, but he held me tight against his body.

"Rest baby," he whispered in my ear and I felt my body relax against him. The exhaustion from the day was quickly pulling me under into a sleep but before I was totally lost to the dark, I managed to say one last thing.

"I love you too."

Chapter 22

Serena

I groaned as the buzzing of my phone pulled me from sleep. Blearily opening my eyes, I realised I wasn't alone in my bed. The warm body pressed against my back was definitely not one of my cats. Memories of last night came flooding back and I couldn't help the smile that spread across my face. Jake. We had... well; we had gotten to know each other quite intimately. I felt my cheeks flush as I remembered. His strong arms around me, his lips trailing kisses down my neck, the way he had looked at me like I was the most beautiful thing he had ever seen. It had been perfect.

As if he could sense my thoughts, Jake stirred behind me. His arm tightened around my waist and he nuzzled against my neck.

"Mornin'," he mumbled, his voice still thick with sleep. I rolled over to face him, taking in his rumpled hair and sleepy grey eyes. He looked so peaceful and content. Leaning in, I placed a soft kiss on his lips.

"Good morning," I whispered back, unable to keep the happiness out of my voice. Jake smiled and pulled me closer. We stayed like that for a few blissful moments, wrapped in each other's arms. I wished we could stay here forever, shut out from the rest of the world.

But the buzz of my phone reminded me that wasn't possible. With a sigh, I untangled myself from Jake's embrace and sat up, grabbing my phone from the nightstand. I looked at the screen and it was empty of any notifications. I frowned, I could have sworn that I heard it. Then the noise came again, and I looked down at the floor where Jake's pants were laid and rumpled where he had left them. The noise was coming from there. I looked over at him with a grin.

"It's not me," I said, and he furrowed his brow in confusion.

"Huh?" I lifted my phone and waved it around.

"The annoying buzzy bee is in your pants," I said. Jake's face cleared as the understanding dropped. He then shrugged and with a devious smile pulled me back into his arms.

"Well in that case," he said, kissing my nose, "Ignore it." He leaned in to kiss me just as the phone buzzed again. I chuckled as he groaned in annoyance.

"Sounds like they want you pretty bad," I said, and tried to wriggle out from under him. He tightened his grip and ran his nose against my neck.

"Well, I want you pretty bad," he whispered huskily, his words sending a thrill through my body. As is on queue his phone buzzed again and I laughed.

I pulled away and sat up on the bed.

"Tell you what," I said. "I will go put the kettle on and you can deal with the angry little phone, and then I can show you how orgasmic my breakfasts can be." I winked and stood up from the bed.

"There's only one breakfast I wanna be eating," he growled after me, sending another shiver of excitement through me as I headed out of the room.

"Good," I called back over my shoulder, "I wasn't going to cook anything, anyway." The sound of his laugh as I headed to the kitchen was surprisingly light and carefree, something I realised I had not experienced with Jake.

I hummed to myself as I filled the kettle and placed it on the stove. Tea always made everything better. I opened the cupboard and pulled out two mugs, pausing for a moment to admire the delicate floral pattern on my favourite one. It had been a gift from Gran on my 18th birthday. I smiled sadly thinking of her. If only she could see me now. Or maybe not, I laughed to myself. But knowing Gran she would be watching from above, probably taking score on form and shit.

The sound of footsteps pulled me from my thoughts. I turned to see Jake entering the kitchen, fully dressed in his clothes from yesterday. I couldn't help the small pout of disappointment that formed on my lips. I had rather enjoyed seeing him in a more natural state this morning. He gave me a lopsided grin as he walked over.

"Sorry to disappoint, but duty calls," he said jokingly. I rolled my eyes but couldn't help smiling back.

"Everything okay?" I asked, noticing the slight furrow between his brows.

"Yeah, I just need to take care of some business. Boring work stuff." He waved his hand dismissively but I could tell something was off. Call it intuition or just being observant, but I could see the tightness around his eyes belying his nonchalant attitude. Still, I knew better than to pry. We had only just met after all.

"Well, don't let me keep you then," I said lightly. Jake stepped closer and slid his hands around my waist.

"Trust me, there's nothing I'd rather be doing than staying here with you." His voice dropped lower as he pulled me against him. My heart skipped a beat as his lips found that sensitive spot on my neck. I melted into him for a moment before gently pushing back.

"As tempting as that is, if you need to go, you should. I'll be here when you get back." Jake sighed but nodded.

"I really am sorry. I'll come by as soon as I can, okay?" He brushed a stray hair from my face, his fingers lingering for a moment against my cheek. I nodded, suddenly at a loss for words under his intense gaze. Then he leaned in and kissed me firmly, stealing my breath away. My hands clutched at his shirt, not wanting to let go. With obvious reluctance he slowly pulled back.

"I'll see you later," he murmured. His grey eyes were dark with desire and I knew mine must look the same. With great effort I loosened my grip and stepped back.

"Looking forward to it," I managed to say, my voice sounding breathier than I intended. Jake grinned and with one more swift kiss, he was out the door. I let out a long breath as I heard the apartment door close behind him. What was I getting myself into with this man? Shaking my head to clear it, I finished prepping our tea, even though now it would just be for me. I had a feeling this was going to be an interesting day.

Less than an hour later I was also showered and dressed and ready for the day. With Jake gone I decided that I needed to tidy up all the mess from the shop last night. I headed down to the shop to see that both of the cats were enjoying a spot of sunshine that streamed in through one of the windows. Obsidian looked up and meowed before resting his head back on Carnelian's body. I smiled and reached down to scratch both of their heads as Looked around the room. There were crystal shards all over the floor from what I could only assume to be Gran's attempt at protecting me yesterday.

I sucked in a shaky breath as I stared at the broken crystals littering the floor. Each shattered piece was a stark reminder of the confrontation with my mother yesterday. After over twenty years of absence, she had suddenly reappeared in my life. Not for a loving reunion, but to threaten me. Her own daughter. The venom in her words had cut deep. She called me an abomination, something evil that needed to be destroyed. Just thinking about it made my chest tighten painfully. I knelt down and began carefully gathering the larger chunks of crystal, dropping them into a bin. The tinkling sound as they hit the bottom echoed hollowly in the quiet shop. Was I really so evil? Evil enough that my own mother wanted me dead? I thought back to the visions Jake, and I had shared during his reading. Flashes of violence and bloodshed. Was that my future? Was that the evil my mother saw in me? My hands trembled, causing the crystal I was holding to slip from my grasp and shatter on the floor. The jagged sound made me flinch.

Obsidian padded over, nudging my hand with his head. I scratched behind his ears absently, taking comfort in his presence. At least someone didn't see me as a monster. But my mother's words haunted me. She claimed Gran had put a spell on her to prevent her from revealing my true nature all these years. And now she had finally found a way to break that spell. Which meant it was only a matter of time before she told the Council about me. Before they came for me. Fear twisted in my gut at the thought. I didn't want to believe my mother's accusations, but what if she was right? What if I really was dangerous? Carnelian joined us, winding between my legs with a loud purr. I stroked his fur, taking a deep breath to steady myself. No. I refused to accept it. Gran had always told me I had a great destiny ahead of me. Not that she told me how great it was but she said that I would bring light and healing to many. That didn't sound evil to me. I had to trust in the gifts Gran helped me cultivate, not the hatred of a woman who abandoned me. I would not let fear and doubt poison me. With a deflated sigh I started to gather up the remaining pieces of crystal and put them in the bin with the other bits.

As I was putting the last of the shards in the bin, I saw the journals on the counter. These were what my mother wanted yesterday. She was pretty insistent on getting them. That told me that there must be something in them that could be of use to me. The shop was looking tidy again, but my thoughts still felt scattered. I couldn't stop thinking about what the journals had said, about Gran working for the Council. Were there more secrets hidden in them?

I made myself another cup of tea, Earl Grey with a splash of milk, just how I liked it. The familiar ritual soothed my nerves. Cradling the warm mug, I settled into one of the overstuffed armchairs near the front window. Obsidian jumped up into my lap, purring contentedly as I stroked his inky fur. I set my tea on the side table and reached for the stack of journals. Gran's elegant script greeted me as I opened the first volume. I skimmed through entries detailing her daily life as a Council Operative, the way they used her gifts to serve the Council, her hopes and worries. It all seemed so normal in her writing, but I couldn't help but feel annoyed at the obvious manipulation that was happening and felt sad that Gran wasn't aware of it.

Until I came to an account from when she was in her late thirties. She had been sent on some kind of mission to Bordeaux, France. Gran wrote about being tasked to retrieve a relic, a lead crystal goblet that supposedly had mystical properties. She was to transport it to a secret Council facility for safekeeping. I sat up straighter, dislodging a disgruntled Obsidian. A relic? Like the pendant I had found in Gran's things after she died? I read on eagerly. Gran described the goblet in detail - its intricate etchings and the way it seemed to glow from within. She wrote about strange visions she saw when handling it, brief glimpses into the past. But before Gran could learn more, she was ordered to wrap up the goblet and hand it over to other agents. Her job was done.

I leaned back in the chair, tea forgotten. So Gran had been searching out relics, just as I seemed destined to do. She mentioned in another journal that four relics were needed to perform the Ritual of the Zodiacs. With the pendant, that made three more I presumably had to find. I chewed my lip thoughtfully. Would I need to go to France to look for it? I was starting to feel like we were running out of time and a trip to France wouldn't exactly be cheap either. But even then, trying to find three magical items, that I had no clue what they even were, and could be anywhere in the world. Well, it was beginning to sound like a needle in a field of haystacks. Frustrated with the massive responsibility and my lack of how to fulfil my destiny I read on, hoping for more clues.

It wasn't until two journals later that things really started to get interesting. Gran wrote about coming across a young woman with the gift of sight. She talked about how the woman was believed to be working with the resistance in helping them find the Zodiacs. My eyes widened as I recognised the name Willow Barton. Wasn't that who Alec had said was who Gran helped? I read through the notes of how Gran had tracked down the girl and was planning on dispatching one of her best assassins Andrew Kirkland to take out the girl, but Gran put in the Journal that she would have to make sure that she had found the right location first.

I settled back into the armchair, eager to learn more from Gran's journal. As I turned the page, the change in handwriting immediately caught my attention. The flowing script I had come to know as Gran's was replaced by something messier, less refined. I ran my fingers over the page, wondering at the difference. The first line made me gasp out loud. Gran wrote that she had made a massive mistake, one she desperately needed to rectify. My pulse quickened as I read on. She described how she had tracked down the psychic, Willow Barton, with the intention of eliminating her. But when Gran grabbed the girl trying to flee, she was hit with an intense vision. I could picture Gran clutching this young psychic, both frozen in place as images flashed before them. Gran wrote of seeing a blonde girl with eyes like the sea, she somehow knew it was her future granddaughter, though they had never met. This girl stood surrounded by eleven others, hands joined as light poured from them. The vision revealed that this girl, me, was one of the twelve Zodiacs, mythical beings meant to heal the damage caused by magic. My hands trembled, making the journal shake. I couldn't believe what I was reading. Gran had seen my destiny, long before I was even born. She wrote of her shock and awe at the revelation. The Council had taught her that the Zodiacs were dangerous, their powers unstable. But Gran now knew that was a lie. The Zodiacs were meant to restore balance to the world.

I continued reading eagerly. Gran described how the vision faded, leaving her forever changed. She knew then that she could not follow the Council's orders. Willow had to be protected, not eliminated. Gran made the decision in that moment to defect, rejecting the propaganda she had been fed for years. My heart swelled with pride for my brave grandmother. I knew it couldn't have been easy, but she chose to follow her conscience and leave the only life she had known. All because of what she saw in that vision, me. I wiped away a tear that had escaped down my cheek. Even then, Gran had been looking out for me. Guiding my path from afar. She gave up everything to ensure I would one day fulfil my destiny. My hands caressed the journal reverently. I wished I could go back in time and hug her tight, thank her for the sacrifice she made for me. Because everything I had just read told me that I was on the right path and despite the ugly words from my mother, I wasn't evil. And I was ready to face the Council of Supernaturals head on if that was what it took.

Chapter 23

Serena

I just picked up another of Gran's journals when the bell above the shop door tinkled as the door opened and Alec walked in. I set the journal down on the table as Alec approached.

"You're not going to believe what I just found," I said. "This journal is from when Gran was working for the Council. She got a vision from that Willow girl you mentioned, about me being the Cancer Zodiac, years before I was even born!" Alec's eyes widened.

"Iris knew about you that early on?" he asked. I nodded, tears of emotion welling up.

"That must have been why she reached out to the Resistance. She made the decision to leave the Council knowing how corrupt they were. I'm so proud she stood up for what was right, even though it must have been hard and so dangerous for her." Alec put a comforting hand on my shoulder and nodded.

"She really was an amazing woman," he said with a smile. "Such a force to be reckoned with. And knowing what you just told me makes so much sense as to why she came to us for help." A warmth spread through my body at how much my Gran loved me even before I existed. But then it turned cold as I thought about my mother.

"Shame that my mother couldn't be as forgiving as Gran was," I said sadly, I felt tears pricking at my eyes at the hurtful things she said yesterday. Alec knelt down in front of me and took my hands in his.

"First off," he said, his face set in a determined expression. "There is absolutely nothing to forgive. You aren't some criminal, no matter what the bloody Council are telling people. You and those eleven other women, wherever in the world they may be, will be the reason that this earth keeps on spinning." A sad look crossed his eyes, and he looked down.

"Clara is just complicated you know," he said looking back up at me. "She grew up living in the world of the Council of the Supernaturals, and even when Iris came to us for help I don't think that Clara ever left the Council in her mind." I tried to smile. I tried to even understand how it must be to be pulled from one way of living to another that was practically the opposite. But I couldn't get my head around the notion that my own mother was willing to kill me, her own child, for something that I was born into.

Then I remembered what my mother had said yesterday, about Alec and him not being my father. I had never even considered Alec being anything more than a friend. Sure he acted fatherly towards me sometimes, but it never once crossed my mind that we were related. But when my mother had said it yesterday, and when she had spoken about my father Alec had gotten pretty angry.

"Alec," I asked quietly. "What did my mother mean yesterday, about my father being evil?" Alec stiffened slightly and then forced a smile on his face.

"It's complicated sweetheart," he said and stood up to cross the room.

"Well, spell it out for me," I said following him. I could tell he was trying to avoid something, but I wasn't giving in. "Is my father actually a bad person, like my mother had said?" Alec spun around quickly and shook his head, alarm on his face.

"Serena, no," he said quickly. "Your father was one of the kindest and most amazing men I knew. He was so far from anything remotely evil that it is absurd to think of him in that way."

"So you know him then," I urged on, "You know my father." I stared at Alec, my heart pounding. All my life I had wondered who my father was, why my Gran had refused to speak of him. Now, finally, I had a chance to learn the truth.

"Alec, please," I said, my voice tight with emotion. "I need to know about my father. If you knew him, you have to tell me." Alec hesitated, his face conflicted. He ran a hand through his dark hair and let out a heavy sigh.

"Alright," he said finally. "You deserve to know the truth about your dad. His name was James. And yes, I knew him very well." Alec paused, as if gathering his thoughts. When he continued, his voice was soft with remembrance.

"Your father was one of the best men I've ever known. He was part of the Resistance, a true believer in our cause. He had an energy about him, people were just drawn to him. He could light up a room with his smile." I listened intently, picturing the man Alec described. A man I had never known, but who was a part of me.

"We were close friends, your dad and I, like two sides of the same coin," Alec went on. "We both grew up together in the Resistance. James was fiercely loyal, he would have done anything for the people he cared about. And he was brave. He never backed down from a challenge, never ran from a fight if it was for the right reasons." Alec shook his head, his eyes glinting with emotion.

"Your father was the life of the party too. He had an incredible sense of humor. Always playing pranks on people, keeping things light even during the darkest of times. It was impossible to stay sad around him for long." My heart ached, longing to have known this man. I tried to imagine his smile, his laugh. Tried to picture myself as a little girl, nestled safely in those strong, loving arms.

"When your Gran and mother left the Council and joined us, your dad worked hard to help Clara adjust," Alec continued. "It couldn't have been easy for her, leaving everything she knew behind. But James was patient and kind. He truly loved her." Alec paused, his expression growing solemn. "They became an item quickly. We all thought Clara had changed, that she embraced the Resistance. Obviously we were wrong." He shook his head, looking pained.

"Your father would have been so proud of you, Serena," he said softly. "So proud of the woman you've become." I felt tears spill down my cheeks. Hearing about my father for the first time was bittersweet. I ached to have known him, but felt so grateful to Alec for sharing these precious memories. Then something about the way Alec spoke about the man struck me and I felt a cold knot in my stomach.

"Was?" I asked and Alec furrowed his eyebrows. I shook my head, not even sure I wanted confirming what I already figured out. "You said was. You only referred to him in past tense." I saw pain pas through Alec's eyes and he looked away. I could see him trying to swallow a lump in his throat.

"I'm sorry Serena," he said. "But James died, he was killed." A tear slipped down his cheek and I couldn't help but feel the incredible sadness that was coming off of him.

"How?" I choked out. "How was he killed?" Alec shook his head and turned away from me. I stared at Alec, my heart pounding. I needed to know what happened to my father.

"Alec, please," I urged. "I have to know the truth. No more dancing around it." Alec let out a heavy sigh, his shoulders slumping in defeat. "You're right. You deserve the full story."

He motioned for me to sit down, then pulled up a chair across from me. Leaning forward, he clasped his hands together and met my gaze.

"It was about a year after your parents got together," he began slowly. "Clara came to visit your grandmother one day, with you as a tiny baby in her arms. When Iris opened the door, Clara barged right past her without a word. Didn't even let your gran hold you." Alec shook his head, his brow furrowed. "When Clara came back out, she was in a right foul mood. She told your Gran that she would never see you again and stormed off. Iris tried to ask what was wrong, but Clara just snapped at her that it was all her fault." I listened intently, picturing the scene. My heart ached for my poor grandmother, treated so coldly by her own daughter.

"The next day, your mother left your father," Alec continued heavily. "She told James he had manipulated her, that he was evil and she wanted nothing more to do with him or the Resistance. James was devastated. He loved her so much, he couldn't understand what had happened." Alec paused, taking a deep breath before going on. "That same day, Clara went back to the Council. And exactly one week later..." He trailed off, avoiding my gaze. Dread pooled in my stomach. "What happened, Alec?" I prodded gently. "Please, I need to know." Alec met my eyes, his own glistening with tears.

"Clara led a group of Council members to ambush one of our meetings. They broke in and dragged James outside..." His voice broke and he looked away. "It was Clara who killed him, Serena. Your own mother." The words hit me like a punch to the gut. For a moment, I couldn't breathe, couldn't think. My mother had murdered my father in cold blood?

Hot tears spilled down my cheeks as the weight of it all sank in. I thought back to her venomous words in the shop just yesterday. How she said I was an abomination, that she would kill me too. Suddenly her threats felt so much more real, so much more sinister. She had already taken my father from me before I ever got the chance to know him.

"I'm so sorry, Serena," Alec said softly, reaching out to grasp my hand. "We never wanted you to have to carry this burden. But you deserved to know the truth." I clung to his hand like a lifeline, overwhelmed with grief and shock. My own mother was a murderer. The woman who gave me life had so callously taken away the life of the man I should have called Dad.

We sat in silence for a long moment as I processed it all. Then a realisation struck me.

"The spell," I gasped. "That's why Gran did it - to stop my mother from being able to reveal me as the Zodiac. She must have known she would try to have me killed too." Alec nodded solemnly. "Iris wanted to protect you, by any means necessary. She knew what Clara was capable of. She didn't tell any of us what happened that day, but said that she was worried for your safety. She did the spell to protect you. Not that she would have known if it could have worked or not."

"Why not?" I asked and Alec shrugged.

"After the attack we didn't see Clara, or you, for another four years. Iris spent so much time trying to find out if you were still alive." Anger and hurt welled up inside me. My mother had betrayed my father, betrayed all of them. And she would have happily betrayed me too. I had so many conflicted feelings towards the woman who birthed me. But at least now, things made more sense. Her hostility, her threats, all stemmed from a deep hatred and resentment.

I took a deep, shuddering breath, trying to collect myself. I felt Alec squeeze my hand comfortingly.

"I know this is a lot to take in," he said. "I can't imagine how you must be feeling right now. But I'm here for you, Serena. We all are." I managed a small, watery smile.

"Thank you, Alec," I whispered. "For telling me the truth. For being here." He pulled me into a fierce hug and I broke down, sobbing into his shoulder as he held me tight. We stayed like that for a long time, mourning the loss of the father I never knew, processing the grim revelation about my mother.

When my tears finally subsided, I pulled back and met Alec's eyes.

"Did he have any other family?" I asked, maybe slightly hopeful that I might have some family I didn't know about. Alec stiffened slightly and then smiled.

"Yeah he did," he said. "And you met them already."

"I have," I exclaimed. "When?" Alec smiled again.

"I want you to know that the decision was made to keep you hidden, and away from the resistance, just in case the spell didn't work and Clara came after you." I narrowed my eyes on Alec.

"What does that have to do with if I had met them or not?" I asked and Alec sighed.

"James' parents wanted to be in your life but they are so heavily involved in the resistance that they are always being watched," he said.

It made sense that if they knew who I was or that I could be in danger that it was safer to stay away.

"But," Alec said with a smile. "You did spend last Christmas with them." My eyes widened as he spoke. Last Christmas was bittersweet. It was the first one without Gran and I was feeling sorry for myself, Alec had invited me over to York for his big family gathering. There were so many people there, but they were all related to Alec. Did that mean...

"But- but I spent last Christmas with you and your family," I stuttered. Alec nodded and smiled again.

"And your family," he said and my heart suddenly started beating faster. "James was my older brother."

Chapter 24

Serena

"Your brother?" I exclaimed, stunned by Alec's revelation. Alec nodded, his eyes glistening. "Yes. We were very close growing up." My mind reeled as I tried to process this new information. Alec was family? I had known him for years, ever since Gran introduced us when I was a teenager. He had been a constant presence in my life, like a protective older brother. In many ways, he was the only real family I had.

"Why didn't you ever tell me?" I asked. Alec sighed, running a hand through his dark hair. "Iris thought it best to keep my true identity hidden. If anyone ever suspected I was related to you, then they could trace it back to your father, it could put us both in danger. Plus, we didn't know how well the spell would hold up."

"What do you mean?" I asked and Alec sighed. He went over to the counter where the more recent of my Gran's journals were and looked through some. After a few moments he came back with one of the Journals.

"Iris told me about the spell and told me the mechanics were written in her records." Alec held out the journal to me and I looked through the notes. In it my Gran said that the Spell of Silence, was a difficult one and was easily triggered. I looked up at Alec, not quite understanding what it meant.

"Yeah your Gran could have been a bit less vague," he said with a chuckle. "Basically from what I knew of the spell was that Clara couldn't come out directly and say who you were, or who was a resistance member, but it didn't mean that she couldn't indirectly find a way. Or if someone directly asked her if her daughter was a Zodiac then that could trigger a break in the spell." Alec shrugged. "The more we kept you off the radar, the less likely that someone would even ask about you." That made more sense than I thought it should. I still didn't understand it all, I did understand that it was for my safety.

There was certainly a lot to take in over the last couple of days. From my mother returning into my life and threatening to kill me, to finding out that I had a whole other family that I knew nothing about. I was starting to feel a little worn out. Carnelian must have sensed my overwhelm because he chose that moment to jump up onto my knee. I stroked his head as he settled down in my lap with a contented purr. I glanced up at Alec and grinned.

"So any more revelations?" I asked "Is Ophelia my great aunt or something." I was making a joke, but a look crossed Alec's face that stopped me.

"What is it?" I asked and Alec shook his head.

"It's probably nothing," he said and leaned over to scratch Carnelian's head. "How about I make some tea?" He stood up and headed towards the office.

"Alec," I asked, stopping him in his tracks. "What is bothering you?" Alec turned back around to face me and grimaced.

"I haven't heard from Ophelia in a while," he said. "I phoned her yesterday after..." he trailed off obviously not wanting to bring my mother up again. "But she didn't answer, and never got back to me." I felt a prickle of unease at Alec's words. Ophelia not showing up or answering her phone was definitely out of character for her. She was one of my closest friends and confidantes. The fact that even Alec couldn't reach her was troubling.

"That's not like her," I said with a frown. "She always calls back, even if it's just to say she can't talk." Alec nodded, his brow furrowed with concern.

"Exactly. And when I stopped by her place, it didn't look like she'd been home all night." My unease grew sharper. Ophelia lived in a little cottage in the heart of Whitby's old town. She rarely spent nights away unless she had told one of us about it. A knot of worry formed in my stomach. Something wasn't right.

"What do you think's happened?" I asked Alec. He let out a weary sigh, raking a hand through his dark hair.

"Honestly, I'm probably overreacting. We're all on edge lately with everything that's going on. Those Council operatives snooping around, your mother turning up..." He trailed off with a scowl. I knew he was still furious about my mother's sudden reappearance and her threats towards me. If I was being honest, so was I. Her venom had cut deep, reopening old wounds I thought had long since scarred over.

"You're probably right," I said, trying to sound more convinced than I felt. "I'm sure Ophelia's fine. Maybe she just needed some time to herself." Alec nodded, but his eyes remained troubled. "I hope so. I know she can handle herself, but with the Council here..." He didn't need to finish the sentence. If the Council had even an inkling of

Ophelia's involvement with the Zodiac prophecy, she could be in very real danger. Just the thought made my blood run cold.

I tried to push down the knot of worry that had formed in my stomach over Ophelia's disappearance. Alec was right, she was more than capable of handling herself. And it wasn't like her to just vanish without a word for days on end.

"I'm sure we're just overthinking," I said with a small smile. "Why don't you put the kettle on while I tidy up down here? Then we can look through Gran's journals again. Maybe we missed some clues about the other relics." Alec nodded, though his eyes remained troubled. I could tell Ophelia's absence was really bothering him. As he headed up to the flat to make tea, I turned my attention to straightening up the shop. I had scattered the journals that I had read into several smaller messy piles.

I was just straightening them up when Alec returned, two steaming mugs in hand. He set them down on the counter and turned to me, his expression grim.

"Before we get back to the journals, there's something else we should talk about," he said. I paused my tidying, instantly wary. That serious tone was never good.

"What is it?" Alec ran a hand through his hair, looking uncomfortable.

"It's about Jake." My stomach flipped nervously at the mention of Jake's name. Ever since our passionate encounter last night, I hadn't been able to stop thinking about him. I couldn't explain the intensity of the connection between us, but it felt so deep, so fated. Being with him had felt...right. Like I was exactly where I was meant to be. And I couldn't get the moment he told me he loved me out of my head. Just thinking about it sent warm fuzzy feelings through me.

"What about him?" I asked carefully.

"Look, I know you two have gotten... close, these past few days." Alec chose his words delicately. "And I understand the draw. But Serena, we barely know anything about this guy. He shows up out of the blue, charms you, conveniently has ties to the supernatural community..." My hackles rose defensively.

"So you think he's just playing me? Trying to get information?" Alec held up his hands.

"I'm not saying that. I just think you need to be cautious. Tread slowly." His expression turned solemn. "Especially with who his uncle is." I bit my lip. Alec had a point there. Alec had told me some of the stuff that he had heard about Stephen Kirkland and told me that even in the resistance circles his reputation preceded him. As a high-ranking Council operative, he was known for his ruthlessness in hunting down unregistered magic users. If he was truly the person who had raised Jake, that connection gave me pause.

"I know," I admitted quietly. "But Jake's not like that. He doesn't believe in the Council's methods."

"Are you sure about that?" Alec pressed gently. "Serena, you've known him for less than a week. And there's been a lot going on to distract you from looking too closely." I bristled, even though a tiny seed of doubt had taken root inside me. "What's that supposed to mean?" Alec held up his hands again.

"Nothing judgmental, I promise. I just want you to be smart. Don't let your feelings cloud your judgement." His expression softened. "I don't want to see you get hurt." I let out a long breath, my defensiveness fading. I knew Alec only had my best interests at heart. And if I was totally honest with myself, I had been moving fast with Jake. Too fast, probably. I barely knew anything about his past, his family, what brought him to Whitby. But every time we were together, it just felt so right. Still...

"You're right," I admitted begrudgingly. "I don't know Jake well enough yet to fully trust him. But I really don't think he means me any harm." I thought of our passionate encounter, the way he had looked at me with such tenderness in those intimate moments. I wanted to believe it had been real. Alec nodded slowly.

"Fair enough. Just promise you'll be careful?"

"I will," I assured him. And I meant it. As much as my heart wanted to believe Jake was as good as he seemed, my head knew I couldn't afford to be blindly trusting. Not with the Council lurking so close.

I looked up the moonstone talisman still hanging from the hook by the office. Jake's last link to his late mother. The one he'd been so distressed over losing. I had been meaning to give it back to him, but something always seemed to be getting in the way.

"I should probably return that to Jake soon," I mused. "But maybe before I do, I'll perform a reading on it. See if I can pick up any unusual vibrations." If Jake did have malicious intent, a psychometric reading on his talisman would likely reveal it. Alec's expression turned approving.

"Good idea. That's a smart next step." I nodded, feeling more settled now that I had a plan. I would proceed with care where Jake was concerned, keeping my eyes wide open for any red flags. And in the meantime, do some magical digging to uncover his true intentions. My heart squeezed uncomfortably. I didn't want to find anything suspicious. But I owed it to myself, and the Zodiacs, to be absolutely sure about Jake before letting him get any closer.

But until then, we had more important things to worry about. I let out an exasperated sigh as I handed Alec a stack of Gran's journals.

"Here, these are the ones that mention the relics. Maybe we can find some new clues if we go through them again." Alec nodded, taking the offered journals.

"Good idea. Finding those remaining relics needs to be our top priority right now, before the ritual time comes." I frowned in frustration, hands on my hips.

"That's just it though, we still don't know when the ritual is supposed to happen! The prophecy wasn't exactly specific. All we know is that it's sometime this year."

"True," Alec conceded. He flipped open the top journal and started scanning through it. "But your Gran seemed to think you'd just know when the time was right. Like it would just come to you intuitively." I rolled my eyes.

"Oh, sure, no problem. I'll just magically intuit the precise date and time for an ancient cosmic ritual I only just found out I'm meant to lead." My voice dripped with sarcasm. Alec shot me an amused glance over the journal.

"Alright, fair point. Let's see if we can find some more concrete clues then." I pulled up a chair beside him with a huff, grabbing one of the journals from the stack. As frustrating as all this vagueness was, Alec was right that we needed to keep searching for answers. The Zodiac prophecy had been kept secret for centuries before being passed down to me. There had to be more hidden in these pages if I looked hard enough.

We poured over the journals together, searching for any mention of the relics or clues about the ritual. The shop was quiet except for the occasional meows from Obsidian and Carnelian as they dozed by the window. I rubbed my temples as I flipped through page after page of Gran's cramped, looping handwriting. So far I'd found nothing useful, just vague references to guarding certain objects and preparations needing to be made. With a soft groan, I closed the journal I'd been skimming through and grabbed another.

"Find anything?" Alec asked without glancing up from the journal he was studying. I shook my head with a huff. "No, just more cryptic allusions. This would be so much easier if Gran had just written down specifics." Alec made a noise of agreement. "Well, she knew the Council would want to suppress the prophecy if they found these journals. I'm sure she was just being cautious."

"I know," I sighed, leaning back in my chair to stretch my stiff shoulders. "Doesn't make it less frustrating." Alec shot me a sympathetic smile before returning to his reading. I flipped open the next journal, hoping this one might finally give us the clarity we needed.

As I turned the brittle pages, a passage caught my eye: I sat up straighter, immediately alert as I scanned the entry. This was the first concrete mention I had found of the relics and what Gran had done with them.

"Listen to this," I said to Alec, before reading the passage aloud:

> *"After my vision revealing that my dear granddaughter is destined to be one of the Zodiacs, I now know what I must do. I have begun travelling the world, following every whisper and rumour that could lead me to the sacred relics needed for the ritual. It has been an arduous search, full of dead ends and false trails, but I persevered.*

Just yesterday, after months of work, my efforts have finally borne fruit. I have recovered three of the four relics necessary to complete the ritual! Even now I can feel their energy thrumming beneath my fingertips, eager to fulfill their purpose. I dare not write more about their exact nature here. I will bring them back to Whitby, to keep under my protection until my blessed girl is ready. The Council must never discover them. I will hide one here in the shop, concealed where only she will find it when the time comes. The others I will secret away somewhere in Whitby, in places tied to the ancient magic of this land. My beautiful girl will know where to look when the moment arrives. For now, they must stay hidden. I will need to help her as much as possible and I want to bring some familiars to help with her search. They are rare but I know that they will come to help their soul keeper."

"Familiars," I repeated the last part. Alec grinned and leaned over to stroke Carnelian, who had taken to laying across another pile of journals as we read. My eyes widened as I looked between Alec and the cat. Carnelian must have sensed my attention as he looked up at me and meowed before going back to sleep.

"Seriously!" I exclaimed. Gran had gotten me the cats when I was almost fifteen years old. I assumed it was because I struggled with friends, but could she have really found me familiars? It suddenly made sense. It was one of the cats that led me to finding the necklace, and the journals. I couldn't believe that I never picked up on it. And now with the revelation of the relics as well. I looked up at Alec, heart quickening with excitement.

"This is huge! Now we know for sure Gran gathered the relics herself and hid them here in Whitby." Alec nodded, his eyes bright.

"This is big. If we can find them all before the Council does, it could make all the difference." His brow furrowed. "Did she give any hints about the locations?" I scanned the entry again, looking for any clues.

"No, nothing concrete. She just says she hid them in places tied to the 'ancient magic' of Whitby." I sat back with a frustrated huff.

"Well, that could be anywhere! This whole town is steeped in magic and legends." Alec tapped his chin thoughtfully.

"True, but my guess is she would have chosen locations meaningful to her personally. Places she had an emotional connection to." I considered that, reflecting back on what I knew about my Gran's history here. She had grown up in Whitby, leaving only for her travels. Most of her life had been spent here.

"Well, there's the abbey ruins of course," I mused. "She used to take me there all the time as a child. Said it was a 'thin place' where the veil between worlds was weaker." Alec nodded.

"Good thought. Where else?" I closed my eyes, picturing Gran as she gave me tours of her favourite Whitby haunts over the years. Our strolls along the pier, browsing the shops downtown, afternoon tea in the quaint cafes... My eyes flew open.

"The lighthouses!" Seeing Alec's blank look, I explained. "It was one of her favourite spots. She said it called to her, made her feel connected to the old magics that guided sailors safely to shore. That their combined efforts created a gateway."

"The abbey and lighthouse, that makes sense," Alec agreed. He tapped the open journal. "Any other places that stood out to her?" I wracked my brain, but nothing else came to mind. "No, mostly just the seaside and the old town. Though..." I paused, remembering something. "She did talk about the whale bones. Said they were infused with ancient magic." Alec snapped his fingers.

"The whale bone arch, yes that could be it! Good instinct." He smiled at me. "I think you're right, those three locations seem like very strong possibilities." I felt a flutter of excitement in my chest. It wasn't much to go on, but having even a vague direction to focus the search felt heartening. We actually had a chance of finding the relics before the Council now.

"So, where should we start looking first?" I mused aloud. The abbey, lighthouse and arch each had potential in their own way. But we couldn't search them all at once with just the two of us. Alec pondered for a moment.

"My instinct says the abbey," he said finally. "It was clearly very special to Iris, and has the strongest ties to ancient magic as a known religious site." I nodded slowly.

"I think you're right. The abbey feels like the most likely place for Gran to have hidden one." I checked my watch, nearly seven in the evening, and it was already dark out.

"Why don't we have some dinner, then head over to start searching? We can keep an eye out for Ophelia while we're there too." Alec agreed, looking relieved to have a solid plan in place. As he headed upstairs to grab some food for us, I quickly tidied up the scattered journals. For the first time since Gran had passed, I was starting to feel like I really was connecting with her purpose for me. Maybe her spirit would even guide us to the hidden relic today.

"Don't worry Gran, we'll find them," I whispered aloud, hoping she could hear me. Wherever her spirit rested, I knew she would be doing everything she could to help from the other side. With luck, her clues would lead Alec and I to the next relic. One step closer to carrying out my destiny.

Chapter 25

Jake

I was getting sick of being at the beck and call of the Council, and of my bloody Uncle. Once again he had interrupted my time with Serena cutting it short. As I stormed down the cobbled streets after leaving a beautiful looking Serena this morning in the kitchen, after several incessant calls from my uncle Stephen, meaning that I had to go before he came looking for me. I got the feeling that Serena didn't like my uncle. Not that anyone would have if he had dropped a bombshell of information like he did yesterday. But here I was running to him, like the good little soldier boy that I was trained to be. I knew that I hadn't completed my mission yet, but I was still working on it. It took time to get someone to trust you enough to get what you needed, and for some reason I had the feeling that Serena was the key to everything. I also knew that meant that what we had together was pretty much doomed from the start. I also knew that part of my annoyance was that I was angry that someone had hurt Serena so much. I might not have known Serena for long but I knew that for someone to reduce her to the broken emotional mess that I had found her in, sobbing almost hysterically on the shop floor, then that person must have been really awful. I shouldn't have these feelings of love for Serena but I did, and I wasn't lying when I said I would hurt whoever it was that hurt her. I just had to find out who I was hunting down.

My boots clicked loudly on the cobbles as I strode towards the B&B where me and my uncle was staying. He had booked in yesterday after turning up unannounced, saying that he wanted to keep a closer eye on things. The sun was already high in the sky, promising another rare warm day for the seaside town this winter. Maybe another effect from the shit show that was a result of the Zodiacs and their misuse of the magic in the world. But I barely noticed the pleasant weather, too caught up in my swirling thoughts. Serena's tear-streaked face kept flashing through my mind. Seeing her so distraught had sparked an unfamiliar protectiveness in me that I didn't quite understand. I was used to being cold and detached, a requirement for my work. Yet this woman had gotten under my skin in a matter of days. I shouldn't care about her pain, but I did.

I reached the B&B and took the creaking steps two at a time to the second floor. I didn't bother knocking, just threw open the door to my uncle's room. He was sitting at the small table by the window, steaming cup of tea in hand.

"Ah Jake, right on time," he said smoothly, gesturing for me to take a seat. I remained standing, glaring down at him.

"This better be important to drag me away from my work," I growled. My uncle raised an eyebrow.

"Touchy this morning, aren't we?" He took a slow sip of tea. "I take it you've made progress with the witch?"

"Her name is Serena," I said through gritted teeth. "And yes, I'm gaining her trust."

"Excellent, excellent." My uncle set down his cup and steepled his fingers. "Now, tell me everything you've learned about the girl and her... abilities." I hesitated. I knew I should tell him about the strange vision Serena and I had shared during the reading. And about the way that I feel connected to her. But something held me back.

"Well?" My uncle prompted. "What useful information have you gathered?"

"Nothing concrete yet," I lied smoothly. "I need more time." My uncle scrutinised me and I had to force myself not to shift under his piercing gaze. After a tense moment, he nodded.

"Very well. But time is of the essence, Jake. We need to identify if this girl can help us before..." He trailed off, but I knew what he meant. Before the Prophecy came to pass. Before the rise of the Zodiacs threw our world into chaos.

"Do we even know for certain that she is connected at all?" I asked. "I mean I know you said in the original report that the source told us that a psychic would have what we needed. Are you sure Serena is the psychic in question? God only knows that this town is full of them."

"It's her." A new voice sounded from the side of the room. I recognised the voice instantly and turned with a big grin on my face, just as the person was closing a second door that probably led into a bedroom.

I grinned broadly as Clara Moore stepped fully into view. She was an agent from a different cell, but we had worked together successfully on several missions over the years. Clara was probably one of the most skilled and dedicated operatives in the entire Council. Her long blonde hair was swept back in its signature braid and her green eyes glinted with purpose.

"Clara! Good to see you," I said warmly, walking over to give her a quick hug. "What are you doing here?"

"The mission I was on went south and Stephen requested my assistance on this mission," Clara replied, nodding respectfully to Stephen. "Especially given my... history with this area." I nodded in understanding. Early in her career, Clara had been part of a major Council operation to take down one of the biggest Resistance cells in York. Her work had been instrumental in crippling the York Resistance and capturing many of their top leaders. If anyone knew how to navigate the tricky local networks of magic users sympathetic to the Zodiac cause, it was Clara.

"Your expertise is most welcome," Stephen said approvingly. He gestured for us both to take a seat at the small table. "Now that we're all here, let's discuss our next steps. Jake, give us both a quick update on your progress with the Ashmoor woman." I quickly summarised my interactions with Serena so far, leaving out the shared vision and my confusing feelings toward her, focusing only on the factual details that could help the mission. Clara listened intently, her brow furrowed in concentration.

"Serena Ashmoor is very much involved," she said. I noticed that she seemed to almost spit out Serena's name like it gave her a bad taste.

"How can you be sure?" I asked. Clara sighed and closed her eyes, before opening them and looking at me again.

"Because I was the source that sent you here in the first place," she said and my eyes widened, although I tried to hide the shock on my face.

"Then why weren't you the one to take this mission?" It made more sense that if Clara had a good understanding and was sure of Serena's involvement, that she would be best fit for the job.

"It's complicated," she said and looked over at my uncle. There was clearly something that they weren't telling me here.

"What?" I asked. "What is it?" My uncle cleared his throat before looking back at me. "Clara has expressed concern over your erm... growing friendship with the witch," he said and I immediately felt a flash of anger rush through me. I tried to conceal it but even I could tell that my tone was very much off.

"No disrespect Clara," I started, knowing I could get in trouble for arguing with someone of higher rank than me. "But how the hell would you know about my growing friendship, or why should you have any concern over it at all?"

"I just do," she said, clearly getting frustrated over something. "Please Jake, trust me on this, that girl is bad news. I'm only looking out for you, like your mother would have wanted me too." The words stung as Clara mentioned my mother. The woman had been friends and Clara had spent many a time around at our house when I was a kid.

"Look at me Jake," Clara said and reached out to take my hand. "I need you to be safe, I would hate for something to happen to you." She glanced down and then back up at me.

"Where's your talisman?" she asked and my hand instinctively went to the place where my talisman should have been, only to grasp at empty air.

"Erm... I lost it," I mumbled, a flush rising in my cheeks. Clara shook her head in disappointment and turned to face my uncle Stephen.

"See," she said, as though this minor detail was irrefutable proof of her position. "You can't send him into that witch's lair without protection. No wonder he's acting like a love struck schoolboy." I yanked my hand away quickly as anger spiked through me again, hot and fierce.

"Whoa, what the fuck," I exclaimed, unable to contain my outrage. I pushed back my chair and stood up abruptly. "You have no right to make that call. Or to judge someone you have never even met." I turned on my heel and strode towards the door, done with this nonsense and ready to leave.

"But I do have the right," my uncle said, his commanding voice stopping me dead in my tracks. I paused and slowly turned back to face him. He was right of course. As a senior commander on the Council, he could order me back to base with a single word, and I would have no choice but to comply or risk being charged with treason. I glared at my uncle Stephen and then shifted my gaze to Clara, who at least had the decency to look conflicted about angering me so deeply.

"Go on then," I said. "Tell me why I can't trust Serena." Clara opened her mouth to speak and then closed it again with frustration flying across her face several times. Finally she deflated and glared at the table.

"Dammit," she hissed, "I need those bloody journals." I narrowed my eyes on her. What the hell was she talking about? I stared at Clara, my anger temporarily giving way to confusion.

"What are you talking about?" I asked. "What journals? And what does this have to do with Serena?" Clara sighed, looking troubled.

"It's complicated, Jake. Your uncle and I didn't want to burden you with the full details." I crossed my arms.

"Well I'm burdened now, so you might as well explain." Clara nodded reluctantly.

"Very well. As you know, years ago I led the operation that crippled the York Resistance cell. One of their leaders was an elderly witch named Iris Ashmoor." My eyes widened in surprise. Ashmoor, the same last name as Serena.

"Iris was a cunning old crone," Clara continued. "She escaped when we raided the Resistance hideout. We suspected she had information that could compromise other cells, but she disappeared before we could apprehend her." I glanced at my uncle.

"You think this Iris is connected to Serena?" He nodded gravely.

"Yes, Iris was a Council Operative before betraying us to the Resistance." It was then that I put the pieces together. Iris Ashmoor was the one that my uncle mentioned to Serena yesterday.

"Serena's grandmother?" I asked and my Uncle nodded.

"Iris was known to keep meticulous journals filled with details about the Council workings and Resistance members and plans. If her granddaughter has those journals, she could pick up where Iris left off." I shook my head in disbelief.

"I can't see Serena being involved with a Resistance cell. She runs a new age shop, for heaven's sake." Clara looked at me sympathetically.

"I know you feel a connection with her, Jake. But she's Iris's granddaughter. The apple doesn't fall far from the tree." But no matter what Clara was saying, I couldn't imagine Serena being a part of the Resistance, sure maybe she was connected to a believer, and probably unknowingly connected to the Zodiac themselves. But the Resistance, I couldn't see it.

I thought back to how distraught Serena had been yesterday. What if her mother was involved with the Resistance too? Is that why they'd argued so bitterly?

"Wait," I said out loud, wondering if the sudden reappearance of Serena's mother was important here. "Serena's mother showed up yesterday. I don't know what happened but Serena was pretty upset afterwards." My uncle glared at Clara for some reason, and Clara shrank back in her chair slightly.

"You didn't tell me you went to the shop," my uncle said with a hint of anger in his voice.

"I wanted to see if I could get the Journals myself," Clara shot back and stared at them both as the realisation hit me.

"You?" I asked and Clara nodded her head.

"Yes," she said looking up at me. "Serena is my daughter." No. It wasn't possible. Clara was the woman who had hurt Serena. She was the one who had reduced her to a broken mess. I stared at Clara in disbelief, my mind reeling from her revelation. Serena was her daughter? How was that possible? The woman who had caused Serena so much pain was her own mother? I sank down into the chair, shaking my head.

"No. No way. Serena told me her mum abandoned her as a child. Left her to be raised by her grandmother." Clara sighed, looking pained.

"It's true. I...I left Serena when she was just a little girl. But it wasn't my choice. I would have..." I searched Clara's face as she trailed off, looking for any hint of deception. But all I saw was regret, sadness and frustration in her green eyes. Still, I wasn't ready to fully believe her.

"That doesn't explain why Serena was so distraught yesterday," I said. "What did you do to her?" Clara glanced at my uncle nervously before responding.

"I went to see her at the shop. I wanted to get the journals. That was all I wanted, but she refused to listen. The darkness has already sunk its claws in her." I shook my head again.

"No. Serena is good, I know she is." Clara reached across the table and put her hand over mine, her expression gentle but firm.

"Jake, you want to believe the best in her. I understand, truly. But Serena is not as innocent as you think." I snatched my hand back.

"What are you talking about?"

"She's a believer, Jake," my uncle said, and I looked over at him, "I don't know how yet but Serena is involved with the Zodiacs."

"I have proof," Clara said and stood up and crossed the room to the door that she had come out of. I stared at the door, dread pooling in my gut as Clara walked toward it. I didn't want to believe her, didn't want to accept that Serena could be involved with the Zodiacs in any way. But the grave certainty in Clara's voice made me fear she had evidence I couldn't refute. With a nod from my uncle Stephen, Clara grasped the doorknob and pulled open the door, revealing a small bedroom. My brows furrowed in confusion which quickly turned to horror as Clara stepped back, giving me a clear view inside.

There, tied to a chair in the centre of the room, was the lifeless body of a young woman. Her head lolled forward, long dark hair obscuring her face. But I recognized the flowing bohemian dress and multitude of bracelets adorning her wrists. It was Ophelia, Serena's friend. I stumbled to my feet, shock and dismay crashing over me in waves as I moved woodenly toward the body. This couldn't be real. Surely my eyes were deceiving me. But as I reached Ophelia and gently tilted her head back, the awful truth stared up at me.

Her eyes were closed, mercifully concealing the terror she must have endured. Bruises marred her delicate face and neck. And her chest...her chest was a ruin of blood and tattered flesh. She had been tortured to death. Bile rose in my throat as the abhorrent image seared itself into my mind. I whirled around to face Clara and my uncle, who were observing me intently.

"What have you done?" I choked out through the knot in my throat. Sure I knew we sometimes had to resort to strong methods, but this was too much even for me. Clara's face was impassive.

"I told you, Jake. We caught one of Serena's friends, a fellow Zodiac believer." I shook my head in disbelief. This couldn't be justified, no matter their reasons. "What proof did you have that she was involved? How do you not know that you haven't just tortured and murdered an innocent woman? This is wrong and you know it!" I shouted, jabbing an accusing finger toward the body. There was a reason why we had specialist assassins. I would be sent out to find the people, and deal with them if needed. But torture was only done in extreme circumstances and only when we were sure that the target was certain. Clara's eyes hardened.

"Innocent? Hardly. She was devoted to the Zodiac cause, intent on bringing about the end of the world as we know it. I did what was necessary to get information." I stared at her, aghast.

"Necessary? She didn't deserve this, Clara! No one does." I knew in part my upset was about how Serena would react to her friend being killed. Clara stepped toward me, her voice low and urgent.

"You're not seeing the bigger picture here, Jake. One life, no matter how blameless, means nothing compared to the millions who will suffer if the Prophecy comes to pass."

I didn't have a response to that. As much as it sickened me, I understood Clara's conviction. The Council's mission had always been the greater good, no matter the cost. Stop the Zodiacs, prevent the Prophecy, save humanity. By any means necessary. I had killed in the name of that mission. But this? This was beyond the pale. My uncle finally spoke, his tone conciliatory.

"Jake, I know this is... difficult for you to process right now. But you must see that your feelings for the Ashmoor girl have clouded your judgement." I turned on him angrily.

"My judgement isn't clouded! This is wrong, no matter what you claim about Serena. She doesn't deserve to be punished for the sins of her friend." Clara moved closer, her expression softening.

"Oh, Jake. I know you care for Serena. Truly, I wish I could believe her innocence too, for your sake. But I've confirmed she's been in contact with known Zodiac agents. She's involved with them, whether willingly or not." I dragged a hand over my face, emotions churning violently within me. I didn't know what to think anymore. Could Serena really be caught up with the Zodiacs? The group who would see the world descend into darkness and death if their mad Prophecy came true? And a group that was responsible for the death of my parents. No. I refused to accept it. I had looked into Serena's eyes and seen only goodness there. She was no villain intent on apocalyptic prophecy. She was just a woman trying to find her way, as lost and conflicted as I was.

I took a deep, steadying breath and fixed Clara with a defiant stare.

"I won't condemn Serena without proof. Not just the words of a tortured woman." I gestured angrily at Ophelia's body. "Bring me evidence that Serena means to enact this Prophecy. Then I will act accordingly. But until then, I will not harm her or allow harm to come to her." Clara started to protest, but I raised a hand to stop her.

"No. I've made my position clear. Now if you'll excuse me, I have work to do." I strode past them and wrenched open the door leading to the hallway. There I paused and looked back.

"Dispose of the body. But don't you dare lay a hand on Serena unless I say so."

With that, I left, letting the door slam behind me. I was shaking with adrenaline and simmering fury as I exited the bed and breakfast. I had no idea whether they would listen to me, But underneath the chaotic storm of emotions, my mind was clear on one thing.

I had to talk to Serena first.

Chapter 26

Serena

I took a deep breath of the salty sea air as Alec and I walked along the harbour towards the lighthouses. It had been a long and stressful day already and it was closing on midnight. And being the week before Christmas and the weather was really beginning to turn bitter. After spending hours scouring Whitby Abbey and coming up empty handed, I was starting to feel discouraged about our chances of finding the relics my Gran had hidden. But Alec reassured me that we just had to keep looking.

"Iris was a clever woman," he said, placing a hand on my shoulder. "She wouldn't have made it easy for us to find these relics. But I know we'll uncover them eventually if we stay persistent." His confidence buoyed me. I nodded, squaring my shoulders. We would find them. We had to.

I always loved the harbour, with its timeworn seawalls and the tang of salt in the air. It felt peaceful here. A reprieve from the chaos that had entered my life since discovering my role in the Zodiac prophecy. We reached the lighthouses, their red and white stripes vivid against the blue sky.

"Where should we start looking?" Alec asked. I gazed up at the twin sentinels guarding the harbour's entrance.

"Let's try the east lighthouse first," I decided. Something about its isolated perch on the end of the East arm of the Harbour mouth called to me.

We headed down the pier towards the end of the harbour mouth and the lighthouse. Seagulls cried overhead, riding the updrafts. At the end I rested my hand against the weathered stone, sensing for any clues or traces of magic. But the lighthouse stood cold and silent. My shoulders slumped. Another dead end. Alec gave me an encouraging smile.

"Come on, let's check around the base. You never know what we might find." We circled the lighthouse, scanning the ground and running our hands along the stonework, searching for anything out of the ordinary.

As we reached the far side overlooking the sea, I stopped short. There was Obsidian, primly seated beside a strange wooden box embedded at the lighthouse's base.

"Well, would you look at that," Alec murmured. I stared at the box in astonishment. It was intricately carved with astrological symbols and inlaid with what appeared to be copper. This was no ordinary box. It radiated an aura of power that raised the fine hairs on my arms. How had I never noticed it before? I must have passed by this lighthouse hundreds of times over the years. Obsidian looked up at me and gave a little "mrrow" of greeting, his good eye glinting knowingly.

That cat always did have a knack for showing up wherever magic was afoot. Another example of the familiar pair that I hadn't known were guiding me. I stepped closer and ran my fingers over the carvings, heart pounding. This had to be one of the relics. But how to open it? There was no discernible lid or hinges. Alec knelt beside me, studying the box intently.

"I think these symbols are clues. See here, the astrological sign for Cancer?" He pointed to an etched image of a crab. My sign. Which meant...this box was somehow keyed to me. I placed my palm flat on the lid. A surge of energy rushed up my arm, and the scent of my grandmother's perfume briefly enveloped me. The box vibrated beneath my hand. Then, with a soft snick, the lid popped open.

Nestled inside on a bed of velvet lay what looked like the base of a box. From What I could see in the dark it was tinted, blue, or maybe green, it was hard to tell exactly in this light. I recognized it instantly from one of my grandmother's journals. This was it, I knew it. We had found the second relic.

"Look at that," Alec said with a grin, but there was something off about it, like it was missing something.

"I don't think this is the whole thing," I said, frustration brewing inside me. "The picture I saw showed a lid as well." I looked inside the wooden box but there was nothing else in there.

"Has someone stolen it?" I asked nobody in particular. Alec looked in the box and then back at me.

"Are you sure?" he asked, and I nodded. What would happen if I couldn't find the lid? Would that make the relic useless? I stood up and searched the sea, which was dark and brooding as my thoughts were right now. When something caught my eye over on the west harbour arm. I looked over to see a flash of orange that seemed to have an unnatural glow in the dark. I turned and looked at Obsidian, who had gone back to cleaning himself, and grinned. I turned to Alec with excitement rushing through my body.

"I know where the second half is," I said before rushing off down the pier, not waiting for a reply. I rushed down the pier, my boots thudding against the weathered planks. The night air whipped my hair as I raced towards the west lighthouse, my heart pounding with exhilaration. Carnelian was there waiting for me, I just knew it. My faithful feline companions had led me straight to the first half of the relic, and now Carnelian would guide me to the second.

As I reached the end of the west pier, I saw him. A flash of orange in the darkness, still glowing with an unnatural radiance. Carnelian sat lazily before the base of the west lighthouse, his green eyes glinting in the moonlight. Just like Obsidian, he had appeared exactly where I needed him to be. I slowed to a walk as I approached, my breath forming frosty plumes in the cold night air.

"There you are," I murmured, smiling down at Carnelian. He blinked up at me slowly, as though this was all perfectly normal and not some magical destiny unfolding before us. I knelt and stroked his soft fur, feeling a rush of gratitude for my faithful familiars.

"Thank you for showing me the way." Carnelian purred, then turned and looked meaningfully at the lighthouse base behind him. I followed his gaze, and there it was, an identical wooden box to the one we had just discovered, carved with astrological symbols and inlaid with copper. My pulse quickened. This had to be it. The second half of the relic, hidden away all these years, was now within my reach.

I placed my hand on the lid, just as I had done to the first box. A spark of energy jolted up my arm, and I smelled my grandmother's perfume in the air. The lid popped open with a soft click. Inside, nestled on rich velvet, lay an ornate glass disk shape. Much like the base that Alec was holding on the other pier, it had a beautiful astrological design etched into it. It glimmered in the moonlight, shades of sapphire and emerald dancing across its surface. The missing lid to complete the first relic. Clutching the lid carefully, I made my way back around the harbour towards where I had left Alec. He was examining the base we had discovered beneath the east lighthouse, but looked up at my approach.

"Did you find it?" His eyes went wide at the sight of the lid in my hands.

"This is it," I confirmed with a grin. "The lid to complete the first half." Carnelian wound his way between my ankles, purring proudly at a job well done. Alec shook his head in amazement.

"Incredible." He reached out to take the lid from me. As our fingers brushed, a spark passed between us and we both gasped. Alec's hand shot back and his eyes widened as he stared at the lid.

"Yep," he said, side eyeing the lid. "I'm gonna leave this to you." I laughed as he backed away from the first box. I pulled the base from the first box and fitted the two pieces together. They clicked into place seamlessly, reunited at last. I held my breath as I waited for something to happen. For a moment, all was still. Then the joined relic began to glow brighter, suffusing the air with warmth and power. The scent of Gran's perfume surrounded me like a loving embrace. We had succeeded.

After midnight, Alec and I headed back to the shop, Carnelian and Obsidian following closely behind. The town was quiet and still, lit only by the occasional street lamp and the lights from the boats that bobbed gently on the dark water. I clutched the Glass Box tightly to my chest, feeling the smooth worn edges under my fingers. Even through my coat, I could feel the gentle thrum of energy it emitted. We had found the second relic. I could hardly believe it. After searching for so long yesterday, it was finally within my grasp. Alec walked beside me, hands stuffed in the pockets of his worn leather jacket. His breath came out in little white puffs in the cold night air.

"We should check out the Whalebone Arch tomorrow," he said. "You mentioned it was one of Iris's favourite places. Could be something there." I nodded, only half listening. My mind was still reeling, thoughts racing. The Glass Box seemed to hum louder, as if responding to my excitement. We were another step closer to fulfilling the prophecy.

As we turned onto High Street, the familiar sight of my shop came into view. Soft light glowed from the apartment windows above, welcoming and warm against the dark facade of the old buildings. Home. After the long day, I was looking forward to collapsing into bed. Alec stepped forward to unlock the shop door. A small bell tinkled overhead as we stepped inside. I blinked, eyes adjusting to the soft lighting within. The scent of herbs and incense enveloped me. My shop, just as I had left it. Shelves lined with jars, books, crystals and charms. The worn wooden counter. My cosy backroom for readings. It all felt comforting, familiar. A refuge. I secured the Glass Box within a cupboard and locked it. Wouldn't want it falling into the wrong hands. My hand lingered on the worn brass knob. The responsibility felt heavy on my shoulders. Were we really ready for this? Alec gave me a tired smile.

"Get some rest. We've got a big day tomorrow." I nodded.

"You too. And Alec... thank you. For everything." He shrugged.

"Of course. Iris was like family, and you are family. I'd do anything for her. And for you." He squeezed my shoulder lightly before turning to leave. I stood in the silence of the shop for a moment, listening to his footsteps recede down the street. Then I headed up the narrow stairs to my apartment.

Carnelian and Obsidian were already curled up on the sofa, eyes closed, purring softly. I envied them for their ability to fall asleep anywhere. I envied their peace. Would I ever truly feel at peace again? I peeled off my coat and boots and changed into pyjamas. As I washed my face and brushed my teeth, I caught my reflection in the mirror. The past week or so had taken their toll. There were dark circles under my eyes, and my face looked drawn and pale. But behind the exhaustion, there was a determination in my gaze. I would see this through. I climbed into bed, snuggling down under the thick quilt. Obsidian joined me, curling up into a little black ball by my feet. His presence was comforting. My mind was still spinning, but sheer exhaustion soon dragged me down into sleep.

CANCER BLESSED

I dreamed I was by the harbour again, standing before the lighthouse. But this time, instead of the Glass Box, there was a woman waiting for me. She wore a long white gown, her steel grey hair rippling loose down her back. Her face was lined with age, but her dark eyes were bright and keen.

"Gran!" I cried out, rushing forward. But as I drew near, her form dissipated like mist. I spun around, searching the darkness. "Gran, don't go!" Her voice seemed to echo all around me.

"The darkness is rising, Serena. The prophecy must be fulfilled."

"But how?" I pleaded into the emptiness. "I still have so many questions!"

"Trust in yourself," her voice whispered. "Trust in your heart."

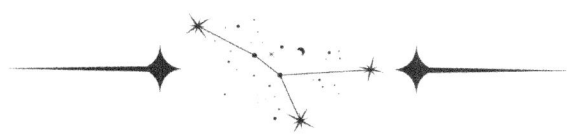

I awoke with a gasp, morning light filtering in through the curtains. Just a dream. My heart ached. I missed my grandmother so much. Her guidance, her wisdom. I felt like a small boat adrift on a vast, unknown sea. With a sigh, I hauled myself out of bed. Time to begin another day. Feed the cats, make tea and toast. Shower, dress. The normal morning routines steadied me as I prepared to head back down to the shop. We had a relic to find today. I needed to focus. Bury my doubts and fears. Like my grandmother said, trust in myself. I gave Obsidian and Carnelian fresh food and water. They blinked up at me slowly, as if saying "Good luck today." Their presence gave me courage. I wasn't alone in this. The Glass Box still hummed faintly in its hidden cupboard. Two down, two to go. We were so close.

I headed down to the shop and prepared to open for the day. It would be quiet but there was always a chance of a last-minute tourist looking for something for Christmas. I raised the blind covering the door and was surprised to see Jake standing on the other side. I couldn't help the smile that grew on my face at seeing him. I unlocked the door and slid it open, the little bell above jingling merrily. But my smile faltered when I saw Jake's expression. His handsome face was drawn into a scowl, his grey eyes stormy. He brushed past me without a word, the scent of his cologne sharp in the air.

"Jake, is everything okay?" I asked cautiously. He paced the shop floor agitatedly.

"I need to find my talisman. The one I lost here the other day." His voice was clipped and tense. I glanced over at the office where the door was still closed, knowing the Talisman was hung on the hook just inside the door.

"I haven't come across it yet." It wasn't exactly a lie. I just needed some time to cleanse its energy first. If anything, I needed to prove to Alec that Jake was a good guy. Jake ran a hand through his hair in frustration.

"Are you sure? I need it back."

"I'll keep looking for it, I promise," I said gently. "But Jake, did something happen? You seem...on edge." He laughed hollowly.

"You could say that." I took a step towards him.

"Do you want to talk about it?" For a moment, his stony facade seemed to crack. I thought he might open up to me. But then the shutters came down over his eyes once more.

"I should go," he muttered. "Just let me know if you find the talisman." He turned to walk out the door again but I called out to him.

"Jake." He stopped in his movements but didn't turn around. "Your uncle? Did you know that he knew my Gran, and that he worked for the Council?" I knew that if I didn't ask that I would still be thinking it. I felt a knot in my stomach as Jake slowly turned to face me, his expression unreadable. His stormy grey eyes, usually so warm, were now cold and hard.

"What did you just say?" he asked quietly, his voice tight. I took a deep breath to steady my nerves.

"The other day when I met your uncle. He told me that he knew my grandmother and that she worked at the Council." Jake was very still, his stormy grey eyes fixed on me, narrowed slightly. I could see the tension in his shoulders, his jaw clenched.

"I remember."

"Did you know?" I asked gently, trying to keep my tone soft. "That he worked for the Council?" Jake ran a hand through his short crop of brown hair and let out a long breath, as if considering his words carefully.

"Yeah, I knew. He's one of their top commanders." I nodded slowly, trying to keep my face neutral despite the unease swirling within me. The Council - it was an organisation Gran had warned me about since I was a child. A shadowy group determined to control and contain all things supernatural. Gran said their propaganda about protecting humanity was a front for more sinister goals. Of course, she didn't tell me that I should stay away since I was one of the people they wanted to hunt down, or that she had worked for them herself. That bit of information had come as a nasty shock when I read her journals after she passed.

"I can guess from your reaction how you feel about the Council," Jake said tightly, a muscle feathering in his jaw. "But they do important work. My uncle has devoted his life to keeping people safe." I bit my lip uncertainly. I knew Jake and his uncle were close, that he had raised Jake after his parents died. I had to tread carefully here.

"I'm sure he believes he's doing the right thing-" Jake's eyes flashed, stormy once more.

"Don't patronize me," he bit out angrily. "You have no idea the sacrifices he's made. The Council protects humanity from very real threats." His hands were balled into fists at his sides now, tension radiating from him. I took a hesitant step towards him, holding my hands up in a placating gesture.

"Jake, I didn't mean... I just think maybe the Council doesn't have the full picture. My grandmother believed-"

"Don't," Jake snapped, making me flinch at the sharpness in his tone. "I don't want to hear it. The Council knows more than you ever could." I felt my own anger rising now, hot and defiant. How dare he dismiss my grandmother so callously?

"More than my grandmother? She worked for them for years. I've read through her journals of the horrible things she did while working for them. She regretted it all, enough that she devoted her life to studying the supernatural from then on. If she believed the Zodiacs weren't a threat then-"

"Well, she was wrong!" Jake exploded, his face contorted in rage. I stepped back instinctively, stunned by the venom in his voice.

"The Council has proof of the danger they pose. But you...you're too blinded by your grandmother's bullshit to see it. The Zodiacs are evil, every single one of them, and if it wasn't for the Council, then this world would be the next one sucked into that damned black hole that the bloody Zodiacs caused." His words stung, hitting me like a physical blow. I stared at him, this man I had so recently started to care for. Had I gotten him all wrong?

Jake seemed to realise he'd gone too far. He passed a shaking hand over his face and let out a long breath.

"I have to go. This was a mistake." Before I could say another word, he turned and stormed out of the shop, the door slamming violently behind him. I stood there, shaken to my core. The sick feeling in my stomach had grown, spreading through my limbs like ice. I didn't know what to think anymore. I didn't know Jake at all, not really.

Chapter 27

Jake

I slammed the door of my bed-and-breakfast room shut with enough force to rattle the pictures on the wall. I paced back and forth across the small room, fists clenched at my sides. The nerve of that woman, defending the Zodiacs as if they were some benevolent force instead of the monsters I knew them to be. After everything my uncle and the Council had told me, how could Serena believe they were anything but a threat? My parents had been killed by the effects that the Zodiacs had caused, and their bloody fanatics. The resistance had to be stopped before more innocent lives were lost. The Zodiac's had to be stopped before we lost the world into a black hole abyss.

A knock at the door interrupted my fuming. I wrenched it open to find Clara on the other side, concern etched on her face.

"I saw you storm out of the shop. Are you alright?"

"What? You're following me now?" I snapped and the look of shock on her face stilled my anger for long enough to realise that I was lashing out at her. I took a deep breath and motioned her inside, too agitated to stand still.

"Jake, are you okay?" she asked again, and I turned to face her.

"No, I'm damn well not alright. You were right, Serena is one of them, a Zodiac sympathiser." Clara frowned and looked away.

"I'm sorry Jake, I tried to warn you," then she looked up at me with an excited gleam. "Did you get proof?" I shook my head.

"No, but she all but admitted it. Started spouting nonsense about how the Council doesn't know the full truth about the Zodiacs. That they might not be the monsters we think they are." I spat the words out bitterly.

"Just like her grandmother," Clara muttered. I whirled to face her.

"What do you mean?" Clara folded her arms across her chest. "My mother had dangerous beliefs too. It's why she left the Council, betrayed us and our plans to the Resistance. I tried to protect Serena from her influence, but..." She trailed off, shaking her head. My hands curled into fists again. I had trusted Serena. Let myself feel something for her. And this whole time, she had been seducing me to get information for the resistance. Just like Clara warned me.

I clenched my jaw as my uncle barged into my room, not even bothering to knock. His face was grim, eyes hard as flint.

"We have new information," he announced without preamble. "Our sources indicate the Zodiacs are planning their attack in two days time, on midwinter's night when their power will be at its peak." I swore under my breath. Two days didn't give us much time.

"It's the solstice," Clara added quietly. "Of course they would choose then." My uncle nodded, his expression stern.

"Which means we need to move quickly. The Zodiac hiding here must be found and eliminated before their plan comes to fruition." His piercing gaze fixed on me. "Any progress in identifying them?" I shifted my weight, avoiding his eyes.

"I'm still working on it." My uncle's mouth flattened into a hard line.

"Work faster. We're nearly out of time."

"I know," I said through gritted teeth. Didn't he think I understood the urgency of the situation? That I wasn't doing everything I could? Clara stepped forward, laying a placating hand on my uncle's arm.

"Jake's doing his best. This Zodiac is clever, covering their tracks. But..." She turned her green eyes on me. "I think Serena may know more than she's letting on. My mother was deep in the resistance after all. And so was the guy who is always around her." My head snapped up at her words.

"Alec?" I asked and Clara nodded.

"I don't know if he is still with them, but when James..." She trailed off and looked away with a deep sadness in her eyes. We all knew about how the Resistance had targeted Clara. Her mother had forced her to leave the Council and then she had been subjected to brainwashing from them. Brian Kale was one of the prominent members of the York cell and he and his two sons were well known for getting in the way of many Council operations. One of his sons, James Kale had taken an interest in Clara and managed to seduce her in his attempts for more secrets. Clara had managed to get away and get back to the Council. She had been instrumental in the operation to dismantle that Cell. She was the one who took revenge on Kale himself. It had taken a lot out of her and she had disappeared for a few years, but she came back to us more determined than ever. I didn't even know that she had a child until I found out she was Serena's mother yesterday.

"Wait," I said and Clara looked up at me, the knowledge of what I was thinking shining in her eyes. She nodded.

"Yes," she whispered. "James was Serena's father. And Alec was his brother." Even though I was already thinking it, the revelation that the woman that I thought I had fallen in love with was the daughter of someone as heinous as James Kale. Yet here I was being caught in the same trap. I sighed and nodded reluctantly. As much as I hated to admit it, Clara had a point. Serena clearly knew things, even if she wouldn't reveal them. And we were running out of options.

"You're right," I said reluctantly. Clara and my uncle looked at me. "Serena is the key here."

"Then you need to get back in there," my uncle said firmly. "Turn on the charm, get her to trust you again. And this time, don't leave empty-handed." His tone allowed no argument. I bristled at the command, feeling like a scolded child, but said nothing. Arguing would be pointless.

"Maybe you could convince her to see reason," Clara suggested. Then her face turned hard as she looked at me. "But you might have to get creative." I sighed, scrubbing a hand over my face. The thought of hurting Serena left a bitter taste in my mouth. But we were talking about the fate of the world. I had to put aside my conflicted feelings.

"Fine. I'll go back and talk to her," I said at last. My uncle nodded approvingly.

"Good. We'll be close by if you need assistance." He checked his watch. "I have to report to the Council. Keep me informed of any developments." With that, he strode from the room, leaving me alone with Clara once more. She touched my arm lightly.

"I know this is difficult for you. But it's for the greater good. Once this is over..." I cut her off sharply.

"Let's just focus on finding the Zodiac first." I wasn't ready to think about after. Not yet. She searched my face and then nodded. "I could come to the shop with you for backup." I shook my head at the offer. After what Clara did to Serena, I could only imagine her showing up with me would make Serena clamp down even more. I had to be the charming one, and if that didn't work, well then... I didn't even want to think of what I would need to do. Clara stepped closer and put a hand on my arm.

"Okay. But you need to be smart about this, Jake. Don't let your emotions cloud your judgement." I took a deep breath, willing the sick feeling in my stomach to pass. She was right. I had to keep a cool head if I was going to get through to Serena. Maybe if I did, she would understand that she was on the wrong side, and come over and help us.

"You're right," I conceded. "So what do you think we should do?" Clara smiled slyly.

"I have an idea..."

I stood outside the shop window watching from the shadows as Serena moved around the room. She looked like she was tidying up for the evening and was getting ready to close up. I felt conflicted as I observed her, knowing that I would likely have to hurt her to get the information I needed if she didn't willingly comply. When my uncle had first given me this assignment, I was eager to prove myself. Hunting down supernatural threats was what I had been trained for my whole life. Plus the idea of being one of the people involved with taking down one of the actual Zodiacs, well that was a good feeling to have. But now, after getting to know Serena, things weren't so black and white. She seemed genuinely good-natured, not at all like the evil beings my uncle had warned me about.

Still, I had my orders. Serena was clearly involved with the Zodiacs in some way. I needed to find out what she knew, one way or another. As I continued to watch through the window, Serena finished cleaning up. She locked the front door, flipped the sign to "Closed," and moved to turn off all the lights. This was my chance. I stepped out of the shadows and into the light of the entrance. I could tell that my sudden appearance outside the shop window shocked Serena. She jumped a little when she noticed my silhouette outside. Her body language changed in an instant, shoulders tensing as she turned to face the window. When she recognized that it was me, her eyes narrowed. She was obviously not happy to see me. I supposed I couldn't blame her. Our last conversation had ended rather badly after I lost my temper. Serena crossed her arms as she stared at me through the glass. I gave her a little wave, and tried to put on a charming smile, hoping that she would at least hear me out. After a long moment, she sighed and walked over to unlock the door.

"What do you want, Jake?" she asked bluntly standing in the doorway, making it clear that she wasn't letting me past the threshold. Her tone was weary but guarded.

"I wanted to apologise for earlier," I began carefully. "I shouldn't have gotten so angry. And I shouldn't have blamed you." Serena considered my words before responding.

"If we're going to keep spending time together, you need to have an open mind. Things aren't as black and white as you think." I nodded while clenching my fist. Why was she so blind to the poison that these people had been teaching her? But I needed her to trust me again, if my plan was going to work. I needed to get back into that shop at the very least. Clara seems so insistent on getting those journals, and I needed the information about the Zodiac in this town before my uncle started breathing down my neck again.

I stood there watching Serena's guarded expression, knowing I needed to tread carefully if I wanted to regain her trust.

"Serena, can I come in, please?" I urged, trying to put sincerity into my voice. "I'd like to talk, if you'll let me. No arguing this time, I promise." She hesitated, clearly debating whether to let me in or shut the door in my face. I held my breath, hoping she wouldn't turn me away. After a long moment, she stepped aside with a resigned sigh, allowing me to enter the shop once more.

"Make it quick," she muttered, moving to re-lock the door behind us. I felt a small rush of victory and gave Serena a grateful look.

"Thank you. And again, I'm sorry about earlier. I let my temper get the better of me." Serena didn't respond, her expression still wary as she crossed her arms. I took a step closer, reaching for her hand in an attempt to connect with her. But she quickly moved away, putting distance between us once more.

"What do you want, Jake?" she asked bluntly. I took a deep breath before responding.

"I've been doing some reading since our argument. Came across something called a locator spell? Apparently psychics use it to help find missing people or objects. Do you think...would something like that help me find who I'm looking for?" Serena tensed at my words, shock flashing across her face. I could tell the mention of magic had caught her off guard. She studied me for a long moment before responding carefully.

"Something like that doesn't always work. This type of thing is subjective." She looked hesitant for a moment. "And I don't think that you should continue to look for this person." I clenched my jaw as Serena refused to perform the locator spell. This wasn't going according to plan. I needed that information, and I needed her help to get it.

"Why not?" I asked, trying to keep my voice even. I didn't want her to realise how desperate I was. Serena hesitated, seeming unsure if she should explain further. Finally she spoke, her voice quiet.

"When we did that vision...I saw something. Something bad happening to you." I tensed. The vision. I had tried to block most of it out of my mind after how unsettled it left me. But she had seen more of it than I had, clearly a lot more given the tremor in her lip as she spoke.

"What exactly did you see?" I asked carefully. Serena wrapped her arms around herself, as if warding off a chill.

"There was fighting. Chaos. And blood. At the end, I saw you..." She trailed off, her eyes shimmering with emotion. I felt a knot form in my stomach. Whatever she had seen had clearly disturbed her. And if it involved me being hurt or worse...that explained why she was so against helping me now. But this only confirmed that I had to do this. This Zodiac, whoever they were, was clearly dangerous, and it was my duty to protect the world from them. I took a step towards her, my voice gentle.

"Serena, it was just a vision. We don't know if any of that will actually happen." She shook her head firmly.

"My visions are always true. Especially the strong ones. You finding this person, it's dangerous. For you." Her eyes met mine, full of concern. "That's why I can't help you with this." I cursed internally. This complicated things. Serena seemed utterly convinced that locating my target would lead to my demise. And that meant she had no intention of assisting me with a locator spell. Not willingly, anyway.

"Serena, please," I asked once again, this time letting the desperation flood into my voice. She looked me dead in the eyes, her own aquamarine eyes a storm of emotion, and shook her head.

"No Jake," she said, her voice resolved. "I know this is important to you but I care about you and I don't want to see you get hurt. I'm sorry."

"Yeah, so am I," I muttered as she turned away. My hand drifted towards the blade concealed under my jacket. I hated to do this, but she wasn't leaving me much choice. I needed the information she could provide, one way or another. And I was running out of time and options.

"But," I said, causing her to look back at me. "I'm afraid I'm going to have to insist," I said quietly, slowly drawing the blade out into the open.

Chapter 28

Serena

I turned to face Jake and my eyes went wide at the sight of the weapon, and I felt fear flood through my system. I took a step back instinctively.

"Jake..." I said in a shaky voice. "What are you doing?"

"I'm sorry," he said, advancing another step. "But this is too important. You need to perform the locator spell for me, whether you want to or not." He didn't seem that sorry, there was a gleam in his eyes that sent a cold shiver down my spine. I backed up until I hit the counter, trapped between it and a slowly advancing Jake. I swallowed hard as Jake continued to advance, the blade glinting in the low light of the shop.

"Jake, please," I said, trying to keep my voice steady. "Think about what you're doing. This isn't you." He hesitated for a moment, uncertainty flickering in his eyes.

"You don't know me," he said roughly. "Not really. I have been using you as much as you have been using me." His words hit me hard, worse than the knife in his hand ever could.

"W-what?" I stammered out as my heart broke into a thousand pieces. He had been using me, was it all a lie? I couldn't believe it, I knew we had only met a week ago, but I knew that what we had was real, I could feel it.

"Don't try to play stupid with me darling," he spat out. "Clara warned me about your manipulative ways, just like your bastard of a father manipulated her." Clara? My mother? Jake knew my mother, how could he know... Then it hit me. Jake's uncle worked with the Council and so did my mother. I felt like I had been punched in the gut. Jake had been lying to me this whole time. He knew my mother, does this mean he was working with the Council? Was this entire thing between us a ruse? The feeling of betrayal coursed through my veins and it burnt me like lava bringing light to my stupidity.

I straightened up and squared my shoulders, forcing myself to meet his cold grey eyes. I had to have answers.

"Tell me the truth, Jake. Who are you really looking for?" He let out a derisive laugh, but there was an element of sadness tinged in it.

"I'm looking for the monster responsible for viciously murdering my parents when I was just a boy." I shook my head in confusion. This wasn't the answer I was expecting. His parents had died in a storm, or so he had told me.

"What? What are you talking about?" Jake's face twisted in anger and he stepped closer, the knife glinting dangerously.

"The evil bastard that ripped my parents away from me," he spat, and then a distant gleam crossed over his eyes again. He pushed his body against mine, trapping in against the counter. The feel of his body sent sparks of electricity through me as my body didn't seem to care that this man had just broken my heart. Jake leaned in and I shivered as I felt his breath on my neck.

"And don't worry your sweet little head, darling," he whispered in my ear. "Because when I find who I am looking for, it's be their cold dead body that you see, not mine." I willed my body not to react to the closeness, and the overpowering scent of Jake's musk as he leaned in and ran his nose against my neck, but I could already feel myself reacting, leaning into him as my breathing quickened. Jake let out a low growl as he felt my reaction, but it was short-lived as I felt the cold tip of the blade that he was carrying against my side. I froze at the feel of it against my skin.

"So be a good girl and do the damn spell," Jake whispered, "Before I have to do something that you will regret."

I felt the tears flowing down my face before I even knew I was crying. My body was battling between the lust and the fear, both fighting for top spot, and both clouding my brain. Jake stepped back slightly, not enough to remove the warmth of his body against mine, or the knife for that matter, but enough that he could see my face. Something like regret crossed his face, and he reached up with his free hand and wiped away the tears on my cheek.

"Come on, sweetheart," he said, his tone almost soft and caring. "Do this for me and I will be out of your life forever." For some reason that I couldn't pinpoint, I knew that he was lying, and this wasn't going to be the end of it. But I had no choice, or none that I liked. I had to do the spell. If I delayed it long enough, then maybe Alec would get here and be able to help me against Jake.

Slowly I nodded my head, and Jake smiled, although there was no warmth in it.

"Fine," I whispered, "I'll do your damn spell, but then you leave my shop and my life and I never want to see you again." I tried to put the anger I felt into the sentence but even I could tell it came out weak and pathetic. Jake didn't seem to care though and nodded his head in satisfaction.

"Good girl," he said and stepped away from me, giving me space to move.

"The spell says you have to-" he stated, but I interrupted him as I turned away and walked towards the back room.

"I know how to do the spell," I spat out at him. "It was my Gran's spell that that bitch told you." I turned to look at him. "That was where you got it from, wasn't it? Clara Ashmore, non mother of the year." Jake looked away and shrugged.

"She goes by Moore now," he said and I let out a derisive snort as I turned away again. I was heading into the office when Jake called after me again.

"How did you know it was her who gave it to me?" I turned back in the doorway and glared at him.

"It was the first spell I learnt," I said, not even bothering to hide the pain in my voice. "I found it in my Gran's journals and tried to use it repeatedly to find my mother." I bit back the tears and shrugged at the memory of vision after vision, trying to find any clue, any reason as to why my mother would abandon me. I looked back at Jake, knowing there were tears shining in my eyes.

"I guess the reason it didn't work was because I never had a mother to be found. It seemed you are both the same in that way, playing a role to get what you want." I turned again and headed into the office before the painful memories caused me to break down completely.

I leaned against the desk and took a deep breath as the tears fell. I hated that I was crying over this. I had spent too many sad moments, too many tears on a mother that never really existed. I didn't want to waste more on a lover that was just as much of a fantasy.

"No funny business in there," Jake called from the shop and I took a deep, shuddering breath as I gathered the supplies I would need for the spell, sage, candles, chalk, and a few crystals Gran had imbued with power. My hands trembled as I arranged everything on the small wooden tray that I used for rituals, anger and hurt swirling within me. I couldn't believe how foolish I had been, falling for Jake's act. Believing his lies about wanting to connect with his late mother's friend, when all along he had been using me. And working with my mother, of all people. The betrayal cut deep, reopening old wounds I thought had finally begun to heal after all these years.

Wiping the tears from my eyes, I steeled myself and walked back out into the main room of the shop where Jake was waiting, an impatient look on his handsome face. How could I have not seen the cruelty behind those stormy grey eyes before now? Taking a deep, centering breath, I set the tray down and began arranging the supplies on the floor.

"We'll need to sit inside the circle together for this to work," I said coldly, not meeting Jake's gaze. Out of the corner of my eye, I saw him shift his weight nervously.

"Together? Is that really necessary?" His voice held an edge of apprehension. I looked up and met his eyes then, letting him see the full force of the anger and pain raging inside me.

"Yes. The connection needs to flow between us for the spell to reveal what you're looking for." Jake hesitated a moment longer before nodding curtly.

"Fine. Let's just get this over with."

Once everything was in place, I settled cross-legged on the floor across from Jake, the chalked circle the only thing separating us. I lit the candles with a whispered word, their flickering light throwing dancing shadows across Jake's stony face.

"Give me your hands," I instructed flatly. Jake complied, his large, calloused hands engulfing my own. I fought back a shudder at his touch, the spark I had felt before still crackling between us despite everything. Closing my eyes, I took myself through the steps of the spell, chanting the words that were seared into my memory. I could feel the magic building in the circle like a living thing, responding to the pain and betrayal fueling my spell casting. The shop around us faded away as the vision took hold, and suddenly Jake and I were standing in a dark, fog-shrouded landscape. Flickering images began to take shape, shadowy figures moving through the gloom. There was a woman with kind eyes, bending to embrace a young boy with a mop of unruly brown hair. Jake's breath hitched, his hands tightening almost painfully on mine.

"Mum..." he whispered. The vision shifted, growing darker. Anguished screams cut through the air as the shadowy figures convulsed in agony. Jake's parents, I realised. This was the night they died. Blood splattered, flames erupted, and a hulking, demonic shape loomed out of the darkness. There was something off about the vision, I knew that things often appeared as symbols in the visions, especially things or people that had a hidden agenda or held a lot of secrets. But something felt almost familiar about this figure.

"Zodiac," Jake whispered, and I flinched as I realised what he was truly looking for. The vision shifted as his mind moved away from the painful memories of his parent's death, and locked on to what, or more like who, he thought was responsible. I saw Jake standing in black Council uniform and him standing with his uncle in a sparse office.

"Your next mission is a high one indeed, son," his uncle gleamed out. "You are to find one of the Zodiac's themselves. You will dispatch of them and bring back the relics that they possess. You understand what an honour this is, boy?" I saw as Jake nodded, his movements stiff but a low tremor of excitement in his limbs.

"Yes Sir I do," Jake answered coldly.

"Good," his uncle replied. "This is your chance to get revenge on those responsible for the death of your mother and father." I tried to pull my hands away from Jakes but he seemed to have an iron grip. Knowing now what he was looking for was terrifying, and I knew I had to get away before he realised who I was. The voice of Jake's uncle carried on as the vision shifted again to the landscape view of Whitby. I could see the Abbey on top of the cliff fast approaching as the spell brought Jake closer to what he wanted to see. I tried again to pull my hands free but I couldn't move. Just as the vision neared the front of the shop I heard a hiss and then felt something land on our outstretched hands. The last thing I saw before Jake pulled his hands back with a hiss was an outside view of us sitting there as we were right now.

My eyes flew open, and I saw that Jake was standing as he cradled his hand, which now sported an angry red set of claw marks in it. Both Carnelian and Obsidian stood between us, their fur on end as they faced Jake. I scrambled to my feet as I stared at Jake's furious expression. Part of me had hoped that he hadn't seen the final part of the vision, but the fury in his eyes told me that he had seen everything.

"You evil bitch," he hissed out as he stalked towards me. "You were manipulating me all along." I tried to back away quickly and made a run for the shop door but I felt and hand in my hair as I got to the door. Jake yanked me back against his body and hissed in my ear.

"I've got you now, you evil Zodiac bitch." Then he yanked me to the side and my head smacked hard into the wall. I cried out as pain shot through my skull and my vision blurred as I fell to the floor. The last thing I saw before the darkness swallowed me whole was Jake's furious face.

Chapter 29

Serena

The first thing I noticed when I woke up was the unbearable pain banging through my head. The second thing was that I appeared to be on something soft with my arms restrained to something above my head. Whatever it was bit painfully into my skin. The third thing I noticed was the sound of Jake's voice. He seemed to be arguing with someone, and I guessed it was someone on the phone since I couldn't hear anyone else.

"I told you," Jake hissed, "I got the journals, or what I could find." Then silence as he listened. He seemed to be in another room, so I took a chance to open my eyes slowly to survey my surroundings.

I blinked slowly, trying to clear the fog from my brain. As I took in my surroundings, a knot of fear formed in my stomach. I was lying on a small bed in an unfamiliar bedroom. My hands were chained above my head to the metal headboard, cold metal cuffs digging painfully into my wrists. I tugged experimentally, but there was little give in the chains. Turning my head, I noticed a wooden chair next to the bed. It was stained with what looked horribly like blood. As my gaze travelled down, I saw more dark stains splattered on the floor around it. My heart began to race. This was not good. Not good at all.

Jake's voice carried in from another room. He sounded angry, hissing into the phone about journals. I strained to listen, but couldn't make out the other side of the conversation. After a minute, his voice faded as he moved farther away. I took a deep breath, trying to stay calm and think. The last thing I remembered was being at the shop with Jake. He had wanted me to do a spell to help locate someone... that's right, the Zodiac! The spell had revealed my own location instead. Jake had realised I was the one he was looking for. He called me a liar, slapped me hard across the face. After that, everything went black. Now I was chained in this horrible little room. Jake had kidnapped me. The Council must have sent him, I realised with dread. They now knew about my role as a Zodiac. I had to get out of here, had to get to Alec before...

"Well, my Uncle said that I was to take her to the Council," Jake's voice interrupted my thoughts and his words sent a wave of fear screaming through my body. The council was clear on the subjects of the Zodiac. They, or we rather, were to be put to death. I needed to get out of here and fast.

"I am not going against Council orders Clara." He was talking to my mother. Or more like arguing. "You take it up with the Council, if you want the kill then you need to clear it with them first." Oh god, they were arguing over who got to kill me. I tried to pull on the chains again, stupidly hoping that this time they would break. I could almost hear my Gran reciting her favourite quote, the definition of insanity is repeating the same actions and... wait. Gran, maybe she could help. Surely she could somehow get a mystical message to Alec or something. Or could she? Would Alec be able to hear her, no let alone understand her? But I had to try. I closed my eyes and reached inside myself to where my gift was strongest, I felt for that familiar spark that would flare to life whenever I used it and... nothing. I opened my eyes again in frustration. It was empty, like some sort of black hole inside me. I wanted to scream in frustration and fear, knowing there was nothing I could do.

"I am going to get ready for the trip," Jake said, only this time his voice was closer. "I'll get her transported out of this shithole of a town tonight." I quickly closed my eyes again just as the door handle began to move. Maybe if Jake didn't know I was awake, I could get an advantage. I heard the door open and my heart hammered in my chest as I laid there, trying to steady my breathing. I could hear Jake moving around the room, the sound of his footsteps echoing off the walls. I did my best to keep really still, praying that he wouldn't notice that I was aware. After what felt like an eternity, Jake finally came to a stop at the end of the bed. I could feel him staring at me, his shadow looming over me. My stomach churned with fear as I braced myself for whatever he had in store for me. Then more footsteps and the bed dipped beside me.

"You really are the most beautiful woman I have ever seen," Jake whispered, and I felt his hand tracing my cheek. I tried my hardest not to flinch away from his touch. He seemed to freeze slightly, and I thought that maybe I had given myself away but then he carried on talking.

"I hated hurting you, you know." The bed moved again, and it felt like Jake had laid down next to me. His hand was back, in the soft caress, only this time it traced the swell of my breast.

"God, your body is a work of art," Jake whispered as he nuzzled his head into my neck. I could feel my body trying to react to his touch, my nipples pebbling at his touch. "It's such a shame that the soul inside is so evil." These last words were practically spit out. His hand left my breasts and moved down to where my top ended.

"What I wouldn't give to feel myself inside you at least one more time," Jake whispered into my ear, and I fought to suppress the shiver that was less to do with fear and more to do with the growing need in my body.

I felt his hand push up under my top, and begin to palm at my breasts. I suppressed a moan as he pulled my bra down enough to gain full access and began to play with my already hard nipples. As Jake's fingers pinched and rolled my nipples, I fought the urge to react. My body was betraying me, responding to his touch in a way that I despised. I tried not to clench my fists or grit my teeth, trying to push the feelings away. But it was no use. The more he touched me, the more my body responded. Jake's lips moved lower, kissing and nibbling down my neck. I could feel his breath on my skin, sending shivers down my spine. I squeezed my eyes closed, trying to block out the sensations. But it was too late. My body had already betrayed me. I felt a sudden heat between my legs, a response that I couldn't control. I wanted to push him away, but it would mean giving me away so I struggled to remain still as his hands roamed over my body.

Oblivious to my stifled reactions, Jake's fingers moved lower, tracing a line down my stomach, making me shiver. He pulled my top up, exposing my breasts.

"Fuck me, These are perfect," he whispered. "I could do anything to you like this. My little sleeping demon." I felt his hot breath on my skin as he leaned in, his lips closing around my nipple. I bit my lip to stop myself from moaning. His hand moved further down my body and up my skirt, his fingers brushing against my thighs. I wanted to push him away, but I couldn't. I wanted to tell him to get off me, but I needed him to think that I was still unconscious. But how far would he go if I didn't stop him?

"I could fuck you so hard, and wake you up screaming," Jake hummed against my skin. "It would only be fair for me to manipulate your body, like you manipulated my heart." His fingers found their way to my underwear, and he began to slide them down my legs. I closed my eyes, willing myself not to respond to his touch. But my body betrayed me, and I felt myself getting wet. Jake's lips moved lower, kissing and nibbling his way down my stomach. His fingers slid along my slit, and I gasped, unable to stop myself.

"I knew it." He paused for a moment, and I fought not to open my eyes, terrified that he had realised I was awake. "Dirty little whore is already wet, even asleep you are begging for it." He pushed in through my folds and found my clit with his thumb and began rubbing. I moaned as a finger slipped into me and froze as I heard Jake chuckle.

"Of course, that was if you were actually asleep," Jake stated in an almost matter of fact voice and he pulled his fingers from me, leaving me empty and on the edge. My eyes flew open, and I glared at him as he smirked down at me. His eyes travelled over my body once more before he moved away and got off the bed.

"For such an evil, manipulative bitch, you really are a terrible actress," Jake said as he headed to the head of the bed. My heart pounded in my chest as Jake began to undo the chains that were holding me to the bed.

"What... what do you want from me?" I stammered, my voice barely above a whisper. Jake's eyes gleamed with a cold, calculating light as he finished loosening the final chain.

"I want you, Serena Ashmoor," he growled, his voice low and menacing. "And I want all your Zodiac friends to die. Preferably slowly. Painfully." His words hit me in the gut and sliced through me like a hot knife through butter.

"You have it all wrong!" I cried, desperation filling my voice as Jake yanked me to a sitting position. "The council is lying about the prophecy, it's fake. They're the ones who are evil, not the Zodiacs." Jake's eyes narrowed, his face a mask of disbelief.

"Don't try to manipulate me again, Serena. I know what you are. You're a monster."

"No," I insisted, struggling against the restraints that bound me. "The council wants to control the world, and they're using the fake prophecy to do it. They've been lying to everyone, making you believe that the Zodiacs are evil when in reality, we're the only ones who can save the world." Jake shook his head, his jaw clenched and pulled me from the bed. He marched me roughly out of the door to the bedroom and into another room that looked similar to his room at the bed and breakfast.

"That's a load of crap. The Zodiacs are poisonous, and they're the reason my parents are dead," he continued as he latched something else to the cuffs around my wrists. It bound my wrist to each other and had a longer chain attached like some kind of leash.

I stared at Jake, stunned as he began to move around the room. I knew his parents had died. The vision that I had last showed how horrific it was. But there was nothing that said the Zodiacs were involved.

"I'm so sorry, Jake," I whispered. Jake snorted. "Yeah, well, it's too late for apologies. I'll make you pay for what they did, Serena. You and your precious Zodiac friends are all going down."

"Please, Jake," I begged. "You don't have to do this. We can work together. We can stop the council and save the world." Jake laughed, a harsh, bitter sound.

"Save the world? You're delusional, Serena. The Zodiacs are the ones who are destroying the world. You're all abominations, and you deserve to die." I closed my eyes, trying to block out Jake's words. His hatred was like a poison, seeping into my soul. I knew that I had to find a way to reach him, to make him see the truth. But how?

"Jake please," I urged. "Please think about this, how do you know it was the Zodiacs?" Jake turned sharply and glared at me.

"Don't," he snarled, "Don't you fucking dare."

"Don't what?" I asked, the desperation in my voice.

"Don't try to manipulate me. Your powers are useless now, Especially with those on." He nodded down to the cuffs on my wrist and I realised what he was saying. Unobtanium. The cuffs were made from the stuff. I had only heard about them in the news, but from what I knew they suppressed supernatural powers. No wonder I couldn't reach my gift earlier.

"Jake, I never once tried to manipulate you," I tried to assure him, but his face twisted in rage.

"Oh, you didn't, did you?" he asked and then pulled something from under his top. "Then why were you hiding this from me?" I looked to see the Talisman that he had lost in his hand. I had planned on returning it to him, but things kept getting in the way.

"I didn't hide it," I said. I was starting to get pissed off at the accusations and my anger was starting to overwhelm my fear. "Plus, you were the one who was lying." I snapped out and noted the faint hint of shock crossed his face. "You came into my shop, and my life and all on a lie, remember." Jake growled and turned away from me.

"Yeah exactly," I spat, "You accuse me of manipulating you, but who is the one doing the manipulating here?" Jake was on me in an instant. I heard the growl seconds before I felt myself slammed against the wall behind me. I cried out as pain laced through my back. I gasped for air as Jake's forearm dug into my throat. His eyes were dark with fury, and I could see the veins pulsing in his neck.

"You don't understand anything, do you?" he growled. "What I'm doing is for good. You're evil, Serena. You and your Zodiac friends are a blight on this world." I struggled to breathe, my vision starting to blur.

"No, Jake," I managed to croak out. "You're just annoyed that you felt something for me. That's why you're lashing out like this." Jake's grip tightened, and I felt a surge of panic. I knew I had to do something, or he would choke me to death. With all my strength, I pushed myself forward, using my legs to thrust against his groin. There was no way he could deny how hard his dick was as I ground against it.

"See?" I hissed, my voice barely audible. "Even now, you still have feelings for me. So how could it be these assumed powers that I have manipulating you?" Jake's eyes widened, and then filled with lust. He pushed his groin further against my leg and I felt his arm on my throat relax. I knew I was getting to him, but he was getting to me too and I could already feel myself responding as he pushed my leg aside and began grinding against my body instead.

Then his lips descended on mine. My heart raced as Jake kissed me with a mix of passionate rage. His lips were rough and demanding, and I couldn't help but respond. Everything inside me told me that it was wrong, that the man wanted me dead, but at the same time, it felt right. It felt like something I had been craving for years, something that had been denied to me. I kissed him back, my hands trapped between our bodies as we both lost ourselves in the moment. His tongue slid into my mouth, exploring every inch, and I could feel his arousal pressing against my core. I moaned softly into his mouth, my body responding to his touch. Jake growled, and pulled me in tighter but the binds on my arms meant that he couldn't get close enough. I gasped as Jake roughly grabbed me and spun me around, my front pressing against the cool sideboard. Before I could even register what was happening, he pushed me forward, my hips hitting the hard wood with a sharp pain. I cried out, my hands flailing as I tried to regain my balance. But Jake was relentless, his grip on my arm tightening as he flipped up my skirt and pulled down my panties in one swift motion. I felt exposed and vulnerable, my heart pounding in my chest as I looked up at him, my eyes wide with fear and anticipation.

Without a word, Jake thrust his fingers into my pussy, hard and fast. I cried out, a mixture of pain and pleasure coursing through my body. Jake grunted in satisfaction as he felt how wet I was, his fingers sliding in and out of me with ease. He leaned in against my back and whispered huskily in my ear.

"I'm not the only one who has feelings, it seems." I moaned softly, my hips bucking against his hand as he continued to finger-fuck me. It was intense, almost overwhelming, but I couldn't help but crave more. I wanted him inside me, wanted to feel his hard dick thrusting into me, filling me up. Without warning, Jake removed his fingers, and I tried to bite back the whine of feeling so empty. But it was seconds before he kicked my legs apart and positioned himself between them. I felt his cock, hard and throbbing, press against my pussy lips. I whimpered, my body trembling with anticipation.

Jake didn't waste any time. With a fierce growl, he thrust his dick into me, burying it deep inside my pussy. I cried out as I felt him stretch me wide. It was intense, almost painful, but I loved it. I loved the way he filled me up, the way his dick slid in and out of me with such force. Jake began to fuck me roughly, his hips thrusting forward with a primal energy. I moaned and cried out, my body writhing against the wood that bit into my hips with each powerful thrust. It was wild, primal, and completely exhilarating. I couldn't believe that I was letting him do this to me, that I was allowing myself to be taken by the man who wanted me dead. But there was something about him, something that made me want to submit to him completely. Something inside me that told me he was mine as much as I was his.

As Jake continued to fuck me, I felt a building sensation deep within my core. It was intense, almost overwhelming, but I knew that I was close. I cried out, my body trembling with anticipation as I felt the orgasm building inside me. And then it happened. A wave of pleasure washed over me, making me cry out in ecstasy. I clung to the sideboard, my body shaking with the force of my orgasm. Jake continued to fuck me, his thrusts becoming more urgent as he felt me come.

Finally, he groaned, his dick swelling inside me as he released his own orgasm. I felt him fill me up, his cum spilling deep inside my pussy as he collapsed against me, pinning me against the sideboard. It was intense, almost overwhelming, but I loved it. I loved the way he filled me up, the way his cum coated my insides. I loved the connection that we had, even if he didn't believe it.

We both stayed there, him still sheathed inside me, panting from the vicious act that had just happened. I sighed as I felt the gentle caress of his lips on the back of my neck. I wanted to stay like this forever, in this haze, but the moment I heard the vibration of his phone, and felt the way his body stiffened against mine. I knew it was over. Without a word, Jake pulled out of me, leaving me empty and bare. A wave of sadness washed over me as he answered the phone. His tone was more strict, almost flat with no emotion at all. I dare not move as he responded to whoever it was.

"Copy that," he finally said and put the phone down. I flinched as I felt him around my legs and realised that he was pulling my panties back on and lowering my skirt. He pulled my body up from the unit and turned me to face him. What I saw upset me even more. Gone was the lust and the fury, even the raw hatred no longer lingered in his eyes. His face was a mask of nothingness. He had shut down his emotions completely, and for the first time I saw the cold hard eyes of a killer in him.

"Jake," I whispered, and I saw a slight flinch as he checked the binds on my wrists.

"It's time to go," he said, his voice as void as his expression. "Transport is here."

"Jake please," I pleaded as tears fell down my cheeks. I knew that if he took me to the Council, I wouldn't come out alive. Sadness flickered across Jake's face and he reached up to wipe away my tears. Then he turned away from me and pulled on the chain binding my wrist.

"I'm sorry," he whispered, "But you are the enemy."

CHAPTER 30

"Jake, please," I begged as he roughly pulled the chains down the stairs of the bed-and-breakfast. The family from the other day opened their door as we walked past and Jake flashed a badge in the man's face before he could even say anything.

"Official Council business," he said, and the man threw me a look of sympathy before shooing his family back into the room.

"Jake," I said again, trying to pull on the chains to get him to stop. My heart pounded in my chest as I struggled against the chains that Jake had attached to the cuffs around my wrists. I knew that if he got me in that van, the Council would kill me without even listening to me. I had to find a way to stop him.

"Jake, please," I begged, my voice trembling with fear. "You don't have to do this." He scoffed at me, his eyes cold and hard.

"Do what? Let you continue to suck the life out the world? Serena, you're a danger to everyone around you. You need to be stopped." I shook my head vehemently, tears welling up in my eyes.

"No, Jake. You don't understand. The Zodiacs are trying to save the earth. We're not the bad guys." He laughed bitterly, his grip on the chains tightening.

"Save the earth? Try brainwashing someone else, I'm not buying it." My heart sank at his words. There was no getting through to him, and the irony of being accused of brainwashing when that was exactly what the Council had been doing to the whole world with their damn fake prophecy.

"Jake," I pleaded again, desperation creeping into my voice. "Please don't do this. You can't just take me away like this." He looked at me for a long moment, his expression unreadable. Then he sighed heavily and rubbed his eyes. He looked back up at me and there was sadness in his eyes.

"Do you think this is easy for me?" he asked, his voice edged with weariness. "I thought I had actually found someone who understood me, but then I found out that you were playing me all along."

"How was I playing you?" I snapped. "You were the one lying."

"You weren't exactly forthcoming about what you are, were you sweetheart?" Jake shot back. I wanted to scream at him. Of course I wouldn't have been honest about who I was. The Council are hunting Zodiacs and all their believers, positioning the world against us, and what for? What would they achieve when the damn black hole they were blaming on us ended up swallowing us all into oblivion?

"Well duh," I snapped and rattled the chain between us. "I mean when you get such stellar treatment, how can you blame me?" Jake looked down at the chains and then back at me.

"You really don't understand," he said. "People are dying in freak weather, my own parents were killed because of your kind and what you are doing to the earth. But no, you just keep telling yourself that you aren't the destruction that you are." He didn't even give me a chance to respond before turning on his heel and yanking the chains dragging me along with him.

I dug my heels into the cobblestones as Jake dragged me out onto the empty street; the cuffs biting into my wrists. My heart lurched when I saw the ominous black van idling by the curb, two expressionless Council operatives standing sentry beside the open back doors. Inside was a small metal cage just big enough for a person to stand in. My breath caught in my throat. Once I was locked inside that thing, I knew I'd never see the light of day again.

"Jake, please," I begged, craning my neck to look up at him. His handsome face was stoic, his grey eyes cold and empty. "You don't have to do this. I'm not the enemy here." He didn't even glance at me, just kept marching toward the van, yanking me along like an animal. Panic swelled inside me as we neared the operatives. I planted my feet, trying to dig my heels in, but Jake was too strong.

Just as we reached the van's open doors, I heard a voice call out.

"Serena? What's going on?" My heart leapt when I saw Violet hurrying down the street toward us, her bright blue hair bouncing as she jogged over. Jake turned, blocking Violet's path.

"Council business, ma'am," he said in an authoritative voice. "Keep walking." Violet's eyes went wide as she took in the scene, me bound in chains, the cage inside the van. Her face seemed to fall into a disapproving expression.

"Why, what did she do?" she asked, moving toward me. One of the operatives stepped in front of her, hand on his belt near his weapon. Violet faltered.

"I said move along," Jake ordered. His tone left no room for debate. Violet's gaze met mine, her eyes full of curiosity and judgement. My own welled with tears as I realised she wasn't going to try to stop them. She turned and looked at Jake and nodded. Then she turned and hurried away without looking back. My heart cracked at the betrayal. I thought Violet was my friend. But now I was alone, at the mercy of the Council and the man I thought I loved.

Jake shoved me toward the van with such force that I stumbled, barely catching myself before falling. I craned my neck frantically, searching the empty street for any other sign of hope, but no one else appeared. The street was desolate, the surrounding buildings dark and foreboding in the night. Jake gripped my arm painfully, ready to force me into the cage that awaited inside the van.

"Please, Jake," I whispered, my voice breaking as the tears spilled down my cheeks. "Don't do this. I love you." His stoic mask finally cracked, emotion leaking through the facade. Pain flashed across his face and he hesitated. For one brief moment, I saw a war raging behind his stormy grey eyes. The hand on my arm loosened just a fraction, uncertainty creeping in. But then the operative cleared his throat sharply. Jake's pained expression hardened again into cold resolution. Without another word, he shoved me roughly into the van. I cried out as I crashed inside the metal cage, the doors slamming shut behind me with an ominous clang that echoed through the empty street. Jake's face was grim as he latched the cage door, the click of the lock sealing my fate.

"I'm sorry," he said quietly, not meeting my tear-filled eyes. "But this is how it has to be." His apology sounded hollow, as if he was trying to convince himself. Then he stepped out into the night and slid the van doors closed, plunging me into darkness. The engine rumbled to life, and the van started moving, carrying me away to an unknown fate. I sank to the cold metal floor, the unforgiving surface biting through my clothes. Tears streamed down my face as my last ounce of hope died. I was alone now, at the mercy of the Council. And the man I loved had betrayed me.

I slumped against the cold metal bars as the sound of the doors to the van slammed; the vibrations reverberating through the van and my heart. Then the final light of hope died as the van started up and began to move, carrying me away into the unknown. I could feel the rough metal floor pressing into my legs through my thin dress as the van rumbled down the road. Would I just disappear without a trace? Would the world even know I was gone? How would my dear Alec feel when he realised I was missing? Would he blame himself for not protecting me better, or would he think that he had warned me sufficiently about the danger of trusting Jake? And what about my cats, Carnelian and Obsidian? Perhaps Ophelia would take them in if I never returned. I knew I was desperately trying to think of anything to fill my mind, anything but the grim fate that surely awaited me once we reached the Council's stronghold. Fear clawed at my throat as I imagined the cold, heartless people who had ordered my kidnapping. Jake had betrayed me completely into their hands. I was alone now, at the mercy of the Council and their sinister plans. It felt like hours but I knew we couldn't have been moving longer than five minutes when I slammed against the cold metal bars as the van screeched to a sudden stop. Pain exploded through my shoulder and I cried out, cradling my arm to my chest. I heard muffled voices from outside, shouting and scuffling. There was a loud bang against the side of the van, making it rock violently. My heart pounded, adrenaline rushing through my veins. What was happening out there? I craned my neck, straining to see through the tiny barred window of my cage. All I could make out were indistinct shadows dancing in the dim light. More shouting, another crash against the van. It rocked again, nearly toppling me over.

Fear coursed through me. Was it the Resistance coming to rescue me? Or something even worse here to finish me off? I shrank back against the corner of my cage, making myself as small of a target as possible. The van doors were wrenched open violently. I threw my arms up, shielding my face from the flood of light. Heavy boots thudded up the steps, and I tensed, waiting for the killing blow.

"Serena!" a familiar voice shouted. I lowered my arms hesitantly, hardly daring to believe it. Alec stood there, chest heaving, face smudged with dirt. Relief crashed over me at the sight of his familiar rugged face.

"Alec!" I cried. He was already at work on the lock of my cage, fumbling with the latch. After a few agonising moments there was a click and he wrenched the door open. I all but fell into his arms, my body shaking with adrenaline and relief.

"Thank God," I breathed into his shoulder. "How did you find me?" Alec pulled back, his eyes urgently scanning the area.

"No time to explain, we have to move quickly before reinforcements arrive. Can you run?" I nodded, still trying to catch my breath. Alec helped me down from the van, keeping a supportive grip on my arm. My knees nearly buckled as my feet hit the road, the events of the night catching up with me. Alec kept me upright, peering anxiously down the empty street.

"We don't have much time, we need to get you someplace safe." I looked around, getting my bearings. Alec had intercepted the van in a deserted industrial area on the outskirts of town. Dim streetlamps illuminated the cracked pavement, but there wasn't a soul in sight.

"My shop," I said urgently, meeting Alec's eyes. "We can regroup there." He nodded curtly and pulled me into a jog down the street. My legs burned and lungs heaved, but I forced myself to keep up with Alec's long strides. We had to get off the streets before Jake or the Council caught up with us.

By some miracle, we made it to my shop without encountering anyone. Alec quickly ushered me inside, locking the door and drawing the curtains. My legs gave out, and I collapsed onto my overstuffed sofa, my heart pounding against my ribs. Alec crouched down in front of me, gripping my shoulders.

"Are you alright?" His eyes searched my face intently. I managed a shaky nod, still struggling to catch my breath.

"Yes, I'm okay now thanks to you." I reached out and squeezed his hand gratefully. A muscle feathered along his jaw.

"I never should have left you alone," he said, anger flashing in his eyes. "When I realised Jake was Council, I knew he would make a move against you but I was too late..." I shook my head, cutting him off.

"You came back for me, that's what matters." Alec's expression softened, his eyes glistening slightly.

"I swear Serena," he said, rubbing his face as he stood up to check out the window. "I came back here and saw the place had been ransacked, I really thought the worst." I looked around the shop and for the first time I saw the mess that it was. The shelves had been toppled and there was broken stock and stuff all over the floor. I could see into my office and my desk was overturned and things pulled off the wall. Tears formed in my eyes at the sight. I knew this was all just stuff, but it wasn't just my stuff, it was my Gran's stuff. All of it destroyed, like worthless rubbish.

"Hey," Alec said as he knelt down in front of me again. "It's okay, I got you now." I shook my head as tears streamed down my cheeks. I wanted to say that I was fine, but the lump in my throat from the sudden barrage of emotions felt like it would suffocate me.

"Serena sweetheart," Alec said and pulled me into a fierce hug and it was all I needed to let the sobs begin to escape my body as I clung to him like the last lifeline that I had.

A sudden pounding on the shop door made us both jump. My heart seized in my chest. Alec leapt to his feet, pulling me behind him protectively. I gripped his arm, fear icing my veins. Had the Council found us already? Maybe coming to the shop was a bad idea. I was surely the first place that Jake would look for me.

"Alec." A voice called from the other side of the door and Alec visibly relaxed as he stepped forward at the familiar voice. I grabbed his arm and shook my head.

"Serena, it's okay," he said with a reassuring tone. "It Violet."

"I know," I whispered, "But she saw them take me and didn't do anything." Maybe Violet was working with the Council, maybe not, but I couldn't forget the look she gave me and the way she just walked away. Alec shook his head again.

"Sweetheart, it was Violet who told me what had happened," Alec said and my eyes widened. He opened the door and Violet rushed in straight past him searching the room. Her eyes landed on me and relief washed over her face as she flung herself at me, pulling me into a fierce hug.

"Oh my god, Serena," she said as she squeezed me tightly. I hesitated slightly before finally returning her hug. "I am so sorry I didn't do anything, but I knew I was outnumbered and if they knew I was with the Resistance, then they would have detained me as well."

"What?" I pulled away from Violet and stared at her. "You are Resistance?" Violet nodded and smiled.

"There are more of us than you might think," Alec said. He nodded to Violet. "Violet found me freaking out in the shop and told me she saw that bastard Jake putting you in the van." He grinned at Violet. "Taking note of the licence plate was a genius move, it meant that we could track the van and intercept it." I stared in awe at Violet, my friend for so long, and she just shrugged and smiled at me.

"I'm glad we got to you in time," she said and I pulled her into another hug, overwhelmed by all the emotions that were running through me.

"Not that I'm not glad to see you," Alec said, "But why are you here, Violet?"

"Oh, we need to move," Violet said. "Millie said she can house you in the safe house until we can secure transport out of here. But the Council is already sending reinforcements."

"Millie?" I asked. The landlady at the local was involved as well? How many people did I know from the Resistance? Did they all know about me? Alec began to move around the shop quickly, pulling things together. He leaned into the office and pulled my weekend bag, which looked like it was pretty full from the way it strained.

"Yeah, she's one of the originals here," he said as he handed me the bag. "It's part of the reason why Iris chose Whitby as her home." My heart hurt a little at my Gran's name and I looked sadly around the destroyed shop again.

"Hey," Alec said, taking my arm gently. "We need to move out, I need to get you safe." He pulled me towards the door as I hesitated. "Serena, it's just stuff."

"It's not just stuff," I whispered as a fresh set of tears fell down my cheeks. "This is all I have left of my Gran."

"I am sure that Iris would rather you be safe than worrying about all this," Violet said, and if on cue a bunch of crystals flew from one of the only shelves that were still standing. I couldn't help but grin. That was my Gran's way of saying "Screw the shop, it's not important." I let out a big sigh and looked around the room again.

"Okay okay," I said, holding my hands up in defeat. "I got the message. Just don't destroy anything else." Alec took that as a cue to head out of the shop, and with one final look I followed him and closed and locked the door behind me.

Chapter 31

Serena

The relief flooded through me in waves as we finally made it to the pub, the familiar lights glowing warmly in the foggy night air. Millie was waiting just inside the old oak door, her eyes full of concern and steely determination. She quickly ushered us inside with a sweep of her arm, leading us past the bustling patrons who paid us no mind. We followed her to a darkened corner of the pub, where she pressed on an inconspicuous wooden panel set into the wall. It swung open smoothly, revealing a narrow stone staircase that disappeared down into darkness. The air wafting up from below was cool and musty, a stark contrast to the cosy warmth and chatter upstairs.

"Quickly now, down you go," Millie said in a hushed but urgent tone, gesturing for us to follow her into the shadows. "We need to get you all out of sight before the Council's reinforcements arrive in town." Her voice held an underlying tone of strength that I found reassuring despite the circumstances. I glanced back at Alec and Violet as we descended into the dimly lit basement one by one. Their faces held a mix of worry for what was to come, and determination to protect me no matter what.

As my eyes adjusted, I saw that the basement was simply furnished with neat rows of camp beds along one stone wall, each with blankets and pillows laid out for us. Lanterns hanging from hooks cast a warm glow over our makeshift accommodations.

"Thank you, Millie," I said, heart swelling with gratefulness for her loyalty. "I can't tell you how much this means to me." She gave me a reassuring smile and squeezed my shoulder firmly.

"You'll be safe down here for now," she assured us. "My staff and I will keep watch upstairs night and day. We'll make sure no one suspects a thing." I watched as Alec and Violet began fussing over the camp beds, rearranging blankets and fluffing up pillows in an effort to ensure my comfort despite our less than ideal circumstances. Their thoughtfulness brought a soft smile to my face.

"Is there anything else we can get for you all?" Violet asked earnestly, glancing around the sparse basement with determination in her bright eyes. But Millie simply shook her head.

"Just rest up," she instructed us firmly. "We've got things under control upstairs, so try not to worry." I felt a surge of gratitude for these brave souls who were risking so much to protect me from the Council's wrath.

"Thank you all," I said softly. "I truly don't know what I would do without you in my life." Millie's expression softened with understanding.

"You'd do the same for any of us, love," she replied gently. "Here in Whitby, we look out for each other no matter what." I nodded slowly, taking in the warmth of her words and letting them fill me with courage and resolve. We would get through this ordeal together, as a family.

Alec finished preparing one of the camp beds and turned to me with concern etched on his face. He reached out and gently brushed a lock of hair from my eyes in a comforting, paternal gesture.

"How are you doing, kid?" he asked, and I rolled my eyes as I smiled at the familiar phrase he often used with me.

"I dunno," I said with a sigh as I sat down heavily on one of the beds, the events of the last few days weighing on me. "Tired, I guess." But that seemed like an understatement. Being hunted by the Council, one of the most influential organisations in the world, and possibly putting my closest friends in danger in the process, required a much weightier word than just 'tired'. A feeling of dread came over me then as a worrying thought crossed my mind. If Alec and Violet were down here with me, who else might be affected by this whole mess? My eyes widened in alarm and I looked up at Alec urgently.

"Oh my god, Alec," I asked, my voice tense with concern. "What if they go after Ophelia?" I stood up, intending to head back up the stairs to the pub. Maybe Millie could get word out to warn her.

"We need to warn her somehow!"

"Serena, stop!" Alec called out behind me. I shook my head adamantly, my hair flying around my face.

"No, there's no time!" I insisted. "I can't have anyone else getting hurt because of me." I had my foot on the first step up when Alec called out again, his voice sharp.

"Serena!" The tone made me spin around to face him, ready to argue. I couldn't fathom keeping myself safe at the expense of others.

"What, Alec?" I demanded hotly. But then I saw the grave look on his face and glanced between him and Violet. I could tell there was something they weren't telling me.

"What is it?" I asked, feeling a sense of dread flooding my body. "What's happened?" Alec stepped towards me with his hands out in a calming gesture. "Maybe we should sit down," he said gently. But I shook my head firmly and stepped back from him.

"No. I don't want to sit down. What is it, Alec?" I insisted. Alec glanced over at Violet briefly and then back at me. Finally he took a deep breath and looked away, unable to meet my gaze.

"Ophelia's dead," he said heavily. I heard the words. I understood them individually. But strung together in that sentence, the full meaning was too horrific for me to grasp. I shook my head in disbelief, trying desperately to shake away the nightmarish thoughts beginning to surface.

"No," I said firmly, my voice shaking with emotion. "You're lying or you're wrong. Ophelia can't be dead." Alec looked at me with a pained expression, his eyes full of regret and sorrow.

"Serena," he said gently, taking a step towards me. "I wish it wasn't true more than anything in the world, but I found her myself." My heart pounded in my chest as he continued. "The damage on her body... It was the Council that did this to her." The words hung heavy in the air between us, each one like a punch to the gut. My knees buckled beneath me as the reality of Ophelia's death hit me like a freight train. I crumpled to the floor, my body wracked with sobs as I clutched at my chest, trying to hold myself together. How could this have happened? How could I have let it happen? Ophelia was more than just a friend to me; she was my confidante, my support system, and my rock. She had been there for me through thick and thin, and now she was gone because of me. The guilt weighed heavily on my shoulders, threatening to crush me under its immense weight.

"Oh my god, what have I done," I sobbed out as the grief and guilt overwhelmed me.

"Serena," Alec said softly, kneeling down beside me and placing a comforting hand on my shoulder.

"It's not your fault." But his words fell on deaf ears as I continued to sob uncontrollably. How could he say that? How could anyone say that when it was so clearly my fault? I knew that being the Cancer Zodiac came with a price, but I never thought it would cost me someone as dear to me as Ophelia. And now that price had been paid in full, and all I could do was mourn her loss and feel the crushing weight of guilt on my chest.

"Serena," Alec said again, his voice more insistent this time. "Please listen to me." He gently shook me by the shoulder until I looked up at him through tear-filled eyes. "This is not your fault." His eyes held a mix of compassion and determination that made it impossible for me to look away from him. "The Council did this, not you." I wanted to believe him; I really did. But how could he be so sure? Hadn't Jake made it clear that he blamed me for everything? And now Ophelia was dead because of it... Because of me... Oh my god, what if Jake had killed her? I couldn't even bear to think about that. My heart felt like it was going to break from the sheer weight of sorrow and guilt that threatened to consume me whole.

"How can you be so sure?" I asked through tears, looking up at Alec with pleading eyes. "Jake blamed everything on the Zodiacs. Maybe we are as evil as what everyone is saying." Alec took a deep breath before responding, his expression filled with determination and resolve.

"Don't you dare say that, " he said, his tone leaving no room for argument.

"Why not?" I asked, "It's what everyone is thinking. If I wasn't bringing misery everywhere, then she would still be alive."

"Because we know who killed her," he said firmly. "And it wasn't you." He paused for a moment before continuing softly,

"It was Clara" The name sent shivers down my spine; Clara. The woman who had kidnapped and tortured Ophelia. The woman who had blamed everything on her own daughter for being the Cancer Zodiac. The woman who had given me life had taken it from my friend. My heart felt like it was going to explode from the sheer anger and despair that consumed me at that moment. How could anyone be so cruel? So heartless? So willing to take another person's life just because they were convinced they were doing the right thing? It defied all logic and reason; it defied everything I believed in about humanity. And yet here we were, living in a world where such things were possible. Where such things happened even daily. Where people like my mother existed. And where innocent lives like Ophelia's were cut short because of it. My mind reeled from the sheer horror of it all as tears continued to stream down my face unchecked. I looked up at Alec, seeing concern in his eyes.

"Are you sure?" I asked, and he nodded his head gravely.

"Unfortunately so," he said. "I recognised the signature of the marks from when she killed..." he trailed off as anger flashed through his eyes. He recognised her style from when she killed his brother, my father. My own mother was responsible for so much grief and still it was me she wanted dead.

"But why did they take Ophelia?" I asked as Alec helped me off the floor and onto one of the camp beds. "Why didn't she just tell them who I was?"

"I assume that the spell Iris put on her, stopped her from revealing who you were. That was probably why she wanted Iris's journals, to break the spell." It all made sense as Alec spoke. I shrugged.

"Well, I guess she will be happy now," I said. "Jake took the journals when he took me." A fresh wave of sadness washed over me as I said Jake's name. I still couldn't believe that he was one of them.

Alec stood up from the floor and placed a kiss on my forehead. I looked up at him and he forced a sad smile.

"Get some rest," he said, "I have a feeling that Whitby is soon gonna be overrun with Council, we need to get you out of here before that happens."

"But what about the last two relics? How are we supposed to find them without my Gran's journals?" I asked, "And the ritual?"

"I have an idea about one of the relics," he said. "And the rest, we will figure out when you are safe, you understand me. Serena, you are top priority right now."

"Alec I don't think that-" I started but was cut off by Violet.

"Alec's right," she said, her face serious. "It won't matter if we find the relics or not if you are captured or dead." I knew she was right, but I didn't like how much the responsibility that was resting on my shoulders was being so dangerous for the people I loved. But I knew I couldn't argue. I was exhausted and needed to sleep before I could think clearer. I laid down on the camp bed and Alec covered me with a blanket, before turning towards the stairs.

"Where are you going?" I asked, and he smiled at me.

"To get everything planned, and to check something out." He glanced at Violet and she nodded.

"I'm staying here with you," she said and sat down on the bed next to mine.

"Go to sleep," Alec said. "Tomorrow we will get plans into action, and get you out of Whitby where you are safe." I wanted to argue, but I was struggling to keep my eyes open. Maybe things would be better in the morning. I doubted it, but how much worse could it get?

Chapter 32

Serena

The whole town of Whitby seemed to be bathed in a blueish ethereal glow as I stood on the cliff top above, looking down. The wind whipped around me, causing my hair and the white lacy dress that I was wearing to fly around me in some form of ancient dance that called upon a sacred power. The ocean breeze kissed my skin as I gazed out over the moonlit water. I knew instantly that this was another dream, but even in this mystical realm, the familiar sight of Whitby brought me a small measure of comfort. But the peace was short-lived as memories of recent events came flooding back.

Jake's betrayal cut me deeply. I had felt such an intense connection with him, one I couldn't explain but knew in my soul. His handsome face and muscular frame had stirred new feelings in me that I'd never experienced before. But it had all been a lie, a ruse to get close and expose me. The anger and disgust in his eyes when my secret was revealed would haunt me forever. And my dear friend Ophelia, murdered by my own mother. Tears sprang to my eyes at the thought. Ophelia had been my rock, guiding and supporting me for so many years and even as I navigated the tangled web of my destiny. Losing her so violently at the hands of the woman who gave me life was almost too much to bear. My grief felt like a gaping wound, raw and aching. But I knew I couldn't let it consume me. I had to be strong, for her and for all the lives that depended on me.

Steeling myself, I turned from the sea. As I did, the ruins of Whitby Abbey came into view. Even in this ephemeral realm, the crumbling Gothic walls radiated a quiet power. I felt called there, drawn by some invisible thread. I made my way across the clifftop towards the abbey grounds. The empty windows watched me like sightless eyes as I passed through a stone archway. The winding path brought me to the roofless nave, open to the moonlit sky. This was the first time, in a dream such as this, that I first saw the Constellation, only such a short time ago. I paused, once again sensing a presence here with me. I took a deep, shaky breath as the ethereal light began to take shape before me. It coalesced into a humanoid form, though somehow still diffuse, as if made from stardust itself. The Cancer Constellation had come.

"Why?" I called out, my voice echoing in the empty ruins. "Why does it have to hurt so much?" The Constellation hovered silently for a moment. When it spoke, its voice was soft and soothing, like a gentle tide washing over me.

"Dear Serena, I know you have suffered greatly. But it was necessary for your journey." I shook my head angrily as tears spilled down my cheeks.

"Necessary? My friend was murdered! By my own mother! And my heart was ripped out and poisoned with betrayal." The Constellation drifted closer, its aura radiating compassion.

"Ophelia's passing was tragic. But her purpose was served. She helped guide you to the precipice of your destiny." I felt the caress of the wind through my body again. I could feel it working at my poor damaged soul. "And the love you think is gone is still here. You will see, when it is time. Everyone has a path and a price to pay to walk it." I scrubbed at my eyes, trying to stem the flow of tears.

"It's not fair," I choked out.

"No, it isn't," the Constellation agreed gently. "But the wheels are in motion now, events moving swiftly towards their conclusion. Your fate is nearly at hand." I looked up, startled by its words.

"My fate?" The Constellation's aura brightened, casting dancing beams of light along the abbey walls.

"Yes, dear one. The time of prophecy is upon us. You have found the relics, awakened your powers. Now you must fulfil your cosmic purpose." My mind reeled. It was all happening so fast. I thought of the journal pages, the glass box, the oval necklace. Pieces of some great destiny I still didn't fully understand.

"But I haven't," I called, "I only have two relics. I'm not ready. Everything is against us. Everyone, the Council," I protested weakly. "My mother, Jake...they'll try to stop me."

"And they will fail," the Constellation pronounced, its voice resonating with conviction. "Trust in your abilities, Serena. You are more powerful than you know." I wanted to believe it was right. But doubt still lingered. "I don't feel powerful," I admitted. "I feel scared. And alone." The Constellation drifted closer still until I was cocooned in its radiance. I felt its light soak into me, fortifying my spirit.

"You are never alone, Serena," it assured me. "I am always with you, as are all the forces of the cosmos. And your eleven spiritual sisters." I took a deep breath and lifted my chin.

"What must I do?" The Constellation pulsed brighter.

"The final relic will reveal itself soon. When the time comes, you must not hesitate. Claim it and speak the words of power."

"And then?" I asked hesitantly.

"Then your destiny will be complete. And the world will begin to heal." I nodded slowly. My hands trembled, but my heart was steady. I was still afraid, but I would not let that stop me. Too much depended on it. On me.

"I'm ready," I whispered, determined to do whatever I needed to get this done. The Constellation flared brighter in response to my resolve and the whole Abbey shone brightly before the light died completely.

The first thing I noticed as I woke up in the basement of the pub, was two small presences at the end of my bed. I sat up and looked at Carnelian and Obsidian patiently watching me, and knew why they were here. I rubbed my eyes and yawned, still groggy from sleep and my mind still fuzzy from the vision that I had just had. Carnelian and Obsidian sat patiently at the end of the bed, their eyes fixed on me. I knew they were here to lead me somewhere, and I had a feeling where. As I swung my legs over the side of the bed, I heard a soft knock on the door.

"Serena, are you awake?" Alec's voice called out. "I have something to show you." I hesitated for a moment, not knowing if I could afford the interruption. But the cats seemed eager to follow him, so I decided to put my faith in them. I pulled on a pair of jeans and a sweater, then followed Alec out of the basement and up the stairs. The pub was quiet as we made our way through the dimly lit rooms. Alec led us to a narrow staircase at the back of the building, which creaked and groaned under our weight. As we climbed, I could hear the cats padding softly behind me, their claws barely making a sound on the wooden steps. At the top of the stairs, Alec pushed open a door to reveal a dusty attic filled with old boxes and cobwebs. The cats immediately darted towards the far corner of the room, where they began to sniff and paw at something hidden beneath a pile of dusty blankets. Alec followed them, his eyes wide with excitement.

"I found it!" he exclaimed, pulling the blankets aside to reveal a silver candle with a cancer Zodiac design etched into it. "It's said to burn eternally." I approached the candle, my heart racing with anticipation. This was the third relic I needed to complete the prophecy. As I picked it up, I felt a surge of power coursing through me, as if the candle was already beginning to work its magic.

"Where did you find it?" I asked, looking around the dusty old room. I heard a disgruntled grunt from the doorway and looked over to see Millie standing there, glaring at the cats.

"These two pests were clawing at the door all day," she said. "Did my bloody head in, they did." Obsidian went and wound his body around Millie's legs and I saw the annoyance melt from her face as she reached down to stroke him.

"As soon as Millie told me, I came upstairs and let them in the room," Alec said with a laugh. "I assumed that after how much they had helped us so far, there was something they wanted in here, and it wasn't a mouse."

"There are no bloody mice in my pub," Millie snapped at Alec and I smiled as she threw an old cushion at him. I looked back down at the candle and then at the cats. They were both back to watching me.

"This is it," I whispered, my voice barely above a whisper. "The third piece of the puzzle. She already knew, didn't she?" Of course the cats didn't respond, but I could feel their approval.

"She, who?" Alec asked, and I explained the dream that I had just had to him and Millie.

"Well, that's a lot of information for my old soul," Millie said after I had finished. "I gotta go get back to the pub, though. Midwinter is a busy night." I looked up at her, my eyes widening as I realised what day it was.

"Of course," I exclaimed. "Midwinter." Both Alec and Millie looked startled at my excitement. "Midwinter, it's now right?" And Millie nodded. "The ritual, it's tonight."

"Are you sure?" Alec asked, and I looked back at the cats and knew for certain that this was it.

"Yep," I said as I nodded. A thrill of excitement rushed through me that we were coming near to the resolution of hundreds of years of legacy. Alec didn't look so excited.

"There is a lot of movement from the Council," he said, his face twisted in concern. "I wanted to get you out of town during the celebrations that we had planned."

"No can do," I said. I stood up with the candle firmly in hand and headed towards the door, followed quickly by my two beautiful feline guides. It was now or never.

As I descended the stairs back into the dimly lit basement, I could feel the weight of the silver candle in my hand. It was heavy, almost as if it held a secret that was eager to be revealed. Alec followed closely behind me, his footsteps echoing in the quiet space.

"Serena, are you sure about this?" he asked, his voice filled with concern. "With the Council on high alert, it's not safe to be out in the open." I paused for a moment, looking up at him with a determined expression.

"I know the risks, Alec. But this is something that needs to be done now. I can feel it in my bones. I can't be selfish when the whole world is at stake." He sighed, running a hand through his hair.

"Okay, but be careful. I couldn't bear to lose you." I turned around and hugged Alec. The intensity of the emotions running through me right now was almost too much to deal with. Finally, I stepped back and nodded, my heart pounding in my chest. I knew that the next few hours would be crucial, and I had to be focused and alert.

I made my way to the far corner of the room, where I knew the other two relics were hidden. As I reached out to touch the first one, a small glass box inlaid with stars, I felt a surge of energy coursing through me. It was as if the objects themselves were alive, and they were responding to my touch. Alec watched me intently as I carefully picked up the box and placed it in my bag. He knew how important these relics were to me, and he trusted my instincts. As I moved on to the second item, the oval pendant necklace, I could feel the air around me growing colder. It was as if the very fabric of reality was shifting, and I knew that we were on the precipice of something truly extraordinary.

With the three relics safely in my possession, I turned to face Alec. "We need to go," I said, my voice barely above a whisper. "It's time." He nodded, his eyes filled with a mix of awe and trepidation. We made our way back up the stairs and out into the night, the cold air biting at our skin. As we emerged from the shadows of the pub, we were greeted by the sight of a full moon, casting a silvery glow over the town. It was Midwinter, and the air was thick with magic and anticipation. We made our way through the crowd, blending in with the revellers as we followed Carnelian and Obsidian towards the Abbey steps.

As Alec and I reached the 199 steps that led up to the Abbey, I could feel the weight of the three relics in my bag and the significance of what we were about to do. I had to trust that the Constellations knew what they were doing and that the final relic would reveal itself to me, just as the Constellation told me in my vision. We were on the brink of something that could change the course of history, and I was both exhilarated and terrified. Alec paused for a moment, looking up at the imposing stone structure before us.

"Are you ready?" he asked, his voice low and steady. I took a deep breath, trying to steady my racing heart.

"Yes," I said, my voice barely above a whisper. "I'm ready." As we began our ascent, I could feel the energy building within me. The air was thick with anticipation, and I could sense the presence of the relics, urging me on. We climbed the steps slowly, each one bringing us closer to our destination. I could hear the distant sound of music and laughter from the town below, but it seemed distant and unreal, as if I were in another world entirely.

Suddenly, we were stopped in our tracks by a figure blocking our path. I was shocked when I realised that it was Jake, his face twisted in anger and determination. He stepped forward, his large frame towering over us.

"What the hell do you think you're doing?" he demanded, his voice low and menacing. "You can't do this. I can't let you destroy us all." I looked up at him, my heart pounding in my chest. I could see the fear and uncertainty in his eyes, and I knew that he was not just trying to stop us, but also trying to convince a small part of himself that I was as evil as he had been told I was.

"Jake, please," I said, my voice barely above a whisper. "We have to do this. The fate of the world is at stake. The Council are wrong."

"You would say that." I noticed movement out of the corner of my eye. I turned to see Clara, my estranged mother, and the woman who had killed my friend along with several other Council operatives approaching us from behind. They were armed and dangerous, and I knew that we were in serious trouble.

"Anything to suck even more magic from the rest of us." I turned to her and glared. My heart hurt with the knowledge that my own mother hated me so much that she was probably relishing the idea of plunging the knife that she gripped in her hand, into my body. Alec moved to stand between us and Clara rolled her eyes.

"You're a fool for thinking that you can go against us," she snarled at him. "What's your plan Alec, gonna fight us all by yourself." I couldn't see Alec's face, but the tension in his body and the air around him was tight with violent thoughts.

"I've been waiting a long time for this Clara," he hissed, "But no, I'm not fighting you alone." He looked over his shoulder and down the stairs behind me. I looked around, confused and my eyes widened as I saw several people standing on the steps. All of them facing us. At their front was Millie, holding a cricket bat. She nodded to me and gave me a half smile. Behind her I saw Violet and Jonathan, who ran the fruit and veg shop, and tens of other people who I knew from living and working in Whitby. All of them looked armed and ready to fight. I realised that I was surrounded by more people than I thought, and it brought tears to my eyes.

I turned back to face Jake and tried to plead with my eyes.

"Jake please," I said. "It doesn't have to be like this. Just let me pass so I can do what I need to do." Jake had so much hatred in his eyes as he glared at me.

"I will go down fighting to stop you, if I have to," he snarled, his tone cold enough to send shivers down my spine. I was about to ask again when the vision from the other day slammed through my mind. The image of Jake, lying dead on the Abbey steps took my breath away, and I looked up at him in horror. This was it, this was the night that I was seeing. Dread filled my stomach as I realised that Jake could very well die by the hand of the person he had come to town searching for, and a tear slipped down my cheek as I realised that person was me.

Chapter 33

Serena

I was still lost in the horrific thought that I was somehow the one that would be responsible for Jake's death, the vision playing over and over in my head. The vivid image of Jake's lifeless body sprawled across the stone steps refused to leave my mind's eye, tormenting me. I barely noticed that the images of the vision had begun to change in my head, so consumed with guilt and dread. It wasn't until I felt the familiar tingle of magic along my skin that I realised I had slipped into another vision.

The image of Jake laid dead on the steps still consumed my reality and I tried desperately to get to him, to see if he still drew breath, to stop whatever was about to happen. But even as I watched helplessly, the scene seemed to shift; the edges going hazy as it rewound before my eyes like a tape playing in reverse. I was powerless to intervene as the tragic events I had witnessed started to unravel.

Jake's body blurred, reforming into an older man who looked so similar he had to be Jake's father. The surprise and pain that had been etched onto Jake's face moments before was now on this man's face instead. I watched in horror as a shadowy figure approached him from behind, the glint of a blade visible for a split second before it was buried in the man's back. Jake's father cried out, crumpling to his knees, next to the dead body of a woman dressed in what looked like a purple ball gown edged with gold, who I could only assume was Jake's mother. The shadowy figure yanked the blade back out, wiping it on their cloak before turning to leave. As they did, the hood of their cloak slipped back just enough for me to see their face. I recognised the person straight away, although they were younger, the hatred and cold anger was still gleaming in his eyes. The shadowy figure I had seen in Jake's vision, and the one now, the one responsible for the death of Jake's parents was Captain Stephen Kirkland, Jake's uncle. I strained against the force holding me, desperate to keep the man there, to see more. But the vision was fading, Jake's father and his killer blurring back into Jake's lifeless form sprawled on the steps.

The force holding me suddenly released, and I stumbled forward with a gasp, nearly losing my balance on the worn stone steps that lead up to the abbey. But Jake's body was gone now, the vision over, vanished as quickly as it had appeared. I was left kneeling alone on those weathered steps, my heart racing wildly as I tried to make sense of the fragmented images and revelations that had just been revealed to me. Though the vision had lasted only moments, the implications of what I'd seen churned through my mind. The shadowy figure in Jake's memory, the one responsible for the brutal murder of his parents when he was just a child, had been shockingly familiar. Captain Stephen Kirkland's face, though younger then, had been unmistakable beneath the hood of that cloak. Jake's uncle, the man who had raised him after that horrific tragedy, was also the one who had caused it. The hatred and cold rage I'd glimpsed burning in the Captain's eyes had chilled me to the core. I strained to recall every detail I could, desperate to understand how this could possibly be true. But the vision had already begun to blur and fade from my mind like a disturbing dream upon waking. I was left with only scattered remnants of those images and my frantically racing thoughts.

That had to have been the moment Jake's father was murdered. And the person who'd killed him, was his own uncle. Why would he have killed his own brother and sister-in-law, and then lied to Jake all these years about it? Is that why I'd had the vision of Jake's death first, was it some kind of warning? A premonition that the same fate awaited him at his uncle's hands? My stomach twisted with unease as I thought back to the chilling vision. I had to find Jake, to warn him before it was too late. I scrambled to my feet, looking around frantically at the fighting people. I could see Alec, mid blow with some unknown operative, and my mother was further up the stairs, but I couldn't spot Jake anywhere in the chaotic scene. Maybe he had already gone down to the town during the commotion, I thought hopefully. I turned away from the fighting above me and hurried down the steps towards town as fast as my legs could carry me. As I reached the bottom, a broad figure suddenly stepped out of the shadows. I stumbled to a stop, my heart leaping into my throat.

"Jake!" I cried out in immense relief, my panic dissolving instantly. It was him, solid and real and very much alive. Before I could stop myself, overcome with relief, I threw my arms around him tightly, so incredibly thankful it had just been a vision and not reality. He staggered back a step in surprise, confusion flickering across his rugged face.

"Serena? What the fuck?"

"It wasn't me," I cried out desperately as he tried to push me away, still disoriented by my emotional outburst. "I didn't kill you, I swear. I had a vision, and I saw..." I pulled back, searching Jake's stormy grey eyes urgently.

"What?" He frowned down at me in bewilderment. I took a deep breath before speaking again.

"I had a vision about your father's murder. And I saw..." I faltered, uncertain if I could really tell him his own uncle might have killed his father. Would he even believe me? Jake's expression darkened, his jaw tightening.

"What did you see?" he asked sharply, his tone demanding. I hesitated, wavering.

"Jake, I think... I think it might have been your uncle who-"

"Don't," he cut me off harshly, his eyes flashing dangerously. "Just... don't." He pushed me away from him forcefully in anger, causing me to stumble and fall backwards down the remaining steps. I landed hard on my tailbone and pain radiated up my spine.

"Stop fucking lying," Jake spat venomously as he advanced on me. "You are trying to manipulate me again. I'm not going to fall for it again."

"Jake, please," I pleaded desperately as I tried to shuffle back away from him across the dusty wooden floorboards. The fury burning in his stormy grey eyes was so raw and uncontrolled that I could feel its heat from where I lay sprawled. "I s-saw it, I swear." I tried frantically to back up further to escape his advance, but my back collided with something solid. I gasped and looked up to see the same cold, calculating eyes from my vision staring down at me. Stephen Kirkland sneered maliciously at me from above, his weathered features twisted in contempt. I tried to pull away from him, but he roughly grasped a handful of my hair and I screamed out in pain as he wrenched me up onto my feet.

"What do we have here then," he sneered, his voice dripping with disdain. "If it isn't the poisonous little bitch herself." I struggled desperately to break free, but his vice-like grip on my hair was too tight.

"Get the fuck away from me, you murderous bastard," I screamed, my voice raw and trembling with rage. He merely laughed harshly in response.

"I hardly think I have anything on you and your other Zodiac witches. Thousands of people, millions even, have perished for your selfish prophecies and deeds over the centuries."

"Jake, please, help me!" I tried frantically to appeal to any part of him that still cared, that still said it loved me, praying he would come to my aid.

"Why would he help the likes of you?" Stephen hissed venomously, his hot breath on my ear making me cringe. "You are the reason he lost his parents all those years ago." Fury welled up inside me as I realised this was the insidious lie that had kept Jake's thoughts chained to the Council all this time, used only to control him. It had been Stephen's doing, not mine.

"I'm not responsible, you're the one who killed them, I saw it," I screamed, my voice rising in pitch as I struggled against Stephen's vice-like grip. I saw a flicker of shock in Stephen's face before it disappeared again behind his usual stony mask. But that brief crack in his facade was enough for Jake to notice too.

"Stephen?" Jake asked, his voice still edged with anger but now tinged with uncertainty as he searched his uncle's face for answers.

"Stop your games, child," Stephen hissed, his tone dripping with contempt as he roughly turned me to face Jake. I could now see the ornate dagger glinting wickedly in Stephen's free hand.

"Finish her off, now," he commanded Jake, his voice brooking no argument. "You failed once before, don't fail the Council again." I knew Jake was starting to doubt everything he had blindly accepted from Stephen and the Council over the years. This was my chance, possibly my last chance, to reach the real Jake beneath the layers of lies and manipulation.

"Jake, I'm not lying," I urged desperately as his hand tightened around the hilt of his own blade. "I swear on my life, I saw it with my own eyes. How would I know your parents were dressed up in their finest clothes for some grand ball or gala when they died, if I didn't see Stephen murder them?" Jake's eyes widened slightly at the revelation and he looked away from me to meet his uncle's stony gaze.

"She's spewing nothing but lies, Jake," Stephen asserted coldly, though I could detect a hint of panic creeping into his voice. "She's trying to turn you against your family, against the Council. Don't let this witch manipulate you."

Jake turned his stormy grey eyes on me, a hint of pleading in them that I had never seen before. This ruthless assassin was silently begging me for the truth.

"What colour was my mum wearing?" he asked, his voice low but demanding.

"What?" I asked, confused for a moment at the sudden question. Then realisation dawned on me. He wanted proof that my vision was real. I searched back in my mind to the haunting memory of the vision, picturing his mother's beautiful gown once more.

"Jake, enough of this nonsense," his uncle hissed, spittle flying from his mouth in rage. But Jake's eyes were firmly locked on mine, his strong jaw set stubbornly.

"What colour?" he asked again, his words coming out through clenched teeth. I saw a muscle feathering in his cheek as he struggled to contain his emotion. Stephen yanked me back violently by my hair and I cried out in pain as I felt the sharp edge of a blade against my throat.

"Fine, I'll kill her," he sneered menacingly, and I felt my body go cold with fear, my fate hanging by a thread. Then I saw it again, the whole awful scene unfolding in my mind's eye.

"Purple!" I cried out desperately, tears streaming down my face. "It was purple silk with gold embroidered edges along the skirt." Jake's eyes widened even further in realisation, his face draining of colour.

"Why would she know that unless you actually saw it?" he whispered to nobody. I saw the truth dawning on him and the realisation quickly turned to rage as he looked up at his uncle's stony face.

"Why?" he whispered, his voice breaking with emotion, "Why would you kill them?"

"Fucking psychics," Stephen snarled, his face contorted in rage as he yanked me back violently by my long blonde hair. I cried out in pain and shock as I went flying backwards, only realising a moment later that Stephen had also gone flying as if an invisible force had struck him.

"Get your hands off her," Alec shouted, his dark eyes flashing dangerously. I turned just in time to see him lunge at Stephen with lightning speed. He made hard contact, barreling into the larger man and sending them both crashing heavily into the brick wall of a nearby house. I saw a brief flash of metal in Stephen's hand and screamed in terror as he suddenly plunged a vicious looking knife deep into Alec's side.

"Alec!" I shrieked, sprinting over to where he had fallen. I could see blood rapidly spreading across his shirt but couldn't locate the exact source of the bleeding no matter how frantically I searched. Alec grimaced in agony as he dragged himself into a sitting position against the wall.

"Serena, watch out!" he called in warning, nodding behind me. I whipped around to see Stephen advancing menacingly towards us, fresh blood dripping from the knife clutched in his fist. But before I could react, something invisible seemed to smash into him from the side and he went flying violently again, crashing heavily to the pavement.

"WHY!" Jake screamed in Stephen's face, his voice raw with anguish, as he began to viciously punch the older man over and over. The searing pain of profound loss and ultimate betrayal was etched all over Jake's rugged features. "Why would you so heartlessly take them from me?"

"Because they were traitors to the cause," Stephen snarled through bloodied lips as he barely managed to block one of Jake's powerful punches before delivering a brutal blow of his own to Jake's ribs. The force of the impact momentarily winded Jake and caused him to stumble back a few steps. But both men were back on their feet in mere seconds, circling each other warily.

Stephen turned and sneered menacingly at me again, his cold grey eyes glinting with malice.

"I've always despised psychics," he hissed venomously. "You all arrogantly think you're better than the rest of us mere mortals, but you're not. And you, Serena, are the most deceitfully evil one of them all."

He began advancing towards me and Alec with lethal intent, but Jake swiftly moved to stand protectively in front of us, blocking Stephen's view and access.

"Stay the hell away from her," Jake demanded fiercely as he landed another powerful punch to Stephen's jaw. I caught the flash of a blade in Stephen's hand a second too late. My scream of warning echoed through the alley just as Stephen viciously lunged at Jake, the knife aimed straight for his heart. But Jake was younger and quicker. He grabbed Stephen's wrist with lightning reflexes and ruthlessly twisted until an agonised yell escaped the older man. The force of Jake's counterattack drove the blade deep into Stephen's own stomach instead. A look of utter shock crossed the commander's hardened features before he dropped to his knees, clutching the hilt protruding from his abdomen. Jake glared pitilessly down at the man who had raised him, the man who had callously betrayed him, before he kicked Stephen brutally in the face, sending the traitor crumpling lifelessly to the filthy pavement below.

I scrambled to my feet and ran to Jake, my heart pounding with concern.

"Oh my god, Jake, are you okay?" I cried out as I tried to check him over for any wounds or injuries. He pulled back from me sharply, raking a hand through his short, dark hair. I could see the muscle in his jaw working tensely as he struggled to contain some powerful emotion that seemed to be raging inside of him.

"Jake?" I pleaded, my voice soft and gentle. Did he still blame me for what had happened? Jake turned slowly to face me, his stormy grey eyes brimming with so much turmoil and anguish that it made my heart ache.

"I almost killed you," he whispered, tears beginning to stream down his rugged, handsome face. "Oh god, Serena, what I did to you..." he trailed off despairingly as his broad shoulders slumped under the weight of his guilt and self-loathing. Unable to bear seeing him torture himself this way, I pulled Jake closer and wrapped my arms tightly around his solid waist in a fierce, protective embrace. I felt his muscular body stiffen in surprise before he took in a deep, shuddering breath and wrapped his own powerful arms around me even more tightly. Jake pushed his lips urgently against mine in a searing kiss that was raw with powerful emotions and need. It felt like something dormant came alive inside of me, some mystical energy that I didn't even know I possessed. A brilliant light seemed to flow through my body, circulating this vibrant energy through every fibre of my being. I gasped against Jake's mouth as I realised this mystical power didn't just flow through me, but also through Jake as well, connecting us together somewhere deep in our souls. The leather bag that always rested on my hip had started to feel hot and I pulled back from the dizzying kiss to see an ethereal glow emanating from within it.

"Well, I'll be damned," Alec said as he stumbled over to us, his eyes wide with disbelief. He nodded to Jake, and I looked up to see the talisman around Jake's neck glowing almost as brightly as my leather bag.

"What the fuck?" Jake looked between me and the talisman, his face etched in confusion as he tried to understand what was happening.

"It's the fourth relic," Alec said, and I gasped as the realisation hit me.

"Are you sure?" I asked, and he nodded with certainty.

"They recognise each other," he explained. "All the relics are communicating." I opened the leather bag to see the ethereal glow was indeed emanating from the three relics nestled inside. My mind raced as I tried to comprehend the significance of this moment.

Out of the corner of my eye, I saw a flash of orange fur around Jake's feet. I looked down to see both Carnelian and Obsidian, my cat familiars, watching me intently. They wound around each other playfully as they turned and trotted toward the stone steps leading up to the Abbey. I followed their gaze and gasped; above the Abbey, the night sky was free of clouds and littered with thousands of brightly glowing stars. They twinkled joyously, as if celebrating this fateful night and what was about to come. I could feel it in my bones, the vibrant energy of the night flowing through me and into my core. I turned to Jake and Alec, a smile spreading across my face.

"It's time," I said with determination. The prophecy was unfolding, and we would see it through.

Chapter 34

Serena

I glanced down at my watch and saw that it was a quarter to twelve at night. I knew without a shadow of a doubt that I had to complete the ancient ritual by the stroke of Midnight for it to work. A smile spread across my face as I thought somewhere around the world there would be eleven other young women all embarking on this same mystical journey as well.

"Jake, you need to get Serena up to the Abbey right away," Alec said urgently as I looked up the stone stairs where several fierce battles between our allies and the Council hordes were still raging.

"What about you?" I asked, concerned for my dear friend. Alec grinned bravely despite the pain clear on his face.

"I'll be there, don't you worry, sweetheart." Alec clutched his side tightly where dark blood was spreading across his shirt from a vicious wound. He winced again in agony. "I'll just be a little slower than usual to arrive."

"Oh no, Alec we need to get you some help immediately," I said, rushing to him and trying to examine the severity of his injury. He brushed my hands away firmly but kindly.

"Sweetheart, I can handle myself. You have the fate of the entire world resting on your shoulders tonight." The impact of Alec's words struck me hard, and a sudden rush of fear shot through me.

"Hey," Jake said softly, taking my hand and pulling me closer until I could feel the warmth of his breath. He gently brushed his lips against mine. "You can do this, I will be right by your side no matter what." I nodded, feeling confident and ready in the face of his unwavering faith in me.

"What the fuck!" I spun towards the steps where my mother was standing on the bottom step, fury etched into every line of her face. "Jake, what the hell are you doing?" Jake took a slight step forward, almost unconsciously positioning himself between me and my mother as the protector.

"Clara," he said, holding out his hand in a conciliatory gesture, "We were mistaken. We need to take Serena to the Abbey to perform the ritual."

"Like hell you do," my mother spat, her words dripping with venom. She sneered at me, and the intense hatred that radiated from her was almost sickening. "So you've worked your evil powers on him too, you little bitch. Like father, like daughter, right?"

"Go fuck yourself," I shot back, barely controlling my own rage. I hated her so much at that moment - hated that she wasn't the mother she was supposed to be, hated that she had killed my father before I ever got the chance to know him, and most of all I hated that she despised me for something she had gotten so completely wrong.

"Clara," Alec growled, his voice low and threatening. "You are not going to stop what needs to happen."

"Oh, aren't I?" my mother pulled out an ornate handled knife from a sheath strapped to her thigh. The silver blade glinted dangerously in the low light as she turned to Jake, her eyes wide with mock innocence.

"What do you think your dear Uncle Stephen is going to say when he finds out about this? And the Council?" she purred. "They won't take too kindly to their orders being defied."

"My uncle is a murderer, and the Council have been lying to us all along," Jake spat back, anger simmering beneath his words. My mother's eyes widened in surprise at the accusation.

"What are you talking about? Stephen only ever took a life when it was necessary, for the cause, to protect us all," she said, her voice wavering slightly.

"Does that include my parents?" Jake said bitterly. "Don't even try to lie to me. Serena saw him kill them in a vision. I know the truth." My mother looked over at me, her eyes filled with hatred, before turning her gaze back to Jake. She opened her mouth to respond, but no words came out. The web of lies was unravelling before her.

"You believe this evil creature over your own family?" my mother said, her eyes flashing with anger and disbelief.

"Stephen confirmed it himself," I replied steadily, meeting her gaze. "Said they were traitors to the Council." My mother took a deep breath, her shoulders slumping in defeat as she clearly realised she could no longer continue the web of lies.

"Fine," she conceded bitterly, "Stephen was right. He caught them talking to the resistance, plotting to leave the Council's service."

"So he killed them?" I asked, shocked that she could even think such cold-blooded murder was acceptable.

"Well, you don't betray the Council," she said defensively. "They made that clear after my mother abandoned her post."

"And so I had my parents ripped away from me," Jake spat, his body trembling with barely contained rage and anguish. I could see he was trying desperately to hold back the swell of emotions.

My mother obviously saw it too and came down the step towards us, towards Jake, her hand outstretched in a gesture of harmlessness despite the other hand still clutching a wicked-looking knife.

"Jake, darling," she said gently, her tone soothing.

"I am sure if we find Stephen and talk about this-" Alec let out an amused grunt, interrupting her mid-sentence.

"Too late," he scoffed derisively, a smug look on his face. My mother's eyes flashed with anger as she glared at him.

"What is that supposed to mean?" she snarled through gritted teeth, her body tensing. Jake stepped back instinctively, pulling me with him, and revealed the now dead Stephen sprawled on the floor, blood pooling around his lifeless body. My mother's eyes widened in shock and horror and she rushed to the corpse.

"Oh my god, no," she cried out, her voice breaking as she tried in vain to pull on the lifeless body. "Jake, how could you do this?" Tears streamed down her face as she looked at Jake accusingly.

"What, like you killed my friend?" I spat viciously, the pain and rage bubbling up inside me. I heard an inhuman snarl before I saw the blur of movement.

"You evil bitch!" my mother screamed, her face contorted in fury. In a flash, she had spun around to rush at me, the wicked-looking knife raised high. "I will enjoy killing you," she growled through bared teeth, madness in her eyes.

"Serena," Alec called trying to warn me, but it didn't matter, I wasn't fast enough and knew she was faster and stronger than me. I stood petrified watching my own mother coming at me with a knife, in slow motion. The gleaming blade glinted in the dim light as she rushed towards me, madness and murder in her eyes. I closed my eyes bracing for the attack, certain this was the end, when I thought I was gone for something blocked my limited light and I heard a grunt and a scream. My eyes flew open to see Jake standing in front of me with his own blade impaled into my mother's chest. Her eyes were wide with shock, mouth open in a silent scream of agony. Blood blossomed around the hilt of the knife, staining her shirt crimson. Jake's face was a mask of fury and determination. With a guttural cry he twisted the knife again, burying it deeper into her chest. I saw the light of life drain from my mother's eyes as she stumbled back, the knife sliding free. Her body crumpled to the ground with a sickening thud, eyes glassy and unseeing in death. Jake stood over her lifeless body, chest heaving, as we both stared at her still form.

I should have been sad. Or horrified, but all I felt as her body fell to the floor was relief and a sense of closure that was calming. It was as if a weight had been lifted from my shoulders. I had dreaded this moment for so long, but now that it was here, I only felt free. Alec rushed to my side and I could hear him asking if I was okay in a concerned tone, but I waved him off, more concerned that Jake was still standing with his back to me several feet away.

"Jake?" I called out quietly. I reached out and touched his shoulder, pulling slightly to get him to turn around. Jake slowly turned just enough for me to see the strained look on his handsome but blood spattered face. I gasped as my eyes dropped to see my mother's ornate ritual blade, the one meant for me, sticking out from Jake's stomach.

Crimson blood had already soaked through his shirt and was dripping down his jeans.

"Jake, no!" I screamed as he dropped to his knees, clutching the jewelled handle of the dagger. His normally sharp grey eyes looked glassy and pain filled as his face drained of colour. I saw him tighten his grip on the handle and with a grimace of effort, he pulled the engraved blade out. It dropped from his fingers, clattering loudly on the pavement below. Jake swayed, his free hand going to the wound as if to stem the flow of blood. I dropped down beside him, pressing my hands over his in a vain attempt to stop the bleeding. Tears blurred my vision as I looked at the man I loved, mortally wounded trying to protect me.

"Oh god, Jake," I cried, my voice cracking as I desperately tried pushing my hand over the gaping wound that was gushing crimson with blood. But the sticky scarlet liquid kept pouring relentlessly through my trembling fingers and I couldn't get the bleeding to stop no matter how hard I pressed down, and Jake was getting paler and paler by the second as his life force drained away. He dropped heavily to the cold concrete floor on his back with me kneeling in the growing pool of blood next to him when he reached a bloodied, shaking hand up and tenderly caressed my tear-streaked face, leaving a red smear on my cheek.

"I fucking love you," he whispered, his voice hoarse and barely audible.

"You can tell me later when you're better," I said, tears streaming uncontrollably down my cheeks as I looked at his ashen face. "Right now we need to get you help, just hold on!"

"Serena." Alec tried to gently pull my crimson stained hands away from the fatal injury. "Sweetheart, I don't think we can save him-"

"No!" I demanded, desperation in my voice. "I will not let him die. Jake please, you need to help me stop the bleeding!" Jake just gave me a sad smile as a single tear slid down his cheek, mingling with the blood.

"I'm glad I met you," he croaked, his breathing becoming more laboured. "You healed my heart when I thought it was forever broken." His striking grey eyes that I loved so much, slowly closed, and his muscular chest stopped moving as his breathing ceased altogether.

"No," I screamed, my voice echoing into the night sky as I looked up at the glittering stars above, pleading with them in desperation to save my love. Alec tried to gently pull me away from Jake's lifeless body, but I clung to him with every ounce of strength I had left, as if the very act would somehow keep Jake's soul tethered to this world.

"Serena, please," I heard Alec say softly as he attempted to pry my fingers away, but I refused to let go. My nails dug into Jake's rapidly cooling skin, leaving crescent shaped marks on his forearms.

"No, you can't let this happen to him," I sobbed, hot tears spilling down my cheeks in rivers. My body shook with the force of my grief as I hunched over Jake's body protectively. As I spoke, I noticed the talisman around Jake's neck had begun to glow faintly. I glanced down at my bag where the other relics lay dormant and dark, but the talisman grew brighter and brighter, until its light seemed to bathe Jake's entire body in an ethereal glow. I pulled my hand away from the fatal wound, watching with wide, incredulous eyes as the glow concentrated on the gash and before my eyes, the ugly wound began to close up miraculously. The torn flesh knitted itself back together as if an invisible seamstress was at work. Soon there was nothing left but a thin white scar, and the rise and fall of Jake's muscular chest resumed.

"Whoa," Alec breathed next to me, his eyes wide with amazement as Jake began to cough and splutter, returning to life before our very eyes. Jake's eyes flew open and tears began pouring from them, trailing down his dirt-smudged cheeks. I pulled him into a tight hug, relief washing over me in waves, and he hugged me back just as fiercely, his strong arms tight around me as if he never wanted to let go.

"I saw her," he croaked, his voice hoarse and cracked from disuse.

"Saw who?" I asked, tears of joy streaming down my face. Jake smiled weakly and wiped away some of the tears with his calloused thumb, only for them to be quickly replaced by more.

"My mother," he said, a faraway look in his misty grey eyes. He touched the talisman hanging around his neck, the silver moonstone pendant that had been a gift from her, and grinned at me. "She said that the talisman was a gift from Iris."

"Iris? My Gran?" I asked in surprise, and Jake nodded, a knowing look on his handsome face.

"Apparently she saw this day coming and infused the talisman with a powerful healing spell, knowing that one day I would cross paths with you and get it back to you when you needed it most."

"But how could she possibly know that?" I asked, astonished. I clearly hadn't given my grandmother's gift of foresight enough credit. She had seen our fates intertwined long before we'd ever met.

"Because we are meant to be together," Jake whispered and leaned in to brush his lips tenderly against mine in a kiss that spoke of destiny. "Soulmates." I gasped softly at his words, that resonated with truth in my heart. Deep down I had known since the first day he walked into my antique shop that we shared a profound connection.

"I hate to break up the love," Alec said, his usual stoic demeanour giving way to a slight smile as he regarded Jake and I locked in an intimate embrace. I reluctantly tore my gaze away from Jake's mesmerising grey eyes to glance over at Alec, noticing him standing a short distance away with an amused grin crossing his rugged features. "But you have maybe five minutes before midnight."

"Oh god," I gasped, hurriedly looking down at my watch to confirm the late hour before lifting my eyes to the magnificent Abbey, which seemed to be emitting an ethereal glow as the fateful hour approached.

"Oh no, we have to get up there," I said, panic rising within me as I jumped to my feet. Beside me, Jake swiftly stood as well, grabbing the bag containing the precious relics.

"Come on, we can still make it," Jake said, grasping my hand firmly in his strong grip. His tone was urgent but his touch tender. "Alec, can you cover us?" Alec gave a curt nod and Jake pulled me forward, drawing me up the ancient stone steps with swift, sure footsteps. My heart pounded, both from exertion and exhilaration, as we raced towards our destiny.

It was like everything timed perfectly as we rushed up the 199 steps. The fights seemed to almost part ways as we rushed past people engaged in combat, creating a path for us to follow. We made it up the stairs; me panting and wheezing in exhaustion while Jake was annoyingly not so much, his stamina holding strong. We rushed towards the Abbey ruins, the ancient stones that had witnessed centuries of history looming before us. I ran into the centre of the Abbey toward the otherworldly light that was emanating from within and stopped short as soon as I saw the source. There, bathed in an ethereal glow, stood Ophelia. She turned to face us, a serene smile upon her face. My eyes widened in shock and disbelief.

"Ophelia?" I gasped. "But...how?"

Chapter 35

Serena

I couldn't believe my eyes. My dear friend Ophelia was standing right in front of me, a placid smile upon her face. Overcome with emotion, I ran to her and threw my arms around her in a tight embrace.

"Oh my god, Ophelia, I thought you were dead," I cried, tears of relief and joy streaming down my face. But she remained motionless in my arms, not responding to my affections. Confused, I pulled away from her and searched her face. She continued to smile at me with an almost blank, distant expression.

"Ophelia?" I asked uncertainly, a feeling of dread creeping over me. The placid smile on her face faltered ever so slightly.

"Oh dear child," she finally spoke, her voice sounding distant and singsong. "I am not Ophelia. I merely borrowed her form to help put you at ease."

"Oh." Disappointment washed over me like a chilling wave as I realised this was not my beloved Ophelia standing before me. "Then who are you?" I asked, my voice trembling slightly.

"Dear child, I am the one who has been guiding you all this time," she replied, her smile radiating a soft, comforting light. "I guided your dear Gran to prepare you, and I sent your other early guides to help you on your quest." She waved her slender arm, and I glanced down to see Carnelian and Obsidian sitting nearby, watching me intently.

"The Constellation?" I breathed in awe, my eyes widening as I took in her celestial form. She nodded, her flowing locks glimmering like stardust.

She looked up and her smile turned sad as she gazed at something behind me.

"I guided you a little too, my dear boy," she said gently. I turned to see Jake's face filled with wonder and shock.

"You are very important to this journey," the Constellation continued, her voice melodic and soothing. "My sweet daughter Serena needed to learn to open her heart, and only her soulmate could help her with that." Jake stepped forward and took my hand in his, giving it a supportive squeeze. "I'm sorry, my friend," he said, his voice hoarse with emotion. "I didn't mean to get so lost along the way." I saw tears glistening on his cheeks once more. The Constellation reached out and touched Jake's arm lightly. He gasped as a visible shiver ran through his body.

"You found each other," she whispered tenderly. "And your parents would be so proud of the man you have become."

The constellation looked up at the night sky dotted with twinkling stars and then back at me, a gentle smile spreading across her ethereal face.

"It is time, my daughter," she said, her voice soft yet resonant. "The heavens have aligned in perfect synchrony and the cosmic forces are poised and eager for the ritual to be completed." I nodded, a wave of confidence and purpose suddenly surging through me. Jake stepped forward and passed me the leather bag containing the first three Zodiac relics we had collected over our journey. I clutched it tightly, feeling the power thrumming from within.

"Each of these relics contains a piece of your own celestial energy," the Constellation explained, sweeping her arm across the horizon. "They embody the four core elements that comprise the universe, earth, air, fire and water. You must place each one at its corresponding cardinal direction to focus their collective power." I loosened the drawstring on the bag and reached inside, the cool materials of the relics pulsing beneath my fingertips. It was time to fulfil my destiny among the stars. I nodded again and set to work, feeling out the energetic circle that was forming as I walked the ruins.

The ancient stones beneath my feet hummed with power, guiding me to align the relics just so. I looked up to the stars above and smiled as I felt the connection with each of the elemental points. First, I placed the oval necklace, the first of the relics that I found, and placed it on the point that represented earth. It seemed to rejoice in its return to the earth. Then I walked counterclockwise around the circle and pulled out the second relic, the small glass box with etchings of the Zodiacs along its surface, and placed it on the point for water. Each of the relics let out a pulse of blue light before settling into a soft glow as they connected with their place in the circle, as if the elements themselves were stirring from a long slumber. I continued around the circle and pulled the third relic, the beautiful candle, and placed it in the point for fire. It too glowed brightly with orange light for a moment before settling into a subtle hue again, its flame flickering as if responding to an invisible breeze. As I walked around the circle to the final point I smiled at Jake who stood there waiting for me, the talisman with the moonstone set in it lying around his neck.

"You look so fucking beautiful," he said, his voice low and husky, as I reached him. I could feel the intensity of his gaze as his eyes raked over my body appreciatively, making me shiver with anticipation. I smiled as something deep in me tugged on my heart and soul, a heady mix of nerves and desire.

"You don't look so bad yourself," I replied, my tone playful and flirtatious. I let my eyes wander over his muscular frame, taking in the way his shirt clung to his broad shoulders. He was dressed simply, but the black button-down shirt and dark wash jeans highlighted his rugged good looks perfectly. I bit my lip coyly as our eyes met again, causing him to raise an amused eyebrow at my obvious appreciation of his appearance. The chemistry between us was palpable, like a living, breathing thing, and I could feel the magnetic pull between us growing stronger by the second.

Jake bent his head downwards, allowing me to reach behind his thick, muscular neck to the clasp of the talisman. I undid the delicate clasp with trembling fingers and pulled the talisman away from his warm skin. Two things happened at once as the moonstone talisman left his body. First, it began to glow brightly, pulsating with ethereal energy, as if it could already sense its destined home on the air point of the mystical circle. But then the second thing happened. Jake cried out in sudden agony and collapsed to his knees on the hard, unforgiving ground. I looked down in horror to see his black shirt growing wet with dark blood.

"Oh my god," I cried out in alarm, my voice echoing around the shadowy cavern. I immediately dropped to my knees beside him and pulled up his soaked shirt to assess the damage. The vicious wound on his abdomen that had only just finished healing minutes ago was now torn open once more, blood slowly seeping from the jagged laceration.

"What's happening?" I cried, my voice shrill with panic as I whipped my head around to face the Constellation. She met my terrified gaze with a mournful, regretful expression in her ancient eyes.

"I am sorry dear," the Constellation said regretfully, her ancient eyes downcast with remorse, "But the fourth relic is what is healing the wound. Without the talisman against his skin, then the wound isn't yet fully healed." I looked down at the talisman in horror, cursing myself for not realising it sooner. How could I have been so foolish? Quickly, I pushed the cool moonstone back against Jake's clammy skin. Immediately, the vicious laceration began to knit itself back together before my eyes, the jagged edges of the wound sealing up once more. Jake gasped loudly, as if he was finally able to get breath into his lungs again after nearly drowning. He leaned heavily against me, his muscular frame trembling with exertion as he panted, his skin icy cold to the touch. I wrapped my free arm around him tightly, willing my warmth into his weakened body.

I looked up at the Constellation with desperation, silently pleading for answers about this mystifying relic that seemingly held Jake's life in its hands. She gazed back at me mournfully, regret shadowing her ageless features.

"What am I meant to do," I cried, my voice breaking as I looked up at the Constellation with pleading eyes. "I can't take the talisman away from him without him dying." The ageless celestial being gazed back at me with profound sadness etched into her starry features.

"I know you have already sacrificed so much, my child, but I am afraid that the stars require one more sacrifice tonight," she said softly, her words landing like blows upon my heart. My eyes widened in horror as the meaning behind her words sunk in.

"What, no," I begged, fresh tears spilling down my cheeks. "I can't lose him, please, there must be another way." The Constellation slowly shook her head, regret and sorrow mingling in her fathomless eyes. I felt Jake's large, calloused hand gently cover mine in a comforting gesture.

"Baby," he croaked, his voice rough with emotion and pain. I looked over at him, my vision blurred by my tears. His stormy grey eyes, the eyes I loved so much, shone with a darkness that scared me to my core, it was a darkness of resignation and acceptance that I couldn't bear to even think about.

"No, please," I pleaded brokenly, shaking my head before he could even say the words I dreaded to hear. He forced a pained smile to his handsome face, though it didn't reach his eyes.

"Baby, it's not just me here," he said softly, his thumb stroking over my skin. "You have to consider the whole world."

"Screw the world," I whispered bitterly as he leaned his forehead against mine in a bittersweet intimacy. "I have lost enough in my life, I refuse to lose anything else. It's my turn to be selfish now." Jake let out a hollow chuckle, though it was filled with sorrow rather than mirth.

"You and I both know that you aren't that person," he murmured knowingly, and I squeezed my eyes shut as a fresh wave of tears spilled free. Even through my anguish, I knew deep down that he was right.

Then a thought occurred to me as I gazed up at the shimmering form of the Constellation, a tiny spark of hope fluttering in my heart like a fragile moth.

"How long does the ritual take?" I asked, my voice tentative yet urgent, as if I were gently coaxing the moth to fly from my cupped hands. "If Jake could just hold on long enough for me to get the talisman back around his neck, if I could buy us even a little more time..." But the mournful look that crossed the Constellation's ethereal face told me that my fragile hope was about to have its wings crushed.

"I am sorry, child, but the ritual calls for another sacrifice as well," she said, her voice achingly sympathetic. "When you complete the ritual, magic will vanish entirely from this world in order for it to reset once more. The relic will be nothing more than a lifeless trinket." I shook my head in despair as fresh tears coursed down my cheeks, dripping onto my hands like raindrops. The moth of hope lay still.

"No," I whispered brokenly, "You can't expect me to willingly let him die." The thought of losing Jake, the man who had somehow cracked through the icy walls around my heart, was too much to bear. I would not, could not, complete the ritual if it meant sacrificing the one person who now meant everything to me.

"Serena, baby," Jake said, his voice strained yet gentle, pulling my attention to him again. His stormy grey eyes, normally so intense, now looked at me with warmth and acceptance. "Remember what I said at the bottom of the steps. You have healed the broken pieces of my heart; you saw beyond the ruthless killer I was moulded into and found the man beneath. I will die happy knowing that you, my fierce angel, have saved everyone else in this world." I didn't want to listen to his words, refusing to accept that this was the end. Jake was persistent, his large calloused hand attempting to pull my own hand away from where I held the moonstone talisman against his skin. I cried out, my voice breaking as I pushed all my effort into keeping the talisman in place. Its cool surface was our only hope, the sole chance of stopping the deadly death from stealing Jake away from me forever.

"Jake, stop it," I pleaded, my voice cracking with desperation. But he didn't listen and instead wrapped his strong, muscular arms around my waist and pulled me in, pressing his lips against mine in a kiss that held so much sorrow and pain from our doomed love, and so much passion all at once. I wanted to live in that electrifying, bittersweet kiss for the rest of my life, and felt myself melting into the hard planes of his body. Jake reached up with his large, calloused hand and caressed my cheek tenderly, before breaking the kiss, causing a heart-wrenching sob to come from my lips at the loss of contact.

"I love you so fucking much," he whispered hoarsely, his smoldering grey eyes boring into mine, "You are my heart and soul, and as long as your heart beats I will be with you in spirit." He then roughly yanked the moonstone talisman, my only hope of saving him, from my grasp and pulled the chain over his head in one swift motion. I screamed in anguish as his muscular body stiffened in agony from the excruciating pain of the wound in his side. Jake leaned towards the final point of the circle and slammed the talisman down with the last of his ebbing strength before I could stop him, his battered, bloodied body falling to the cold stone ground.

"Jake," I screamed, my voice cracking with desperation as I tried to get him to reconsider his reckless actions. He tilted his head up towards me, a pained yet peaceful smile crossing his battered face.

"Go on and complete your destiny, my love," he croaked weakly, his voice barely above a whisper. Blood continued to pour from the gaping wound in his side, his hand futilely trying to stem the crimson flow.

"It is time," the swirling constellation intoned, its cosmic voice reverberating around the stone circle. I glanced around, watching as the four elemental relics began to glow and pulse with vibrant light and energy, the circle finally complete. I shook my head in denial, even though I knew in my heart I had to see this through to the end. Bending down, I tenderly kissed Jake's sweat-slicked forehead, taking his blood-slicked hand in mine and pressing it against his side in a vain attempt to stop the bleeding.

"Hold on for me, please," I pleaded, tears streaming down my face as I cradled his battered body.

"For the rest of my life, baby," he vowed, his voice growing fainter by the second.

I stood up and walked through the lights into the centre of the circle and stood looking up at the stars. I could feel all the elements calling to somewhere deep inside me, connecting me with the stars and funnelling energy through me. Even though I had read the words for the ritual countless times, I had thought that I would struggle to remember them when the moment came. But my worry was for nothing as the ancient incantations flowed effortlessly from my mouth as if they were meant to be known only now. The words spoke of cosmic forces beyond my comprehension, yet they felt as familiar as my own name. I could sense the power in them, the power to rend the veil between worlds and summon powers primordial. My voice grew louder, filled with conviction and authority. This was my destiny; I knew that now. Whatever came next, I was ready. The stars swirled overhead as if responding to my call, and I raised my arms to embrace my fate. This was bigger than me, bigger than anything I had ever imagined, but I would see it through.

> "Divine Constellation, hear my plea
> Four relics of Cancer I bring to thee
> To undo the selfish wonder,
> That has torn the sky asunder,
> I draw upon your divine magic,
> I worship at your altar,
> The wrongs are most tragic,
> But still I do not falter
> My heart is pure,
> My soul complete,
> Take all that I give,
> So a new world we can meet."

I gasped as the energy built inside me with each word, rising up from deep within my core until my whole body tingled with power. On the final word of the incantation, the energy burst forth, shooting straight upwards towards the stars and pulling every last drop of my essence with it. I was bathed for a long moment in the ethereal essence of the universe as the magic swirled around and through me. I could almost feel the delicate threads of reality shifting as the spell worked to heal the rift torn in the fabric of space and time. It was as though the very seams of creation were being gently stitched back together under the guiding hand of some divine seamstress. The feeling was overwhelming and amazing all at once. I was at once insignificantly small and infinitely connected to everything. For the briefest moment I glimpsed the inner workings of eternity and understood just how delicate and precious this life truly was.

And then, nothing. It stopped. The last of the energy drained from my body and the air became still and dark in the night. I fell to my knees, no longer being held up by the cosmic power of the universe. I could feel the rough stone floor of the old chapel below my hands, and feel the gentle night breeze stirring my hair, but even though I couldn't quite pinpoint the feeling I could feel that the magic had gone. There was a big empty feeling inside me that for a moment made it hard to breathe, as if the very air had been sucked from my lungs. I looked up as I heard the distant sound of the church bells strike midnight, their solemn tones echoing through the darkness. The glowing magical circle and shimmering image of the Constellation had vanished completely. All I saw around me was shadows and moonlight streaming through the empty hole of the ruins. The only sound now was my own ragged breathing.

The only thing I could see was a dark still form just outside the circle.

"Jake," I called, only he didn't answer as I scrambled to my feet, my heart pounding, and ran to him. I reached him and fell to my knees, finding his handsome face pale, his eyes closed and his hand limp by his side. His breathing came in short, ragged gasps as I pulled his muscular but lifeless body onto my knees, my vision blurring with tears. I pressed desperately against the slowly bleeding wound on his abdomen, trying to stem the crimson flow.

"No, no, no," I choked out between sobs, clutching him close, his head lolling limply against my shoulder. I screamed into the darkness for someone, anyone, to help me save my soulmate, my one true love. Jake had risked everything for me, had turned against the Council to protect me, and now he was paying the ultimate price. As I rocked his cooling body, weeping, I swore I would not let him die in vain.

Epilogue

Serena

Six Months Later

Six months had passed since that fateful night when I was forced to make the hardest decision of my life. As I flipped the sign on the shop door, signalling the end of another busy day catering to tourists in the seaside town of Whitby, my heart still ached with grief. The summer months were always hectic here, with crowds flocking to experience the picturesque harbour, imposing abbey ruins, and winding cobblestone streets. But no amount of bustling activity could distract me from the profound sense of loss that plagued my waking moments. Though my rational mind knew ending things was the only way forward, my heart rebelled against this truth. Each morning I awoke feeling the raw absence of part of my soul as keenly as a physical wound. Going through the motions of my daily routine was a struggle, even after half a year had elapsed. A piece of my soul had been torn away that night on the cliffs, and the ragged edges still bled.

I turned off the shop lights and headed into the back room where Carnelian, my beloved ginger cat, was sitting on my desk. I reached out to stroke his soft fur as I locked away the day's modest takings in the old iron safe. He responded affectionately by rubbing against my hand and practically vibrating with his distinctive purr. The profound connection to the spirit familiars that had been my trusted guides and companions was one of the many things lost that fateful night, along with all access to magic itself. The world had been plunged into a bewildering magic blackout and there was widespread panic and fear until almost a full month later when the first faint signs of magic began to slowly return. It would likely have been an extremely scary and chaotic time for most people if not for the news that the ominous black hole that threatened our very existence was inexplicably disappearing. The general population saw it as a miracle, but I knew much better. If the other eleven women sacrificed as much as I did that night on the cliffs of Whitby, then the price was definitely paid in full for this supposed miracle, though at great personal cost.

I had hoped with a naïve optimism that when magic came back, it would somehow magically heal the deep pain and loss inside me, but my own personal magic never returned. I hadn't had a single vision, premonition, or magical experience of any kind since that fateful night on the cliffs of Whitby. And more importantly, I hadn't been able to feel the comforting, familiar presence of my Gran. I wanted so desperately to know in my heart that she was okay in the afterlife, that her spirit lived on, but no matter how much I called out to her in anguish, all I received in response was cold, empty silence. It was as if the black hole that threatened our very world had instead been swallowed up into the depths of my soul, steadily consuming all that I was from the inside out. I had spent many long, lonely nights down in the solitude of the shop, curled up on the floor in tears as I cried out time and again for any small sign or reassurance that I hadn't lost everything that ever mattered. The reassuring voices of my spirit guides and guardians remained mute, leaving me more lost and alone than I had ever felt.

A noise brought my attention back to the present, and I looked up to see Alec watching me, the sympathy screaming in his eyes.

"How're you doing, kid?" he asked, and I rolled my eyes at the familiar greeting that I had heard so often from him over the past few months. Though I had lost so much, I had also gained family. Discovering that Alec was my paternal uncle and finally being able to celebrate holidays and special occasions with him, his parents, and my newly found grandparents was an unexpected silver lining amidst the darkness that had consumed my life. Their warm embrace provided a sense of belonging I hadn't known since Gran passed away.

"Dinner is ready upstairs," Alec said, breaking me from my reverie. I smiled gratefully and nodded my head in acknowledgement. Carnelian leapt down from his perch on the desk where he had been intently observing me and padded across the floor to join Obsidian, who had been patiently waiting for him. The two cats took the lead as we turned off the lights in the shop and headed up the stairs to my apartment above, the inviting aromas reminding me that despite all I had lost, there was still warmth and light to be found in this world.

I was immediately hit by the aromatic scent of Italian herbs and garlic bread as I walked into the living room of my cosy apartment above the antique shop. The small dining table was set up and ready for our intimate dinner, with three plates neatly arranged and my glass of chilled white wine already poured.

"My god, this smells divine," I said, my stomach rumbling in anticipation as the tempting aromas of homemade lasagna wafted through the air.

"Just wait until you taste it," came the reply as two strong arms wrapped around my waist from behind. I leaned back into the familiar warmth of my soulmate's embrace. Jake had really taken to the kitchen with gusto since he got out of the hospital, challenging himself to provide as many orgasm-inducing meals as possible, his words not mine.

"I dunno," I said with a flirtatious smile, turning my head to meet his gaze. "That chocolate molten cake you made the other night will be a hard one to beat." Jake growled playfully in my ear as he nuzzled into my neck, sending delicious shivers down my spine. "There are plenty of things I could use chocolate for, my love." I bit my lip, my imagination running wild with all sorts of tantalising images and ideas.

"Guys, please," Alec groaned from his seat at the table. "Save it for the bedroom." I couldn't help but giggle at his mock annoyance as Jake nipped at my earlobe again, his warm breath tickling my skin.

The relationship between Jake and Alec was a strained one, full of tension and distrust borne out of their opposing allegiances. However, it was certainly helped along the road to repair when Alec and a few other resistance members came rushing to the cliff that fateful night, practically carrying Jake's broken, bleeding body between them as they raced to get him to the hospital. The doctors said that it had been incredibly close, and they had nearly lost Jake a couple of times on the operating table as they worked tirelessly to stitch and seal his grievous wounds. But somehow, against all odds, they were able to stabilise him, and after the longest two days of my life spent pacing the hospital corridors, he finally emerged from the induced coma. It had been another two agonising weeks of watching him lie unconscious, hooked up to tubes and monitors, before he was well enough to be released from the hospital's care. And then another week of no contact, no word at all as he went through intense interrogations and debriefings with the Council, who were furious that he had betrayed them. I had been so overjoyed to see him almost a month later when he came walking back into the magic shop, looking weary but resolved, and declared that he was no longer working for the Council. Now he was allied with Alec and the rest of the resistance, working to try to negotiate better terms and magical practices with the Council in hopes that we didn't find ourselves in the same deadly position in a few hundred years' time.

I sat down at the old oak table and grinned at Alec as he rolled his eyes in mock exasperation. Jake joined us a moment later, carrying a piping hot lasagna fresh from the oven and placing it carefully in the middle of the table. He sat down in the chair next to me and took my hand, bringing it to his lips for a gentle kiss before reaching for my plate to dish up some of the amazing, cheesy pasta layered with rich bolognese sauce and herbs that was steaming temptingly in front of me.

I was about to start tucking into the delicious, cheesy pasta when I heard a faint noise from downstairs in the antique shop below. All three of us looked up in surprise and Jake glanced over at the sofa where both of the cats, Obsidian and Carnelian, had curled up together earlier.

"Did you lock up the shop?" Jake asked me with a furrowed brow. I nodded my head confidently.

"Well, it's clearly not the cats making that noise," Alec deduced, a wary tone in his voice. I stood up from my seat to go and investigate the sound, but both men quickly shot up to block my way.

"Whoa, hold on," Jake said, gently grasping my arm.

"Don't you dare go down there alone," Alec warned, his protective instincts in full force. I couldn't help but grin at the way they both immediately moved to shield me from potential danger.

"Oh shush, both of you," I chided lightheartedly. "It's probably nothing and I'm not in any real danger." In truth, I knew they both cared for me deeply and were just looking out for my safety, as they always did.

I headed down the stairs to the shop with both men supporting disapproving looks and following close behind me. The first thing I noticed when I reached the bottom was that the lights were still on, illuminating the cosy space. I could have sworn that I had turned them off before heading upstairs. Perplexed, I slowly looked around the room but nothing seemed out of the ordinary. The antique books and curios were all neatly arranged on the shelves, just as I had left them. After crossing the worn wooden floorboards to the front door, I checked and confirmed that it was indeed still locked. I turned to face the men and gave them a reassuring smile.

"See, nothing to worry about here," I said warmly, hoping to set their minds at ease. I playfully shooed the two of them back up the stairs. "Better go on back up before the cats get into our dinner." Though still seeming a bit uneasy, they obliged and headed upstairs.

I crossed the worn wooden floorboards once more and was just about to turn the lights off when a familiar tingle hit me. Nothing big, just a slight tingle in the back of my mind, the kind Gran would send when she wanted my attention. I heard the scraping sound again and turned in time to see a small trinket, an antique brooch shaped like a crescent moon, on one of the shelves fall over the edge to the floor with a clatter. Then the unmistakable scent of lavender wafted through the air and I couldn't help but smile.

"Serena, was that you down there? What was that noise?" Jake called down the stairs, his voice tinged with concern.

"Nothing to worry about!" I called back up to reassure him with a grin. I turned slowly, taking in the room. The scent still lingered, conjuring up memories of my grandmother.

"Goodnight, Gran," I said softly before turning off the lights and heading back up the creaky stairs to rejoin Jake and the warmth of our little family.

Dawn of the Zodiac

D awn of the Zodiac is a shared world series, each book written by a different author.

Other books in the series
Capricorn Blessed – Rachelle Bonifay
Pieces Blessed – Remy Cavilich
Aquarius Blessed – Georgina Stancer
Leo Blessed – S Lucas
Virgo Blessed – Ella J. Smyth
Libra Blessed – KD Fraser
Scorpio Blessed – Mia Davis

Sagittarius Blessed – Charli Rahe

About Aisling Elizabeth

Hey there! I'm **Aisling Elizabeth** (yep, that's pronounced ASH-Ling). A Yorkshire lass through and through, I juggle the fun chaos of two kids and two mischievous cats. I've always been the storytelling type. Before getting my name on an actual book cover in 2022, I dabbled with sharing my tales on reading apps. Turned out, people kinda liked them!

Dark paranormal romance is my jam. In my stories, you'll find threads of resilience in the face of tough times, characters whose lives are all tangled up (in the best way), and some nods to mental health – something close to my heart, given my own ups and downs.

My first published piece? "Beyond Beta's Rejection", kicking off The Divine Order Series. But trust me, my brain's always buzzing with a bunch of new story ideas.

Outside of spinning tales, I'm all about belting out songs (quality not guaranteed), hopping into gigs, and geeking out at TV and Film fan conventions. If you share my love for any of the above, we'll get on just fine!

Website - www.aislingelizabeth.com

Facebook Reader Group – www.facebook.com/groups/aislingelizabeth

Also By Aisling Elizabeth

Current and future releases by Aisling Elizabeth. Please check www.aislingelizabeth.com/books for more updates and release dates.

The Divine Order Series
Beyond Beta's Rejection
The Alpha's Tainted Blood

The Key Stone Pack Series
Bound by Prophecy (Prequel)
Bound By Fate

Bound By Rivalry
Bound by Curse

Dark Heath University
Dark Ashes *(coming soon)*
Dark Flame *(coming soon)*
Dark Inferno *(coming soon)*

Standalones & Shared Worlds.
Cancer Blessed *(Part of the Dawn of the Zodiacs Shared World)*
Enemies to Wife *(Part of the Wife for Hire Shared World)*

Printed in Great Britain
by Amazon